THE SHALLOW'S DEEP SECRETS

THE SHALLOW'S DEEP SECRETS

VOLUME II

D. RUDD WISE

TATE PUBLISHING
AND ENTERPRISES, LLC

Published by Tate Publishing & Enterprises, LLC
127 E. Trade Center Terrace | Mustang, Oklahoma 73064 USA
1.888.361.9473 | www.tatepublishing.com

Tate Publishing is committed to excellence in the publishing industry. The company reflects the philosophy established by the founders, based on Psalm 68:11,
"The Lord gave the word and great was the company of those who published it."

Book design copyright © 2013 by Tate Publishing, LLC. All rights reserved.
Cover design by Rodrigo Adolfo
Interior design by Mary Jean Archival

Published in the United States of America

ISBN: 978-1-62746-437-6
1. Fiction / General
2. Fiction / Action & Adventure
13.09.24

Acknowledgments

I appreciate everyone who had a part in editing and guiding me with the research on this third in a series of Jess E. Hanes's adventure stories.

First and most of all, I thank my loving wife, Rachel Marie, for her patience and endurance with long hours of editing my stories. Her persistence in trying to understand my thoughts once they were written and squeezing out of me the words I were trying to use really showed her great gift of patience.

I thank you, sweetheart, for your loving support during these past years of novel writing.

Special thanks to Mr. Jerry Husted, founder of the Nordic Tug Incorporated, for his approval of the Tug's use in the story. He is the manufacture of America's favorite trawlers and practical pilothouse cruisers in Burlington, Washington. His helpful correspondence and literature was great reference material for learning more about his boats before I ever stepped aboard one.

Dick LaVanture, another gentleman I appreciate and owe special thanks to for his approval to go aboard his forty-two–foot Nordic Tug, the Marla D.

We cruised on Lake Michigan with him one rough morning. Then another time, I took a trip from Traverse City north to Charlevoix with him and Marla, his wife, to a Nordic Tug owners' convention with the factory.

Dick is the CEO and owner of LaVanture Products, Incorporated and LaVanture Plastic Extrusion Technologies in Elkhart, Indiana.

Thanks to the authors of Honey, Let's Get a Boat, Ron and Eva Stob, for their expert directions on the America's Great Loop and for his encouragement to keep writing on my third novel, which includes a cruise around the eastern United States on the Intracoastal Waterways.

Another special thanks to Taffi Fisher-Abt, director of Mel Fisher's Treasure museum in Sebastian, Florida, for the authorization to copy the diver photo and the reprint her father's quote—Mel Fisher, The Story of the 1715 Spanish Plate Fleet from the Fall/Winter 2000, Discovery Day Treasures souvenir magazine.

Another special thanks to the U.S. Coast Guard in St. Joseph, Michigan. They were a great help with the courses offered for civilian power boaters, especially Auxiliary Officer J. D. Ryan.

Thanks to Joe "the Finder" Shepherd, skipper of the dive/salvage boat the Royal Fifth, who taught me the methods of boat handling and how the research of Spanish galleons' salvage was done. Thank you, Joe, for allowing us to be a part of your crew.

Also, thanks for his patient instructions on diving the 1715 Spanish galleons; for teaching with samples and artifacts on how to identify the difference between black incrusted metals on the ocean floor from the black incrusted metal of silver coins and encrusted objects (EO), which could cover coins corroded to themselves; for his firmness for safety of his crew, divers, and the boat, and for being forever vigilant with no less than two divers in the water and an alert crew on board.

I still have a lifetime of learning about diving and salvaging in these retirement years.

A big thanks to pilot and aircraft owner, the late James E. Rogers for the rides in his Super Widgen G44, Frankly My Dear and permission to use his name and photos in this novel.

I regret his passing in 2007 before this manuscript was finished. We all lost a great pilot and good friend.

Chapter 5 is dedicated to James E. Rogers, with permission from his son, Atty. Richard W. Rogers.

Another Jess E. Hanes Adventure Continues

Other novels in the series:

Operation: Eyewitness
Amarillo Mariposa

Contents

W ell into the second leg of their cruise, Jess and Marie Ann dive on Spanish galleons, search the beaches and meet unexpected difficulties with drug runners, and of course the Coast Guard, FBI, and U.S. Marshal's Service beome involved. Fantastic finds are uncovered, which brings more danger to *The Shallow's* crew.

THE SHALLOW'S CONTINUES

D. Rudd Wise

The Shallow's

Deep Secrets

Another Jess E. Hanes adventure;
This time on the Great American Loop Cruise
A fictitious treasure hunter cruising
The American lakes and rivers in the Eastern USA

CHAPTER ONE

Fort Pierce, Florida

At daybreak the next morning, both Jess and Marie Ann were out on the beach swinging their metal detectors, searching for any item that would have been tossed up from the sunken Spanish galleons of 1715 by hurricanes. They stayed close to each other, watching each other's back for security along the beach; it was always a good thing to hunt in pairs, not alone.

"Over here, Jess!" Marie Ann was knelling next to a hole she had dug in the wet sandy beach, waving to Jess. They were using a small earpiece from pocket walkie-talkies under the detector's headsets and a tiny throat mike.

"What ya got, love?"

"Sweep your detector over this hole and see what it shows on the screen."

He moved the detector loop across the target hole in different directions. "It shows thirteen inches down and silver."

"That's what mine indicated too. I'll keep digging." Jess moved away because of interference with Marie Ann's detector when she turned its back on.

"Jess, I've got it! A silver dollar…" She could hardly control her emotions while washing it off with some of her drinking water a few minutes later.

"1880!" she yelled, rubbing it between her wet fingers, making it shine. "How about that?" she whispered. "It's my greatest silver coin find! I wonder who lost it. There might be more."

"That's great, sweetheart. Make sure to check that area good before moving farther down the beach. There may be more."

Jess watched her as she methodically swept the detector loop across the moist sandy beach. He moved up to the dry part of the beach behind her and then began a slow sweep of the sand back down to the water's edge. He then searched back up to the dry grassy area away from the wet beach.

"I have four more silver," she called. "They're all three-cent pieces with a small hole near their edges. Maybe someone had them on a chain for a bracelet!"

"Write down your GPS position."

"I have it already! Did you find anything?" Marie Ann asked.

"No, nothing worth writing home about, just rusty junk pieces of iron. I'll clean them when we get back."

"Are you sure they are just rusty iron?"

"Yes, sweetheart, that's what the detector indicates," Jess replied. "But that's why I dug those targets to get the iron out of the way. Remember how many times we moved the junk target and found precious metals under them?"

"That's the way you taught me," she said, smiling at him. "I remember, with the new detectors that identify the target, 'Just dig it anyway.' It could be hiding something underneath." She nodded her head. "I don't have to be reminded, 'Instructor!'"

He waved back to her, "Yes, dear, just a habit. I tell everyone to do that on the beaches."

Jess' years of using, selling, and demonstrating detectors could irritate some people by his always wanting to help get the best out of the detectors for a person. Marie Ann was accustomed to his advice, and she was just as knowledgeable about the use of metal detectors as he was. His persistent instructions could be unnerving to most folks.

"I'm on it," she replied and gave him a thumbs-up.

Marie Ann was detecting the wet sand lower down the dunes to the water's edge and then back up to the dry sand. Suddenly she stopped and checked the indication on her detector.

She liked the White's MXT for its better target ID and spelling out what it could be. She was hunting in the Coin and Jewelry mode. The indication was not a high number, only 10 to 12 foil and ring range, but the audio was loud over the target.

"You better not be a wad of tin foil from someone's lunch," she said and read the depth indicator of 8 inches. With her sand scoop, she carefully dug into the sand a few inches at a time. Targets larger than coin size will give erroneous depth indications, like mashed soda cans for a silver half or dollar.

She dug to about 6 inches and used her hand-held pinpointer, a White's Bullseye. It was dead and Jess had the fresh 9-volt transistor batteries in his backpack.

"Where's my standby?" She zipped open her backpack and felt for the other pinpointer, a Garrett Pro-Pointer. On her knees, she took the handheld detector and turned it on. "Great, this one works!"

She reached down in the hole and searched the side and bottom for any targets, nothing. She then got the MXT and ran it over the target again and got the good signal and laid the unit down. She dug with her gloved hand deeper into the sand and felt something hard. She got a hold of the target between her fingers just as a large wave washed in, filling the hole with salt water and more sand. She was up to her elbows in the hole, being held down with wet sand in the hole. She did not want to let go of her target and began scooping the wet sand back out of the hole with one hand.

Looking back out to the surf, she made sure she had time to get her target with both hands. Whatever the target was, it was not large and was thin. She held it in the palm of her left hand and set back on the heels of her shoes. With her fingers, she moved the wet sand off an object that looked like a cross. She could see that it still had gems of some kind still mounted. Taking her water bottle from her fanny pack, she washed her treasure clear of sand.

Yes, it was an unusual-looking cross and its entire fifteen gem stones were still in place, none missing.

"Jess, hey, Jess, come here," she hollered as loud as she could over the noise of the surf, waving her empty hand high.

He had a headphone covering his ears and didn't hear her, but she was ahead of him about twenty feet on the beach; he was always watching around them. Plus, he wasn't finding anything except trash. His nail apron was getting heavy and needed to be emptied again. He waved back and turned his detector off and propped his sand scoop's handle against his chest.

Jess could tell by the excited motion of her arm she needed him. He took a small plastic bag from his nail apron and dumped all the trash into the bag, tied a knot in the open end, and set it in the sand between his legs. This would mark his spot to continue detecting there and he could dump the bag in the trash on the way back to the condo.

"What you find, love?" he said, dropping to his knees beside her. He would not have done that without his knee pads on; there's too much trash on the beaches that could cut up his knees.

"Jess, I've found my million-dollar cross," she said with her broad smile. Pouring some more water over it in the palm of her hand, she held it up to him. "Isn't that the prettiest thing you ever saw?"

"Sweetheart," he said, "turn it over so we can see the other side. Any mint or essayer's marks on it?"

"I can't tell, there's too much crusty corrosion on it."

Reaching out for the cross, Jess was all smiles. "That's a fantastic find, love. Can I hold it closer?"

She started to hand it to him and drew back. "I don't know, should I?"

He moved closer to her and pulled a wet bath towel from off his back pack, spread it across his folded legs, and smoothed it out. She slowly laid it on the towel. He picked it up and examined it closely.

"I bet you have one of a kind." He took a jeweler's loupe out of his shirt pocket and checked the cross closer. "I don't remember this many stones in the ones in the museum. Plus, what type of metal is this, copper, pewter, lead? It sure doesn't appear to be silver or gold."

He put the loupe away and pulled out a small plastic bubble-wrap bag and placed the cross in, folding the plastic over it, making a double layer of protection.

"Sweetheart, you've got a keeper for sure," he said and leaned over and kissed her on the forehead. "Now, while we are sitting here, take a GPS reading over your sand hole. It's almost filled up."

He leaned back, folded the wet towel lengthways and put over his backpack. She put her treasure into her fanny pack for safe keeping. After they drank some water, Jess patted her on the shoulder. "Just think, out there a few hundred yards is still the remains of the eleven 1715 Spanish fleet that sank it that hurricane."

Pointing out passed the surf breakers, he continued, "Joe Shepherd from home, Hank Haardt and I dove on the *Nuestra Señora de las Nieves,* one of the eleven vessels that was sunk. Remember the photos at home?"

"Yes, I do. Do you suppose this cross came from it?" She giggled and pressed him for more information on the galleon. A cool breeze made it comfortable in the shade of the clouds.

"Well, it sure is a good possibility that it is from the *Nieves.*" He was thinking of the museum treasures in Key West, Vero Beach, and Sebastian. "I don't remember anything that looks like what you have found, especially with all the stones still mounted."

"What kind of stones are they? I don't think any are diamonds."

"I bet Taffi will know," Jess said, standing up and offering his hand to help her up. "We've got a lot of beach to cover. Ain't this fun?"

Pointing toward a walkway up on a dune, he said, "Let's take a break for a snack of peanut butter crackers. Hope there's no bugs in the shade."

"Taking any bets on the bugs being gone?' She wanted to shake his hand for a bet and he refused, shaking his head.

After a few more hours of searching the beach, they stopped to eat sandwiches under the shade of small beach trees. The beach was secluded, causing them to be ever conscious of the area around them, always scanning the water, open beach, and the brush areas inland behind them.

Marie Ann handed Jess a spray can of insect repellent from her backpack. After spraying each other, they stretched, checked their map, took another swallow of water from their bladder backpacks, and began searching again.

They were on the beach area where eleven 1715 Spanish galleons had sunk off shore during a hurricane. Since then, storms had tossed debris and coins up from the bottom of the ocean. It was not their first search along this beach and had marked GPS locations on their map of previous finds.

It was now low tide and the corral reefs were sticking up out of the ocean water. They had arrived at one specific spot Jess wanted to use the detectors. Three more hours of sunlight was plenty of time to search. Jess removed his backpack and took out a snorkel, full-face dive mask, and gloves.

They helped each other pull on wetsuits.

"I don't think we'll need fins right now, but better put on those rubber slippers," he said, pointing to a Zip-lock bag. After putting them on, she took his detector and installed a shorter rod on it for being in the water. She left hers on the longer rod. Both of their detectors were fully submersible.

While he was floating between the reefs searching the shallow sandy bottom, up their jagged sides, in their holes and crevices, Marie Ann waded around them searching the exposed tops. They found soda cans, beer cans, and pieces of aluminum foil pie pans. For over an hour, they searched without finding any good targets.

She tried the waterproof Garrett Pro-Pointer down in the corral holes. They were both getting fatigued fighting the waves.

Suddenly, Jess stood up in the chest deep water and yelled, "Over here, love! Be careful stepping between those two corral. It's over waist deep on this side."

She eased over to him. "Look down there!" He pointed, sweeping his detector over the target. He steadied her while she pulled her full face-mask into place.

They both bent over looking under the water with their dive masks on and snorkel in their mouths. Jess pointed at the bottom of a corral and something glistened from the sun through the water. Jess took a deep breath and pulled himself down to the sandy bottom reaching out for the shiny object.

Just as he did, the surf washed over them, pushing Marie Ann up onto the top of the corral. It caused him to release the object stuck under the corral, bobbing him to the surface. He stood up, grabbing her thigh to balance himself.

She sat up on top of the jagged corral, spit out her snorkel mouthpiece. She was lucky that the corral did not cut through her diver's wet suit.

She began laughing. "Maybe someone doesn't want me to see what you found."

"Are you all right?" She was holding onto her knee. "I know you don't like your head underwater."

"Yes! Yes! I'm fine. Your hand gripping my knee hurts more than the corral I'm sitting on."

Jess released his grip and grabbed a smooth section of the corral. "Sorry, love! I didn't want you to wash off there. You could scrape and cut your legs on the corral."

"That surf just lifted me up and sat me on top. I didn't touch a thing."

Jess patted her thigh. "The tide must be changing. I don't see a surge or high breakers. It's still pretty smooth." He moved back, giving her room to slowly make her way off the corral back into water. "You ready to try again?"

"Jesus, give us direction and your safety," Jess said, watching her adjust her mask again.

She nodded yes, putting the snorkel back in her mouth. They both looked back out to sea and then gave each other thumbs-up. Pulling himself down to the sandy bottom edge of the corral, Jess fanned the sand away from his find. While standing on the sand between the corral, but bent over, she watched him through her mask. She held her position by gripping the corral.

She let out a breath of air in excitement and squeezed his arm, pointing at his find.

He began carefully pulling a heavy gold chain from under the corral. With her underwater camera she took his picture with a loop portion of the chain. It kept catching on the sharp ragged edges of the corral underneath. Being very careful not to scratch or damage the treasure, Jess handed his collection of the gold chain to Marie Ann and motioned for her to standup. It was about three feet in length.

When they stood up, Jess held his hands over hers and turned her away from the beach, looking out to sea. Two strands of the chain hung down into the water where the other end was still under the corral. "There is more than one length. You have one piece of it now."

His heart was beating up into his throat, "Don't bring it out of the water, just in case someone maybe watching. Shove it into this mesh sack.

Its weight should help hold you in place. It may take both of us to carry all this weight to the beach."

Jess looked up at Marie Ann and broke out in a big smile. "This must be our day! There's more of it under the corral."

He motioned for her to watch under the water again. He pulled himself back down by holding onto the side of the corral and slowly, carefully pulled another length of gold chain from its hiding place. It was another heavy length of gold chain. One link was cut and opened, catching another gold chain's link; that length dropped loose falling back down in the sand and slid under the corral again. He took the broken link and shoved it up under the wrist of the wetsuit.

He put all the chain lengths in the black meshed sack laying on the sand between the corral, and pulled it closed with a nylon cord which was sown in its opening. The sack was porous, so when it was lifted, water would flow from it. Together, they could not get a good grip on the sack.

Out of breath, they stood up again. Marie Ann slapped him on his good shoulder, laughing, "Now what, Professor? I'm speechless!"

"I don't think it going to move all wadded up in a heap, like that!" He turned around looking in toward the dry beach, "Can't see anyone on the open beach, but it's hard to see into the shadows of those mangrove trees."

She was still giggling about their newfound treasure.

"It's sure heavy. How much weight, do you suppose?" She was still gasping for air in her excitement.

"I don't know, sweetheart, but there is more gold chain under the corral." Jess started to laugh at Marie Ann, "You sound like a school girl on her first date."

She leaned over and kissed him on the cheek, "You say the sweetest things in a time like this?"

He motioned for her to give him her mesh bag and then took a deep breath. Under the surface again he continued to pull short lengths of chain from under the corral putting them in the bag. He surfaced clearing his snorkel, taking another deep breath and submersed again. The bag was full of gold chain short lengths. When he stood, he laid it next to her bag on top of the corral in front of them, on the ocean side.

"There are more down there," Jess said with so much excitement that he stuttered, "If we tie the two bag openings together, I can lift them up around my neck with my shoulders. I should be able to walk with it. Let's try to slide it up my back under water. This wetsuit may help slide it. Let me kneel in the sand underwater. I'll reach back over my shoulders for the nylon rope and pull."

"Don't strip your gears trying to lift it by yourself. I can lift some too!"

"Okay, let's try."

The first attempt did not work; they had to come up for air. Jess said, "While we're catching our breath, get the Global Positioning System (GPS) out."

Marie Ann took it from her waterproof fanny pack and saved their geographical coordinates, so they could come back to the same exact spot for later discoveries. Then, she returned it to its secure storage place. "If you stretch it out on the bottom making a couple or three loops of it? Would that help you lift it better around your neck? Let it dangle down your back?"

"That might work if it was all in one piece, but anyone looking at me would see it." Jess said, "But, if I knelt down again and you put loop lengths of it around my neck, and then down the inside of my wetsuit in the front. Then, if it takes more than one loop draped around my neck it will all be under the wetsuit?"

"That might work, but the tide seems to be coming in," she said and took a deep breath of excitement. "This water is getting deeper. You may not be able to stand up to walk out! With all this weight, you could drown, sweetheart!"

"Cancel that thought, love. I'll leave half of it here and come get the second bag later. Well, let's get with it!" It only took five minutes to get the heavy longer gold chain draped and zipped closed in the wetsuit. "I'll need your help standing up."

He moved the second bag against the bottom of the corral, "I'll be back for you."

She grabbed his arm and knelt down beside him, putting his arm around her shoulder, "You ready?" she asked.

"On the count of three!" Jess nodded his approval.

They counted together and felt their muscles strain as they lifted the weight of the gold chain. They edged around a gap in the corral and headed for the beach. Once on dry sand, they began to laugh.

"What now?" Marie Ann asked. "You can't carry that all the way back to the condo by yourself...not even with me helping you!"

"Well! It's for sure we can't leave it here," he continued to laugh. "I look like a beached whale!" he said, patting his wetsuit. "If I take this off, everyone in the world will know what we have. Can't you feel the eyes burning to get a closer look at this chain?" He waved his hand dismissing the thought, "Even so, we got to contact Philip, and then Tafi."

"You have eight lengths around your neck. If someone walks up to you they will certainly see the chain." She pulled her waterproof cell phone from under her wetsuit which had been hung around her neck. "I have his number listed. You want to talk to him?"

Jess shook his head, "Tell him to come get us with his four-wheel drive dune buggy."

He looked up and down the beach to get a fix on how far they had come. "Tell him to come where he and I had last been on the beach. We don't want to advertise any more than we already have. Tell him I'm worn out!" Philip understood Marie Ann's message.

They headed up higher on the beach to get in the shade of cedar and palm trees where they previously left their backpacks. There was a lower area under the trees where they could not be seen from the beach or the highway to the west.

Jess slowly lowered himself to his knees and leaned back against his backpack laying on the incline of the sand dune. They were both breathing hard from carrying the weight of the gold chain, plus they had to move the two backpacks and metal detectors, and then walk in the loose dry sand. The heat and humidity, plus the extra exertion were getting them both dehydrated.

She smiled and leaned down kissing him on the cheek, "This has been a profitable stroll. I found some worthwhile coins and cross, and then you found those gold trade chains."

"You're right, their heavy enough to be used as an anchor," he said patting the front of his wetsuit. Then he zipped it open to let some breeze blow the white hair on his well-shaped chest He. then opened the sleeves and ankle zippers, rolling them up. "Got a fan in your backpack? You better pull your suit off and blow the stink off!"

She was ahead of him with her removal and laughed shaking her finger at him, "Hold on there! Watch your mouth young man! You're not off this sand dune yet!"

After assisting him with the removal of his backpack, she noticed blood oozing from under Jess' wetsuit wrist band and dripping into the dry sand. "You're bleeding! We must have broken open that incision the doctor made on your shoulder wound."

She helped him remove the upper part of his wetsuit and removed the gold chain lengths and put four of them into her backpacks.

He handed her the one single link of chain, "Put this somewhere safe."

She weighed it in the palm of her hand and smiled at him. Then she put it under her swimming suit against her belly-button. "Secured, Captain!"

Jess opened their first-aid kit and held it for her to use. She dressed his wound and covered it with a new gauze bandage.

"There, that'll do until we get to the condo," she said lightly patting the bandage.

"Now, I need to go back after the one bag left between the corrals," Jess said and stood up. "I'll half a bar of 'fast energy' with you."

"That might not be a good idea with that bad shoulder," she shuffled over to him in the sand. "Let me look at it again.'

He pulled the shoulder of his wet suit back for her to take a look.

She tenderly pressed around the wound. He flinched, "Get a wide Band-Aid and put across it."

She shook her head, "That's not a good thing to do." But, she turned and retrieved the first-aid kit.

Once it was in place he zipped the wetsuit and headed for the corral. She reluctantly put her wetsuit back on. Catching up with him, she matched his stride into the water. They secured their treasure bag from the corral and returned to the dune, storing it in her backpack.

They took off their wet suits and put on dry clothes in the privacy of the dunes and trees.

Sitting in the sand under a palm tree, they drank water. They snacked on a half cold cheese/meat/crunchy peanut-butter sandwich.

They had a total of eight long lengths of chain. He tossed his wet suit over the backpacks they were in.

Waiting for their ride back to the condo, trying to calm down and relax, discussing the weight of the chains, and about which 1715 Spanish galleon it could have been on, possibly the *Nuestra Señora de Las Nieves*. They suspected it would show up on the galleon's manifest copy that was at the museum. Was this location marked on their computer treasure maps? Does the chain have Spanish mint marks on it? Each individual link looked to be at least an ounce of gold, which could have been used for trading purposes.

What other treasures were in this location? It could be found further out in deeper water on the ocean side of the corral reef… perhaps amongst the corral where the gold chains were found. It was possible treasure could still be found on the beach between the low tide line and the high tide line. Or, it could even be found in the dune they were resting on or further inland on the other side of the island.

Spanish treasures had been found up and down the whole eastern beaches of Florida. That is why so many beach hunters swarmed the beaches after storms passed through…treasures were scooped up from the oceans bottom and crevices and then tossed up on the beaches.

Jess stood. "Wish we had those laptop computers that can be hooked up to a ground-penetrating radar [GPR]," he said and then turned on their White's submersible metal detector called a Beach Hunter. "Those GPR units show a three dimensional color pictures of what's in the ground sixty feet."

"That would be nice, but we don't have the twenty-six thousand bucks to tie up in a unit like that, "Marie Ann said. "Plus, we can't take off to Oregon for two weeks of training. You're limited to three or four feet with that unit you got there."

"Yeah, but look what we have already spent for beach hunting. I wonder if there's rental stores around here that would have a GPS," Jess said, moving about ten feet from Marie Ann so his detector would not interfere with her electronics. He put on his headset and carefully began scanning the base of the sand dune.

In the distance to the north, they could hear the roar of a dune buggy. The dunes were high enough to block the noise of the surf. Marie Ann ran up to the top of the dune as Jess came up behind her. She began waving to him when Jess grabbed her by the arm and violently pulled her down the side of the dune. They rolled together to the valley between the large dunes.

"Sweetheart, you hurt?"

"No! But I broke the rod on my detector," she said. "Why did you yank me down like that?"

"That wasn't Philip's dune buggy, sweetheart! I hope the driver didn't see us!"

They returned down in the lower part of the dune. He grabbed the backpacks with the gold chains inside as Marie Ann got the wet suits. "Let's move further inland and call him again." He pointed to a group of low cedar bushes, "Over there!"

They had just disappeared under the brushes when the dune buggy topped the one they had been on. The driver was so close Jess could have grabbed her and pulled her into the underbrush with them. She was looking back toward the dune where they had run from, following their tracks back to the brush.

The young lady, perhaps in her twenties, turned toward the brush, looking directly at Jess, but could not see him and could not hear anything over the roar of the dune buggy engine.

Jess moved out of the brush and hollered, "Yes? Can't we have some privacy?"

She gasped, floor-boarded the dune buggy. It dug a hole in the sand and stalled out. Frightened, she looked back at Jess who stood with his hands on his hips as Marie Ann came up from the girl's blind side.

"Hello! We didn't mean to scare you so much. We won't hurt you," she said smiling and leaned in taking the keys out of the ignition and tossed them to Jess.

He tossed the keys back to the young girl, "We thought you were a friend of ours, but this isn't his buggy. His is all yellow and not noisy like yours."

"I'm Philip's friend," she said with a shaky voice while trying to put the keys back into the ignition. "Why did you hide from me?"

"We don't want others to know where we are," Jess said and sat in the passenger's seat. "How do we know who you are?" Turning to Marie Ann, "Sweetheart call his cell phone again."

She could not reach him on his cell phone, but left a voice mail and then called the condo number. Still no answer and left a message on his answering machine. "I wonder what happened to Philip."

Jess hopped out of the seat. "If the three of us lift the rear of this buggy, we can move it out of this hole you dug."

With hardly any effort they moved the rear of the vehicle. The young lady stuck out her hand, "I'm Vickery Wadesworth, a neighbor of Philip. My Mom and Dad own the condo complex and restaurant. Would you like to drive us back, Mr. Hanes?"

"How do you know us?" Jess asked and accepted the handshake. He then helped Marie Ann load their backpacks and detectors in the rear storage box. He pulled a piece of netting over everything to keep it in place.

"Everyone calls me Vic," she said, climbing in the single bucket seat in the back. "I'm buckled in!"

Jess and Marie Ann glanced at each other and got in and buckled up. "You know where Philip is?"

"He went to the restaurant to meet someone and asked me to find you!"

"Are we to meet him there?" Marie Ann asked.

"Yes, after you shower and change. Someone is throwing a party and we are all invited," she said with a girlish giggle.

"Okay, let's get going," he said and started the dune buggy. "Who's the party for?"

"Don't know! Philip wasn't too happy about it! It was on short notice!" she said between the bumps as they headed for the smoother sand of the beach.

Once on the hard surface of the beach, Jess increased the speed to the limits, 45MPH and headed north carefully watching out for wood pilings or any obstructions in the sand.

He thought to himself, *Now is not the time to have an accident. Really Jess, when is the best time? You have more than material treasures on board. You have your sweet wife and the young lady in the back. Remember, none of this has come to you, except the Lord permits it.*

"Thank you, Lord, yes, Lord, I'll slow down. Thank you for your protecting hand and mercy. Thank you for the bounty of our discoveries, even though there were lives lost in 1715," he said aloud, but not so the two ladies could hear him over the noise of the buggy he was driving.

CHAPTER TWO

Hutchison Island, Florida

By the time the three got the dune buggy parked, Marie Ann and Vic were well acquainted and laughing.

"Thank you Vic, we will see you in a little while," Jess said and shook her hand. He and Marie Ann got their gear out of the back and headed for their condo.

"Pretty little thing isn't she?" Marie Ann said with a snicker, looking out of the corner of her eye at Jess.

"Didn't notice!" he said with a smile on his face and not looking at her.

"Jess," Marie Ann laughed, "since when have you stopped noticing beautiful women? Liar, liar, pants on fire!"

He laughed, "You're right! I'm old, but I'm not blind."

She bumped against him, poked him in the ribs with her elbow.

While Marie Ann took her shower, Jess put the eight long lengths of gold chains in a cemented waterproofed vault-safe in the top of the closet. It was built into a cement column, six feet off the floor. Hopefully, it would be protected from storms and high water during hurricanes.

They were told about the third hurricane when it hit in September of 2004, the safe was underwater, but did not leak.

He took his shower and dressed. It was after sunset when they left the condo. Arm in arm and snuggled close, they walked across the lawn to the Tiki restaurant next to the swimming pool.

As they crossed the patio next to the pool, Jess noticed no lights in the restaurant and no one was inside. He put his arm around Marie Ann's waist and pulled her gently with him behind a brick pillar. They noticed two men coming out of the palm tree shadows between them and the parking lot. The men were arguing about something and did not see the two hiding.

"Sorry, love!" Jess said and pulled her even closer, kissing her hand. "I've sure gotten jumpy since we found…"

Marie Ann put her finger across his lips, looking toward the dark shadows of the restaurant and whispered, "Shush…Jess!" Then she screamed as Jess crumpled at her feet.

Someone had come from behind him and hit him in the back of the head with the butt of an automatic pistol. Two men grabbed her from behind and covered her mouth while another held her around her waist, lifting her, carrying her to a car.

One of them had used a lot of after shave or cologne like Jess used. Squirming and twisting, she tried to escape, until they chloroformed her and tossed her in the backseat. They smoked the tires leaving the parking lot and left Jess laying in the shadows.

When Jess became conscious he rolled over and slowly got to his knees. Holding the back of his head with his left hand he pushed himself up the side of the rough brick pillar, staying in the shadows.

Unsteady on his feet, he spoke out for Marie Ann, "Love, where are you?"

He moaned and continued to lean against the bricks. Suddenly, a bright light shined in his eyes. He covered them with both hands, "I can't see with that shining in my eyes."

Mr. Hanes, what are you doing in the shadows? What happened?" A familiar female voice said. "You look terrible!"

"Is that you Vic?"

"Yes, sir! Let me help you," she replied as he knelt in the grass and passed out. The last thing he remembered was the perfume she wore. His brain was in a whirl, spinning, falling into a black hole, no light, no sound, just silence.

Vic ran to her condo and called the sheriff's department. She told them she had found a gentleman beaten. Then she went back to Jess, but he was gone. It was not five minutes and two county sheriff's cars arrived.

She motion with her flashlight and yelled at them, "Over here! Over here!"

Four officers ran to her. By now, some of the residences from the condos were standing on their terraces, watching the excitement. Two officers stayed with Vic and questioned her. The other officers talked with the people on the terraces.

"Here's where I heard him moaning and tried to help him stand up, she said with a frightened voice. "Then he got wobbly and passed out over here on the grass."

The officers found blood tracks on the grass and on the brick pillar.

"Has he been drinking? Can you I.D. the man? How old? Did you know him?" one of them asked her as fast as he could. He was a young officer, excited with the crime scene and was trying to empress the beautiful young lady. "Did he touch or hurt you?"

Waving her hands, she interrupted him, "If you would please shut up long enough for me to reply, I will be glad to answer your questions." She replied with her hands on her hips.

Her folks arrived while she was giving him the information. The other officer began following the blood trail with his flashlight.

Her father questioned the officer, because he was not in uniform. He asked for the officers identification.

"My daughter will cooperate, but enough questions for now," he said and put his arm around Vic. "She is a minor."

"Do you have any identification on you?" the officer asked Vic. "I'm Lieutenant Fred Barns of the Hutchinson Island Sheriff's department." He showed her his badge because he was in civilian clothes. "Why is a young lady out so late?"

"She had our permission to be out Officer." Her father was getting aggravated.

She handed him her Florida driver's license.

"So you had your eighteenth birthday last month? What was the date and year you were born," he asked.

She frowned, wondering why he asked such a stupid question. He could read it on her license. He was watching her facial expression for a response.

"It right there, September 2, 1982." She put her hands on her hip impatiently. The *next thing he'll do is hit on me*, she thought.

"Daddy," she said looking up at him with a helpless expression.

The officer used his portable radio mike fastened to his belt, "Central! This is Barns."

"Go ahead, Lieutenant!"

"We have a missing person." He turned away from Vic giving his report and walked in the direction of another officer who was trying to follow the blood trail. The other two officers came over to them.

Vic and her Mom and Dad could not hear the police's conversation. They sat down at one of the restaurant's patio tables and she opened her cell phone, pressed a few numbers and waited.

He answered, "Yes Vic."

"Philip, where are you? We have a problem! Someone robbed Mr. Hanes and Mrs. Hanes is missing." She had not told the officer about Marie Ann being taken by force. Her parents listened closely to the details as she told Philip what she heard and saw from her fourth floor condo terrace.

"Call your folks and get back to your apartment. Don't talk to anyone else until I get there." He said with urgency. She tried to interrupt, but he talked too fast and she had to wait for the cell phone transmission to catch up. "Let me know if they find Jess, if I don't get there first. I'm on my boat and leaving now. Bye!"

"Bye!" she replied, and turned off her cell phone. "I couldn't get a word in edge-wise."

They headed for her condo/apartment cutting across the large grassy yard and parking lot. She kept turning around walking backward, talking to her folks and watching the police.

She hurried ahead of them. Her pace picked up the closer she got and was in a brisk walk when she started up the stairs. She took two or more steps at a time. Stopping short, Vic moved back into the shadow of the weeping willow tree branches that blocked the night light of the condos. There was a strange noise and her folks had not caught up to her.

"Oh my!" She grabbed her cell phone hanging around her neck "How did that ringer get changed?" she said softly to herself. "Yes?"

No answer. "Hello, whose calling?" Then she got a disconnect tone. She ran for the apartment door, hurriedly unlocked it and slammed it behind her, locking and bolting it. The apartment phone rang. She knocked over a kitchen stool getting to the phone.

"Yes Daddy?"

"Hello, sweetheart!" He said, "Are you okay? Do you want us to come up?"

"I'm fine, Daddy, I just ran up the stairs!"

"Okay, we are just locking the car. Do not unbolt the door until you see us on the outside camera monitor," he said.

"Yes, Daddy!"

Vic watched the monitor and then let her folks in. She told them about what had happened, talking as fast as she could. They finally got her to calm down and sit down, while her mom made some iced tea.

"Again, sweetheart, start from the beginning."

CHAPTER THREE

Missing Person

Philip contacted the sheriff's department and then headed to the condos. He took a back road from the marina through the mangroves, tall grass and cedar trees, using only the parking lights on his jeep. Taking a short cut to the top of a high sand dune, he turned its lights off and left it parked in the shadows. With his binoculars, he scanned the whole complex of condos. He could see Vic and her parents in their living room from his vantage point on the sand dune.

He called them on his cell phone, watching them answer their phone, "Hello."

"Charles, this is Philip! Don't talk, just listen. Your telephone may be tapped," he could hear Peg ask him who was calling. "The sheriff's department has the situation under control. If you do not have to go out tonight, please stay in. I'll call you later or come by. I would suggest turning your lights off. I can see you clearly from the south."

"Okay! That will work!" he hung up.

The sheriff's department told Philip that Jess had been jumped and was missing. Also, that Marie Ann had been kidnapped by someone in two black vehicles. The police were in Jess' condo apartment, but he was not there. Because they did not have a search warrant, they did not stay long.

Philip got approval from Charles, the owner of the complex, to get into Jess' condo. He began his own search of the condo complex, looking for Jess. He had a key to Jess' condo and waited for the police to leave the area before entering.

He did not have to use his flashlight because he knew the apartment layout like the palm of his hand. He could not find anything disturbed or out of place, except Jess' pistol and extra ammunition magazines (clips) were missing from under the bed. He also found blood stains on the closet safe's combination tumbler.

He was clueless to why Jess and Marie Ann were in Harm's Way. The earlier 'staged' run-in with the authorities at the swimming pool may be a starting place. He needed to call in favors from both sides of the law.

Suddenly, Philip froze in his tracks. He could feel someone very close to him. So close he could feel the body heat of the other person. Was he fast enough to jump away and protect himself. He was not armed except for his six celled flashlight.

"Don't move Philip!" Jess whispered, holding his .45 auto to his friend's neck, searching him for a weapon. "What ya doing in here, friend?"

"I've been looking for you, Jess!"

Jess jabbed him in the neck with his automatic, "Hold your voice down. There may be listening devices in here."

He pushed Philip toward a stool at the kitchen island serving bar, and then stepped away from him, "Have a seat!"

"Why are you so rough with me Jess, and with a gun?" Philip asked, laying the flashlight on the bar and folding his arms.

"Right now, I wouldn't trust my own brother roaming around my apartment with the lights off." Jess put his weapon in its concealed holster. "I need answers! I can't find Marie Ann. She has disappeared..." He leaned against the serving bar, light headed from losing blood.

"Philip..." losing his grip on the bars edge, he slid to the floor, leaning his back against the bar's wall.

Philip rounded the end of the bar and knelt next to Jess, feeling for a pulse. Jess' pulse was rapid and he was hot. Philip found a dishwashing cloth, soaked it in cold water. He washed Jess' face, neck, and bare arms to cool him down.

Jess finally opened his eyes and only saw a blur in the dark.

"Hold still!" Philip whispered. "Let me take care of these wounds on your head and neck." Turning on his flashlight, he laid it on the stool next to Jess' head.

Jess could feel a cold wet clothe on his forehead and held still.

"The only thing I could find in the bathroom was this iodine to wash these cuts and some Band-Aids. This is going to sting."

"Ay! Ay!" Jess grit his teeth and tried to relax. He grasped Philip's wrist. "You're a good friend, Philip. Forgive me for my reaction earlier. I wasn't in danger from you."

"You didn't know, no problem, Jess!" He put three Band-Aids on the head wounds. "It's our normal reaction to circumstances like this." He scooted away from Jess into the beam of light on the other side of Jess. "Your color is coming back. I think you'll be all right. Why don't we go to my apartment and get something to eat?"

"I don't think so, I'm not hungry and Marie Ann may call."

"Jess, I have some details for you," he reached around to turn off the flashlight. "Marie Ann was kidnapped. Vic saw it all from her balcony. She was the one who called the police."

"I didn't see any police," Jess moaned as he leaned his head against the bar's wall. "Wait!" He said trying to clear his fuzzy mind, "Marie Ann was kidnapped, by who?" With Philips help, he got to his knees.

"Take it easy old man!"

"Hey, you're right!" Jess moaned again while getting to his feet, "I remember we went to the restaurant for your party, but it wasn't open and no one was there. Then we got jumped. Vic told us to meet you there!"

"I don't understand why she told you that," Philip said and stood next to Jess to catch him if he would faint. "I only told her where to pick you up, because I had to go to the boat. Someone called telling me it was listing badly. I got there and it was okay."

"What's going on, Philip? What's all this rough stuff and kidnapping Marie Ann?" Jess slowly walked over to the bay-windows of the condo apartment which overlooked the abandoned beach front. "Does it have anything to do with where we are diving on the 1715 fleet?"

"Possible, but I really don't know! What would be their purpose, money?"

Jess groaned again and grabbed his neck with his left hand, and then slowly turned toward Philip's voice in the shadows of the living room, "Why are we targets and not you? I know you have no family, but why take Marie Ann?"

"This could be the work of terrorists, local gangster treasure hunters or even modern day pirates? I don't really know at this time." He moved over next to Jess at the window, "Let's go talk to Vic and her parents."

Jess sort of snorted, "Yea! But she's a minor. We can't pressure her to talk to us."

"I'm sure once they see you; I can persuade them to cooperate." He turned to Jess, "By the way she's in her early twenties, somewhere around twenty-one or two." Philip tried to make a point, "Cute isn't she?"

Jess shrugged, "I think she's still a minor, but not cute enough to get away with lying and setting us up like that." Jess was getting his dander up and started to shake. "Philip let me calm down a second." He took a deep breath, slowly letting it out, "I've not openly done this in your presents, but I'm overdue."

He bowed his head, took another deep breath, slowly let it out. "Father in heaven, forgive me for becoming so bitter toward people I don't even know that may be involved in this or not. Continue to keep Marie Ann safe in your arms and forgive where we have sinned against you. Keep Philip and me from being deceived and misdirected by the works of Satan. I claim this victory in Jesus precious name, Amen."

Philip cleared his throat. "Well, thank you, Jess. I even feel better." He placed his hand on Jess' good shoulder. "I'm sure we'll find Marie Ann in good health and get this all settled."

"For her sake, the sooner the better," Jess said and shook Philip's hand. "Lead the way partner, I'm right with you."

They took the back elevator down to the ground floor and headed to Vic and her parents apartment.

Chapter Four

Hutchison Island, Florida

Lying on her side, Marie Ann opened her eyes and the room began to spin. Her neck hurt and she had a throbbing headache. Closing them, the room stopped moving. She could not move her hands or legs, they were tied. A cool breeze blew across her bare legs below her knee length skirt.

She could hear the surf of a nearby beach. Voices became louder, approaching from a distant room. She slowly tried to open her eyes, but she could only squint. It was difficult focusing on anything, so she kept them closed.

"Good! Mrs. Hanes, you are finally awake?" a voice said with heavy British accent. Laughing, he said, "I am George, your body protector."

He came closer to her, she could smell his cologne. It was like what Jess used, but this man must have taken a bath in it. It was too strong. He sat next to her on the couch and began to stroke her shoulder length hair. He made a guttural sound like a hungry dog.

She tried to turn her head away, but he held her head in place by her hair. She wanted to move her arms, but she could not feel anything. They were numb and tied behind her. She wanted to speak, but her mouth was covered.

She began to pray for Jess' safety, remembering the expression on his face before he was hit on the back of the head...a look of being trapped.

"Turn her head so the light is not in her eyes," a younger British man's voice said with authority. "And extinguish that lamp!"

"Charlie, you back off!" George said holding Marie Ann's hair. He swore, "Young punk, who put you in charge?"

The back door to the room slammed shut. "Hey, you two!" Then something hard hit a tabletop with a loud bang. "Turn her loose and untie her... now!"

Marie Ann jumped and opened her eyes wide just as the brighter lights were turned off. The short stocky bearded man grabbed George by the shirt. "Let her go!"

Wide eyed, George let go of her hair, and then he was slung to the floor.

"No one told you to gag and tie her! Get out of here!"

Charlie punched George lightly on the arm, "See! I told you not to tie her!"

"Shut up you little weasel," George said and shoved Charlie away from him. The two moved to the door entering the other room, George turned, "She could get away, Dud."

"Don't call me Dud!" he pointed his finger at them. "Both of you go sit in there with Lemi. I've about to run my course with you two, scum-of-the-sea!"

He turned to Marie Ann as her eyes became focused on him. Turning her over, he untied her wrists and then her ankles. Then he gently sat her upright.

"I am so sorry about the rough treatment you have received at the hands of these roughnecks. I will assure you it will not happen again. They will make it up to you. That is my promise!" He knelt down in front of her gazing into her pretty hazel eyes. "Good, you can see. I was afraid they used too much chloroform on you."

He tilted his turbaned head looking into her face. His narrow, deep wrinkled face was kind and seemed sympathetic toward her, and she could see a concealed firearm in its holster under his light jacket. "This may hurt when I remove the gray tape from your lips or would you rather do it?"

Marie Ann fingered the tape until she found the edge. She slowly prayed inwardly as she carefully removed it from her tender chapped lips, *Jesus, I'm in your protecting hands. Greater are You in me than he that's in this world!*

"My name is Dudley. Here, use my clean handkerchief. Your upper lip is bleeding, right there," he started to touch her lip where the blood was coming out.

She jerked back from him dropping the tape, but took the handkerchief, "Should I thank you or will you hit me too?"

He suddenly turned toward the other room and stood up, shaking a driver's license at them. "Who hit Mrs. Hanes?" No one answered. He went in to the three men,

"Better tell me, now." The younger one pointed to George, who had washed Marie Ann's face. "Why did you hit her? There is no reason to be a brute bully. She's not a London whore like you are so accustom being with."

He stood in the doorway gripping his hands tightly, the knuckles turning white, "I don't think we have the right woman. She does not look like the one in the photo you have!"

The oldest of the three, George, stood up, "Sure I did! And, I burnt the photo! What are you going to do about it?" He stood, waving his arms in defiance. "Makes no difference to me what she is! She's just a broad…" No sooner had he turned away and spoke the last word, Dudley swung a round-house punch, snapping the man's neck. The big guy hit the floor.

"Check him; I may have broken his fool neck!"

Then he went back to Marie Ann. She held the handkerchief to her lips and was staring at what had taken place in the other room. She made no attempt to move.

Sliding a chair away from the table, he sat facing her from across the room. He then leaned back in the chair, placed his elbow on the table and leaned sideways against his hand with the side of his face.

"I need for you to call Mr. Hanes, he should be in your apartment...if, he's not in the hospital. These men of mine worked him over good! That I do not mind, but not a lady!"

He went over to Marie Ann and handed her driver's license to her and his cell phone, "I took that out of your purse earlier."

He stood, "The call cannot be traced. So, please tell him anything you wish." He smiled walking away from her, "I just want him to know you are not really being harmed. Afterwards, I will then address him with my list of demands." He pulled out a wrinkled piece of paper from his shirt pocket, smoothed it out and laid it on the table.

She called their apartment, no answer. Then his cell phone, "Your party cannot be reached at this time, please leave a voice mail message."

She sighed, "Jess, please answer the phone, it's me." Still no answer and she hung up.

"You may try again later." He stood, "Would you like hot or cold tea?"

"Cold if you don't mind," she said and stood. "If I can have my purse, I'll get a couple of aspirin for my headache."

He turned and motioned for her to sit back down. "Yes, the chloroform gave the bad headache. I can see it in your eyes." She did, as he went into the other room. While he was out of her room for a short moment, she scanned the room for possible clues as to where she was and how she could escape. When he brought back her purse and a glass of iced tea, he sat the glass on the table. He then rummaged through her purse and handed her a small envelope marked aspirin.

She drank the tea slowly while taking the aspirin. Closing her eyes again, she prayed for the Lord to help her find Jess. She sat back on the couch leaning her head back. The tall thin man went back to the other room, partly closing the door behind him.

CHAPTER FIVE

Hutchison Island, Florida

Vic and her parents sat transformed, looking at the bruises and cuts on Jess' face. They were very polite and let Vic tell her story.

She told them Philip had asked her to go after Mr. and Mrs. Hanes for him, because he had an emergency at the boat dock. On the way out to her dune buggy, one of her friends stopped her, telling her there was to be a big party at the restaurant for everyone. Somehow, she misunderstood the Hanes' were to be there too. So when they got back, she showered and changed clothes, and then walked out on the terrace balcony to see who the band was and listen to the music. That was when she saw no lights and heard no music.

Then, she saw two men jump into the shadows as the Hanes' walked over to the restaurant. They beat Mr. Hanes and took Mrs. Hanes forcefully to their two black cars. Vic went down to help Mr. Hanes, but he was no longer lying against the pillar of the restaurant. With her flashlight, she looked in the brush, but could not find him. That was when she called the police and met them there.

"You couldn't identify any of them or the vehicles?" Jess anxiously asked.

"Yes, but I didn't tell the police. There was something strange about them, I don't know what!" she said with self-confidence she would be of some help now. "But, one of the men who beat you

I've seen around the swimming pool watching the sunbathers. I had assumed security let him through the gates."

Her father, Dr. Charles Wadesworth spoke up, "Sweetheart, you should have told them anyway. Any strange men hanging around like that should be your first warning something was wrong."

"Yes, Victoria, by all means let us know also," Peggy, her mother requested with an air of sophistication. "We normally do not have such trash within the confines of the condominiums."

"Peg, don't be so snobbish in front of our friends," her husband said. "We are just uptown city slicker from Atlanta. Vic is our only child and she lives here the year around."

"Yes, Charles! Whatever!" She said and went to the kitchen. "Would you gentleman care for iced tea or coffee? Sweetened?"

Vic went in to help her.

"Unsweetened, please," Jess replied as he stood and stretched. "Woo! Can't do that yet! I think they may have ripped my shoulder stitches out." He reached under his t-shirt to check and brought his hand out with blood on it.

Vic went over to Jess, "May I look at it Mr. Hanes. I'm in my third year of nurses training at Florida State."

"Yes, thank you," Jess said. "I thought your name was Vickery?"

"Mom likes Victoria better!" she answered.

"Mrs. Wadesworth, I would enjoy some tea. Please," said Philip and he also stood. "I bet you have broken ribs, Jess."

"Daddy is a nuclear physicist and physician. He works at the nuclear power plant down the road near here. He can look at your wounds, if you like," Vic offered.

Her mother brought the drinks on a tray into a room off the terrace. "Ya'll come out here. The ceiling fan is stirring the air better. It's not so stuffy as the living room."

"May I suggest that you close your blinds on the terrace before we come out," Jess said.

"What in heaven's name for?" she asked bringing in another tray of crackers and cheese. "We will not be able to see the waves."

"Good idea, Mr. Hanes." He turned to answer his wife as he closed them, "Security! Security purposes, Peg!" He turned and motioned them out on the porch, "It is not just for gentlemen, come on out."

"Can we dispense with all the formalities? Please, use our first names…as you now know, Mom is Peggy, Peg for short. Dad is Charles, and I'm yours truly, Victoria." She laughed, and tried to mock her mother's southern accent. "I much rather be called, Vic! Mom insists on Victoria, but that's so starchy and high society! Like Vickery!"

"Daddy, would you look at Mr. Hanes shoulder wound. It's opened where the stitches pulled out and puffy," Vic asked, and turned to touch Jess' injured shoulder. "I'll get the peroxide to wash it out, antiseptic and adhesive spray." Smiling to herself, she turned to get the medicine. "I will be a senior in nursing school this fall."

Jess nodded to Charles. "We certainly need nurses."

"Mr. Hanes, would you remove your T-shirt?" He turned. "Bring a couple of towels too, Vic." He helped Jess with the shirt. "What happened here, my friend? That is extremely deep!"

"Charles, please call me Jess. We were diving and I got too close to a sea urchin. The doctor at the hospital…"

Suddenly, someone's cell phone rang. Everyone who carried one reached for where they usually carried it. Vic and her father continued working on Jess' wound while he answered his phone. It was Jess' phone; he was hoping it would be Marie Ann calling.

"Hello!" Jess said, apprehensive to talk, but anxious to hear her voice. No reply. He put it on the speaker, "Love, is this you?" He held up his finger for all to be quiet.

"Yes! It's me! I don't know how long they'll let me talk, but I'm not hurt. Except for a bloody lip where they covered it with tape. I'm getting over a severe headache from the chloroform they knocked me out with." She hesitated, and they could hear voices in the background. "They wouldn't let me use my own cell phone…"

Marie Ann lay the phone down against the back of the couch and turned on its video camera. She tilted it so Jess could see and hear what was going on. She stood up and held her hands in front of her.

They heard someone who was not happy about Marie Ann using the telephone. Jess put his cell phone on speaker and put it on the table so everyone could hear and see. He put his finger to his lips to quiet them. They could only see two of the men, one with a turban on his head and a shorter man standing next to him.

Vic jumped up pointing at the cell phone and shaking her finger. She turned to Jess and whispered, "That man grabbed your wife. He's the same man at the swimming pool."

Jess motioned for her to be quiet and to sit down. He leaned closer to the picture on the cell phone to get a better look.

Marie Ann spoke, "There is one man here, who wears a turban and seems to have my interest at heart…" she began breathing heavily, "… but, the other three are British seaman, and mean."

"Yes, love. Keep talking as long as they let you," Jess said softly, motioning Philip to get him something to write with and have him call his CIA friends on the Wadesworth's cell phone.

Marie Ann sat down on the couch next to the cell phone and began to cry, "Jess, I love you. They told me this phone can't be traced. I'm scared, but I know Jesus will take care of us!"

"We have already claimed His safety for you. Your help is there with you and more on the way. Keep talking to me, love!"

There was silence on the other end, except for some muffled sounds. "Mr. Hanes, your beautiful wife is in good health. As a God-fearing man, you'll continue to hold her good health in your hands. So follow these instructions to the letter..." The dial tone was heard.

"Love! Marie Ann, are you there?" Jess was hollering into the cell phone. He almost panicked. "Lord Jesus, please continue to keep your arms about her."

He hung up, hoping they would call back. Jess sat down, whispering more prayer, softly reciting Psalm 91 for Marie Ann. The others in the room bowed their heads and offered their own prayers to God.

Then he dialed *69 on the cell phone, just by chance it would give him a number. It did and it was not Marie Ann's number. He called the CIA and local sheriff's department and brought them up to date.

Chapter Six

Kidnappers

"What's wrong with you guys?" the tall turban-headed man said with a heavy British accent. "This is not the woman I told you to bring?" He turned away from Marie Ann and tossed a photo at the men on the couch. It landed on the floor between them.

"Does that look like this woman?" he demanded.

"Mr. Sully, her name is Hanes and she was at the condo restaurant with her husband," George said, sitting on the floor. He leaned back against the couch, holding his neck where he had been punched by Dudley.

Defiantly he said, "It sure looked like her to me!"

"I wrote down the name! You cannot read?" Sully moved over to George, "Where is that photo?"

"I burned it!" George reminded him again and then tried to stand.

Sully shoved him back to his knees. "You did what! Her name was on the back of the photo!"

George reached for a gun under his belt, but Sully kicked him in the pit of the stomach and pulled the gun away from him.

"Do you remember the name on the photo?" Sully angrily asked.

He yelled at the other two, "Do you remember the name?"

They both shook their heads.

"I didn't see the photo until George started burning it," Charlie said, pointing an accusing finger at George.

George threw a coffee mug at Charlie. "Shout your mouth, you little liar!"

"Dudley, you and Charlie take her back to where you picked her up. And, get out of there quickly!"

Sully turned to Marie Ann, "My apologies, Madam!" and then bowed toward her.

'What about George?" Dudley asked.

"He is my responsibility," Sully said, and made a motion with his finger pointed in the air. "You return her unharmed or I'll have your head." Then, he said turning away from Marie Ann. "Meet me at the dock, refuel and run-up the Lake."

"The what?"

"Did I stutter?" Sully shouted, "Refuel and start the engines on the seaplane," the turban headed man replied as he turned his back on Dudley, and then shook his head while rolling his eyes.

"Why, where am I going Mr. Sully?" Dudley asked and shoved his hands in his hip pockets.

"Never mind, I'll do it myself when I get there. Stay with the seaplane until I get there. In one hour, we fly out of here."

"You don't want to take this pretty lady?" George said and started to reach for her.

Sully shoved him toward the door, "Dudley, take this lady to the car and keep her safe. Take her back to where you kidnapped her."

"Yes, sir, Mr. Sully. We will...," he stuttered. "I have George's gun now," Dudley said and offered his hand to Marie Ann.

She reluctantly took his hand to get up from off the couch. He motioned to follow George out the front door. Dudley got into the back seat with Marie Ann and tapped the back of George's front seat with the gun barrel.

"Put your seatbelt on, we don't want no tickets if we're stopped." Dudley tapped the seats headrest behind George's head. "Now, don't forget, I still have your gun. Now, drive back to where we got her!"

George frowned at Dudley looking in the rearview mirror on the windshield. "Okay big man with the gun." He put the car in gear and they sped away from the house, leaving Mr. Sully with a soon to be dead man.

CHAPTER SEVEN

North End of Hutchison Island

Two of Philip's CIA contacts were listening to the details of Jess and Marie Ann's attack and kidnapping. Suddenly, they heard tires screeching in the parking lot. Vic got up and parted the shut blinds.

"Hurry, hurry!" she screamed at them in the room. "There's the big black limousine. Hurry, there's Mrs. Hanes!"

The five men in the room ran out the condo terrace. One of the CIA agents started talking on his cell phone as the other agent and Jess ran through the condo to the side door leading to stairs to the first floor. Charles and Philip stayed on the terrace to watch with Vic.

The two men had heard Vic scream and ran back to their vehicle parked in front of the restaurant, leaving Marie Ann standing on the sidewalk. The first try of starting the limo did not work. By the second try, Jess was almost on them. It started and they floored it in reverse, spun it around, and smoked their tires getting out of the parking lot.

Jess and the agent were left standing in the cloud of burnt tire smoke.

"Ray!" the other agent on the terrace hollered. "We got them sighted and in chase!"

Jess turned to the agent and shook his hand. "Let's get Marie Ann."

She was still standing where they had left her, arms open and tears flooding her eyes. Jess swung his arms around her and held her.

"Thank you, Jesus! Oh yes! Thank you, Jesus!" he said in unison with her.

He did not feel the pressure on his wounds as she almost squeezed the breath out of him. He put his hands on both sides of her face and turned her toward the restaurant flood lights.

"Love, did they hurt you? Your lip is bleeding."

"Not really. Just emotionally!" she said. "I made my lip bleed when I took tape from across my mouth too fast."

Jess tenderly kissed the split in her lip. "We have a doctor and nurse upstairs, Vic and her dad. Let's go!"

The agent with them continued to survey the grounds as they went to Charles's condo.

After talking with Marie Ann and getting her details, the two agents left.

The sun was coming up over the calm waters of the beach when Jess and Marie Ann finally got to their own condo, showered, prayed, and crawled into bed. They went to sleep in each other's arms.

Jess took the condo telephone off the hook and turned both cell phones off.

CHAPTER EIGHT

Early Flight Cancelled

"I'm not waiting any longer for those two wharf rats," the turban headed Sully said over the roar of the seaplanes engine.

He looked north and then south toward the west bank of the Indian River and sat down in the pilot's seat, buckled in, rechecked the instruments, and whispered to himself, "The engine temperature and oil pressure is correct." He tossed the rope back on the pier.

Sully closed the aircraft's canopy and taxied the Lake amphibian seaplane away from a make-shift hiding place. Then he headed out toward the ship's channel into a light southern breeze. After taking off, he flew low, south down the inland waterway between the buoy markers.

Flying only for a short distance of a half mile, he abruptly turned due east to cross Hutchison Island. If he had banked much sharper, the left wing tip would have been in the water. He flew just high enough to skim over the palm and mangrove trees. Then out to sea just far enough to still see land out his starboard window he turned to a starboard course 158 degrees, staying below the coastal radar.

He did not have Dudley to help with the instruments, so he canceled his plans to fly to the Grand Bahamas' Islands. He would now head down to Havana, Cuba. He would follow the coast to Florida Keys, and then make his usual contacts for fuel.

Dudley and Charlie sat behind bars in the Coast Guard brig at the Fort Pierce harbor entrance. They were being held for INS and Interpol agents to arrive. The Coast Guard was to only hold them temporary, five hours maximum, before releasing them to the local authorities for kidnapping. The CIA did not want to waste time with them; they had bigger fish to fry.

That fish was headed for Havana, hopefully they would be able to intercept him before he flew out of the U. S. territorial waters. A Coast Guard vessel on early morning coastal watch sighted the low flying Lake seaplane and contacted a U.S. Navy Hawkeye Airborne Early Warning aircraft on maneuvers from Mayport, Florida, which was flying north along the eastern coastline.

They were high enough that ground clutter and waves did not interfere with the radar response back from the lower flying aircraft. In fact, they only had a few hundred feet separation below them as the smaller aircraft passed underneath them headed south parallel with the beach. They slowed and made a sharp turn south, dropping down and behind the civilian seaplane.

They slowed to 120 knots, slightly behind and above the slower aircraft. After notifying the Coast Guard, who immediately sent two helicopters to meet them out from Miami, the Hawkeye slowed to 100 knots. There was a headwind that slowed the smaller aircraft.

It took only thirty minutes for the military aircraft from Key West to arrive and the Hawkeye turned on landing lights. It was just twilight and the bright lights surprised the seaplane's pilot.

Sully thought he had come out from under a cloud and the sun was up. He looked back through the left cockpit window and could not see anything behind him or to the east, because the Hawkeye was in a blind-spot. It did not dawn on him that he was now surrounded by military aircraft; one behind and one above and off each wing tip.

The two helicopters dropped down to the seaplane altitude, 200 feet above the water, and turned their search lights on. Sully was suddenly wide awake and froze on the controls. He did not have his radio volume turned up. Otherwise he would have heard them trying to contact him before turning on the flood lights.

They turned off the lights so he could see them. A crew member seated at the doorway of both helicopters motioned to their earphones for him to operate his radio. He dipped his wings and then turned up the volume.

"Come to a heading of 270 degrees and follow the helicopter off your starboard wing."

Sully did not speak, but dipped his wings again and slowly banked his aircraft to right to follow the SA365 Dauphin 2. He climbed about fifty feet to get out of the blade wash of the helicopter.

The following Dauphin told the lead aircraft what the seaplane had done and came along side it. The crew member gave him a thumps-up for an okay. "There is a United States Coast Guard vessel dead ahead. Land your aircraft for inspection. I repeat, land your aircraft for inspection."

Sully dipped his wing again and scanned the water ahead for a ship. He saw it and turned his landing light on, slowed his seaplane and circled the vessel.

"Land on the port side, port side; we will hover until crew members are on board."

He was clean of drugs and firearms, so that did not bother him. He did not have a passport or papers for the aircraft. But under his flowered Florida shirt he did have his CIA credentials in a black watertight leather carrier hanging under a big gold chain around his neck.

The morning ocean was flat and smooth. He could see the skyline of Miami to the west as he taxied alongside the U.S. Coast Guard cutter. He cut the engines and slowly began to drift with the waves. A small craft was already in the water heading toward him with heavily armed sailors.

Sully, unbuckled his seatbelt, opened the canopy side door and stood up in the seat with his arms raised. His black beard fluttered in the wind and the royal blue turban glistened in the early morning sun.

He whispered to himself, "Why didn't I stay at home; Ohio is so beautiful this time of year."

He was an undercover agent working the drug routes out of South America.

CHAPTER NINE

Hutchison Island Condos

Around ten the next morning, after two days with kidnappers, Marie Ann made sure the telephone ringer was off and put the phone back on its cradle. If someone called they could leave a message on the answering machine. She slowly made her way down the hall by aide of the hall plug-in night light to the bathroom. She wanted to take another shower.

She left Jess peacefully sleeping in their queen size bed. He felt her get up and rolled over, dozing off again. An hour later, he was awakened by the smell of bacon and onions cooking.

Bright eyed and bushy tailed she began breakfast making a four egg, double bacon, cheese, onion, jalapeño pepper with Pepper Jack cheese omelet. A side order of Texas toast and a large pot of Cubana coffee were ready.

Jess was showered and dressed by the time the coffee was poured.

"Good morning, love. How do you feel?" he said as he sampled the hot coffee.

She changed her frown to a beautiful smile, back to a frown, "Light headache, but the shower helped relax that somewhat!" she began pouring her coffee.

"Sure smells great!" Jess said and reached for her hand as she sat next to him at the kitchen lunch bar. They bowed their heads while Jess prayed, thanking God for their continued safety and for His wisdom for them during the coming day.

"And a special thank you for bring Marie Ann back safely. Keep us from being deceived by these people. We certainly need your wisdom about the gold chains. Thank you, we ask Father in Jesus name, Amen."

"You know what the onions remind me of?" Jess asked with his mouth half full of omelet.

"Yep, the onions at the fair," she replied passing him the butter for his toast.

He took his table knife and spread butter and grape preserves on the toast. "Nope, but close; remember what the diner cook told us in Springfield, Missouri? He would cook onions early before breakfast and turn the exhaust fans on high. It would attract the workers and drivers at the next door truck stop."

"Then at the Indiana State Fair in the ole Exhibition Hall, when the cookie booth would spray vanilla in the air when their cookies were ready." She nodded her head, "And, the people would flock around their booth to buy."

Their conversation was light, letting Marie Ann continue to settle down from the events of the last two days.

After they took care of the breakfast dishes, they weighed the gold chains on the bathroom scales for a total weight. Then measured and weighed the individual eight lengths. Total weight was forty-seven pounds.

Jess took the single link he had put in his pocket and weighed it. It was one ½ pound. Each link was 2 inch long and was ¼ inch twisted thickness.

Total length of the eight chains was forty-six feet long; 276 links in all. This amounted to 138 pounds of gold according to the condo scale in the bathroom.

Jess handed Marie Ann a plastic numbered I.D. tag to attach to each of the eight chains. These tags were number by the museum for research and tracking. They photographed each length separately, and then together.

"This looks like the same gold chain that's in Mel Fisher's museum at Sebastian," Jess said. "I'll have to call Taffi with these dimensions and weight."

They finished taking photos with a digital camera and then transferred them to the computer for e-mailing. They would eventually take the gold chains to the museum at Sebastian for further research and value appraisal.

"I'll get on the Internet for current gold prices," Marie Ann said. "Wonder what value the salvage market will tag it with?"

"I couldn't even give you a good estimate," Jess replied as he draped the chain around his neck. "Last we checked, it was pushing $1,000 a troy ounce."

He stood up and stretched. "We may not get to keep this find. It was in the water and I think it was in one of Mel's 'exclusives' on the 1715 Plate Fleet. That gives Taffi the salvage claim rights to it."

"Some of your diver friends would tell you not to tell where it was recovered. But I know you wouldn't do that."

"Right, we can't do that! One lie would lead to another to cover up the first," Jess replied. "That hasn't been our life style for over forty years. I know you're not suggesting that we do that, because it would put us in direct conflict with our Lord. Plus, it would be breaking a written contract with the Fisher's museum."

"You found it on the beach in waist deep water at low tide," Marie Ann said. "Then the state of Florida would lay claim to it and take you to court if you don't turn it over. But, it was in Mel's exclusive and you're a part of the crew for that exclusive. You would be protected as one of her division divers."

"You're right, sweetheart. And now that we have that settled, we'll get it to the museum ASAP."

Jess removed one of the chains from around his neck after putting the tag on it. "I wouldn't want to carry that for very long. It would definitely give me a sore neck."

He stretched the chain out on bath towels, and then rolled each one separately in a towel. They were all returned to the condo safe.

"We'll do some extensive research before anyone knows about it. By then, we will know what our options are." Jess stood back putting his hands on his hips, before closing the safe's door. "Look at all those white towels of gold; can't believe it's over 100 pounds of gold."

"No wonder you're all stoved-up and sore. You wrestled, tugged and lifted it all the way to the dunes on the beach," she said and rubbed him between his shoulder blades.

"With your back problem too; we need our heads examined! I could have carried more than I did." She sat down at the computer desk.

Jess walked over to her, "You're right, but we did what we did and there it is," he said and nodding at the open safe. "Did you find out anything on the gold price?"

"I can't get on-line. My computer is locked up," she said very annoyed and frustrated with it. "One more time it does this to me, I'll use it for a boat anchor."

Jess massaged between her shoulders in return for her massage, "Let's go over to Philip's. He may have info on those crazies that grabbed you yesterday."

They locked the safe, set the alarm system and left.

While walking over to Philip's condo, someone shouted and waved from the Wadesworth's light blue Chrysler "Bat Mobile" Cruiser. Jess and Marie Ann waved back and continued on to Philip's place.

"I've been wondering," Jess said, squeezing her hand. "Those idiots kidnappers the other night could have been after that family and not us."

Philip and Charles were in a quiet discussion when Jess and Marie Ann approached Philip's screened-in porch. The two men did not see them coming and both jumped when Marie Ann knocked on the door.

"I didn't mean to startle you guys!" Laughing she pointed at Philip, "You look like you've been shot or seen a ghost!"

"Come in! Come in!"

Both men stood as the couple came in and seated themselves at the porch table.

Marie Ann pointed at the car lot, "I thought that was you and your family in the 'Bat Mobile' that just left."

"No, that was Peggy and some friends." Philip gave her a hug, and then poured them iced tea from a sweating pitcher. A breeze from the ocean and a large fan hanging from the ceiling circulated the humid air through the porch. The expressions on the men's faces were stern with anxiety.

Jess put his elbows on the table and leaned toward Philip, "Now what's wrong?"

Charles slid transparent folders with a photo and papers in them across to Jess. Marie Ann scooted close to him in order to see what it was. Leaving it in the individual folders Jess passed the photo to her and began reading the faded wrinkled papers.

"Vic is certainly an attractive young blonde," Marie Ann said looking on the back of it. She caught her breath and put her hand across her mouth, "Oh! No!"

The photo of Vic had a bloody thumb print and a scribbled note on the back, 'Doctor Wadsworth, Is this your daughter's blood? I will be in contact with you. No police!'

"Who are these people, Charles?" Jess gritted his teeth, eyeing every detail of the photo. "And, what do they want?"

Marie Ann reached for the photo and studied it again. She nodded her head, "Here! Look at this, these three men in the background..." Turning to Charles, "Do you have a magnifying glass or something I can use to get a better look at this?"

"I don't really know who they are, but they probably think we have money to burn!" Charles motioned them into his office where he had a desk lamp with a magnifier in the center.

He turned it on, "We are well off financially, but I certainly can't get my hands on 4 million." Folding his arms, he took a deep sigh, "I don't even have friends or family with that kind of money lying around."

He walked over and looked out toward the parking lot and came back to the desk. "Just because I work at the nuclear plant doesn't mean I have access to confidential or secret information. Taking Vic as a hostage can't get them money!"

"Those are the three men who had me tied up, and this tall one is their leader. He's the one with the blue turban headdress!" she handed the photo to Jess and the other two looked over his shoulder.

Jess slapped the table top in front of him, making everyone jump. "Look at those guy's again! They were the same men in the seaplane the other day." He stood and put his hands on his hips. He leaned over to Marie Ann to say something to her.

"I was so groggy from that chloroform when they had me tied up. I didn't recognize them as those in the aircraft," she said.

Philip took the photos and used the magnifier, "You're right! That's the same men in the Lake seaplane."

"Philip, I bet they're not really interested in Victoria, money or..." Jess said, pointing at the photo. "I bet you're right; they will hold her for information about the nuclear plant. Money is secondary and Vic will be discarded when they get what they want from you."

"Jess, you don't have to be so blunt," Marie Ann said and continued to look at the photo.

The others shook their heads, not recognizing any of the three in the photo and walked back out to the porch.

Charles made more iced tea, poured the others glasses full and sat with his back to the porch outside door. The wind had come up and the sea mist became thicker.

"I haven't told her mother yet! This was all on the porch table at home when I went in." Charles stood, "I'm afraid to call the local island police over here. Not right away, we need to discuss this some more..."

Jess gently stacked the photo and papers. "Do you have a large folder to put this stuff in? Everyone has their fingerprints on it now."

"That means we all will have to get fingerprinted?" Charles asked frowning.

Philip answered nodding his head. "I'm sure you're correct, I'm afraid so."

"We'll need to get something with Vic's prints to compare with the one on the photo," Marie Ann suggested.

"That may be one of their prints too," Jess suggested. "That sure is a large print for it to be Vic's"

John and Philip looked at the photo again and agreed.

"When will your wife get home Charles?" Marie Ann asked. "Would you want us to be here when you tell her?"

"Probably in a couple of hours," he wiped his forehead. "Yes, that would be appreciated."

"We can do something right now," Marie Ann said reaching for Jess' hand. "We can pray for Victoria's safety and quick return. Jesus knows what needs to be done! We're to trust our Lord Jesus and Father in heaven."

She bowed her head and the others followed her lead. Jess knelt and prayed aloud. Then there was a long silence.

Nothing was further said as they listened to the surf from the beach.

It was quiet for a long time when Philip stood up and walked over to the porch screen. He took another long swallow from the glass, leaving only the ice cubes, and turned back to the table. "Jess, I don't trust those law enforcement people who were here the other day. Do you have contacts?" he poured a refill into his tall tea glass and offered the others more.

Jess looked at Marie Ann, they both smiled, "The very best! We know some fantastic law enforcement people. Thank you, Lord!"

Jess pulled a cell phone from its resting place on his belt and stepped outside. Marie Ann followed with a pad of paper for notes. They walked under a shade tree talking. It did not take five minutes and they returned, both smiling.

"Let me have this photo and those papers. Stay here, love. I'll be right back!" He pulled out his T-shirt and pushed the folders underneath, then tucked it back in his pants. "There is a fax machine at the pool snack bar. We shouldn't use your office fax."

"Wait, Jess! I'll go with you," Marie Ann said. "I have some more questions."

"By the way, Charles, it is all right that I take these?"

With a smile, he motioned with his hand. "Sure! Can we be of help here?"

"Not yet! But I'm sure we all are about to become a tight-knit team!" Jess said over his shoulder as the two headed for the restaurant. Marie Ann wrapped her arm around Jess' waist and he pulled her close to his side as walked across the lawn. The sprinklers had started covering the sidewalk.

She looked up at him, "Why didn't we think about this night before last, when those idiots brought me home? We have a wealth of support to tap into!"

Jess nodded, and they both said at the same time, "U.S. Marshall, Madilene Ash!"

CHAPTER TEN

Another Kidnapping

Jess and Marie Ann started into the restaurant when she noticed someone get out of the bus and walked toward the front of Charles's condo. She grabbed Jess' arm and pointed, before she could say anything Jess took off running toward Victoria.

Marie Ann yelled as loud as she could to attract Vic. She stopped, turned and saw Jess coming waving his hands. Charles and Philip heard Marie Ann and came out into the yard to find out what was going on. They all ran to Vic standing on the front steps. She was startled from all the excitement and backed up leaning against the front door.

"Sweetheart, are you all right? Are you hurt anywhere? What did they do to you?" Charles asked out of breath as he wrapped his arms around her, holding her tight. The others gathered around and quietly waited their turns to talk.

She pushed away from her father, "What's wrong with everybody? You scared me silly!"

Philip and Jess scanned the area for unfamiliar cars and people. Jess motioned them all to Philip's screened porch. No one talked until settled around the table or in chairs.

"Sweetheart, where have you been," Charles asked, trying to calm down. "We have been so worried…"

Marie Ann put her hand over Vic's, "We have had a fright not knowing what was happening to you." Moving the photo in front of Vic, "Where was this taken and do you know who these men are in the background?"

She looked at Marie Ann and then her father before looking at the photo. She smiled and pushed it over to her father, "This was on the boardwalk along the bay. I don't know those men."

Charles pushed the photo back to her, "Look long and carefully! Have you ever seen these men anywhere?" Looking at Jess who nodded back, "Please turn it over!"

"Oh yes, this is the guy I saw at the swimming pool last week. He thought he was a ladies man, Creep!" she said as she turned the photo over. Then she gasped after reading the note and seeing the bloody print, "How did it get out of my album upstairs at home?" Scooting the photo away from her, "That's not my blood! What is this all about? Who are they supposed to be, terrorists?"

Marie Ann moved close to Vic and softly informed her they were the ones who hit Jess on the head and took her away. They put their arms around each other and cried.

"What do they want with me?" Vic finally asked and poured ice tea into an empty glass on the table. Charles walked behind her and put his hand on her shoulder brushing away her long blonde hair from her face.

Leaning down he kissed her on the forehead. "Well, sweetheart!" He paused and continued, "I suspected they want to take someone as ransom and demand I give them classified information from the nuclear plant."

Philip leaned his chair back against the frame of the screened porch, "They are the same ones who tried to come aboard our boat at sea; kidnapped Marie Ann and returned her; got this photo from your room and put someone's blood print on it." He stretched his arms and put his hands behind his head, "What's this all mean, Jess?"

"Well, it's hard to second guess terrorists! And that's exactly what we have here" He smiled at Vic, "They have been in your room, so when was the last time you were in it? Do you remember if anything was out of place, anything unusual about your room?"

"No, I haven't since before breakfast." She frowned looking at her father. "You and Mom were at home when I left."

"Where did you go, sweetheart?"

"Daddy, you know I went to the hairdresser. Mom had made the appointment for me."

"That reminds me, she should be back by now," Charles said turning around to look toward the parking lot. "We were out of bread and milk. She went to the Quick Shop two miles south on A1A." Pointing at a vehicle parking, "There she comes."

"By the way, Vic," Jess said. "Don't go back in your room, only if it is absolutely necessary. Take someone with you if you do and don't touch anything. The authorities may want to dust your room for fingerprints."

"What authorities?" she asked.

"U.S. Marshals," Jess replied. "We have some good friends with them."

"We have two nephews who are Texas Rangers, but they have no authority here in Florida," Marie Ann said. "But they may have though the governor of Florida. It was just a thought, just a thought!"

"I would not ask that man for anything!" declared Charles. "He—"

"Charles!" Philip butted in. "Not even for your own family's protection? That's being a mighty bit selfish, don't you think?"

Jess stood up waving his hands at the other two men. "Okay, guys! Politics aside for now! We have to work as a team to get this problem taken care of before it gets worse. Agreed?"

Charles got up, shook Jess and Philip's hands, and then walked over to Marie Ann to do the same. "I am sorry everyone. You're correct, Jess. It's just so much to handle. I've not been in a situation like this before!"

Putting his arm around Vic, he kissed her on the forehead. "I am sorry, sweetheart. What should be done now, Jess?"

CHAPTER ELEVEN

Diving Off Hutchison Island, Florida

A week later, after talking to U.S. Marshal Ash, tensions subsided and things got back to some sort of normalcy. The Marshal's Anti-terrorists Service had sent two of their people over, interviewed everyone and took the papers and photo, and then searched for fingerprints in Vic's room.

They also took a statement from Marie Ann and Jess about the kidnapping.

Charles and his family continued their life style as if nothing had happened.

Philip, Jess, and Marie Ann were back diving close to the Sebastian Inlet from their trawler. It was more than fully equipped and supplied with all the amenities for a lengthy stay at sea, plus every item needed for diving and enough room for six.

It was calm and clear. The sun was barely up when they dropped and set two stern anchors and then the bow anchor—in that order.

By that time, everyone was ready for divers to get in the water.

Marie Ann had double-checked the divers' equipment before they put on their regulators from the low air pressure Hookah breathing unit. It could accommodate two men with full face mask and communications at depths of 150 feet. So now working in the shallow 30 feet, they had sufficient capacity.

Working the hard pan, coquina,[1] or bottom which was under the sand for two or three hours, they were ready to come up for lunch.

If they broke through this 3- or 4-foot crust, a black muck of decay would be found. They had no way of determining the depth of the black stuff. They did not dare stir it up, because it was like thick oil and would drift up toward the surface and stick on everything it touched.

She would bring them up at noon. But in the old days when the treasures of the 1715 fleet were originally found, the divers would be bringing it up to the surface even as it was found

---

[1]   A soft, whitish limestone made up of shell fragments and corral.

Once in the water, Jess went under aft of the boat to check the lock/fastener to the lowered mailbox. The mailbox is the name for a mechanism to direct the backwash of the propeller down toward the surface of the ocean floor, moving sand and small debris from where the divers were to hunt for treasure.

Descending to the bottom, Jess checked the communications back up to Marie Ann. Verbal communications was kept short in order to eliminate misunderstandings. Sometimes bubbles from the regulator would interfere with what was spoken.

The signal given, "Number One.," was to put the boat engine in low forward rpm, so the downwash of its prop would blow a hole in the sand.

Jess slowly moved his special, White's Electronics BeachHunter 300, diver's metal detector, across and up the sides of the sand crater made by the downwash. He was patiently waiting to either hear a tone of a detected metal: iron or precious metal.

It detected ferrous and nonferrous metals. This White's Electronics detector was a submersible Beach Hunter that indicated, iron, rings and coins; red LED for iron/steel; green for coins, and copper, silver, gold, brass, aluminum and other nonferrous metals; and yellow for mid-range jewelry and nickels. If the water was clear, the LEDs were handy; otherwise he just listened for the tone. Working the detector in Discrimination, additional tones help identify the type metals; high pitch for silver, middle tone for gold, and low base tone for junk/trash iron. But there were times the iron targets were special and were kept.

If they did not work fast enough, sometimes the sand and sea shells would slide back down into the crater, covering the coquina again on the bottom, covering the heavier metals. Then it would have to be blown again or keep the prop turning.

Philip did the same on the outside of the hole, using a Garrett Sea Hunter Mark II. If the two divers got too close, the two detectors would interfere with each other. They would work back over the area the other had been across, double checking.

It's impossible to cover every inch in the time allotted to be down. That is why research is so important.

Working inside the crater, the downwash held them in place, but it was too much effort to control their movements. There were multiple beeps of targets the detector loop moved over, but Jess couldn't see anything. The downwash kept moving them.

Jess signaled to Marie Ann to lower the rpm of the engine, "Number Zero; back down on rpm."

She immediately replied as she adjusted the throttle to a lower rpm, "Number Zero, rpm down."

The two divers backed out from under the downwash. Philip motioned he had a problem with his detector and went to the surface.

"Philip, do you hear us okay?"

"Yes, Sir Jess. You made a good investment on this full mask with being able to talk. I'm going topside."

Jess gave him an okay with his thumb and finger, and then continued searching the hole. He extended his arm with the detector along the crater's wall. He could not see for all the silt and debris stirred up. He again gave the signal for no rpm, "Zero on the rpm; Stop!."

Marie Ann answered, "Zero on rpm; stopped!"

When the downwash stopped, he could hear the sand and sea shells slowly sliding back into the crater hole. Working fast before the sand filled the hole, he found six black pieces of metal. His heart raced as to the prospects of silver coins, each piece was heavy enough to be an 8 reale. He put them up the inside of his wet suit sleeve; pushing them passed the tight wrist band.

"Take a GPS position of this hole," Jess hollered. He could feel his heart beating in his neck. "We have hit pay dirt."

Picking up more black pieces of metal and safely storing them in his mess bag, he continued moving the detector over the sand and shells. He uncovered two hands full of small corroded black metal, shaped like the irregular cut Spanish coins of the 1715 mints. His meshed pouch was getting heavy.

Then, in the bottom of the blown sand pit was a louder beep from either a large item deeper or several silver coins stuck together near the bottom's surface.

Jess' thoughts were of the possibility of one target being his first gold coin to add to his own personal collection from the oceans bottom. The 1715 Spanish Plate Fleet lost tons of silver and hordes of gold coins right here in this area from the hurricane that sank eleven of their galleons at one time.

Jess could not fan the sand and shells away fast enough to uncover more targets. Suddenly, there was a bright glitter of light reflecting off the bottom. He held his breath as he picked up two items that were as clean as the day they were minted... GOLD COINS.

He shoved them into the palm of his left hand under his glove.

Jess then pulled a lead weighted pouch full of 'double-ought' buckshot from his weigh belt and put it over the target position. Then he took his air regulator out of his mouth and with it he inflated a rubber sack, which was attached to the buckshot pouch by nylon rope.

He was getting too much weight under his wet suit sleeves and the meshed pouch was full of coin size black metal. It was time to surface.

"I'm coming up." Jess shot out of the water with a shout, "Hey, love!" He startled her.

She slid over the boats transom holding on to the line attached to the mailbox and stood on a wooden platform just barely out to the water. Leaning down to take the metal detector from him as he flipped his way onto the platform, she remarked, "I've seen that big smile before, what did you find."

Philip leaned over the transom. "It must not be too much. His hands are empty."

They laughed while Jess grabbed the platform railing and scooted up on it and then was not very steady standing up. She pointed at the bulging mid-drift under his wet suit and laughed. Very dramatically he spread his arms and slowly brought his hands together showing them they were empty.

"Philip, may I have that wet towel hanging over there?" Jess said swaying and pointing at a dirty rag that once was a nice beach towel.

It was smoothed out on top of the wide transom. Jess lifted the meshed pouch of black metal from under the wet suit and laid it on the towel. Then he leaned down on his left forearm and un-zippered the rubber sleeve of his dive suit. With his right thumb and forefinger, he tried to push the objects from under the sleeve, but they were stuck to his skin. He then rolled back the sleeve exposing the six black crusted round metal objects. They were a little over an inch and a half across and a 1/4" inch thick. He judged them to be 28 grams in weight, 8 reale (silver). They would know for sure once the coins were cleaned.

Then he revealed a deep green jade ladies ring under the other sleeve. It was stuck to his skin. Jess removed it and laid it on the towel. He took his left hand and removed the right glove. As he slowly slid the glove off, he held his left hand over the palm of his right hand so the other two could not see what he had. He dramatically unfolded his hand, placing two gleaming 1747 8-Escudo "pressed" gold pieces next to the ring.

By now they were all wide-eyed and laughing with joy. "We've hit it! We've a glory hole!" Jess shouted and slowly moved the objects on the towel and then rolled them separately. That would keep them from rubbing against each other. He handed the towel bundle to Marie Ann who was grinning ear to ear.

He took his regulator, weights and fins off, dropping them on the floor next to the transom. Jess steadied Marie Ann and followed Philip under the boat's canopy. She put their finds inside the salon and came back out on the rear deck.

"Jess, while I'm thinking about it, I'll take a GPS reading over that marker you sent to the surface," Philip said.

"I did already," Marie Ann said, "And I entered it into my laptop computer.

Jess nodded his approval and looked at Philip. "Is your detector working?"

"Yes! We're ready to go again," he said. "It only needed fresh batteries. I didn't change them after our last dive."

Jess put his arm around Marie Ann, "You'll have to be our watch again, sweetheart. We need to get back down before it gets too late. Looks like clouds are forming to the west and we're losing daylight. There's more treasure down there." He pointed to the yellow rubber sack floating on the surface. "I'll pull that just under the water where you can see it from up here. We don't want anyone else to see it."

"Anything else we need to do before we get back in?" Philip asked.

"Nope," replied Marie Ann. "I don't think so."

Philip pulled his wet suit up over his arms and shoulders. Marie Ann checked the air pressure being pumped into the hoses to the two regulators. The compressor was running smoothly and its fuel tank was ¾ full. She moved the two sets of air hose coiled for better excess for her handling their feeding down to the two divers as they prepared to get in the water.

"Marie Ann, put your cell phone on your belt and turn up the volume of the ship-to-shore radio," Jess said, as he searched the horizon with the binoculars. "You should bring the portable radio back here too. You'll be alone and I want you to have everything you need within reach."

"I'm a step ahead of you," she replied and tapped him on his good shoulder to turn around.

She pointed to a closed cabinet mounted on the salon's outside bulkhead. "I'll secure the doors open. It's all in there."

"If we lose communication in these masks and you need assistance, take that pressurized horn and stick it in the water. Give it three long blasts underwater. We'll hear it."

Marie Ann waved her hands. "Captain, I've got control up here! Get back in the water!"

"Yes, dear!" he replied with a snappy hand salute.

"Who's captain?" Philip laughed.

The two men got on the platform and put their fins and full dive mask on. Jess turned to Marie Ann. She had her headset on.

"Testing, one, two three."

"Sounds good to me Jess, Philip?"

"I can hear you both." He nodded okay.

Jess pointed to the west, "We'll not be long. I'll be calling to run the rpm up for about one minute. Depends on how big that target signal is as to how long we will be down." He gave thumbs-up to Philip and they jumped into the water together.

Marie Ann watched their bubbles and their idle talk as the two divers descended and disappeared in the murky green water. The swells of the water were increasing with deeper troughs as the tide came in. Jess called for the rpm change and then off. The water turned a chalky brown as the sand churned and mixed with it. Then the swirling stopped at the water's surface.

She straightened up and took the binoculars, scanning the ocean surface to the north, east, south and back west to the shoreline, which was a mile away. No vessel or aircraft in sight.

She made her report, "The surface is clear of vessels."

"Okay, Captain," Jess replied.

"Sounds good," Philip said as he continued sweeping the ocean bottom with his metal detector.

She then leaned over the starboard side looking forward and then the port side. Everything looked quiet. Returning to the transom, she maintained her watch.

It seemed an awfully long few minutes before Philip surfaced. He motioned and instructed her on their communications for her to move the hoist arm out on the starboard side. She let hoist line out to him. He took the hook on the rope/line and dove with it. She feed out the coiled line from its storage until it floated on the surface. Then she pulled the slack out wrapped it around the winch pulley and tied it off or belayed it to a cleat.

"Okay, start the winch." Jess called out.

Slowly the line tightened and the treasure lifted from the bottom. The boat began to tip to the side and then settled back level as she kept a steady pull.

Finally, she could see both divers and once the netting broke the surface she stopped the winch from taking in more line. This was to use the load in the netting as resistance in the water so it would not swing excessively with the sea swells.

Philip got out of the water and took his fins off and the regulator mask. He climbed over the transom and threw Jess a rope to tie to the netting. With Jess holding onto the load in the water and pushing, Philip pulled the crane's extended arm toward the boat. At the top of a wave they moved the load to the rear of the boat.

"Okay, sweetheart," Jess said and gave Marie Ann a thumbs-up to bring the load out of the water. It swung easily up and over above the aft fantail deck. It was lowered onto a wooden pallet without incident.

Marie Ann secured the crane and winch, and then coiled the rope on the deck next to the bulkhead. She helped spread open the netting that held the treasure.

It was shaped like an oblong box, but no box. The pile of corrosion covered coins container had decayed from many years of soaking in the salt water. The coins were a black mass, hundreds of round metal pieces the size of silver pieces of eight that had corroded together.

In 1715, this was cargo from one of the eleven Spanish galleons shipwrecked during the hurricane they tried to out run. Perhaps it was the *Nestra Señora de las Nieves*, Taffi Fisher would know.

Jess' research had not yet revealed which galleon of the eleven it was down there on the bottom. Previous salvagers working the 1715 galleons had brought up many of these hulks of silver weighing 200 to 250 pounds. The price of silver was pushing $20 a Troy ounce, which would estimate their treasure could be worth $32,000, plus what it would bring on the collectors market for antique value. Some single coins valued for one could be in excess of $2,000. That price would depend on how perfect the stamp of the coin surface was and what vessels it came off.

Of course this is all based on the 2006 silver price.

Jess mauled this around in his mind. He smiled to himself, but even knowing how much the state of Florida would get and then the museum, he and his crew would get a nice percentage of its value or coinage.

Marie Ann went into the pilothouse for the camera and returned, "Okay you two, I want a good pose for these photos. Knell down at each end. Then break off some of the coins and put them in your hands." She circled them taking at least a dozen angled shots of their treasure.

Laughing and talking about the bulk of silver lying on the wood pallet, Jess said, "This may be part of the main ballast load of the Cabin Wreck, the *Regla*. But again, it could be off the *Nieves*. Taffi will know."

Marie Ann brought out three styrofoam cups with ginger ale in them, "Gentlemen, congratulations on our Glory Hole find."

They all touched cups and said, "Here, here."

Jess looked up to the sky. "Thank you, Lord, for our safety and abundance."

Then there was a round of, "Amen, thank you Lord Jesus."

"Philip, the sun is sure getting further down on the western horizon. I think it's getting too late to get back in the water." Jess said and nodded to him, "Before we get these suits off, we need to get in the anchors and get underway before sunset?"

"Aye, Captain," He said.

Marie Ann took a tarp and draped it over the heavy silver mound of coins, securing it to the wood pallet. "We also need to get these coins in the museum as soon as we can, and secure this equipment on the deck in their proper places."

Jess got back in the water and tied a buoy on the rope where the rubber sack was, but made sure it could not be seen above the water and was well below propeller depths. He then unlatched the mailbox so Philip could raise it up to its traveling position and strapped/bolted it in place.

Once Jess was out of the water again, Marie Ann took the handheld GPS and cell phone with GPS, and held them over the buoy for its coordinatces. This updated the info for their location. Then she plugged the handheld GPS into her laptop computer, and then transferred the updated info on the latitude and longitude of the buoy position. Then she sent that info by satellite to the museum's computer. This updated the computer so they could get a color printout from of the holes they blew. That did not have any details about the treasure found, other than silver and gold.

The digital color monitors were ready with surface radar, weather, water depth and speed, wind direction and speed, course waypoints, channel markers. The Nordic Tug was outfitted for cruising any waters the pilot wanted to venture into. Satellite communications, GPS and all the modern up-to-date instrumentation and equipment had been installed. The vessel could be operated on full remote control or switched to manual. Just set the course, mark the waypoints and enter the information, and then go get a cup of coffee or iced tea.

"Did the two match?" Philip asked her as he and Jess pulled in the aft anchor ropes.

"Sure did! I'm good!"

"You're the lady!" Jess hollered over his shoulder.

Philip leaned toward Jess, as he headed to the pilothouse along the outside walk way. "She sure makes a great crew member. We usually don't have to repeat the routine for her."

"Yeah, she's sharp!" Jess laughed. "That's why she married me! She knew a great guy when she saw me!"

"I heard that, swabby! He that tooteth not his own horn the same shall not be tooted," Marie Ann said.

"I never heard that before!" Philip said in his Australian accent while taking off his gloves. He laid them on top of the instrument panel in the pilot's house.

"Anchors are all on board," he said while taping his finger on a couple of pressure gauges, and then adjusted the radio for weather reports.

Jess backed away from her on the aft deck, "She's full of sharp-ones like that, never know what's coming." He held his arms up to shield any object that she might throw at him. "She slashes and cuts, beats and bruises..."

She grabbed a bucket of water and dowsed him with it from a distance. Before the water hit its target, Jess throw out his chest, "I'm a man of steel! Water will never..." He spit and sputtered, then wiped his face off in his hands, "That felt good! Glad it was fresh water, needed that wash down."

Laughing they continued preparing for heading in to Fort Pierce.

Underway, they had not scanned port-aft to the south with the binoculars and did not see the fast speedboat heading for them. It suddenly veered away and headed inland. Its turbo engines screamed from the high speed turn. The noise and sudden wakes of the water coming from their blind side caused a sudden panic. The boat was gone as fast as it appeared.

"Who and what was that?" Philip yelled and added full power to the boat and trailed the speedster. "That idiot, we'll never catch him! He almost broad-sided us! Did anyone get a good look at the boat?" He backed off to half power.

"I'm topside," Jess hollered and headed for the flybridge.

He grabbed binoculars from its storage and scanned ahead of them. They were heading into the sunset. The 100x75 binoculars had a color lens attachment he snapped in place which filtered the bright sun. Now he could see the speedboat.

Marie Ann had climbed the outside ladder to the flybridge control deck and joined Jess. She watched with another pair of binoculars. The wind had come up and the sea was becoming rougher as they headed for the inlet. Philip turned on all the boats running lights so he would not forget when the sun went completely down.

"I can't make out any markings. It's too low in the water," Jess said holding onto the railing. "Stay up here, love. I'm going below to get a bearing with the radar.'

He no sooner got in the pilothouse when there was a noise from the overhead.

Marie Ann yelled something, but the other two could not hear because of all the waves and wind noise with side doors open. She stomped the deck, twice. Philip grabbed the intercom headset and barely got it on when the front of the boat lurched upward. The bow came down with a loud thundering slap of the water. Philip cut the engine.

"What did we hit?" he yelled to Jess as Jess swung up on the starboard gunwale.

Jess stuck his head above the deck she was standing on. "Are you all right? Did you see anything?"

"Yes!" she screamed and pointed aft of their boat. "What's left of it!"

There were small waxed packages washing out of a larger burlap bail.

"Call the Coast Guard!" Jess yelled as he took the outside walkway aft to the transom deck and grabbed a long handled large fish net from a storage bend.

Philip slowly turned the trawler around and came up alongside the bail and protected it from the wind and waves, then cut the engines to idle. While he talked to the Coast Guard, Marie Ann grabbed a tarp and tossed it open on the fantail deck. Jess dumped waxed covered boxes from the busted bail. He suspected drugs.

Before they got it all on board, the wind became stronger and the ocean choppier, making it harder to net the remaining containers. By the time the last one was on board, they had been blown further northwest and the sun was down.

The Coast Guard Cutter had pulled up alongside with an accompanied helicopter overhead. They asked permission to get on board the *The Shallows*.

Philip and Jess motioned at the same time for them to do so. Three petty officers and a Master Chief came on board, wearing their life preservers. Then the helicopter departed and headed in the direction of the speeding boat's exit. Photos and statements were taken and then they left with the drugs.

The diving crew headed for their home port at Fort Pierce. They were surprised the Coast Guard asked no questions about what was under the tied down blue tarp on the transom deck.

Jess figured they had more important things to attend to with the drug problems. Anyway, they usually keep a sharp eye watching the salvage vessels on the Mel Fisher's museum 'exclusive' dive areas. He sort of expected a visit from Coast Guard once they got tied up in port.

CHAPTER TWELVE

Fort Pierce, Florida

Secured to an inter-harbor marina, *The Shallows* was protected from coastal winds. Marie Ann grilled steaks on the open aft sundeck; Philip made Teriyaki salad, while Jess took sun brewed tea and poured it over ice in tall thick-walled glasses.

Jess finished securing the aft deck canopy enclosure which covered the entire fantail/transom deck and fastened to the upper deck. It kept that area private, dry and comfortable from the outside elements.

He made a makeshift supper table from a converted miniature octagon pool/card table, which had holes for glasses or pop cans. He set it over the chunk of black silver coins which was draped with a blue tarp. The blue tarp was covered by an oily canvas tarp to keep inquiring minds and eyes away.

"I've been thinking," Jess said putting the sugar container and paper napkins on the table. "I'm surprised they didn't want to search the whole boat."

He sniffed the air and moseyed over to the steaks sizzling on the grill and lifted the hood. He closed it and reached for a handful of corn chips. He immediately got the message reaching for more, when Marie Ann tapped the back of his hand with her large steak fork.

"They will be ready in ten minutes if you keep that lid down," she slid her free arm around his waist. "Maybe we should call the museum to send their truck over, even if it is after nine?" She said standing ready to open the lid of the grill. "I thought for sure the Coast Guard would want to know what was under that blue tarp."

The two men agreed with her.

"You're right on that account, but, nay!" Philip said carrying his big salad bowel to the table. "They wouldn't come this far with the truck tonight. It would be faster and better ride from Sebastian in an open speed boat; especially in the heavy sea and wind tonight." He shrugged taking a crackers box from under his arm and said, "Of course, we may have other state government come aboard, but not likely tonight. I'd be surprised if anyone shows up."

After the main meal and their speculating what drugs were dumped out of the speedster that almost rammed them, Marie Ann cleared the table. She filled the tea glasses and asked if anyone was ready for homemade apple pie. The two men sat up and looked at her.

"It's on the menu if you're ready," she said with her hands in her red apron pockets. "It won't take but two minutes and I can heat up three frozen pieces from last weekend."

"Now you tell us," Jess said waving off the desert and rubbing his full tummy. "I know it's still good, but I'm stuffed."

Philip waved it off too and shook his head.

"Anyone want coffee in a little bit? After I get the dishes done?"

Jess had left the table to check the grill for cleaning, "Later would be fine with me. Use some of that flavored stuff."

"Philip, you have a taste for a cup or two? So I can make a full pot."

"Sure, I'm easy."

"Philip, while we are waiting for coffee and Marie Ann's doing dishes, why don't we take a look at some of those coins that came off the bigger pile."

"That's a great idea."

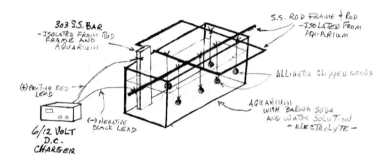

They went in the salon and looked in the converted fifteen gallon fish aquarium filled with water and dissolved three cups of baking soda. There was only room for two dozen black corroded pieces of eight to hang down into the solution. They used electrolytic reduction action with a battery charger. The electrical current ran through the solution and coins.

The coins had not been in the aquarium long enough to even start to come clean from the 200 plus years of corrosion and encrustations of the salty ocean.

A slow rate of bubbles come off the coins as the cleaning process continued. Once the bubbles stop, the coins are removed after turning off the charger. They had mounted a window fan in the slide window above the aquarium to suck out any fumes the solution would create.

"Philip, I know we have been busy all day," Jess said as he stretched. "I think we should be able to relax a few days or until this heavy weather gets out of here. Stay in port, restock our supplies and research our prospects on our gold location."

He stretched in his chair, "Remember, what we are finding could cause another Gold Rush on the 1715 galleons like back in the '60's when Mel Fisher's and Kip Wagner's dive groups hit the 'Carpet of Gold' on the *Nieves*."

Philip settled back in his lounge chair, "That could happen. Once you plug in the coordinates of our location of targets into the museum's computer, we should have a better idea where we are on the bottom."

Jess lifted the coins out of the aquarium by the stainless steel frame's rod and turned off the battery charger. "The computer map we have now is from last year's dives, so fitting our GPS marks into the map should give us good info."

Philip held a coin between his thumb and forefinger, rubbing it. Some crust came off, exposing the silver metal, "What's on your mind Jess?"

Jess looked up the stairway. "I'm concerned about Marie Ann's safety." He turned his back to the stairs. "Once we get this pile of coins to the museum, I'm thinking on heading north along the intracoastal water ways. We want to be off the Great Lakes and home for Thanksgiving."

While checking some of the coins, he continued, "If the water is conducive for diving, we will hang around. But, this tension with illegal aliens and terrorists on the high seas right in our backyards ... and at the condo has me upset."

He walked over and peered out the starboard porthole. "I feel like we're sitting ducks here in port and not much better out at sea."

Philip put the coins back in the solution and turned the charger on. They watched the bubbles starting their ascent to the surface of the solution. When the bubbles began their slow rate he turned to Jess. "Let's not forget our Lord's protection He's promised. I know we put His angels through a lot..."

Jess interrupted with a nod of agreement, "And He will continue to keep all His promises." He bowed his head and placed his hand on Philip's shoulder. "In Jesus name, Father, we claim victory! Now! Satan, get away from Philip, Marie Ann, and me! And stay away from Charles and his family back at the condos. We don't belong to you, Satan, go back to hell where you came from. We have been purchased by the precious blood of Jesus, which was shed for sins on His cross."

Philip followed with a hearty "Amen, Brother Jess! Thank you."

"I've been toying with the idea of taking the trawler north to Hudson Bay through the Great Lakes and then put it in storage at Benton Harbor, Michigan, for the winter. That's if the diving comes to a halt," Jess said yawing. "We could fly back and visit the store and then fly out of South Bend back here. Don't really know, but I'm becoming uneasy here. I'm thinking of moving on up north."

Philip nodded his acknowledgment of Jess' comments.

"Will you do any treasure hunting or diving on the way back home?"

"I'm sure we will be in the water again, somewhere along the way. There's a few hot spots to consider, but it all depends on the how unsettled the weather may become before we get on the rivers." They shook hands and then Jess went up on deck with Marie Ann.

The moon could be seen coming up under the eastern clouds, she pointed at it. "Why is it always so big on the horizon? I know, I know, they say it is atmospheric conditions, but that's far above my little old mind to comprehend." There was a moment of silence. "Anyway, isn't that a beautiful deceiving sight. Storm clouds above the moon and then to the west it's clear. Right here it's quiet in this safe harbor and away over there where the moon is shining it looks deceivingly peaceful."

Philip turned the deck lights off so they could be in the dark and Jess closed the cabin doors, and locked them.

A harbor patrol boat slid slowly by, heading toward the inlet as two other larger vessels were coming into port. There was heavy vehicle traffic crossing the bridges to the islands, but their noise was off in the distance. Crickets and buoy marker horns could be heard.

"Well, before it gets too late, suppose we load this pile of treasure on that cargo cart and get it ready for the museum truck?"

"Jess, I'm sorry! I forgot to call for the truck," Marie Ann said slapping her hands together and turning to the two men. "Is it too late, it is almost ten? I'm sorry!"

Jess held his hand out for hers, "No problem, sweetheart, we can go in the morning. It's waited years now, it can wait a few more days. What do you think Philip?"

"Sure! There's no real rush tonight. Plus, I'm sure you're both just as tired as I am. Why don't we turn in?"

"Being I didn't make the telephone call when I was supposed to, I'll take the first watch." She put up both her hands in the moonlight, "No arguments gentlemen! Go take a three hour nap Jess and I'll wake you about one."

"Well, good night you two; see you at sunrise." Philip went down to the crew's stateroom.

Lounging together on the deck, inside the flybridge collapsible canopy, on a weatherproof couch, Jess pulled her close to him, "What a day! What a good day at sea and a perfect quiet evening. Thank the Lord Jesus."

"Yes, it has been a great day. We should all be able to rest tonight," they lingered an hour or so. No talking just enjoyed the peace of the marina. They eventually went below to the galley. Marie Ann put on a fresh pot of coffee and turned on the radio, hunting for an FM station with 50's and 60's music.

"I'll find that station when we go back up." They both went to the restroom and then got two light weight yellow windbreaker jackets out.

Jess handed her up the coffee mugs and then pulled out a lounge chair with thick cushions and lifted it to her. He set it up on flybridge deck.

"I'll stretch out on this so I can be up here with you."

"Okay, we can talk if you're not real sleepy," she said and found the FM station and turned the volume way down; just enough for them to hear and talk over it.

They pulled the convertible top canvas covers closed around the fly-bridge and the back of the upper deck and then the lower main aft transom deck cover; zippered and snapped them secure. That would help keep out the dampness from the morning dew and make it warmer for them topside.

The pile of silver coins was their item of discussion until Jess said, "Sorry, love. I'm about to go to sleep while you're talking. Wake me in an hour or so."

She got out of her deck chair, laid a small blanket across his bare legs, leaned over, and kissed him on the lips, "I'll freshen up my coffee and be right back." She felt his sigh and his muscles relax.

When she returned he was lightly snoring away. She took a couple sips from her cup and strolled to the upper deck flybridge wheel control panel.

From that location she surveyed the other vessels in the marina and the piers between them. She could see any vehicle entering or leaving the marina. There was a coded electronic gate that stayed closed at night. So the only way to the marina was by water.

The next morning, Jess waved to the drivers of the museum truck as it drove down the pier and geared down for the steep incline to the street above the marina. The artifacts were headed to the museum at Sebastian, less the unclean silver coins and heavy lengths of gold chains in the safe at the condo.

The additional loose silver coins and the gold chains had not been shown to the two armed museum drivers, but a padded envelope with a letter inside was to be delivered to Taffi Fisher at the museum.

It had digital photos on a SD (Secure Digital) flash-memory card from Jess' laptop computer of the gold chains. He had taken close-ups of each link and told her they each had a code stamped on them he was not familiar with.

Since breakfast, Jess, Marie Ann and Philip had exhausted their limited research reference material and photos relating to the unusual symbols on the chain links. So far the Internet did not reveal what was needed. They wanted to talk to Taffi and get her permission to use the resources at the museum and perhaps make a fast trip to Madrid, Spain. But first, they had to go to the museum to show Taffi what they had taken from her 1715 Spanish galleon exclusive.

Jess and Marie Ann wanted to hand their finds to her in person.

CHAPTER THIRTEEN

Sebastian, Florida

The Mel Fisher's Treasure Museum is located on the east side of U.S. Highway 1 at 1322, Sebastian, Florida. Its president and director, Taffi Fisher-Abt, is the daughter of the world-renowned treasure hunter, the late Mel Fisher.

The museum is a large building with a huge collection of Spanish artifacts and treasures from years of salvaging sunken ships and galleons. The main attractions are on display from the 1715 Spanish plate fleet's treasures, plus a gift shop with authentic items off of the eleven vessels that were sank in the 1715 hurricane. Some of these Spanish galleons were sunk off of Hutchison Island and Fort Pierce, Florida. Diving arrangements can be made for the public through the Fisher's museums.

Philip let Jess and Marie Ann borrow his extended cab pickup truck. They parked in the employee area in back of the museum. Taffi Fisher, the director of the museum met them at the entrance of the research department. She was all smiles to see the two and congratulated them on their successful dive.

"So, let me see the additional excitement that you found," she stepped back and motioned them into the conference room. They laid a big wooden crate they carried between them on the floor and uncovered the contents of a big plastic container inside.

Marie Ann reached in and handed Jess one end of a gold chain and she took the other end. Together they began to lift it arm's length high and motioned Taffi toward them. They placed two loop lengths around her neck on her shoulders, another one around Marie Ann and then Jess. He reached in and continued loops until the three of them were standing with four loops of gold chain hanging from their necks to the floor. They were careful to not drag it on the floor.

Marie Ann said with tears in her eyes, "This is the longest of the group…"

Taffi giggled and spread the trade gold chain out arm's length from her side. "Beautiful, and were did this come from, out of my exclusive? It looks exactly like Dad's chain in Key West, but longer." She fingered the chain lengths and hollered down the hall toward the offices. "Gold, we've got gold everybody!" She looked Marie Ann in the eyes. "This is the longest…you have more?"

Someone stuck their head out of one office doorway. "What about gold?" He saw them standing down the hall in the open conference room with the gold chain draped around them. "Lord a' mercy!" he exclaimed. He turned and yelled back into the office, "Get the cameras and everyone back here."

"Taffi," Jess said putting a chair under her to sit in and stepped back to the wooden crate. With a lot of effort, he lifted out a large duffle bag. "Here are eight more lengths for you." He laid each length across Taffi's legs as she sat holding the other longer lengths.

"Spread out that table cloth on the conference desk and put these chains on it. My legs are going to sleep from the weight." Taffi said with amazement.

Then Marie Ann spread out the other relics and coins next to the chains.

It did not take long to assemble a dozen employees with cameras. Some of the staff were taking notes and talking to Jess and Marie Ann.

Taffi asked to have them lay each chain in a pile, they were getting too heavy. She took them from around her neck and draped them across her lap.

Jess and Marie Ann laid their chain lengths across Taffi's lap. The staff pulled up a couple of chairs and just watched as the gold chains were examined by the museum experts.

"This didn't come off the 1715 fleet, it is mint marked from Mexico. There is nothing on the Spanish's manifest for a chain like this," one of the men said to Taffi. "These are bigger links than the one in our showroom. These links must be at least two ounces or more."

Taffi laughed, "At this point I don't care if it is or not. It could have been contraband for all we know."

She turned to Marie Ann, "Where did you find it?"

"Well, to make a long story short, we found them three miles south of the Fort Pierce inlet, between there and the power plant," she said and turned to Jess.

"They were in waist deep water off the beach under a stretch of corral," Jess said grinning from ear to ear. "We have all the GPS coordinates and photos in my laptop."

He stood up from off his knees where he had knelt next to Taffi, and took something small out of his pocket and handed it to her. "Here is a 3-gig external storage. It has all the info on it of all the things we brought up yesterday, plus all these items and the gold chains."

Taffi motioned to a couple of security men. "Put this all in the safe for now. It looks like everything is tagged." Trying to keep from laughing for joy about the treasures, she said, "We will get the research department on this immediately." She caught her breath once they removed the gold chains from across her legs. She slapped her legs. "Wake up dummies; it's time to go to work."

She stood and shook hands again and motioned for the two treasure hunters to follow her to her office. Her secretary gave them a receipt for the block of silver coins, the gold coins and gold chains after insuring they were all tagged, closely weighed, examined and photographed.

Three hours later, the excitement and crowd of the museum's employees got back to work, Jess and Marie Ann went back to Taffi's office.

Knocking on her opened door, she motioned them in and immediately hung up the telephone.

"Oh, one more thing," Marie Ann said walking to the end of Taffi's desk. Taking a small pocket purse from her blue jeans, she said, "Open your hand, please; this is yours too." She laid a blue felt pouch in Taffi's hand.

"Oh my, what is this?" she said with her great smile and red hair shining in the beam of sun coming through her office window. The green emerald solitaire gold ladies ring slid into her palm. It had a Fisher's museum salvage tag tied to it.

"This came out of the same glory hole where the silver coins were found yesterday," Marie Ann said proudly.

"Another fantastic trophy from the 1715 fleet," Taffi giggled like a little girl. "Dad would have fallen in love with this one." She tried to slide it onto her finger and it was too small. "This is almost like another ring we have in our showcase up front."

She smiled and took Marie Ann's hand, laying the ring in her palm, "If this is in anyway close to the ring up front, it's yours and we'll get the documents of authenticity signed for it with all the pertinent info of the vessel it came from. It is very beautiful and it will match you hazel eyes."

Marie Ann was stunned, "I'm speechless Taffi, thank you so very much." She tried it on for size and it fit. "Well, look at that Jess Hanes, what do you think of that?"

He put his arm around her shoulder and pulled her close. "Thank you Taffi, you've made her first diving experience unforgettable," he replied as he held Marie Ann's hand.

She then removed it and put it in the blue velvet pouch Taffi handed her. Then she put it in her blue jeans front pocket for safe keeping.

Taffi hugged her again, "Come on, let's get our work done and then we can go celebrate.

She led the way to the area where the open vats were for cleaning the silver coins. Three staff was already taking the black silver hulk apart; coin at a time hung from an alligator clip and hung them in the vat. It would be a long process of electrolysis removing the black corrosion.

Eventually, the coins would be polished, weighed, and graded. Then each coin categorized by size, weight and quality of the hand stamping, date and where it was minted and which 1715 vessel it was on.

During the evening catered supper celebration at the museum, Jess shared with Taffi and her staff what his and Marie Ann's intentions were on continuing their diving on the 1715 galleons.

With the understanding that the museum would be having their 'Division' party sometime the following year prior to the diving season, Jess and Marie Ann said their goodbyes and spent the night in Sebastian. They spent the next day working in the museum, researching the treasures they had delivered.

The coins, ring and emeralds were off of the *Nuestra Señora de las Nieves*, but they could not tie down the gold "wedding/trade" chains to a specific ship's manifest. That may cause a trip to Spain with one of Taffi's research experts. At this point, the lack of information on the ship's manifest was pointing to the gold chains as contraband or from another vessel sunk in the area.

CHAPTER FOURTEEN

Weigh Anchor Norfolk, Virginia

The Shallows quietly moved north on the intracoastal Waterway ICW from Fort Pierce on a heading of 250 degrees at the 965 mile marker. Following the red on the port and green on the starboard channel markers, the crew was right in the center of the channel.

After their restful night, big breakfast and all ship shape, they were underway before five. The sun would be up on the distant horizon in another hour, hopefully they would be ahead of the speedsters who get underway around ten.

For a Monday morning, the day should be uneventful; except for storms in the Gulf of Mexico were building. Hopefully it would be further north, off of the Florida peninsula and would not be moving into the Atlantic.

Marie Ann set Jess' hot cup of coffee in its holder forward of the pilot's wheel where Jess was at the helm. He was half seated on the captain's chair with one hand slightly nudging wheel's extend handles to keep the pulpit on the bow on course. With the red interior lights on and the monitors' brightness low, they had a 180-degree view straight ahead.

They left the outside doors closed, because of the low fog banks on the water; its mist chilling the air. The windshield wipers cleared the moisture.

The mooring lights of other vessels, buoys, piers reflected very little ripples in the water ahead of them. The greenish foam spread behind them as the Nordic Tug's semi-displacement hull cut smoothly through the water. The low rumble of the marine diesel below decks could barely be heard. The ringing of the buoy bells could be heard behind them as their wake woke the silence. The navigational radios were silent and the two crew members searched the channel ahead of them for debris and other vessels.

Vero Beach and Sebastian were slowly left behind as the sun's rays broke the darkness in the east. It was another clear morning and the weather reports gave them good passage to Jacksonville. But, if they could watch a NASA launch at the Kennedy Space Center at Cape Canaveral, they would anchor or tie up at a marina near Patrick Air Force Base. The base may be able to handle their NT42.

Marie Ann contacted Patrick AFB's directory for the contact of the base marina. They could not handle the 42 feet length of *The Shallows* nor the 4½-foot draft, but they could anchor at mm 883 and watch a shuttle launch. There was a scheduled launch of the space shuttle, if the weather held. If the gulf storms postpone the launch, *The Shallows* would continue on north on the ICW.

By the time they arrived in the Patrick AFB area, the launch was cancelled and they increased their speed to 16 knots in order to be in St. Augustine before dark.

On the AICW they would have some eleven or twelve bridges to contend with in raising them or swing open before getting to St. Augustine. Some of them were only operated at certain times of the day and others on demand. They wanted to avoid having some raised if they could arrive when the tides were out. That too would help keep the cost down.

The only long delay was at the Haulover Canal/Allenhurst Bridge where a barge had broken loose from a tug and was cross-wise in the channel. Jess and Marie Ann anchored *The Shallows* at mm870 for a couple of hours, ate lunch and then washed salt spray marks off the pilothouse windows with fresh water. Sometimes the window spray solutions did not do the job good enough using the wipers. So, he did the outside with vinegar and water, and she used a lemon mixture for the inside of the windows. They both used wadded up newspapers to help remove the moisture of the solutions, instead of rags or towels.

The Channel Master called *The Shallows* and gave approval to leave anchorage and move into the center of the channel after the south bound traffic cleared. Marie Ann acknowledged the call. They weighed anchor and let the auto pilot/GPS hold them over their anchorage spot at R2; the wind had picked up from their port quarter aft (from the west) and the current was moving with the outgoing tide toward the channel This would give them additional bridge clearance, but the bridge had to be opened for a higher mast vessel anyway. Jess would not have had to lower their radar mast for this bridge, even though it was down.

This was the only delay getting to the anchorage mm778. They had ten hours travel from Fort Pierce to St. Augustine, 87nm; two hours of that ten was at anchor. Once at the anchorage, they contacted the City of St. Augustine Marina for a slip and fuel. Their diesel fuel was $2.94 a gallon and the slip was $1.95 a foot for overnight, and would be ready in an hour. The anchor was not even in the water, so they got the directions for getting to the marina and slowly moved out into the main channel.

The city marina had all the necessary hookups as quoted from their Internet web page: Nestled in the heart of St. Augustine, just south of the Historic Bridge of Lions in the city's historic district, is a true treasure for anyone traveling the Intracoastal Waterway, the St. Augustine Municipal Marina.

This ideal location provides a picturesque and convenient harborage for both sail and power boats with a friendly and helpful staff that is on duty 24/7 year round. Fuel, oil, ice and two complimentary pump-out stations are conveniently located on the fuel dock, and the marina has clean and secure restroom/shower facilities and a Laundromat.

It was to be an expensive overnight (24 hr.) stay, because Jess wanted to top off both the starboard and port fuel tanks and load up with fresh water. He wanted to do some sight inspections in the engine room before using shore power. Marie Ann had already made out her long shopping list prior to docking.

There was a young gentleman and his girlfriend who helped set the side bumpers, tie up *The Shallows* with bow, stern and spring lines, hookup the electric shore-line cables, fresh water hose and gave Jess an invoice with detail cost for the slip's rental.

It was late in the evening when they finally sat down to share a cold meat sandwich with peanut butter, half a glass of milk, before going to bed. The trip from Fort Pierce was slow and easy with no problems, but they were more than ready to rest.

Jess rose earlier than Marie Ann the next morning, which was very unusual, and completed the engine room inspection. By the time he was finished, she had breakfast ready. They took showers at the Municipal Marinas facilities, toured the gift shop and returned to the dock. There was a young couple standing on the dock admiring *The Shallows* when approached.

"You have any interest in a Nordic Tug?" Jess asked offering a handshake and introduced himself and Marie Ann.

He smiled, "I'm in the Navy on leave from the West Coast and came in from Michigan and have seen this model trawler at a show in Traverse City."

"I'm Patti and my husband-to-be Gale Splizer." She said and shook Marie Ann's hand. "We are here for a few days and are heading to Mayport where Gale is assigned to his new vessel..." She looked at him for help.

"It really is a new super carrier, the USS *George H.W. Bush*, CVN-77." A handsome young man standing straight and tall, continued with his very southern accent, "I transferred from the West Coast, San Diego. I'm coming from the *Corral Vinson* CVN-70 to the newest nuclear carrier. I was on her four years. That gives me eight years now. I'm waiting to put on the 'brown' in six months."

"That's fast, good for you," and Jess shook his hand.

"So, you're going to be a new chief, what's your specialty?" Marie Ann asked.

He smiled that she knew what he was talking about, "Nuclear Propulsion Electrician's Mate."

"Our wedding is this weekend at my Mom's home in Jacksonville." She smiled and laughed, "We grew up together in Jacksonville before he joined the Navy."

"So you're down here working for the city until this weekend?" Marie Ann asked with a worried look on her face. "Shouldn't you be home helping with all the wedding plans and stuff?"

They all laughed. "Sweetheart, that's their personal business," Jess said, hoping they would not misunderstand. "Marie Ann is an organizer and wouldn't think of taking off when such plans and activity was going on."

"My lands, we've had this wedding planned for four years," she said with her southern draw; they hugged each other. "Mom kicked us out because we were in her way. She sent us down and said she didn't want to see us until Saturday morning. And, by all means, we had better behave ourselves down here."

Jess gave them a short run down on the Nordic Tug and invited them on board. During the visiting, Gale had shown Jess his military identification card, leave papers and some of his folk's photos. Jess in turn showed Gale his retired military ID. After finishing the tour, they settled down in the salon for snacks and something to drink. It was getting close to noon.

"I better let my brother know where we are. He is to pick us up at noon in front of the marina," Gale said and made the cell phone call, no answer. "I'll try again in a few minutes."

Jess was showing Gale the navigational maps of their cruise and where they were going and Marie Ann was going through family photos with Patti. Jess motioned for Gale to bring his ice tea glass with him and go down to the salon with the ladies.

"I have a proposal to make with the captains permission," Jess said to Marie Ann and made a sloppy salute toward her. "What would you think of taking on a crew up to Jacksonville? We could leave within the hour?"

"You mean a ride on this vessel to Jacksonville?" she said with a smile and clapped her hands. "Could we, Gale?"

"How long would the trip take, and are you sure?" He looked at Jess and Marie Ann.

"As soon as you let your brother know, we could be launched in thirty minutes."

Jess and Marie Ann opened their navigational charts for Jacksonville and Mayport for the AICW along the Atlantic shoreline north bound.

"Okay, we're here near the mm778 anchorage area," Jess said and moved his finger across the map following the ICW north.

Marie Ann marked Mayport as approximately mm740 for a quick location. "That is 38 nautical miles at ten knots, gives us three hours and eight tenths, so round up to four hours."

"Add onto four hours for the bridges between here and there, what's their vertical clearance?" Jess said and grabbed a scratch pad on the table.

Gale and Patti came up stairs to the pilothouse to watch Jess and Marie Ann use the charts.

"What can we do?" Gale asked.

Jess took the chart and placed it on the table behind them in the pilothouse. He turned the map to face north and showed them the location of the marina.

"Here we are at this mile marker, 778. The Intracoastal Waterway goes up through here. Let's make a list of bridges we'll go under and if they are tolls to pay. That information will determine if we'll need to stop to have them opened," Jess said.

Marie Ann began to show Patti her listing of bridges and their vertical clearance above the water, explaining what *The Shallows* mast required without having to lower it.

"Where in Jacksonville do you live Patti?" Jess asked.

She looked at the navigational map which had no street markings, "Not far from the ferry crossing to Mayport from Fort George Island."

"That 740 mile marker is a good reference. So, we know that if we average ten knots, we'll have four hours from here. Work your bridge information, love, and see what delays we have."

As Marie Ann followed the ICW north to Jacksonville, the other three watched and kept track of the info she was giving them. They were finished in less than fifteen minutes and it looked like a great run to Jacksonville.

"My brother will meet us at the public boat landing north of the Heckscher Drive Bridge. It's across St. John's River from Mayport."

Patti clapped her hands, "I live about five minutes up the road off A1A on Fort George Island. Daddy bought a home there twenty years ago after I was born. He eventually got it paid for before I went to college."

"Daddy's two brothers own a dry dock boat repair and landing on the island, right on the St. John's River." Patti continued with a big smile, "I can call them and tell them to meet us there and it shouldn't cost you a thing." She was beside herself with joy and could hardly sit still. "Is that all right with you, Gale?"

"It sure is, sweetheart, and tell them what type of vessel this is," he replied and hugged her.

Marie Ann wrote down *The Shallows'* name and type for Patti.

"If you'll need to dump or get water and fuel, I'm sure Uncle Carl will be happy for the business," she said and opened her cell phone.

While she was making those arrangements, Gale continued with his part of their first meeting at college.

"That's where we met in the Johnston State College downtown. I was taking a undergrad's course in aeronautical physics. I'm sorry to say I didn't finish the course. I couldn't agree with one of my professors who taught the class I needed."

Jess laughed, "And what was the disagreement over?"

Marie Ann put her hands on her hips, "Jess that's none of your business, plus I'm sure failing a course is no laughing matter for Gale."

Gale waved his hands. "I had fun disagreeing with the big snob. He always tried his best to bully everyone in class. I wouldn't put up with it when he determined what my thesis was to cover. It had nothing to do with aeronautics: 'Why Is the United States 3rd Best in Aircraft Design?'"

"Why, did he want you to prove the U.S. is the best, number 1?" Jess asked and continued his check list up to Jacksonville.

"Nope, he's a socialist and didn't like the way the U.S. government was dominating other countries with their political military powers. I got into some heated arguments with him which marked me from the start of the class." He helped Jess roll up the maps and stacked them on the pilothouse dashboard. "I wouldn't put up with his trash talking about our country and when I came to class in Navy uniform, he blew his lid and left the room."

He tapped his fingers on the counter top, "I made such a commotion in class, that Patti cornered me in the hallway afterwards. She liked how I stood up to the professor and she asked me for a date. We met later at the campus library where they had a nice snack bar. Then later on we got serious about our relationship at the same time I dropped out of school after Junior College was over. So, I only got two years and an Associate's Degree in Aeronautical Science."

"That's a big step in your education, plus the Navy probably helps with it when you enlisted," Jess said and made some notes on a sticky pad and put it on the monitor above the wheel. It was a reminder to contact the Mayport Naval Air Station.

"Yes, sir, I have an opportunity to finish college under the Career Enlisted Program. They will put me through school with an addition of six years to my enlistment. I don't know if I want to graduate as a Warrant Officer or Ensign."

"I would think you would have more clout as a Warrant Officer?" Jess said and motioned for them to join the ladies.

"You're probably right, sir," Gale replied.

Patti was talking to her Uncle Carl Wallenburger who was trying to help her understand he had no docking space for any vessel at this time, maybe in a couple of days. "Uncle Carl, are you not coming to my wedding tomorrow afternoon?"

She put him on the cell phone speaker, "Yes, Honey, we will be there in the front row, but I'll have to work all night on a river tug to get him back in the water by 6:00 a.m. The space I could let you use is not available until noon. I'm sorry."

"Well, I guess we can get off at the public landing north of the RV park bridge across Heckscher Drive." She said with a little girls disappointing sound in her voice. "I was so hoping to see you and Uncle Ben before the wedding."

"You missed the great rehearsal last night with all the eats and men around." Teasing her, he continued, "Is Gale behaving himself, he better be?"

Gale leaned toward the cell phone in her hand, "I certainly am as always, Uncle Carl."

"I didn't know you were on the speaker. I better not let out any of your secrets," he continued to tease her.

"Everyone on the Intracoastal Waterway in St. Augustine can hear you. I'm also using the outside speakers," she teased back.

"Enough young lady, remember sweet ladies don't tell lies to their Uncles."

"Yes, sir, I will see you at home tomorrow. I do love you anyway."

"I would certainly hope so. We will make arrangements to pick you up at the landing. Bye."

"Love you too." She then closed the cell phone and looked at the other three. "I'm sorry, I was hoping to get us close to home."

Marie Ann grabbed Patti's hand. "That's okay, everything will work out for the wedding. It always does."

Patti helped Marie Ann with securing the loose items in the galley and salon.

"Captain, we're ready to shove off when you are." Marie Ann called up to Jess. The two women went out on the aft deck and loosen all the lines and made-them-up on the deck. "We can store these later," she said and motioned for Patti to follow her along the main deck railing and up to the bow.

Jess slid the pilothouse doors open on both sides, then went to the starboard side to the ladies. Marie Ann had jumped out to untie the line from the pier and then came back on board.

"All lines on board and bumpers stored, Captain," she called out to him from amidships. Patti must have had some experience on a boat by the way she assisted Marie Ann.

Jess had the diesel engine running in idle and moved the throttle in reverse at a very slow rpm and used the bow thruster to move it further away from the pier. Their bow was pointed upstream against the river flowing to the ocean.

"Clear starboard," called out Marie Ann.

"Clear starboard aft," called out Patti as she waved to her shipmate on the starboard bow. Marie Ann returned the wave.

"Captain, we all clear to come about," Marie Ann called to Jess.

Jess blew the air horns twice to get attention of anyone around and headed for the Bridge of Lions. It was up and they already had received permission to go through the opening at 8 knots.

Gale held onto the overhead railing in the pilothouse watching every move Jess made: radio operations, navigating the channel markings, marking their waypoints as they headed north. He watched Jess' routine and began to help with the channel markings and sighting them prior to getting there. They settled into a routine together and everything smoothly fell into place. By the time the ladies had finished outside *The Shallows* was well up the ICW toward Jacksonville.

The ladies had sandwiches and tea ready, placing everything on the chart table behind the captain's chair in the pilothouse. They scooted in next to each other as Gale slid next to Patti.

Jess asked Marie Ann to pray over the meal and for their journey to Jacksonville, 38 nautical miles north. At ten knots, they should easily be there in four hours. But as any good aircraft pilot or boat captain would do, he added an hour for any unexpected delays. That is just good practice.

At mm765, they pulled into the anchorage to let a tug with two large barges pass through the narrow channel from R20, two miles north of them. It was less than a half mile away and they could see it coming.

"I hope he isn't in that big a rush for us. He's pushing up a big wake with those barges." Jess got on the radio and called the tug pilot to let him know they were at the mm765 anchorage and well out of the way.

"Thank ya Boss, we's sees ya." and blew his horn twice and long. "I've got emergency on board, crew member has appendicitis. Helicopter will meet us at mm765 in five minutes."

Sure enough a U.S. Coast Guard helicopter flew pass *The Shallows* at pilothouse level and hovered until the tug had his barges out of the channel current into the anchorage area. It did not take five minutes for the transfer and the helicopter was on its way to a hospital somewhere.

The tug pilot blasted his horn twice and eased out into the channel current and headed south with his barges and a long blast on the air horns.

"Thank you NT42 for waitin' sees ya'all later."

He was making enough of a wake behind him that small craft banged against the piers. Jess answered back with a long blast of his air horns.

"I'd bet we won't see that happen again on this trip," Jess said as he helped himself to half a sandwich, stuck in his mouth, and stood at the wheel again. They were back in the river's channel current again heading north.

MM758, the Palm Valley Bridge was up and out of operation for repairs, so there was no delay there. MM754, Palm Valley Landing had no traffic to contend with and they scooted on north.

Jess left Gale at the helm while he studied the ICW to Norfolk, Virginia.

He turned to Gale and asked, "You and Patti attend church in Jacksonville?"

"No we don't, but there's a little Bible Church at Jax Beach where we go ever so often," he said and pointed to a waypoint. "There's a green marker off the starboard bow, Captain. Depth twenty feet, cruising at ten knots, radar shows no vessel ahead of us."

"Great, we should be in Jacksonville in no time at all." Jess replied and asked, "Is that were you two are getting married?"

"No, we're having the ceremony at her Mom's home. Her Dad, John who I never knew, was killed in Vietnam and her Mom request we have it at their home," he said with an agreeing attitude. "My father is a MIA in Vietnam."

Jess turned to him and put his hand out to Gale, "Young man I'm sorry to hear that. Has there been any new information on his whereabouts?"

"Mom receives information ever so often from the Missing In Action headquarter out in Kokomo, Indiana. They can't go into an area of Cambodia where his Skyraider crashed."

Jess prayed silently for Gale, asking the Lord Jesus to touch him, his Mom and his bride to be. Tears welled up in Jess eyes, "Is there anything you can think of that we could help you with?"

"You mean finding Dad or our wedding?"

"Either one or both," Jess replied and folded up the maps again.

"There just might be, but I would want to talk to Patti and her Mom first." Gale replied and turned the helm over to Jess. "I need to go to the 'head' and then I'll go ask her."

Marie Ann came into the pilothouse and stood next to Jess at the helm. "I've been relieved of my bow duties. Gale said I needed a break; you two men must have had a lengthy talk."

"He's an impressive young man. He seems to have his head screwed on right; in my opinion," Jess said and put his arm around her shoulder. She snuggled up closer, "They make a nice looking couple, don't they?"

"Yes, they do; we had some good girl to girl talk," she said and looked up at Jess. "She's concerned about her Mom, after she and Gale get married. Her Mom wants her to live with her in her big home on Fort George Island. That would help her Mom and financially help this young couple. She has seen some of her young friends who got married and lived with their parents and it always seemed to end in a big fuss and division in their families."

"I asked her about Jesus our Lord and if she had ever asked Him into her life," she continued and moved away from Jess so he could handle the helm.

They had to cross an area of fast mixed currents from a river flowing into the ICW, and he needed both hands on the wheel.

"She did ask Jesus into her life, right before meeting Gale at college. He had accepted Jesus as his Lord and Saviour while in high school. I told her we would help support them in prayer as to what Jesus would have them do in decision with her family."

She did not talk while Jess called out orders for the young couple on the bow. "The waters rougher than I thought it would be. Attach your safety lines for a while, until we get through this area."

She went back out to assist them until they were clear of the turbulent water.

It must have been the aftermath of the heavy rainfall up stream in that area two days prior to their crossing. It did not look like the land was high enough to create such a fast run off.

Marie Ann told the young couple how she and Jess had come to know the Lord Jesus. Her Mom led her to the Lord at home and Jess was introduced to Him during a tour of Naval duty in Morocco. They were both surprised with her testimony for the Lord. It did not seem to go along with their current life-style of treasure hunting.

Farther north, at the Porte Vedra Beach ICW landings, there was a city celebration of sorts along the waterway supporting the local baseball team. There were brightly colored decorated pontoon floats with drinks and free hotdogs with walkways and piers back to the land. Any small vessel could come along side and be served refreshments for free, and then be on their way. The local Chamber of Commerce financed the gala and expected donations.

Marie Ann and Patti were standing at the pulpit railing waving to people when Jess told Gale to join them and pick out the float they wanted to pull up to.

They picked the girl's ball team to support. All four of them got a blue baseball hat with a white Pelicans symbol and name on the front.

They gave a sizeable donation for the team and the teenage girls screamed and hollered, waving at them for a long time after *The Shallows* left their float.

"Jess that was a huge donation left them in our boats name. I know those six pieces of eight, Spanish Reales, will get to the needed families," Marie Ann said and kissed him on the cheek. "I've asked Jesus to bless them."

"I've never seen Spanish coins before. Where did you find them?" Patti asked and held Gale's hand watching their new found friends.

"Well, it's a long story," Marie Ann told them. "We are professional treasure hunters and some years ago we started looking for lost items as a hobby. It has grown to be our everyday quest."

"Those coins we gave them came off a Spanish galleon off the coast of Fort Pierce. It sank back in 1715 with ten other galleons during a big hurricane." Jess said and continued to share some of their hunting tales and showed them some of their treasures they had on board. Before they could finish the story about the cruise they were on, the St. Johns River came into view.

"Sorry, but we may have a lot of traffic coming in from the ocean or going out. Marie Ann, take the helm. I'm going topside to the flybridge. You two come up with me." Jess ordered and he lead them topside.

At the helm of the flybridge, Jess called down to Marie Ann to go to the pulpit.

Once she had transferred operations to him, was ready with her safety harness around her, she waved up to him.

They now wore headphones with microphones to communicate.

Jess motioned for the young couple to come closer to him, "Every one keep your eyes on our surroundings and let me know if we need to change course. I'm going straight across to the ICW on the other side." Then everyone went to their assigned spot to observe from.

There was a huge ocean freighter coming in to dock, so Jess hollered to everyone that he was coming to port and move toward an anchorage at mm740. They would not drop anchor, but he would use the GPS 'auto' stationary waypoint. Hopefully it would be enough to keep him from having to manually fight the wind and currents at anchorage to stay in one spot. The bow and aft thrusters would help keep them in place.

Once they got there, he marked the waypoint on the GPS and engaged the auto pilot. There was a light wind from the east, but the river currents swirled at their location. Jess hollered to his crew that he would move out of the swirling water for a better, calmer location in the anchorage.

Patti was the first to see a spot. "Captain, back here on the starboard side aft." She was pointing to get his eye contact at the flybridge aft railing.

Marie Ann went back below her on the main fantail deck. They agreed for Jess to slowly reverse the prop. Ten feet away from the other location, the GPS kept them steady in one spot. Jess then called the Port Authority to let them know where he was and why he was there.

Jess heard the freighter's two long blast of its air horns and answered it with his. He then contacted the freighter and told him his intentions. A small pilot tug was following the massive vessel.

He hollered at his crew, "We're in no hurry. We'll stay right here until that white freighter is up stream. It may take thirty minutes or so, but I wanted to watch him. Marie Ann, got your digital camera?"

"Yes, Captain, I'm coming to the bow to take pictures."

The white vessel must have been a thousand feet long. He took his binoculars that had a field gauge in the lens and focused in on the ship. It was just short of a thousand feet in length and it was low in the water with evidently a full load. Its freeboard, (distance from the water to lowest point of the vessel where water could come on board), had to be as high as a six story building. It was almost comparable to the super carrier docked across the way at the Mayport Naval Station.

At the angle Jess was looking he could not see the numbers on the side of the island structure of the aircraft carrier. He assumed it was Gale's ship the USS *George W. Bush* CVN77, a nuclear super carrier.

When they finally got across the river, they pulled up to the public landing north of the Heckscher Bridge crossing onto Fort George Island. There were two vehicles full of people waiting on the pier for Gale and Patti.

The young couple introduced everyone and the party began for the two. Balloons, songs, dancing, and soda pop began along the pier. They were whisked away by the bridal party to Patti's home on the island.

Patti's two uncles stayed behind with Jess and Marie Ann to get some details worked out with them for docking space at their marina.

The two uncles apologized for the short answers given to Patti on the cell phone about a vacant space at their boat business.

"We've a surprise at our boat yard for them and didn't want them at the dock. A three-mast schooner is docked for their honeymoon cruise," Uncle Carl said and continued, "Yes, ah, we do have space for ya and can accommodate any service needs ya may have for ya's nice-looking Nordic Tug."

"Well that's great, but we don't have passengers to deliver now and shouldn't take up space for your customers," Jess said and shook their hands again.

Marie Ann jumped in with her thoughts, "I want you to know that those two were great coming up on the ICW and handled duties like an experienced crew. We've enjoyed our short visit with them."

"Thank ya's, they're ah sweet couple, that they are." He cleared his throat and looked at the other uncle who was not saying much. "We have a proposition for ya, sir, ma'am."

He did not bat an eye when he made the offer. "If ya will honor us by comin' to the weddin' this evenin', ya's stay at our facility's free, and the fuel ya's need is at a discount... ours cost."

Putting his finger in the air, Uncle Carl continued, "Any repairs ya's need will cost only the price of the replacement part; at ours cost."

Jess looked at Marie Ann, "I guess we have to get out our best 'bib-and-tucker' for a wedding."

"If'n ya would permit us, being ya has accepted our offer, I kin come aboard and directs ya into our docks. Uncle Greg kin take our van back," he said with a big grin and nodded to Uncle Greg. "See ya there, brother."

He turned back to view the Nordic Tug, "I'm lookin' at my leisure retirement. What a grand looking vessel ya's got. Beautiful line's she's got."

Jess motioned Uncle Carl toward *The Shallows*. "Let's get aboard, times ah' wasting."

While Jess was at the helm, heading *The Shallows* back to the ship's channel of the St. John's River, Marie Ann gave Uncle Carl a tour of the NT42. She was very thorough in the details of their home on the water. But of course, it was not the first vessel Uncle Carl had been on.

Once they were up in the pilothouse with Jess at the helm, Uncle Carl spoke in his deep Irish accent, "Ya has very comfortable quarters, sir. I kin see where ya leisure time is spent... when ya's in no special hurry." He winked at Marie Ann, and hurriedly turned to Jess who had a broad smile. "What is ya's max speed on still water, sir?"

Marie Ann grabbed her notes lying on the helm's desk. "Our best was in the Gulf of Mexico, for a straight six hours on auto pilot, we held a steady 23.4 knots, no wind and but smooth seas."

"That was not max rpm, but I would assume we could push her to over 24 knots on glassy seas." Jess held up his hand. "But I wouldn't want to hold it at that high rpm for a six-hour run."

Uncle Carl smiled and patted the wheel. "Ya have a diesel engine that can take that speed for a week without any damaged. Do not be timid with your engine. Push it to the limit when you have the opportunity."

"Fuel consumption would be high, but I'd betcha it'll ride nice and steady. Of course the high speed would be for an emergency only, I'm sure," Uncle Carl said and winked at Marie Ann again. "Are ya havin' any complaints with the diesel engine or drive bearings? The reason I ask is that we could put ya vessel in dry dock and run ya engine on the dyno and check it fer any problems. The test might save ya from some down time up the ICW. I have a night crew who's ah sittin' idle tonight, and it will not cost ya ah thing to have us check it out."

"We're not in a big hurry, so an engine check would be great, thank you." Jess extended his hand. "We're not accustomed to such red carpet treatment."

Marie Ann nodded. "We were anchored for the night in Tennessee and our propeller was stolen while we were on board."

"Ya're in the Deep South, sir, and we're more than happy to fix ya up, and check ya prop," Uncle Carl said and pointed to a pier off the port bow. "May I use ya radio and put her into our dry dock slip?"

Jess stepped back and motioned for Uncle Carl to take the helm and let go of the wheel when he felt a grip on it. He only took ten minutes to be aligned and ready for dry dock.

"Once we're locked in the building ya electric will be plugged in and ya'll be all set fer preparing to go to the wedding," he said and added. "Don't eat too much before ya's leave. There's hoard of food to eat tonight. Ya'll be picked up in a couple of hours. The wedding starts at 6:00 p.m. Ya'll come'n wet ya's whistle."

Slowly and easily *The Shallows* came up out of the water. It rested comfortably in the dry dock's special cradle rigging while being moved into a building. Ten minutes later, the noisy docks hoist engine was shut down with the vessel stable and in place. When the shore electric was connected the day shift crew moved to another vessel they had next to *The Shallows*

Marie Ann and Jess were in the master's living quarters looking at his gray western suit. He took out a dark gray shirt and picked out three red designed ties laying them across it.

"Sweetheart, which one do you think matches the gray shirt?"

She turned around. "The red and gray striped or the light gray would match your jacket color." She stepped over and took the solid gray tie and put across the jacket. "That's a good match, but it doesn't stand out like the red one."

"Do I want to be noticed or fade into the crowd? Where's my red tie that glows in the dark?" he said kidding and leaned over and kissed her waiting lips.

She backed away, "If they have any black lights at the reception that would be one tie to take along. But you're kidding, aren't you?" She gave him a three-quarter side look.

"Would I really do a thing like that?" And then he sneezed holding the back of his neck. He frowned and waited for the second one, but it did not happen.

"God bless you and to answer your question, yes. I think you would, if you thought you could get away with it, yes you would! Think twice though!"

She moved behind him reaching up and messaged his neck, "You don't need another of your famous neck aches from sneezing."

He moaned with the pleasure of her tender caressing, she said, "Can you purr for me?"

"I would if I could, love, thank you, that feels great."

"Let me put some of that blue muscle cooling salve on it before you put your shirt on" she said and went to the medicine cabinet.

When they finally stepped out on the aft salon deck, they looked like a couple ready for an uptown party, Jacksonville style.

Jess pointed at three masts of the schooner strung with lights that could be seen above the building next to them. The newlyweds would be leaving on it for their honeymoon.

A full size custom van drove up on the dry dock and opened the side door. Someone inside motioned for them to come down.

"Beautiful lady, will you be my date tonight?" Jess offered his arm which she took. They stepped off the diving platform onto a pallet on forks of a forklift and were slowly lowered to the cement ramp next to the van. They looked up to the bottom of *The Shallows* underside.

Jess walked over and patted the hull of the crusted red bottom. "We'll get you cleaned up tomorrow," he said, turned and took Marie Ann's hand, escorting her to the van.

She laughed, "What a beautiful sight to behold, classic, classic. I should have brought my digital camera."

Jess smiled not knowing what her remark was about and gave her a questionable look.

"You're all duded and dressed up, patting your other girlfriend's bottom. The nerve of you, and right in front of me." She squeezed against his arm, "I'm not jealous… yet."

Ten minutes later they were driven into a fenced yard of a beautiful two story white home with a four pillared drive under porch. Young children were escorting people inside.

They arrived at the ceremony on time and were introduced to everyone in the vestibule of Patti's mother's home. Mrs. Elyana Wallenberg met them in a side room, where Uncle Carl introduced them. He was in a black tux and she was in a very tight white laced floor length dress. It caused her to take small steps, but as she held onto Uncle Carl's arm, she kept her balance. She was noticeably uncomfortable in the tight dress.

Marie Ann was wondering who selected the dress for her; it might take the attention away from the bride.

Jess wondered if she would be able to sit in a chair without something having to give. She was a very attractive tall lady that made all the men's heads turn when she passed by.

She approached Marie Ann and put her arm through Marie Ann's and asked her to go with her for a few minutes. With Jess' nod of approval they went upstairs. Everyone watched them go up.

"Jess, I see ya have a taste for beautiful ladies too." Uncle Carl leaned toward Jess and snickered under his Rum breath, "please come with me."

Uncle Carl took Jess into a large guest room full of friends and family members. He was introduced to everyone as a most important dignitary from the Midwest and a close family friend.

He kept Jess occupied with the family members and finally excused himself, "I must get the pastor in his place up front. Ah yes, Jess, will ya and ya's missis honor us by sittin' with family in the second row on the starboard side."

They were seated in guest room, and Jess promptly asked Marie Ann, "How in the world will Patti's mother be able to sit in any chair? I know you don't like tight clothes." He snickered, "she was in a dress that must have been shrunk around her."

"That's what she wanted me to do, help her get out of it and put something else on," she said and lightly elbowed him. "I saw you and the others goggled-eyed at her."

"That dress was not what she had fitted for and paid for at the boutique." She spoke quietly, "Elyana was ashamed that she wore the dress and I'm sure she will apologize at the reception. She looks fantastic in her blue dress suit, you'll see."

Stewart 'Stew,' Patti's only and young brother, took Jess to his seat and then Marie Ann was escorted separately to sit next to him. There were special decorations, but not gaudy or out of place for a special wedding. No pomp or pageantry, just simple, loving touches only a mother could give her only daughter.

Her mom was calmer and much more at ease in her blue dress suit. "It doesn't fit her like a glove either," Marie Ann whispered to Jess. "I'll tell you more later."

She does look much prettier and relaxed in blue, Jess thought to himself.

Patti and Gale were a good-looking couple and their wedding was a success. The reception lasted another two hours. Afterwards, Jess and Marie Ann rode with Uncle Carl. They followed a line of other vehicles behind the newlywed's limo taking them to the dock, where the two-masted American Brigantine Sailing Vessel was waiting for them at their uncle's dry dock pier.

It was strung with lights from the most-forward of the bowsprit to the foremast to the top of the middle (main) mast to the aft mast to the stern railing. All the twelve crew and captain were in white uniforms and greeted the couple on board with a boson's pipe welcome. No one else was permitted to board and it immediately cast off lines and headed down river to the ocean.

Only Captain Swift and his crew, and the two uncles knew where the cruise would take them. Special arrangements had to be made with the U.S. Navy for Gale to have leave aboard another vessel.

The captain of the *O'Henry Swift* obtained the necessary paperwork from Gale's commanding officer. He personally spoke to him face to face aboard the nuclear carrier at Mayport.

"What a dazzling send-off for Patti and Gale," Marie Ann said holding Jess' arm tightly.

The wedding party was asked to return to Mrs. Walsenburg's home for midnight snacks. But, some of the party wanted to see Jess and Marie Ann's vessel in dry dock first. This was prompted, of course, by Uncle Carl.

"I didn't mention this before, cause I didn't know what was happin' after the weddin'. Hope ya's don't mind."

Jess put up his hands in surprise, "Sure, well that's great, but everything's not put away and stored," Jess said and nodded to Marie Ann.

She responded with a low curt, "It always happens when I haven't straightened up things," and then led the way.

The pier was parallel with the dry dock building and the big overhead door was open and the lights inside were on. It was quite a parade of well-dressed people in single file following them to *The Shallows*.

Jess turned, looking behind them. "There must be a lot of boat lovers behind us, look at the line."

He helped her onto the fork lifts platform and motioned for two more to get on with them. Uncle Carl operated the lift and they stepped off on the dive platform and unlocked the salon door.

Uncle Greg was with the next group lifted up and he stayed on the aft deck to direct everyone on and back off. Marie Ann set out a guest pad for everyone to sign and then led the first group down stairs to the master's stateroom, pointing out things of interest. They left going back up to the pilothouse where Jess was trying to answer all the questions for them. Patti's mom and her son Stew directed the groups to the bow and aft. No one was permitted up on the flybridge.

Marie Ann's guest book count was one hundred and twenty one, not counting the four Wallenbergs.

When the last guest had been lowered down, Uncle Carl came up alone. Elyana went into the salon and straight over to Marie Ann. "Thank you so much for helping me at the wedding. I couldn't have survived without you." She kissed her on the cheek and stood back arm's length, "I owe you an apology for all this aftermath of people from the wedding. May I have a glass of water and sit down?"

"Yes, ma'am," Marie Ann replied, "sit over here in this big lounge chair and I'll get you something cold. Do you like iced tea with lemon?"

"Yes, I do, and bless your heart. Do you have it made already?" She asked and flopped down in the chair. "I'm running out of steam."

The two uncles came in with Stew and Jess from the aft deck. Jess said, "Wow, what a group of friends and family you have. I haven't had so many questions thrown at me, and not just about why we are living on this vessel."

Elyana sat up on the edge of the cushion and pointed a long finger at Uncle Carl, "What in the world was this all about, having all those people tromping through their home like this? My heavens, did you ask them first?"

"Now, Ely, I had me purposes. I know it was sudden, but it was me only chance to show off our new vessel to sell." He put up his hands to hold off her talking, "I have wanted to take on the Nordic Tug line of yachts for years and just haven't taken the time to think about it. Then when Patti and Gale floated in here on this one, I just thought I could…"

"Carl, you had no right to impose on the Hanes this way, and you owe them an apology." She said shaking her finger at him, forcing her issue with him.

"Excuse me please," Jess said, waving his hands in the air, "as the captain of this vessel, I respectfully request a moment of silence. Everyone catch their second breath and let it out easy."

He eyed the two uncles and then the mother. "Thank you, would anyone else like a nice tall glass of sun brewed iced tea? Thank you, sweetheart, please." He nodded to Marie Ann and pointed to Stew. "Young man, we have some soft drinks as well."

Marie Ann motioned for Stew to help her in the galley. "Take this to your Mother please. And, I'll have you a choice of drinks when you come back."

She turned to the uncles, "Gentlemen, iced tea with lemon or soft drinks, Spring Cola, Ginger Ale or a fresh cup of black coffee with caffeine."

Uncle Greg put up his hand, "Do ya's have ice cubes? If so I'd like a glass of iced coffee, please."

"Sure can, but we don't have cream; I can use milk or French Vanilla Cappuccino instead of cream," Marie Ann said and motioned him over to the galley counter. "Here's your pick of Cappuccino and I'll get the chipped ice. Uncle Carl, what would you like?"

"Let me apologize for all this confusion and forwardness on my part," he said with his eyes looking down at his hands. Then he looked directly at Jess and then Marie Ann, "I 'm sincerely sorry for taking unfair advantage of you good folks tonight. There's no real excuse for what I started this evening; it could have waited until tomorrow."

"Apology is accepted with no hard feelings Carl," Jess said and continued. "No harm done, plus we don't mind showing off our pride and joy."

Elyana got up and put her arms around Carl's neck and kissed his cheek, "You are a real gentleman Carl, no matter what anyone else says." She laughed and patted his cheek and returned to her seat.

"Now that that issue is settled," Marie Ann said, "would anyone care for homemade chocolate chip cookies?" She turned and took them out of the microwave and passed the plate around. "I made them while we were in Key West and then froze them."

Another hour passed by and Stew walked over to his mother, "Mom it's after midnight and I'm sure these good folks need their rest too."

"Oh my, see what happens when you're having fun. I hope no one is waiting at the house for us. Oh my, I forgot about the offer to have everyone over. This may turn out to be an 'all-nighter'. Oh yes, let's do get home." She hugged Marie Ann and Jess, "Don't leave town too soon, I'd like to get to know you both much better. Call me later this morning, here's my business card."

The Wallenberg family all left with Uncle Carl.

It was all quiet with all the lights off other than the small interior night lights. Jess and Marie Ann went up to the pilothouse and out on the deck to the bow. This gave them a fantastic skyline few of Mayport and downtown Jacksonville, from the Fort George Island. The moon was not out and the night lights glistened off the water surface. The light breeze from the ocean was chilly even though it was 72 degrees.

She put her arms around his waist and snuggled tight. He held her close.

"Love you, sweet lady," he said, brushing a curl away from her eyes. "I don't see any night shift workers. Maybe they're not going to do the engine tonight. It's only 12:30 a.m." He hugged her closer to him. "You want a windbreaker from inside?"

"No, you're my windbreaker."

Suddenly, the interior lights of the building dimmed and went out; only the outside dusk to dawn lights of the building were on. The overhead doors toward the highway were lowered and the one between them and the river lowered.

The doors to the office were closed by a night watchman who shouted at them. "I'll check out here every hour on the hour. Good night."

"Good night," Jess hollered back to him.

"Shall we go below, my Love and put it all to bed?"

"I'm with you young man," she said and grabbed his arm. They secured all their external doors and went to bed, said their prayers and snuggled in. It had been an exciting, long busy day. It did not take long before they were both sound asleep.

The next morning, Marie Ann fixed a light breakfast of scrambled eggs, chopped onions, bacon and potatoes. She had all the windows and doors opened for a breeze, but there was not any, even with the buildings overhead doors open. They just sat down for breakfast and someone called below them in the dry dock.

"Ahoy, aboard *The Shallows*, coffee on?" A female voice echoed in the dry dock, "I can smell the bacon and coffee from down here. May I come aboard?"

Marie Ann looked at Jess with a puzzled expression, and went to the fantail and opened the transom door, "Come on up, coffee's hot." She waited for Elyana to arrive on the platform; one of the dock crew operated the fork lift for her. She and Stew stepped out on the diving deck. "Come on in and make yourselves at home. Had breakfast yet?"

"Yes, we have, thank you anyway. I will have a cup of your coffee again, please," she said and looked at Stew. "You want anything, sweetheart?"

"No, thanks, Mom, your breakfast does smell good," Stewart said and sat next to his mom on the salon couch. "Ya'all don't hurry for us. We got all morning to mess around."

"Sweetheart, we really don't, but I do have a request of you. You both have been a big help to me with Patti and Gale, and I want to show my appreciation in some way. I understand you're treasure hunters?" She said and took a large folder from Stew. "I don't know if this will be of interest; you could perhaps find a lot of treasure. These maps have been in our family for centuries. Would you please look at these, after you're finished breakfast?" She laid it on the galley counter and took the coffee cup Marie Ann handed to her.

Stew was a senior in high school and was a good looking sturdy built young man. He sort of felt out of place tagging along with his mom, he would like to have been out with his friends this morning for the afternoon football game. He got hurt and could not play for the rest of the year. Jess knew this from all the conversations from the night before at the wedding and reception afterward.

"So, you play football, by your build I would think you're either a linebacker or a running back," Jess said and pushed away from the table taking his coffee cup with him. He picked up the coffee pot and refreshed Elyana cup.

"Yes, sir, I'm better at tackling than blocking and I've been able to read the quarterback's plays before they run the play. That's how I hurt my knee, getting blocked from the blind side." He laughed and stood when Jess went into the salon.

"I like your manners, young man," Jess nodded to him. "Keep your seat." Jess motioned for him to set back with his mom.

"What horsepower do you have below in your diesel, Mr. Hanes?"

"It's a 650 hp Cummins. Interested in marine engine?"

"Yes, sir, I work on them in the shop here when I'm not in school or studying. I make straight A's too. I'm not just a sports jock," Stew said and gave his mom a big smile.

"That he does, Mr. Hanes. I'm very proud of my son." She reached over and patted his hand. He did not seem to mind her doing that, they enjoyed each other's company.

Jess was thinking they really miss her husband and his dad. "Would you like to look in the engine room?"

Jess scooted the deck rug covering the manhole to the engine room. It was right forward of the salon's aft door.

He reached down to open it and heard someone's voice. Someone in the dry dock was trying to get their attention. Jess went aft to the boarding deck and hollered, "Good morning."

"We would like to move you out in the water at the pier. If you would fasten everything down, we can have it down in five minutes," the man said with a red reflective vest on.

Jess gave him thumbs-up and hollered at Marie Ann, "Is everything secured enough for getting in the water?"

"Aye, Captain, yes, let's do it," she replied and turned to their guest. "Get a good hold, I don't know what to expect. I thought we would have to get off of the boat."

"Okay," Jess yelled and stepped back onto the aft deck and held onto the ladder railing to the upper deck above the salon.

Like the man said, they slowly slid the Nordic Tug back down into the water and they floated off the submersed dry-dock supports. Two workers held the lines as the man in red told them where to tie-off the vessel. It was all a smooth ride into the water. They secured the bow, spring and aft lines.

Jess stepped out on the pier and shook their hands, "Is either of the Mr. Wallenberg's in their office?"

"Yes, sir, Mr. Carl will be right down," rhe man in red replied and the three men went back up to the big building they removed *The Shallows* from.

Jess could see him coming down the pier and welcomed him on board.

"Mr. Hanes, ya's sure gave me a delay in work production this morning when ya made breakfast," Carl said and smiled at Jess as he went into the salon.

"There's the cook," Jess said and offered him coffee; he declined. "It wasn't me this time; it was good while it lasted."

"Just want to give ya's this detailed receipt for your Nordic Tug's time in dry dock." He said and nodded to Elyana and Stew. "How was breakfast ya's two?"

"Ours was good at home," Stew said, "but it seems we missed a good one here."

"I could smell onions frying all the way out to the parking lot," Carl said laughing, "and my crew were standing outside the office staring at your vessel."

"I didn't think I cooked that many onions to attract attention like that," Marie Ann said laughing with the others. "I know that's how some of the fast-food diners do it and then turn on their outside vent fans. It brings in the outside customers for miles around."

Jess turned to Carl after reading the invoice. "This is not correct, sir. The total at the bottom is zero." He showed Marie Ann. "Look at all they did. Carl there's no cost listed anywhere. What do we owe for these parts and labor work?"

"That's why I was sent down here by the big boss," he turned to Elyana with a big smile. She said, "Ya's know, it was to be added to the wedding expense. Ya, she pays the bills and writes the pay checks, I'm just an adviser and messenger."

"And, Uncle Carl, what did you advise your sister-in-law about this bill?" Marie Ann asked and pointed a finger at him.

"Ya's know, she didn't give me a chance. I was going to agree with her, but she didn't wait around long enough." He laughed and continued, "We appreciate the attitude and kindness ya's showed the youngsters coming back to Jacksonville."

"I was told how you took them into your home on the water, no questions asked," she said and put her hands on her hips and sighed. "The majority of people wouldn't do that at their home, much less aboard ship."

She stood and put her hand on Marie Ann's shoulder, "My spirit testifies with your spirit that you are children of our God and know our Saviour Jesus Christ. And being such, I'm compelled to share confidential information that is only privy to our family. I've secured a quick background check on you both and your treasure hunter business. There will be no charges for the work done on your vessel, or for any parts that may have been used."

Jess started to protest again, but she held up her hand for him to wait, "In exchange for guidance with our search limitations on a buried cache on the island."

"This island that you are on now, Fort St. George, is the one in question?" Jess replied.

Stew spoke up for his mom. "Yes, sir, we own a large amount of the island, but there are portions that are Florida State Parks. Our lawyers have not been able to obtain permission to dig on our own land, mainly because we are not state approved archeologist or legal certified salvagers."

Uncle Carl added, "Our property borders all the state land. Ya's know, they are afraid we will hire someone to tunnel under the line to their property and find treasure on their side."

"I wouldn't think, under the state of Florida and the U.S. Constitution, that they have control over you as property owners doing whatever you want to on your land, unless it endangers someone in some way," Jess said with a tone questioning his own comment. "Do you own the mineral rights to your property?"

"Yes, it's detailed on this land grant," she said and handed him the copy of abstracts.

"They have some screwy lawyer language that causes our young attorney to have nothing to do with the salvaging of treasure and artifacts on the island," she said and asked for some water.

"In fact, the Florida Indian Nations Affairs is in support of our desire to search. Because of their tribal history, the Indian villages and burial sites on our property are in question; they have never been professionally scrutinized by anyone of professional experience and knowledge."

"Have you talked with any salvagers on Florida's east coast; Taffi Fisher in Sebastian or her brother in Key West? Their lawyers took the state of Florida to the U.S. Supreme Court in order to retrieve relics, gold and silver the state took from the Fisher's museums," Jess said and offered drinks to everyone.

Marie Ann served them as they continued to talk about the cache hunting on the island.

"No we haven't, not personally, but our lawyer was supposed to have researched this for us. My lawyer's boss said they didn't want to get involved with the federal government over petty digging in the dirt," Elyana said laughing. "He wouldn't even come out to the locations where we were going to dig, He sent his most-junior lawyer, our lawyer, who was right out of lawyer's college."

"If we are financially able to we can hire him away from the larger attorney firm and put him into business. Retaining him to take charge of this investigation could put a feather in his hat for the future." Uncle Carl said.

Jess pressed on with a few of his own touchy points, "There are people in every state administration that make the rules as they go. If no one bucks them, they will continue on their merry way. Many times, they are breaking the laws themselves and are lining their own pockets as they go."

He cleared his throat and sneezed. "Sorry about that."

"God bless ya's," Uncle Carl said.

"Thank you, Carl." Jess smiled and got a handkerchief.

Uncle Carl replied, "And, at the same time, ya's know, the historical value of the artifacts stay buried in the ground." Shaking his head, "I just don't mean the monitory value. Ya's knows, our children will never know the history unless it's dug from the ground."

Jess nodded to Carl, and Marie Ann asked, "Is there a group or just one person who may be hiding something on the land they don't want the authorities to know about? Perhaps the authorities already know and don't want the public to know."

She slapped her hands and walked over to Ely and patted her shoulder. "Oh my, secrets, secrets, who knows the secrets men hide from others?" She winked at Uncle Carl.

"Not that I can think of right now, ya's know of anyone, Ely?" Uncle Carl replied with a look of surprise that he was not the one to think of such a thing.

"Yes, I can, Carl, and you know it has been a thorn in our side," Elyana said and turned on her bar stool looking directly at him. "Remember, all the way back to when John W. was home before leaving for Vietnam the second time." She looked toward Marie Ann. "I always called my husband John W. I don't really know why the 'W,' but it had significance when I used it. Anyway, when I did, he knew he was in trouble."

They all laughed and Carl cleared his throat to get back to the point she was trying to make with him. "Okay, what am I supposed to remember that involves John W. in this discussion about the Indian shell mounds?"

"I didn't say anything about the Indian shell mounds, Carl." She cocked her head and squinted at him as she stood up. "Carl, what do you know about the shell mounds?"

He would not look directly at her, but turned to Jess. "Ya's know, I've said all along we would eventually have problems with our land that bordered the state parks. Especially, ya's know, where the shell mounds are located." He shifted his gaze to Elyana. "Yes, that spot has been a problem with undesirable trespassers. Ya's all know about the ones sneakin' at night on ya's land."

"Come on, Carl, quite trying to snow everyone. Tell them the details of the missing Indian couple that maybe buried on our land, or somewhere on the island." She was pushing for something specific.

"Anyway, ya's know, according to our old maps there is some gold in the ground close to those mounds." He cleared his throat again and Marie Ann filled his water glass.

He took a good swallow and continued, "Well, back then, early fifties, John and I were out hunting cottontail rabbits. Ya's know, we hadn't seen anything to shoot at and were getting close to the north tidewater channel near the old fort ruins. We heard a woman scream, but your dad said it was probably a cougar upset about something."

He looked at Elyana and smiled. "I told him that they were not out in the daytime and they only screamed like that at night." He shrugged. "What did we know back then, we were only twelve. Anyway, ya's know, we'd then heard the roar of a fast speedboat that was going south on the channel."

"And, later, after we'd all married and children of our own, ya's two told the story again at our family reunion before your mother died. She'd never heard such a story, but your dad said he heard of a young couple disappearing in the swamp. But he didn't know they were Indians or that they were anywhere's near the mounds."

Jess walked over to her. "Are you sure this isn't just a story that these two brothers conjured up?"

"No," Carl said. He smiled and pointed at her. "She's right, it was only recently ya's know, a story came out. Gossip I 'spect, ya's know." He hesitated, looking down as if he had lost track of his thoughts. "In the local papers about an Indian couple's bodies being found in that area. Hurricane supposed to wash them up. I dismissed its being on the state park land." He shrugged his shoulders again. "What would that have to do with anything connected with our wanting to extract relics and historical items back near the fort?"

Trying to shorten his story, he continued, "Ya's know, that property around the fort now belongs to the state, and borders our land. Back in the early fifties, it was state park land, but it belonged to Sidwick Junior, the ole-timer who had the whiskey stills in operation. It's a wonder we hadn't been shot messing around out there." Carl shook his head.

"Every time you turn around and want to build, add on, tear down, dig a hole, somebody wants to tax or fine you for doing it—permit here, permit there," Elyana said and smiled while standing up. "If I remember, there was a halt to construction digging because they found Indian bones on the shell dumps along the river. And the construction was five miles away. The state and federal people were all over our farm until the Indian Affairs took over the investigation."

"Sounds like your property was state park property at one time?" Jess asked.

"No, but they wanted to buy it and run us off the island. My father-in-law told my husband that he would cut him out of the family if he sold to the state. John was not hurting for money and didn't sell."

She laughed and slapped her hands. "Then they were going to turn the whole island into a wild-life refuge and that didn't work, so they tried to condemn the island or claim it as an 'eminent domain' so they could turn around a get the land for nothing."

Jess walked over to her and held her hand. "We understand and sympathize with you all," he said and put his arm around her shoulder. "Unless you have mountains of money to spend on good lawyers, you're not going to get around them taking your land if they really want it. I think, without your digging further, you'll have to sit on this project for a while longer."

He continued while opening the salon windows for cross ventilation, it was getting warm without the air-conditioning on. "I would limit physically digging, excavating, or building on your island acreage."

"Put I know there's history on this island that hasn't been seen or heard of and it's a shame," she sidled up next to Jess and kissed him on the cheek, and then walked over and sat next to Stew.

Carl threw up his hands. "Ya's know, I'd should make a trip down to Sebastian and Key West. They've had years of experience in this line of business. I don't need to wait a couple of weeks. Tomorrow I'll go."

"Let us know if we can be of help," Marie Ann said giving them her business cards. "If we are still in the area, we'll come over."

"Or if we're at home, we'll fly down from Indiana. I'm interested knowing what the museums have to say," Jess said and extended his hand to Elyana, Stew, and Uncle Carl. "Good luck with your Nordic Tug dealership when it starts."

"Thanks ya'll," he said as he helped the other two onto the dock and left in one of their two vans.

"Goodness, what a family!" Marie Ann said while waving good-bye. Jess had his arm on her shoulder as she leaned against him.

"Groceries, we need to restock. Let's lock up and find a place to eat and then get some supplies," he said and they did.

CHAPTER FIFTEEN

Jacksonville, Florida, to Lanier Island, Georgia

The Shallows slowly moved north up the ICW, following six other vessels going under Hwy 105 Heckscher Drive bridge. The Fort Saint George Island, off the starboard side, slowly fading away in the morning mist. At the intersection of St. George River at mm 735; they caught the high wake wave of a speedster going south, which did not rock them too much.

All six vessels were staggered in formation turned to port taking the wake straight on the bow. The turn would have been a nice picture taken from above, showing the white foam turn in the green of the ICW. Then all came back on course in unison.

It was now the middle of June and the weather was still trying to settle down from a harsh cold and snowy winter on the east coast. Jess and Marie Ann had to wear windbreaker jackets during the mornings and evenings when the sun was down. The weather forecast promised lower fifties at night and lower sixties in the daytime if the sun was out. Winds would continue to be brisk and higher prior to sunset and calmer in the early mornings; good for cruising.

The trawler was fully loaded with fuel, fresh water, and groceries. The Hanes felt rested starting out on this leg of the Great American Loop.

They had missed a group of loop-cruisers, Americas Great Loop Cruise Association (AGLCA). The annual east coast

Rendezvous in Barefoot Resort in North Myrtle Beach, South Carolina, was on April 25-28. They had never been to an AGLCA Rendezvous. Many Looper friends were there; but they only knew them through e-mails, snail mail, and the *Great Loop Link* newsletter, and telephone calls. A few they had met coming and going on the AICW. Still in Georgia, they had a long cruise ahead to get north to the Hudson Bay and then through the Great Lakes to get back around to Benton Harbor on the west shores of Michigan.

The morning was too cool to stand on the bow, so Marie Ann stayed in the pilothouse answering the radio. She used the binoculars to watch for debris that had been missed by the six vessels ahead of them. Sometimes they would call on the radio to warn the others in line.

Ahead of them were two trawlers fifty-two feet in length, the third vessel was a yacht of sixty feet. Behind them were four trawlers of various lengths. *The Shallows* was the last of the group. So far the convoy had no debris to contend with on the AICW.

At the 730mm it was suggested by south bounders to the north bounders to increase the groups speed to 16 knots to help cross the Nassau River. Some may have to use maximum speed/rpm's until passing marker R46 to go up South Amelia River. They said to watch out for heavy surface debris and suggested the distance between vessels in our fleet should be further apart until in the Amelia River.

All skippers agreed to the suggestions and Jess called them, "This is Jess on *The Shallows*, if anyone has problems we will linger to assist."

"This is Dodger Roger with the lead. Let us know when you clear marker 46."

"Roger that Dodger," snickering to himself at what he just replied, sat down and buckled into the captain's chair at the helm.

Marie Ann buckled into the lounge bench behind him and grabbed an overhead railing. "They didn't say how rough the water would be, but I don't expect it to be calm as this Sawpit Creek."

"You're probably right. Is everything ready below for a rough ride?" Jess asked.

"We always are, Captain!" she replied, smiling. "As always, Captain, we're shipshape!"

Jess gave the vessel ahead of him a ten minute lead as he maneuvered *The Shallows* in a circle inside the channel, and then again followed the squadron of leisure vessels ahead of them.

The water was dark brown, choppy with a westerly 20 knot wind across the port bow, and a strong river current from the same direction; making Jess make the his Nordic Tug crab to the port with the bow 25 degrees upstream from their course. To stay on course he had to almost use maximum power to hold the course. The waves slapped the side of the trawler and at times rocked her violently.

With Marie Ann trying to keep a steady watch with one hand holding binoculars, the other hand holding the overhead railing and stay in the seat, she could not keep steady enough to spot any debris on the water surface.

"Jess I'm getting sick to my stomach using the binocular." She put them in the armrest of the bench seat, "I'll move over to the door and hold onto the overhead railing."

"Sweetheart, be careful. Is it too stuffy in here for you?" he asked and stood up, restrapping himself to the captain's chair. "It will take us about thirty minutes to make this crossing. This water looks like they have had some heavy rains up river."

Suddenly she pointed and yelled, "Port bow!"

Moving with the current, barely above the surface was a huge waterlogged tree trunk with a general store sign nailed to it. Jess pushed the throttle to reverse and engaged the bow thruster for port thrust. The trunk scrapped along the port side as they just missed a straight on collision. Almost at the same time the propeller began to make loud noises, like rocks were hitting it.

Jess put the throttle to neutral, turned off the thruster, swung the bow to port, upstream with the help of the starboard thrust. They could hear a sand bar scrapping the belly of *The Shallows*.

"Hold on, love, we may run aground backwards real hard."

They braced for a hard hit, but it did not come as they floated across the sand bar into deeper water. Jess immediately adjusted the throttle to full forward and cranked the rudder hard to starboard. They were finally in the channel of the Amelia River. With the bow upstream they began to make good headway and gained on the vessel ahead of them.

"That was close, Jess. If that tree had hit us broad sided, we could have been sunk and washed out to sea," Marie Ann said and went over to him, putting her arm around his waist. "You did great, young man—I mean, Captain."

"Thank you, love, our Lord Jesus kept us from that disaster. We're keeping his angels busy today." He took a deep breath and let it out. "I don't think we would have floated out to sea, look at all those crooks and turns in the river on the monitor. We'd probably be on one of those beaches with the alligators and snakes."

"Jess, don't even think about such a thing," she said and slapped his backside, "The thought sends chills up and down my back."

"No, that's just from the excitement you get being so close to me," he laughed and slowed the Nordic Tug matching the speed of the vessel ahead of them. "Ain't this fun?"

"Would you like a snack and something to drink?" She patted him on the shoulder, "I'm hungry."

He looked at his watch, "We should be in port in a couple hours, how about some cheese and crackers; pepper jack, something spicy, and iced tea."

"And what else, Captain?" she said teasingly and kissed him on the cheek.

"Please, sweet lady of mine," pulling her close and gave her a long tender kiss. "Second thought, I think we should check for damage ASAP. We only have about four miles to an anchorage or marina to check where that tree scrapped the port side. When we get there, we better check below the water line for leaks, inside and out."

"Aye, aye, Captain, be right back," she said and went down to the galley.

Jess unbuckled from the captain's chair and locked the helm wheel in place with two short 'limit ropes'. He stretched and walked around the inside of the cabin. He took out AICW charts looking at the Amelia City. Then he set in the seat again. After removing the ropes he called the five vessels ahead of them about their cross behind them. Everyone had made it across without a scratch, except *The Shallows*.

Jess noticed a vibration when he put his hands on the wheel again and could feel it on the cabinet top of the helm's compartment. He slowly moved out of the wash of the boat ahead of him and the vibration went away. Then the vibration increased when he moved back behind the other vessel.

Thinking to himself that the vibration could be coming from the backwash of the other vessel, but he did not feel it earlier in the morning when they had started out. He slowly increased the rpm's and heard a pounding from underneath in the aft section. Slowing the engine again stopped the pounding, but the vibrations continued.

When Marie Ann came back up with their snack and put it on the table, he motioned for her to take the wheel, "Feel anything unusual in the wheel?"

"What was that banging underneath a while ago?" she said and put both hands on the wheel. "Yes, there is a light vibration."

"If I increase the rpm's it creates that banging from underneath the aft area. It's like something maybe wrapped around the prop shaft," Jess said a little bit discussed of having to get back in the water.

Marie Ann found a marina five miles up the river from them on the north side of the Thomas Shave Jr. Bridge. They would have to go under a smaller bridge right after passing under the state road bridge. It was listed in the charts as Amelia Island Yacht Basin; they had all the necessary amenities needed for cruiser repairs.

She called ahead while Jess contacted the other vessels in their flotilla and advised them they would be tied up for a couple of days.

Leaving early after breakfast, the sun was barely up. They enjoyed the two day layover even if it was for repairs. One of the other cruise couples had rented a car and they all toured the north end of the island of Old Fernandina to Fort Clinch. They spent some time looking for the oldest dated grave marker in Bosque Bell Cemetery. That was for further historical research of the area. They always investigated relic hunting the Civil War areas.

Jess figure they had visited all the antique shops in between, and would have a boat full of 'stuff' had they not managed to keep their money in their pockets. They certainly would not have had room for it all; and, it was agreed upon no shipping of any 'stuff' home.

Marie Ann figured six or seven miles they would cross the state line into Georgia at the center of the Cumberland Sound where the rivers emptied into the Atlantic Ocean. Most of the cruise on the AICW keeps land between the channel and the ocean. The crossing into Georgia would give them a glimpse of the Atlantic off the starboard beam. They had just crossed the 715 mm, and were heading north.

The Cumberland Sound seemed calm at this early hour of the morning and not a lot of commercial traffic. Even though Jess and Marie Ann were aware of the U.S. Submarine Base just off the west side of the AICW; they were surprised to meet one coming toward them after they entered the shipping lane at the R28 marker. They heard the air horns of the submarine blast and they returned the signal.

As they got closer, Jess tied the helm wheel in place and stepped out on the port deck next to Marie Ann and gave the American submarine and American flag a snappy hand salute. They were close enough to see the faces of each man above deck as they returned a hand salute back and a long blast of their air horn. The sub's Skipper had slowed their speed to keep the backwash down and promptly increased it after quietly slipping passed the NT42. Jess stepped back in and unfastened the tied helm wheel and set *The Shallows* to ride out the backwash of the sub, which was a slow roll to ride. Marie Ann was taking pictures with her digital camera.

"What a nice surprise, sweetheart," she said as she put her hands on each side of his face and tenderly kissed him. "I'm proud of you, Jess, and love you so very much. Again, thank you for your service to our country and me." She wiped her tears and then his.

"You're most welcome, love. I'm happy that I could do it. Yep, I'm just an ole softy." He said and hugged her with his left arm. "Thank you Lord for those men on that sub, keep them safe and return them home safely. Thank you for the freedoms we still have because of our men and women in service, and for your Saving Grace."

It was not long before they could see two submarines tied up at the Kings Bay Naval Submarine Supply Base. One was at the northern pier and the other was inside the Navy Degaussing pier on the east side of the AICW. Using binoculars, they could see naval personnel on the docks.

"Now I think of it! They may have a base tour for veterans and retires," he said and slapped the wheel at the helm. "Dumb! Sorry, love, I wasn't thinking. It probably would be very interesting. I bet there's a lot of history around here that's connected to the Civil War."

She sat on the pilothouse lounge bench seat behind Jess. "Let me check the Internet on tours. Let's see...that is called U.S. Naval Submarine Base, Kings Bay, Georgia."

She continued checking her references as Jess slowed their progress north; just enough to keep them in one spot against the currents that wanted to move them down river to the south.

"It says that there's a museum on the base that takes one to two hours to complete on your own. Also, because of the heightened security levels since 1986 and September 11, 2001, it may take six months to get permission to tour the docks or go on board a Triton Submarine." She tapped her fingers on the table top, "I wonder, being your retired Air Force with 12 years of active duty in the Navy...I think I'll just give the base register's office a call and get more info."

While she was doing her investigation, Jess glanced at the AICW channel north for marinas to tie up to, but he could not concentrate on doing that and handle the currents. A fast scan showed no marinas close and this was the last weekend in May coming up, which meant Memorial Day with the crowded ICW with speeding boats. He best settle for an anchorage away from the Intracoastal Waterway.

Marie Ann got off the telephone looking a bit disappointed. "Looks like the base is closed for tours and we will have to dock at least an hour car ride north of here. I thought we could get to the Base Exchange for groceries, but the cost of a vehicle is outrageous."

"Plus, we have the holiday weekend coming," Jess said, and pointed to the charts. "We better find a place to anchor for the weekend. I haven't found a marina yet."

She checked charts and marina references further up the channel near Savannah. "We've got thirty miles to the nearest marina at the Torras Causeway Bridge; there maybe others between here and there. We can be there by two or two thirty, should I give them a call?"

"Sure, find out if they can accommodate us through the weekend. I don't want to be out here cruising with all the speedsters over the holiday," Jess said as he made adjustments to head up the channel. The water was clear and calm with no clutter of debris, so he set their speed for sixteen knots.

After three hours of steady northern cruising, *The Shallows* pulled up to a double pier jetting out into the Fredrick River from Lanier Island just south of the Torras Causeway Bridge. There were two men at the slip where Jess was to dock, who were motioning him in. Marie Ann was on the bow with the lines to toss them. Jess put the Nordic Tug into the fuel berthing without touching either side.

Putting the 650 horse-powered diesel engine in neutral, he and Marie Ann dropped the rubberized fenders over the edge. The starboard side was pulled close to the pier by the man on the pier. Then he helped Marie Ann pull the shore electrical cables from their storage on the bow and laid them on the forward deck.

"Captain Hanes, thanks for choosing Morningstar Marina. Welcome ashore, sir." The southern accent came out real strong as he held out his hand to Jess to step out on the pier. "I'm Willy George the Third and that guy on the port side pier is Howard Bailey. We're the best docking crew on the river."

Marie Ann stepped out on the pier as Jess shook Willy's hand; he took his hat off and smiled. "Welcome to Morningstar, ma'am. We aim to please while you're with us."

Jess waited for Marie Ann's reply. "Thank you, Willy, we are happy to be here. This southern hospitality can be contagious."

"Yes, ma'am, it does happen." He turned to Jess. "The boss said you want the tanks filled with diesel fuel with no additive. You'll add your own, correct, sir?

"You're correct Willy, I'll come aft to give ya'll a hand," Jess said as he stepped back on board and walked aft to remove the fuel tank caps, one on each side. "Which side do you want first?"

"It don't matter Mr. Hanes, we can pump both sides at the same time," Willy said as Howard prepared the other fuel lines. They worked as a team and made sure the fuel lines did not scrap the boat and no fuel was dripped on the deck. It only took ten minutes to fill the two tanks, three-hundred gallon tanks.

When they were finished, Howard told Marie Ann that he would be going to the slip that was picked for the 42-foot Nordic Tug and Willy would help Mr. Hanes get there. He handed the lines back to her as Jess and Willy finished securing the refueling aft. The three moved to the pilothouse.

"There's Howard over there with the yellow flag," Willy said pointing out the port doorway. "Just ease her back into the channel and bring her to port. That's the closest slip we have tonight to the marina office and facilities."

"Marie Ann, how are we back there," Jess hollered to her.

She had moved back to the aft deck on the boarding platform.

"Looks great Skipper," she replied and came back up into the pilothouse.

Maneuvering the 42-foot vessel's bow around to port with the thruster, he made the response look easy. Then he reversed it to starboard thrust as the vessel straightened in the channel, working with the river current. With a little rudder movement, they slowly kept a straight course in the marina channel and around to their slip. In ten minutes they were secured in the slip. Shore electric power cables were connected. When Marie Ann finished with the water lines, the pier crew left. Jess tipped them generously.

After washing up and putting on clean clothes they walked over to the marina office to check in.

"Sweetheart," Jess said as they walked hand in hand, "I asked Willy about what I wanted to have done to the diesel; also who's the best diesel mechanic in this area for the job. He wasn't sure, but he would ask Mr. Morningstar, Junior, his boss. Willy would let us know when we get inside."

"Refresh my memory about the diesel. Is there something wrong with it?" Marie Ann replied with a wrinkled forehead.

"Nothing to worry about with the diesel, love," Jess said. "But remember talking about the struggle we had against some of those fast river currents? And then, when our maximum speed was only at the most 18 knots."

He took her arm and supported her down the decking of the pier. "If we get caught in the middle of a large bay area and a storm would come up or an emergency like yours when we had to get you to port to the hospital; we need some way to increase our power and speed when we need it."

He continued, "That's what your brother Dino was telling us about the electronic diesel engines. If the engine has a blower, a specific electronic chip could be inserted into the diesel's computer, which would give us the added power and speed. I really don't understand it all, but I think we should check into it."

Jess opened the marina's office door and he followed her in. "But didn't he say doing that would void the diesel warranty?"

"Yes, he did, but in an emergency I don't care about the warranty," he said as they were approached by a tall thin gentleman wearing a loud red tie against a light blue short sleeved shirt.

"Welcome to Morningstar, I'm Slim Jones, and the boss' son." He said and shook their hands. "No, I'm not a Morningstar family member. I'll tell you the story behind the Morningstar name later if you're interested." He motioned them to the counter in the back of the store, "But right now, what can we do for you? That's a right nice looking Nordic Tug you have in slip six."

He smiled, "Will you be here for the Memorial Day Sunday parade?"

Marie Ann spoke up first, "Yes we plan to be here. And thank you, we try to keep our vessel in ship-shape."

She handed him the docking form Willy gave to her, which covered the amenities of the marina. Slim glanced over it and then initialed the bottom then put it on a clip board.

He turned and motioned for one of his crew to take the board, "Make sure Mr. and Mrs. Hanes requests are filled promptly, and bring this back to me personally. Your name precedes your arrival. A Mr. Jefferson Davis Whiley in Mobile, Alabama, left a message for you."

Jess and Marie Ann looked at each other, "How would he have known we would stop here?" Jess asked.

"We have a network of marinas from Brownsville, Texas, all the way up to the tip of Maine. Mr. Whiley owns a controlling interest in our complexes. His title is CEO of our accounting departments. He sent an e-mail to all our marinas to cover any chance of your docking with us. Also, he sends his best wishes for a comfortable stay at any of our marinas, no charge for anything. We are to send him the bill."

Jess was all smiles and clapped his hands, "That is most generous of him. Would you have his telephone number handy, so I don't have to back to our boat?"

"Here it is on the back of my business card." Slim pointed to a phone on his desk in his office. "You may call Mr. Whiley in there, sir. Be pleased to close the door for your privacy."

"Thank you, Mr. Jones," Jess said and shook his hand. Marie Ann followed into the office as Slim closed the door behind them.

She put her hands on her hips. "What's this all about? We didn't do that much business with him at the bank."

As Jess talked to Mr. Jeff in Mobile, Marie Ann scanned the office taking in each detail of the hanging pictures and posters, family photo on his desk and the late Mr. Morningstar portrait, founder of the marinas.

The conversation was short; Jess turned, placing the phone back in its holder. "Remember the gold coins we helped uncover and then put in his bank at Mobile. Well we may have hit the 'big find'."

With a big smile, he took off his baseball hat, "Remember, we thought it may have been part of the Gold Rush minted gold coins from California. One third of what was minted was cargo on a paddle steamer, the SS *Central America*. It was sunk in a hurricane off Cape Hatteras, North Carolina in 1857."

"But how did it get up the river from Mobile?" Marie Ann asked. "Unless it was an overland shipment minted at the same time."

"Love, you hit it on the head. I think if you're correct, we won't have to share it with Great Britain after all," he said with a big smile. "Mr. Jefferson Davis Whiley is continuing the investigation and wants us to head for Cape Hatteras.

"Around here, let's keep this hush-hush for right now," he said and reached for Marie Ann's hand, "until we get back on *The Shallows*. I don't want you to wet your britches when I tell you more. I hope this office is not taped or bugged."

Marie Ann looked puzzled about something. "I don't understand what Great Britain has to do with those gold coins."

"They owned part of that gold shipment the SS *Central America* sank with," Jess replied and smiled. "But their insurance company paid them for the loss, so I don't think they can claim ownership. I don't know about the insurance company though. They may have owner's rights to the gold when recovered."

Marie Ann put her arm around his as they went to the office door. "Okay, now that that is over, and only because I'm hungry for an ole fashion cheese/bacon hamburger with onions, and then a piece of apple pie…," she replied and squeezed his hand.

Mr. Slim Jones was waiting at the counter for them. "By the grin on your faces, Mr. Whiley was in?"

"Yes, Jeff was," Marie Ann said, putting her arm under Jess'. "But more important, Jess has promised me the biggest and best hamburger in town. Where do we go?"

Slim was anticipating their need for a map, which he slid across the counter to them. "Here are the keys to my AMC H2 Hummer or you can walk next door to King's House for burgers or sea food. Farther on about 50 yards is the Coastal Kitchen for great home-cooked food. Off the island to the east on Torras Causeway, you'll find a bunch of eating places on the 'big island' all the way to the ocean. The best seafood is along the waterfront." He marked a few place with a colored marker.

"Maybe tomorrow morning, but she has whetted my appetite for a good hamburger," Jess replied and folded the map and scooted the keys back to Slim. "I don't think we will need transportation this evening, maybe pancakes in the morning."

"We have a continental breakfast here in the waiting area from five thirty to ten," Slim offered.

"Thank you again. We'll take you up on that later, see ya," Jess said as they walked out the front door of the Morningstar marina.

They walked slowly on the sidewalk toward the fast-foods places next to the marina. Jess was all smiles, a purpose not to share his secret with Marie Ann until they got there, but she was insistent all the way.

"Why won't you tell me more about the phone call from Mr. Jeff?" she teased back. "You can't hold yourself any longer."

He spread his arms and let out a rebel yell, "Glory halleluiah, thank you, Lord Jesus, for all your mercy and blessings."

Marie Ann looked shocked and looked around to see if anyone heard his outburst. "Come on, hot shot, give me the news. It's a good thing no one saw you, but I bet they heard you across the river."

She pointed. "Those people saw you up on the bridge and are waving at you."

They waved back and continued walking to the burger place. "Those coins we found at Jeff's place on the river could be very valuable, because some were minted in 1855, '56, and '57. At the price of gold now, above $1,000 per Troy ounce, and the great shape they were in, it's a big find!"

They did not discuss it until they were back on *The Shallows*. They first checked over the marina's work against what they marked on the checklist. Jess signed it and took it topside while Marie Ann poured two glasses of her famous sun tea over ice cubes.

He waved at Slim up at the marina office with the clipboard. Slim sent someone after it. Once it was retrieved, Jess took a slow, leisurely walked around the outside deck, scanning the surface for any problems. He wanted to make sure nothing had been moved and nothing was out of place. He continued to sip his iced tea and scan for out-of-place deck items.

He had started at the port railing aft and completely circled his vessel on the main deck. He took a small black plastic key chain device from his pocket and moved a small recessed switch on the bottom with his thumb. A small green LED came on.

Putting it back in his pants front pocket, he strolled back around to where he started, and then went up on the aft ladder to the sundeck to the flybridge above the pilothouse.

The little keychain was an electronic frequency listening device, a freebie from the CIA down in Florida. If there was a transmitting/listening device on *The Shallows*, it would vibrate. After scanning the marina, he noticed a couple of 100-foot yachts had moved into Morningstar slips.

Laying the empty iced tea glass down, he opened a storage compartment under the flybridge helm. He took out night-vision binoculars. The sun had set and he just was a little curious about the larger vessels docked about two hundred yards north of them, up the river.

He felt her body warmth when Marie Ann came up behind him, putting her arms around his waist and snuggling her lips along his neck, kissing him.

"Is she a blonde or redhead?" she asked, squeezing him tighter.

"Well, love, I've not gotten that far yet!" He pointed up river. "See those two large yachts to the north? Here, take a look across the river first with the binoculars and then move to those two yachts. Tell me if you see anyone familiar."

"They supposed to be someone we like or dislike?"

He snickered, "You'll know when you spotted them."

She slowly scanned across to the yachts and watched the people on the sundeck. The canopy was out over the aft sundeck with Med. Lights strung from bow to mast to fantail. The lights were enough to brighten the sundeck and guest. With night-vision binoculars, she could see their faces distinctly.

"With your right index finger, feel for the rocker switch for the camera and take a couple of photos for our computer," Jess said. "Isn't that Dick and Marla LaVanture from home? If that's his vessel, he jumped to a bigger one than what he had on Lake Michigan."

"John and Karla Forgey, you got to be kidding me," Marie Ann said laughing. "What are they doing way out here from Indiana? There's Jake too."

"It must be Geb Conn's yacht, unless Dick came into a fortune because he would not put his 42-foot Nordic in salt water," Jess said laughing. "Remember when he found out we were going to us the same type vessel in this novel and he said he wouldn't put his boat in any salt water?"

"I wonder if they're going to the Nordic Tug factory rendezvous in July at Charlevoix, Michigan," Marie Ann said. "I certainly enjoyed our running around with them up there a few years ago."

"Wonder what that slip number is. We could call them on the landline," Jess said and turned to go down to the salon to get the marina pamphlet. "Jess, it's after eleven here. It's a bit late, don't cha think?"

"They're night owls anyway, it wouldn't matter."

She pointed. "Someone is looking at us from their vessel. He's up on their flybridge. Should I wave at him?"

Jess leaned against the rail and waved before she did and he returned the wave. "Can you tell who he is?"

"I only met Geb once at the air show…Here." She handed the binoculars to him.

"I can't really tell. That gentleman is slender like Geb," Jess said and moved forward for a better position. "He yelled to someone on the sundeck and he went down there. He's standing next to John and gave him the binoculars."

"Is that our landline ringing?" Marie Ann said and walked over to the helm, opened a compartment underneath, and took the phone off the hook. "Hello. Yes, it is. We just recognized you guys over there. Wha'cha doing down here? Sure, come on over."

Jess watched as the crowd moved down to the pier to shore and headed for *The Shallows* along the river front. The Hanes secured the flybridge and moved down to the boarding deck aft to pull the lines closer to the pier for their visitors' boarding. The crowd could be heard heading down the pier, laughing and carrying on.

John Forgey was in the lead and gave Jess a snappy salute. "Permission to come aboard, Captain?"

"Permission granted, Senior Chief. You and your guest are most welcome." Jess returned John's salute.

He stepped aboard and Jess gave him a big hug.

Marie Ann gave him a hug and then Karla followed by Jake. "What a pleasure ya'all!"

Jake saluted Jess. "Permission to come aboard, Captain?"

"Aye there, mate, come aboard." Jess saluted and shook his hand. "You're cruising with a rough crowd there," he said as he waved Dick, Marla, Geb and his family of four on board and then shook hands and gave them hugs.

"Welcome aboard *The Shallows* everyone," Jess said with a big smile. "Let's move into the salon so the bugs don't carry us away." Turning to Marie Ann, he said, "Lead the way, love. I think we have something to drink for everyone."

"Us old folks brought our own, Jess," Dick said holding up his wine glass. "The young folks have to speak for themselves. We remembered you two don't consume the hard stuff."

"Thanks, Dick, for remembering that. Go right on in. How are you doing, Marla, staying out of trouble?" Everyone got a laugh with that question.

Jake and Karla sat on the deck next to the kitchen bar. "That question needs to be answered by anyone else but her."

"You got that right!" Geb replied and introduce his family to Jess and Marie Ann.

Marla helped Marie Ann with the drinks for the kids and Jess got out the throw pillows for those who wanted to sit on the deck or stair steps up to the pilothouse.

"What brings you all to this marina," Jess asked waving his hand to include everyone once they were all settled. "And whose mega-dollar yacht were you on?"

"Dad's going to buy it, I think," one of Geb's sons said and laughed. "He's got everything else except a yacht."

Everyone laughed.

Geb settled back on the salon couch next to his wife, "It seems to handle smartly, but it's not fast enough. It took us eight and one half hours at an average of 20 knots for 175 miles. That's too slow and expensive."

He frowned. The others knew he was calculating his next remark and it got real quiet. "Yes, I believe the 75-foot stern drive would get us here in half the time."

His wife elbowed him in the ribs. "No, sir, you will go alone. At the speed that boat goes it is too dangerous, plus it is not comfortable to walk around in it on rough water. You can have your fast aircraft, but this purchase is for family too."

"Goodness, I didn't mean to cause a family feud," Jess said and stood next to the galley counter. "Hey, anyone for chilled watermelon? Just happen to have two in on ice in the cooler topside."

John stood up. "Sun deck, port or starboard cooler, Jess?"

"There is one in each cooler, thank you, John."

"Jake, give me a hand bringing them down," John said. They both could be heard climbing the ladder to the sundeck.

"I apologize, Marie Ann and Jess," Geb said. "I shouldn't have stated those facts so harshly, especially in front of you, sweetheart." He put his arm around her shoulder. "I know speed is a sore subject."

"Accepted and forgotten sweets," she said and turned to Marie Ann in the galley. "Is there anything I can do to help?"

"There sure is," pointing at Karla. "Right behind you in the bottom of that cupboard are some servicing trays. If you would get those and stack them here on the counter, then everyone can take one and serve themselves. There should be plastic knives and forks too."

"Are paper plates and paper napkins okay for everyone?" Jess asked as he set them at the end of the counter.

"Here's a container of fresh mixed nuts; pickled eggs and wieners, mixed chilled veggie plate; assorted crackers; mild and hot banana peppers; and assorted slices of cheese." Marie Ann handed them one at a time for Marla to put on the galley counter and salon table.

"Love, what else can you set out for a midnight snack?" Jess asked and squeezed her hand.

"That's about it on a quick order. Cut the watermelon and we'll be ready to eat," she said and put out the silverware and kitchen knife for the watermelon.

Dick, Marla and Marie Ann talked at length about the comparison of their Nordic Tug, the Marla D, and *The Shallows*. They still lived up in the northern part of Michigan and had their trawler docked at Traverse City. They had Jess and Marie Ann on board prior to the purchase of this NT42.

Jess moved to the sink and held out his hand for the melon Jake had. "Can everyone handle narrow slices of water melon on the rind?"

Everyone agreed as Jess masterfully slices the melon and set it in a large plastic bowl. He washed and dried his hands and asked everyone to stand for prayer. He asked the Lord to bless the food they were about to eat and to give them His special travel protection for the holiday weekend.

It was one-thirty when the crowd left and no dishes to wash and put away. They all pitched in to clean up.

It was a quick decision made by Geb to rent the yacht for an overnight trip to find out if he wanted to purchase the yacht or not. They would be heading south at dawn and would see Marie Ann and Jess when they returned to Indiana.

"That was quite a nice surprise visit of unexpected guests," Marie Ann said and turned off the outside lights, secured the salon's aft door and turned to have Jess circle his arms around her.

"You sure nipped that situation with Geb and his wife. Proud of you, sweetheart, and the way you handled the surprise."

"We need to thank the Lord for time spent with them," Jess said.

He kissed her. "Proud of you tonight too, love. Let's get to bed before Slim calls us for breakfast."

All lights were out and *The Shallows* was secured again for another peaceful morning, at least what was left of the morning.

Chapter Sixteen

Lanier Island to Wrightsville, North Carolina

After a leisurely trip of 265 nm, 12 or 13 bridges, one night and two 16 hour days, Jess and Marie Ann located a small marina near the 310 mm, Southport, North Carolina. They fueled, ate a hamburger dinner at a local diner, and stocked up groceries from the marina.

They wanted to be in the Morehead City area 100 nm north in two days to beat a storm in the south Atlantic that could give them major problems if they were not further inland on the ICW. They would turn north at Beaufort, 204mm.

When they returned to *The Shallows*, a Coast Guard Master Chief and two Second Class Petty Officers with dogs were waiting for them on a Coast Guard Cutter tied up at the pier next to them.

The chief got out, saluted Jess, and showed his ID. "Captain Hanes, I have orders to board your vessel to search for drugs and firearms. We have searched the other vessels here and yours is the only one to finish this marina."

"May I see your orders, Master Chief?" Jess asked as he returned the salute. "Master Chief, may I look at your ID a little closer, please." Jess took out his reading glasses. He did not take the identification from the chief but stepped closer to read it.

"You're with the NCIS?" Jess asked and led Marie Ann with her arms full of groceries onto *The Shallows*. "Come aboard Master Chief."

The Chief motioned for his two assistants to bring their search dogs, "Be sure you put the boots on them," he ordered, as they approached.

"Got them Chief," one of the Second Class Petty Officers waved a canvas bag.

Before they boarded the dive platform, the dog's paws were fitted with a special boot that would not permit the dog's claws to mar the deck or inside teak wood; and the boots would give them good grip on a wet deck.

When the Coast Guard crew were finished, Jess asked the Master Chief, "What's the latest info on the storm in the Atlantic; is it going to come up the coast or go into the Gulf of Mexico?"

"Captain Hanes, two hours ago the experts didn't know what it's going to do. It's sort of stalling around losing some of its strength." He shrugged, "It may be reduced to a low grade tropical storm by now. I've received no small craft warning, everything seems to be smooth sailing for a couple of days."

"Now that's what I like to hear," Marie Ann said and shook his hand. "Thank you and your crew for your service Master Chief."

"You're welcome Mrs. Hanes." He nodded, saluted and followed his men down the pier to Coast Guard cutter.

The inspection was over in ten minutes and the Coast Guard crew departed. They did not even look over any of the vessel's papers or ask Jess for more information.

Jess went up into the pilothouse to check on the navigational charts to Morehead and Beaufort, North Carolina. He turned on the radio to listen to a local FM station with "elevator/doctor office" music playing; just background music that doesn't blare, but can soothe the soul.

It was getting cloudy and *The Shallows* was in the shadows of a warehouse on the pier. He turned to switch on the inside lights when his cell phone rang. He had it on vibrate and for a double ring tone. It startled him and drew back his hand from the light switch.

"Did it get'cha Jess?" Marie Ann laughed as she came up the stairs from the salon. "Good reflex, I could almost imagine an electric arc coming out of that switch to bite you."

He began to laugh with her as she handed him a fresh brewed cup of black coffee.

"It is so quite up here, I thought this would wake you up." Pointing at his telephone, "But that did, didn't it? Are you going to answer it or not?"

He finally stopped laughing and flipped the cell phone open, "Hello, Jess here."

"Who, certainly," he handed the phone to her, turned, and slid the port door open just wide enough for someone to come in.

A crouched dark figure quickly stepped into the pilothouse as Jess closed the door. The shivering figure leaned against the bulkhead and slid to the floor.

Jess snapped his fingers for Marie Ann to hand him the coffee cup she had on the table.

"Easy now, this is really hot," Jess said and carefully handed it to the individual on the deck.

A low voice could barely be heard while sipping the hot coffee, "Marie Ann… Jess… thank you again."

Marie Ann was on her knees beside the still shaky wet person leaning against the wall. "Jess there is a blanket under the settee bench seat," she gave the coffee cup to him.

"Who do we have here," she asked draping the blanket across wet shoulders.

"Here's a dry towel for her hair," Jess said.

"Oh my, this feels good," she said as Marie Ann soaked up water from the long stringy red hair. The woman looked up at Jess and grabbed his hand, pulling him down to her on the floor. "Be careful, I may have put you in danger. Can you leave port, right now?"

She sneezed and continued, "I was trying to find your boat slip when someone hit me from behind. I came to after hitting the water; I think I swallowed the whole river."

"Madilene Ash," Jess said and pushed the hair away from her face, "What in the world happened."

He helped get her to her feet. "Love, take her down to the crews cabin and I'll bring in the lines," Jess said and stood. "Let me make sure that no one else is aboard and I'll be right back in."

As the two women went below, Jess took his revolver from under the helm's counter and put it under his waist band. With a four-cell LED flash light, he went out on the deck. He closed the door behind him.

He reached outside and above the door to the above deck level. Then he swung up to stand on the main deck hand-railing outside the pilothouse. He could then see across the flybridge deck, sundeck and aft to the boom/crane where the dingy inflatable boat was lashed down. He scanned back to the stainless steel ladder going down to the aft cockpit deck. He slowly let himself down to the main outside deck and walked up to the pulpit. He backed into it so he could see all the way aft on both port and starboard side at the water level, no one to be seen.

On the pier, he unplugged the power cables and then pulled them on board, stored them.

He then loosens the forward port lines all the way aft; loosening the aft lines released *The Shallows* to drift backwards out of the slip. He quickly secured the lines and headed forward through the salon, locking the door behind him. As he climbed the stairs to the pilothouse, he called down to the ladies in the crew's compartment that they were getting under way.

He turned on the ignition for the updated powerful 650 hp diesel engine to come alive. Its low vibrating throb could be felt as Jess added a little aft throttle to help clear the other vessels, then he straightened the rudder amidships and increased the rpm slowly.

Now they were out in the AICW channel when he brought the throttle to enough rpm to keep a steady 16 knots north bound on Cape Fear River to Carolina Beach cross over. They had only a ten mile run to collect their thoughts as to what had just happened.

Jess turned on the night running lights and checked the function of the spot light on the mast.

The internal system's panel indicator lights showed no malfunctions; the fore and aft TV cameras and monitors, all pilothouse monitors for the ICW channel, weather and navigational charts were stable; and *The Shallows* moved easily to the north.

It was not dark yet, but it was twilight enough to see the western horizon. Jess slowed the rpm's for ten knots and called down to Marie Ann on the intercom.

"How's everything down there with the wet U.S. Marshall?"

From behind him, "Shush, she is asleep now. I talked her into taking a shower, and gave her a pair of my new pajamas. She's covered with a light blanket now, and she's sleeping."

She put her arms around his waist as he stood at the helm's wheel. "She didn't talk much other than she was frightened and cold. She also wanted to make sure she still had her government issued automatic sidearm. And, also her I.D. and passport in her underarm waterproof pouch..."

Jess nodded, "She still carrying a .40 or 9mm Glock?"

"I didn't check, it was still in its holster," she said and sipped her coffee. "She said her luggage was still on the pier, unless whoever knocked her into the water took it. I'll call the marina to check for it and hold it until we contact them."

"I wonder what this is all about. The last time we saw her was back on Hutchison Island and she was a brunette," she said and poured Jess more hot coffee. "Systems all on line and gear put away?"

"Nope, the lines are lying on the aft deck, didn't get them put away. They can stay there for now. I'll get them put away in a little bit," Jess said and turned on the spot light to see what was ahead of them in the channel. Surface radar did not show anything, but he liked to see for himself.

"How are you doing, love?"

"I'm fine, just a smidgen hungry. How about you?" she said and stretched, reaching for the overhead teak rails. "I'll make a soup, tossed salad and BLT's when she gets up. She might like some solid soup."

"That sounds great," he said and adjusted the ship's heading, and then scanned the surface ahead of them for lobster pots. "Would you check the charts for a good place to anchor after we do the cross over at Carolina Beach, please?"

She had an answer in no time at all. "Captain, we should be able to anchor at 295.5 mile marker."

She pointed it out to him on the channel on the pilothouse monitor.

"It shows 5 or 6 feet of water and the outer shore should shield us from off-shore winds. The town's not too far in case we need anything."

"That should work, so check on our new crew member," he said and gave her a kiss on the cheek. "Please," he whispered in her ear. "I'll let you know when I'm about to drop anchor, so the noise doesn't frighten her."

At the anchorage area, when Jess had finished setting the anchors fore and aft, he made sure the lights were all on for being anchored. Going up to the flybridge, he checked if everything was secure and then scanned their anchorage. He felt they would be safe from winds coming in from the east.

When he finally finished securing the topside, he entered the pilothouse and locked its outside doors and windows. He turned on the interior night lights and went down to the galley.

Jess took a second look at the ladies, especially the guest of honor. Both ladies had just seated themselves for supper, "It's good to have unexpected company. How are you, Marshall

Madilene Ash? Sorry I didn't recognize you with short red hair and wearing my wife's bathrobe."

She looked extremely tired, but she afforded Jess a nice smile. "I'm very happy to be here, I'll be glad to bring you both up to date when we finish chow. I'm starved!"

Jess stood up from the table, stretched and excused himself, "I would suggest continuing light conversation for right now, specifically no talk about you, Madi, until I come back in."

He nodded to Marie Ann, who rose from the table and went in the galley and down the stateroom. She closed the blinds and curtains at the windows and went back up to the salon.

Marie Ann did not think Madi had a weapon on her when she came up from below. The only things she had when she came aboard was her passport, government marshal's ID badge and weapon in a black concealed underarm shoulder pouch/holster. It was all on top of the washing machine, where Marie Ann put her wet clothes. They could hear the washer working.

"Jess is checking for hidden electronic devices and will be right back in," she said and handed Madi the folded black pouch/holster. "Unless you carried another weapon into the shower, you have only one."

"You are correct, thank you for being so thorough," Madi said and put the pouch in place under her right arm pit. She did not open it, trusting everything was in place. "Whoever hit me and dumped me in the water didn't take my weapon and purse." She put her hand over her nose and mouth, then sneezed.

"God bless you, here's some tissues." Marie Ann handed her a box.

"Thank you, hope I don't get chilled from too much time in the water," Madi said, holding a tissue to her nose and pulling the bathrobe tighter up around her neck.

"You look like a lady that takes care of herself. Do you use vitamins?" Mari Ann scooted to the end of the couch, not waiting for an answer. "My vitamin department is sufficiently filled with our most used supply."

She pulled a drawer from under the couch and put it on her lap. "Let's see here: B12, E, Q10, C, Calcium, Magnesium…and much more."

"Yes, I do use vitamins," Madi said. "It sounds like you have what I need for the sniffles." She moved closer to look at the vitamin bottles.

"By the way, I called the marina and had them look for your luggage," Marie Ann said, showing Madi the second layer of vitamins in the box.

"Thank you. By the way, I have two very important things to tell you and Jess that has happened to me this last year. But I'll wait for him to come back in. I'm so excited to tell you," she said with a special gleam in her eyes.

"I think he is making sure everything is okay topside. He should be down shortly."

Someone was running across the upper sundeck and then there was a loud splash in the water on the starboard side.

They heard Jess walking around the main deck and enter the pilothouse. He came down the outside ladder/stairs to the salon aft door and walked in with a grim look on his face.

"We had an unwanted visitor topside. Someone jumped into the water when I went on deck." He turned on his electronic sensor key chain and put his finger to his lips.

He then handed it to Madi and motioned for Marie Ann to go to the pilothouse and start the engine. "Check us out inside, Madi. I'll get the anchors up."

Jess opened the freezer and took the 'Judge' .45 revolver from a plastic bag and handed it to Madi.

Madi held the weapon in her open palm, examining it. "This cannon weighs a ton, I wouldn't want to carry this for long. My .40 isn't this heavy," she said and slapped her holster under her armpit and handed it back to him.

"If you can't shot them, club them with it," he teased as he put it under his belt and went back out of the salon's aft door.

"Inside night lights only, love," he called to Marie Ann and closed the door as he stepped onto the dark aft deck.

She flipped switches turning off the galley, salon and passageway day lights to night lights. Then she turned on the red lights in the pilothouse and quickly went up to the helm.

In five minutes they were underway for the AICW channel.

Once they got settled in the pilothouse cruising north on the channel, Jess suggest Marie Ann make some soup for Madi and then find another location for them to anchor. It was almost midnight.

Madi was still in Marie Ann's housecoat standing next to Jess at the helm using the binoculars searching the surface ahead of them for lobster pots and debris. Using the flood light/spot light on the mast Jess kept the surface lighted.

"Madi, do you need to contact anyone or go anywhere special?" Jess asked and scanned his instrument panel and compass heading. Fog banks began to form and Jess was getting uneasy trying to navigate.

As Marie Ann came up to the pilothouse, Madi laid the binoculars on the chart table and accepted the bowl of soup and crackers.

"No, Jess, I haven't been able to explain much of anything to you two. I was coming to see you, just a visit to try to volunteer on as a crew member. My clothes are in storage to be sent to me wherever I found you. Just a small makeup bag was left on the pier."

Marie Ann handed them soup bowls with handles and laid another bowl of crackers on the helm console table. Jess and Marie Ann were surprised about her wanting to be part of the crew, but kept quiet until she was finished.

"I just started my four week vacation and have spent two days tracking you down. I used some government connections and satellite to pinpoint your location." She sipped from the side of her soup bowl. "Oh boy, this hits the spot, Marie Ann. This is great…homemade I bet."

"Nope, right out of the can into the microwave oven."

Madi laughed and then continued, "I got a taxi from the airport in St. Simmons to the marina you docked. I just left the security gate office where they showed me your slip location. When I got to the edge of the wharf to walk down your pier…" she took another sip her soup.

"The next thing I remember is trying to keep from drowning. It's a good thing the water wasn't over my head, but only waist deep."

"She still has a lump on the back of her head where someone hit her," Marie Ann said and poured more soup.

Madi put her hand gentle on her head, "It's not as swollen and isn't cut, but it's still sore."

"We've got some salve to put on that before you go to bed," Jess said and turned to a new course in the channel. "It sure takes care of our bumps, scrapes and small cuts."

Once in a while, Madi would use the binoculars to scan behind them and then watched out the pilothouse windows to the east and west at the night lights of the road traffic parallel with the channel.

"One of the most important things that have happened to me recently was while waiting to interrogate a witness in jail down in Big Springs, Texas...on a murder of a Texas Ranger and U.S. Marshal..."

She paused, sitting in the port seat facing aft looking through the binoculars. "We have any soup left?"

Marie Ann leaned over and removed the lid to the stainless steel bowl. "Just enough soup for half a bowl. Hold still and I'll pour it for you."

She took the bowl to Madi. "That was good enough to make another helping all the way around. I'll open another can for us, be right back."

All was quiet in the pilothouse while she was in the galley, only the vibration of the diesel engine could be felt and the occasional transmissions on the VHF radio could be heard on low volume. Jess was in his own thoughts while scanning the channel ahead and scanning the overhead monitors.

Madi continued watching behind them of any questionable fast moving vessels approaching. She began lowly humming a song that she had heard for years, but never really paid too much attention to the words until recently at an old fashion tent revival in Houston.

Jess started singing the words along with her humming, "Amazing grace how sweet the sound, that saved a wretch like me, I once was lost but now I'm found, was blind but now I see; when we've been there ten thousand years, bright shining as the sun, we've no less days to sing God's praise, than when we first begun…" he began to miss some words and started to hum along with her.

Singing from the galley got louder as Marie Ann brought up more soup and crackers, "… and saved a wretch like me, thank you Jesus," she said and began to harmonize with the other two. "Hey, we don't sound bad at all. Let me get my accordion out, be right back."

Madi stood up to sip her soup, lay the binoculars down on the seat welcomed Marie Ann up the stairs from the galley. "You sure have a lot of talent on this vessel Skipper."

They sang old songs as they could remember them and an hour later someone coughed and suggested this session was over.

"Wow, that was great; we could make a CD and have it with us all the time," Madi said, she grabbed Marie Ann and hugged her. "I found someone who had been looking for me all my life; Jesus Christ my Lord and Saviour… two months ago in a jail in Big Springs." Tears were running down her cheeks and she hugged Marie Ann again.

Jess hollered, "Praise the Lord!"

And Marie Ann shouted, "Amen, thank you Jesus!"

Madi moved away and sat back on the seat, "One of the jail's Negro matrons was witnessing to a young girl that was brought in to the empty cell next to the one I was in with the prisoner and guard. She finally calmed the girl who was no more than twelve or thirteen years old, and started talking to her about Jesus."

Madi put the bowl on the tray on the console. She wiped her eyes and blew her nose again.

"That is the best decision I have ever made in my life. Thank you Jesus!" She paused and took a couple of deep breaths.

With a big smile, she continued, "That lady talked to the child so sweet and softly, not gruff and course, that that section of the cell block was dead quiet… but alive in the Lord."

"This is shoutin' time, Madi," Marie Ann said, clapping her hands.

She held up her hands to the overhead ceiling. "Oh yes… when she was finished, there were sniffles from most of the cell mates, including me. That lady started a revival meeting right there and brought four of us sinners to Jesus."

Marie Ann stood up and shouted, "Halleluiah, thank you, Jesus!"

Marie Ann started playing her accordion and singing. Jess took his hands off the helm wheel and clapped them for joy. "We've got us and ole fashion joy-feast revival right here on *The Shallows.*"

"There's another marker, Jess, starboard green," Madi said and began humming "Amazing Grace" again.

She and Marie Ann stood next to Jess at the helm and shared their experiences about Jesus in their lives. It did not take long for time to pass getting into port.

There was idle talk for less than an hour when Jess slowed the trawler to six knots.

"We're coming up to Wrightsville; the satellite monitor shows two marinas on the west bank and one on the east. What's that Alert warning in red?"

"We can't get to those two anchorages east of the channel. There're some problems in the channel. Let me check the marinas on the cell phone for an available slip for tonight," Marie Ann said and took the phone out of its charger.

"What can I do Skipper?" Madi asked and moved next to him at the helm.

"I don't know how much debris will be in the water, but help me keep track of other vessels, especially ones that are larger and crossing ahead of us. I don't know how busy this port is this early in the morning, but the satellite shows the marina slips are full." He picked up his remote and selected a current view of the channel area in Wrightsville.

"Most of the time I can't read the small print at the bottom of the screen to know how current the information is, unless I zoom in. Then I sometimes have trouble backing out of it."

Jess set the rpm to idle speed. "How does it look 360 degrees for approaching vessels, Madi? Is it too cool out on the deck?"

"Not with this bathrobe on," she said. "No vessels moving our way."

"Aye there, mate, keep a sharp eye for me," he said as Marie Ann nudged his arm.

"We have two choices and I told them I would call back in five minutes." She put her notes under the plastic console pad. "The first one on the port side has only one tie up on the channel itself; nothing in the enter marina. The second one has two slips at $1.75 per foot which is $73.50 for the night. If we top of fuel of more than 500 gallons they will reduce a nickel per gallon."

"Go ahead and have them save a slip, we'll be right there," Jess said.

She stepped back to the pilothouse bench seat and table to talk to the marina.

"They're ready for us, Captain"

"Aye there, mate," he replied and gave her thumbs-up.

"A smaller vessel is approaching from the starboard side aft," Madi called out. "It's marked Harbor Patrol."

"Okay, does he want to come along side," Jess asked and stepped out next to her and waved.

"Are you having problems?" They called out on a megaphone.

Jess cupped his hands around his mouth. "No, we're trying to pick a marina for the night."

"You must keep moving in the channel or move to one side. Try the second marina on the port side and watch for the speeders."

"Aye, Aye, Captain," Jess said and waved. Stepping back to the helm he increased the rpm to minimum speed, just enough to get out of the deep channel and head for the Bridge Tender Marina.

It was three in the morning when they finally got to bed. Arrangements were made for diesel fuel after lunch around 1:00 p.m. The noise level was low that early in the morning and they all promptly went to sleep.

Jess was kept awake by vessel horns signaling the bridge tender for bridge passage at seven a.m. He got up made a pot of coffee, washed the pilothouse windows inside and out, and then went up on the flybridge to watch the vehicle and vessel traffic.

When the ladies finally got out of bed and dressed, Jess escorted them to breakfast at the Bridge Tender Restaurant. All three were dragging by the time they got back to the marina.

They were back to *The Shallows* by one o'clock in the afternoon. Jess' plan was to be inland on the AICW in two days. So they turned in early for an early morning run the next day to Moorehead City and Beaufort.

CHAPTER SEVENTEEN

Wrightsville to Moorehead City, North Carolina

The Shallows was on the way north out of the Bridge Tender Marina before sun up. Marie Ann was preparing breakfast underway while Jess and Madi were at the helm. They planned to take turns training Madi the art of navigation and how to maintain the Nordic Tug, and still have fun cruising.

For now, they had to keep a keen eye on the weather. The forecast was good for the next two days, but a 'cat 4' hurricane was brewing in the south Atlantic with a predicted course to hit the Carolina's. If that were to happen they had to find a safe harbor inland as far as they could go, which looked like the New Bern or Washington, NC area. If they could maintain 18 knots on the open straight a ways they should be able to find that protected haven.

They were not on any special time period other than getting into Benton Harbor, Michigan, in decent weather and not have to put their vessel in a dry dock somewhere for the winter months. They were aiming for October or November. If it works out that way great, and if not, no big deal. They had no immediate family to get home for, so they were not keeping a schedule of any kind.

Marie Ann brought a tray of fresh baked bacon, egg, cheese, biscuit sandwiches and hot coffee up to the pilothouse. The aft settee table behind the captain chair at the helm was a perfect place for breakfast.

"Breakfast is served. We can take turns back here at the table," she tapped Madi on the shoulders. "You are relieved at your observation post for breakfast. I forgot to ask if you like bacon and eggs on biscuits."

"Thank you. I love biscuits anytime three times a day." She handed the binoculars to Marie Ann and scooted into the booth behind the table. "This sure does smell good. You guys are gonna spoil me."

"I aim to please," Marie Ann said proudly. "There are two biscuits for each of us and more if we need them later. I sure didn't rest good last night, how'd ya'all do? I got up with a good headache."

She refilled the coffee cups in their holders, and then set the coffee pot back on its secured coffee maker's hot plate.

The other two said they slept soundly; it was just too short a night.

"Hopefully, tonight will be a longer night of rest," he said and set the rpm's for 20 knots.

"Captain, how's our new crew member working out?" she asked and scanned the channel ahead of them.

"Well, I'm not sure, because I don't have to explain things twice to her. She just might make a good fit to this cruise." He waited for a comment from either of them, but nothing, not even a snicker.

Madi was too busy stuffing her face and Marie Ann just stood there staring at him with her binoculars.

"You're not too far for me to take a swing at," she said and turned to look out at the channel marker ahead of them. "If a certain person would not mush-mouth, we would not have to ask for a repeat. Just because you have that Texas accent doesn't mean you can't speak clearly and distinctly to us foreigners from the north. The only reason our new crew member can understand you is because she is from the Republic of Texas too." She gave a little fake whimper to continue teasing him.

He scanned the channel ahead insuring there were no problems close by and slowly locked the helm wheel, reached over and grabbed her around the waist. Taking the binoculars at the same time, laid them on the aft facing console seat on the starboard side of the helm, he held her.

Turning her to face him, nose to nose, eyeball to eyeball, he spoke with a captain's authority, "Once more, I will not have rebellion on my vessel and I will continue to nip it in the bud every time it happens. Now, missy, there will be no discussion in response to your punishment…Pucker up, First Mate, I'm gonna plant one on ya."

She placed her hand across her lips. "Have mercy, Captain, please don't punish me in front of the crew," she begged, and fell limp in his arms.

Madi's mouth was full. She snickered, clapped her hands, and sputtered, "I'll look to port, Captain, and keep my mouth shut. I'll have to make a full report of what I have heard, but I didn't see a thing. I was eating breakfast through the whole scandal."

He picked Marie Ann up in his arms and sat her in the captain's chair in front of the helm wheel. She pretended to come out of her swoon, pulling his face down to hers. "Lover boy, you best behave in front of the crew."

"Always at your service, love," he said, laughing as he turned and unlocked the helm's wheel, checking the rpm. "We will refuel, replenish the galley, and dump both black and gray water at the next marina. I didn't have the fresh water tanks topped off in Wrightsville."

She sat with her arms crossed, staring at his back, sort of expecting him to sit in her lap.

He took a note pad from his shirt pocket and handed it to Marie Ann over his shoulder. "Here is my supply list to add to yours. Pick out the best marina at Moorehead City or Beaufort for our replenishment and contact them for a boat slip…Please."

He leaned back and gave her a long wet kiss, stood up straight, turned facing forward and let out a rebel yell. Jess grabbed the lanyard for the trawlers air horns and blew a long burst.

"Show off," he whispered under his breath.

She grabbed him around the waist and gave him a bear hug as tight as she could. He gasped, trembled, and began dancing a jig while holding the wheel. And then, he froze in place.

It was quiet for a few minutes, except for the vibration from the engine below decks and the splashing of the channel water along the waterline.

"Jess E. Hanes, you're a show off," Marie Ann said and hopped off the captain's chair. She turned to Madi and whispered, "I sure do love him."

He asked, "Second Mate, are you finished stuffing yourself and ready for an assignment?" Madi slipped out of the settee and Marie Ann opened her cell phone and planted herself at the port chart desk.

"Yes, sir, Captain, as soon as I move these dishes down to the galley."

He turned, still with one hand on the wheel. "I think not!"

He grabbed a biscuit sandwich, turned back as if nothing had happened.

"First Mate, did you see that biscuit disappear?" she asked and place the remaining biscuit on a paper napkin on the console next to the wheel.

She began to clear the settee's teak table and then went down to the galley. From there she hollered back up the pilothouse stairs, "I need to visit the ladies room for a short minute or two."

"That's fine, no rush up here," Jess replied and turned to Marie Ann. "Love, I apologize for all the clowning around a while ago."

"Anytime you want to clown around with me, Captain, I'll be most obliging," she replied, stepped over, kissed his cheek, and then continued contacting the marinas.

"Thanks, sweetheart," he said and checked off another channel marker on the navigational chart. "It looks like we have close to 80 nautical miles to Moorehead City. If we can average 15 or 16 knots per hour, that gives us 5 or 6 hours to be cruising, if all goes well."

He checked the satellite monitor for their speed through the water and it indicated 19.5, so he bumped up the throttle a little to get it closer to 20.

"You still have your headache?"

She had sat on the settee bench seat to eat breakfast. "My headache is gone, thank you very much." She smacked her lips, and drank some coffee. "This is good thick sliced bacon. Wish we had some more from home."

"That hurricane development in the southern Atlantic may take six or seven days to get here, but the weather channel predicts North Carolina Outer Banks is the most likely target," she said as she pulled up the weather map on her laptop beside her breakfast tray.

She pointed to Jess' overhead monitor which had the same weather info as she did.

173

He glanced up at the monitor and nodded his acknowledgement to her.

The twilight was getting brighter as the sun wanted to push up over the eastern horizon. It made it difficult to see anything in the channel ahead. Jess took the dark sunglasses from its holder stuck underneath the weather monitors.

"Boy, that helps a lot to sharpen and detail even the small water chops," he said and reached for his coffee cup.

There was a sudden thud from down below them, as if they had hit something in the water. Jess immediately put *The Shallows* at idle.

"Check below where Madi is, make sure she is okay," he said opening the port pilothouse door. "I'll check the surface along the water line."

When Marie Ann suddenly got up, she was dizzy. She leaned against the settee table top, regained her balance and went down the steps to the galley and then to the stateroom passageway.

Jess went aft with a flash light checking the waterline in the shadows and on the aft lazarette deck. He checked the water behind them. He did not see anything.

He then opened the transom door out onto the boarding platform, knelt down looking back under it toward the hull-channel for the propeller and shaft area. There was still nothing to be seen. He returned to the aft deck, locking the transom door and then climbed the stainless steel ladder to the upper sundeck and flybridge.

At the flybridge helm console he turned on the flood light mounted on the mast and shown it aft where the white foam from the propeller could still be seen, nothing floating in the water... no debris. He turned it off and stayed at the helm to run the trawler. He leaned over and pressed the 'talk switch' for the intercom below decks in the crew's quarters.

"Is everything okay down there?"

He waited and tried again. "Sweetheart, is everything okay?" Still no reply from below; this was beginning to worry him.

There was at least two hundred yards from shore to western shore and fifty to the east. Jess turned west to port and slowly moved to shallow water. The depth indication was six feet of water and Jess dropped the forward anchor and waited for it to hook. He noted on his flybridge log of dropping anchor at mm260. They had only covered twenty miles up the AICW.

He thought to himself, *Lord, keep that anchor loose enough that it can be raised.* He turned on all the outdoor lights so they could be seen by other vessels in the morning dimness, and went below.

He entered the aft main deck door to the salon and hollered toward the passageway down to the berthing staterooms. "Hey you two, is everything all right?" He gasped for air. He latched the salon door open.

Immediately he knew what was wrong, exhaust fume from the engine room filled the salon and galley. He opened all the windows and made his way forward.

The crew's stateroom was closed; he knocked. "Hello you two, can I come in?"

He tried the door handle and opened it inward. It opened only a few inches and stopped. He pushed his head against the opening and could see Marie Ann's legs where she lay on the floor against the door. Looking to the left where the closet was and its door was partly open.

"Madi, you in there?"

There was a moaning in the crew's stateroom where she was. Jess lifted the door out of its hinges and leaned it against the bulkhead/wall in the hall/passageway. He leaned down to Marie Ann and felt for a pulse, it was not rapid, but unsteady. He knelt on the bed, reached up and opened the porthole window.

"Sweetheart, can you hear me? Where do you hurt?" He did not have a lot of room to get down beside her. There was a big bump on the side of her head where she was cut. It had not bled at all.

"Love," he patted the back of her hand while with the other hand he brushed the hair out of her face. "Marie Ann, talk to me, love."

She stirred and immediately wanted to sit up. "I'm so dizzy."

Jess propped her against the wall under the port hole and turned on a small fan to help blow the fumes out. "Let me get a wet towel. You're hot and soaked. I'll be right back."

He opened the vessels control panel console across from the crew's stateroom and flipped the switches to kill the diesel engine, and started the emergency vent fans in the engine room, and then switched to the electric generator. Jess grabbed an oxygen bottle and mask from under the console.

He went back to Marie Ann and put the oxygen mask across her face and turned the bottle on, leaning it upright against her side.

"Love, take a few deep breaths of this oxygen."

Suddenly her eyes got big and then she coughed, pulled the mask down and smiled, nodded and closed her eyes and held onto Jess' hand.

"I love you," she said and squeezed his hand.

"Love you too, angel of mine. I'll be right back," he said and patted her hand. "Got to check on Madi."

He started across the passageway to the crew's head/restroom and found Madi sitting on the shower floor, leaning against the forward bulkhead/wall. Her eyes were open, but looked dazed. "Hey, Captain, am I in trouble? I can't get up. I don't drink, so I know that's not the problem. How did I get in here?"

"Are you dizzy?" Jess reached in for her hand. "Can you stand up on your own?"

"Too many questions, Captain. Yes, I should be able to stand if you help me. Where is Marie Ann? She was to get me out of this dang shower I fell in."

She moaned and put her hand on her forehead. "Who hit me?"

"You're not undressed to be taking a shower, too many clothes on," he said trying to make her laugh. "You must have been what made all the noise earlier. You have a cut on your forehead."

"Really, do you think so…overdressed?" she sounded almost like she had been drinking too much booze.

"Let's go get Marie Ann," he said and put his arm around her waist to help her stand. She put her arms around his neck as he lifted and propped her against the wall. He held her steady until her eyes became focused on him.

"So, there you are… hold still a minute until the boat stops rocking."

"Let me take you to your room. I've got a fan running in there to get the engine fumes out," he said as they shuffled down the passageway to her quarters.

Marie Ann was sitting on the edge of the bed with the fan blowing in her face, and the oxygen mask still in place. "This feels much better," she said and tried to smile at them, "Wha'cha doing hugging my husband that way?" and started laughing.

"You two sound like you've been on a toot or inhaled too much laughing gas.

"All of the above doctor, now where's my wash cloth you were bringing to me," she pointed at Jess and giggled. "She don't have one." Marie Ann lay back on the bed.

"Okay girls, keep moving, Marie Ann on your feet. Hold onto that oxygen bottle," he reached into the room and grabbed her wrist, setting her up on the bed's edge again, leaning her against him. "What a sweet deal I've got here, two lovely ladies not navigating too good."

He finally got them through the salon to the aft deck, both seated in lounge chairs. The sun was just coming up and it was in their eyes. Jess helped them vomit over the side and got some food back in their stomachs.

"Ladies, can I depend on you both to stay out here without getting into trouble while I go check the engine?" He gave the oxygen bottle and mask to Madi. "You two share what's left in this bottle. I'll get the other one down in the engine room."

He lifted the deck plate over the engine room from inside the salon. He then lowered himself down into the engine room and checked for fumes as he grabbed the oxygen bottle and mask from their storage container on the bulkhead.

Jess thought to himself, there must be a bad crack in one of these exhaust flex pipes.

The overhead lights were not enough for him to inspect underneath the engine without a flashlight. He was also looking for any evidence of oil leaks or burnt marks on the outside of the exhaust pipes.

It was too cumbersome carrying the bottle and physically get to where he needed to inspect. He went back up to the salon. He took off the mask and set the bottle on a chair. Turning the bottle off, he moved a large floor fan over the opening in the deck opening to the engine room to suck out the fumes. Then he went back out to check on his ladies.

The color was back in their faces and they were laughing about something.

He leaned against the transom. "You gals look a lot better with those rosy cheeks. Anything else I can get for you right now?"

They both shook their head no.

"I think you both could use a headache powder. Wha'cha think?"

They both approved and he started forward. "We don't need all these outside light on. So I'll check around and get us ready to move on up the AICW. I should get you two to a doctor?"

Madi shook her head. "I don't think I'll need one right now."

She stood and shook his hand. "You may have saved both our lives Jess. Thank God for the oxygen."

He took them the box of headache powders and some water bottles.

"Jess don't we have a carbon monoxide detector in our stateroom and in the engine room?" Marie Ann asked standing next to him. "Aren't they on our check list for leaving port?"

"Yes, we do and yes they are on the check off list. I pushed the test buttons on them, but no indication of low batteries." He put his arm around her. "I'll replace the batteries and test them again once I get the engine room full of fresh air."

"Try to keep me aware of any vessels that would leave a big wake behind them. I'll hurry to get this problem fixed; I don't want to tarry here any longer than necessary."

He stepped up on the starboard walk-around side deck and turned around. "Love, would you use your cell phone to check the latest weather forecast for us?"

"Yes, sir, Captain."

He went out on the pulpit, leaned over to inspect the waterline on both sides of the vessel toward the fantail. It all looked clean and undamaged.

"I wonder what caused that loud bang earlier," he said to himself. "Did Madi get overcome with fumes and fall into the shower or did we run over something?"

He then went up to the flybridge to inspect that everything was secured, and then he went back down to the salon.

He moved the fan just inside the door to blow outside. "Hey ladies, do you still smell engine fumes?"

Marie Ann leaned over and hollered down the stairs from the pilothouse, "Nothing up here, Captain."

"Okay, what about you, Madi?" he called from standing on the engine room deck and leaning out the hatch in the salon deck.

She was coming aft from the crew's stateroom up to the galley. "It all smells fresh down here and here in the galley."

"The alarm indicators are clear in the engine room, which I don't understand. They are wired directly to the workstation/power distribution station across from your stateroom."

He held up the two battery operated detectors. "I've put fresh batteries in these. Madi, would you mind remounting this one up in the forward stateroom."

She took it. "No problem, Captain. Its location is above your bed?"

"You're very observant, Madi, thank you."

"That's part of my job," she said and went.

Jess found the crack in the flex exhaust pipe and wrapped it with special high temperature tape. Then he rechecked the engine room using the check list and secured the area. Then he set the salon deck plate back in place. He secured the aft main deck and closed the salon door.

"First Mate, are we ready to get underway?"

"Aye, Captain, we're ready. Do you want me to start the engine?" Marie Ann called out.

"Yes, turn it on and watch its indications on the console. I'll be right up," he said and tarried just long enough to know the diesel engine was running smoothly. He then went around and closed all the windows and doors. As he closed the port pilothouse door, he called out, "Ready to weigh anchor?"

"Aye, Captain," she said and blew him a kiss.

"Thanks, I needed that," he said and went up to the pulpit to wash the chain and anchor with a high pressure water hose. He signaled a thumbs-up for her to retrieve the anchor. He washed off the chain and anchor as it came out of the water, secured the anchor with a latching device and washed the deck.

He stored the hose, and shouted, "Bring her around into the channel and head up the AICW at 16 knots."

"Aye, Captain," Marie Ann replied as she stood at the helm.

Madi joined her and stood at the starboard side of the helm against the console teak counter top. She took the binoculars from its container and focused ahead for debris in the water and called out the next channel marker.

"Passing the two sixty mile marker; coming up on Green sixty five channel marker on starboard bow three quarters of a mile," she said and smiled to herself. She was catching on to the cruise life real well.

"That was very well done, Second Mate," Jess said as he stepped into the pilothouse from the starboard railing. "First Mate, steady as she goes .... What's our ETA for Moorehead City?"

"Mile Marker 210 should take us less than four hours at sixteen knots for fifty nautical miles, providing the wind doesn't kick up from the east. I think the land will slow it down some off our starboard side," she said and shifted her weight and leaned against the pilot's chair, while lightly gripping the wheel.

"The current isn't bad here and we're holding this speed real well. By the way, Captain, earlier I contacted a marina in Beaufort for tonight."

She handed him the Internet Cruiser's Net Satellite view pictures of the Beaufort area and the AGLCA charts of the area. The marina is across the road off the end of the airport runway 3. She hoped they didn't have a lot of night flights.

Jess was concerned about the health of his two shipmates. He was milling over the idea of taking them to an out-patient clinic for testing. Carbon Monoxide poisoning can be real serious.

When they got into port, he wanted to top off fuel, water and get the groceries they would need for a long stay on *The Shallows*.

The weather channel was still showing four hurricanes developing in the Atlantic. One of the four, shows a tracking could possibly hit the Hatteras coast line. The surge of the ocean could trap them inland for a while, but he wanted to be in Norfolk at least in seven days.

This did not leave them a lot of time for researching on shallow water diving or Civil War relic hunting inland, much less actual time doing the hunting. Finding a good safe haven would give them some good days of relic hunting. Maybe even find some beaches to hunt on inland waterways and beaches long the AICW.

The transit slip at the Town Creek Marina was full service, so they tied up, refueled, dumped, watered, and then headed for a restaurant, and grocery store; afterwards they stormed the laundry mat.

Jess talked them into a physical checkup at an out-patient clinic not far from the marina. With being a retired military and civil service, it helped reduce expenses for Marie Ann with Medicare and Tricare. Madi had her civil service insurance card. Two hours later, results were back and the two ladies had no lung or liver damage. Their blood tests were good and they were anxious to get back to the trawler for a restful evening. The facility was able to recharge the oxygen bottles for them.

Once back on their vessel, they stretched out on the upper sun deck with their favorite choice of drinks. It was now getting close to sundown and they leisurely watched it set in the West. The wind increased after sunset and they retired below in the salon.

Madi brought them further up to date as to what she had been doing since they saw her last. She reminisced about the flight from Morocco with Jess not knowing she was an undercover U.S. Marshal assigned to protect him on his way back stateside. Then she continued working with the Texas Rangers after leaving Jess and Marie Ann's ranch in Central Texas. Madi transferred to work the east coast from Key West to New York.

She had kept track of Jess and Marie Ann in their border adventures in the Big Bend country of Texas. Their twin nephews also transferred to the Arizona Rangers working the state and national parks. She had lost track of them until Jess opened the sporting and treasure hunting company in Indiana.

Madi was excited to know they were cruising on the Great American Loop and made arrangements to take a month off and surprise them when they started north on the AICW. She was delayed with marshal business and couldn't meet them in

Key West, but heard about the problems they had in the Gulf. Finally when she caught up with them, she had not planned to knock on their door sopping wet. She was still puzzled as to what had happened, because her luggage turned up at the marina with her firearm. Nothing was moved or taken from her luggage. She apologized again for the way she dropped in on them.

"If we didn't want you, we would not have offered for you to drop in anywhere or any time," Marie Ann said leaning over to her and hugged her. "We're having some fun, relaxing some and have someone else to enjoy the cruise with us."

"Not only that, you're also a great crew member. You sure picked up this navigational stuff quicker than I did," Jess said and turned up the volume on the satellite channel.

"Look at those hurricanes down in the southern Atlantic. What do you two think about leaving at sunrise again for another run north? Sure don't want to get stuck on the shoreline in one of those. Maybe we should try getting to Washington, North Carolina, tomorrow night."

The ladies looked at each other, and then Marie Ann nodded yes and Madi said, "Sure, let's do it, what time?"

"Let's try for six and eat breakfast on the way like this morning. I like those biscuits," he said and stood up.

Marie Ann offered her hand to him to get up off the floor. "Let me get them out of the freezer so they'll be thawed by morning. Do you want your peanut butter, Graham crackers, and sweet milk before going to bed?"

"That sounds great. I'll go topside to make sure everything is still secure. You want to help me, Second Mate?"

"Sure, unless First Mate doesn't need me down here," she said as Marie Ann shook her head no shooing her out. "We will be right back."

Jess took Madi up to the sundeck and pointed out things that needed checked every morning whether in port or not. "It's mostly common sense stuff to observe and check. We don't have a specific list for up here, but it might not be a bad idea. I'm always overlooking something, but catch it a few days later that I've overlooked it." He showed her the outside light switch panel that can be used from the flybridge, and left her there. He went down on the main deck to check things.

"Dog gone it, I forgot," Marie Ann said out loud and went to the aft salon screen door and opened it, stepped out on the aft deck and called up to Madi.

"Hey, Second Mate, you almost finished up there? I've got a message for you."

She was coming down the ladder to the aft deck when Marie Ann called, "You scared me for a second. I almost lost my grip." She slid on down the ladder on the railing. "Here I am. Whacha got?"

They stepped inside and Marie Ann shut the outside door to the screen door. "Just want to make sure our neighbors don't hear our conversation. You got an e-mail from the marina where you were knocked into the water. They will UPS your things to wherever you are."

Madi was happily surprised and then frowned. "But, do I want them to know where I am. Just in case this isn't correct. I think I'll have them send it to the marshal's office up closer to where we are going on the AICW. I can have a friend bring it to me."

Jess got in on the last part. "Someone coming to see you? That's great, male or female?"

"Jess, you're too nosey," Marie Ann said and tapped Madi on the shoulder. "Don't tell him, keep him guessing. He thinks you got a feller somewhere that's keeping track of you."

"Well, actually I do, but he's not the one who will meet us," she said and smiled. "I haven't told you everything, see here," she pulled a chain out of her shirt that was hanging around her neck. On the end of the chain was a beautiful six diamond engagement ring.

"O' my Lord, that's stunning!" Marie Ann said as she held Madi's hand holding it out for them to see.

She hugged Madi. "Congratulations, when's the date set for?"

Jess stood waiting his turn, she turned to him. "Jess, I've got a wonderful gentleman like you that wants me to marry him the first of December." She was beaming with joy.

"God bless you Madi and we will certainly keep you in our prayers," he said as she grabbed him around the neck and kissed him on the cheek.

"Jasper Rasputin the second!" she snickered and clapped her hands.

"What a nice surprise! May I see your ring?" he asked and then pointed at it. "Sweetheart," he said, looking at Marie Ann, "do you think that's real diamonds?"

"Oh, Jess, be nice to her. He's just teasing you, Madi," she said, turned, and opened a drawer at the salon desk. "I have it and you're not going to tease her anymore. I know what you were going to do." She took out something black and put it in her hip pocket.

Jess laughed. "No, no, that's the furthest thing from my mind, love. I wouldn't do that to a U.S. Marshal."

"I think it's bed time for all of us," he said and hugged Madi again. "Good night, young lady, and sleep well."

Marie Ann hugged her again and told her good night and then returned the diamond tester to its drawer.

It turned out to be a quiet night for the crew of *The Shallows*, no low flying aircraft from the airport, no air horns from vessels. The three tired souls slept peacefully.

CHAPTER EIGHTEEN

Moorehead City to Belhaven, North Carolina

The trip from Moorehead City, mm 205 on the ICW to mm 170 was smooth cruising until southeast winds kicked up across the open waters of the Pamlico Sound. By the time they got to the Neuse River Junction, Jess had to fight to stay on course because of the winds hitting the starboard bow.

Now, the winds were following him to G1. If they had a sail, they would pick up 10 knots of speed. Once they got north into the narrows at mm160, the land protected them from the winds. Jess had reduced the rpm's 8 knots of speed, but the wind had them moving across the open water 18. When they made their turn toward the narrows, he kept the rpm's at 8 knots.

"I'm worn out," Marie Ann said as she unbuckled from the settee seat and stood up. "Anyone hungry or thirsty?"

"Iced cappuccino, please," Jess said and unbuckled from the captain's chair and stretched. "Madi, would you take the helm for a few minutes while I visit the little boys room?"

Pointing, he said, "The G23 channel marker is up there, I'll be right back. We've got a cannel to go through. Don't look like much to see around here."

"Yes, sir, I can do that," she said and moved out of the aft facing seat on the starboard side of the pilothouse. "And, yes, I would like to try whatever you two are mixing up."

While Jess was below deck Marie Ann explained the drink Jess had come up with some years ago. "We make a fresh pot of coffee and mix Cappuccino in it while it's hot, and then pour it over crushed ice or ice cubes. It's a good picker-upper."

She paused, thinking out loud, "We have English Toffee, French Vanilla, Hazel Nut, Double Mocha and the other one is my favorite, Dark-Dark Chocolate. And, I'll make up a light snack with pepper jack cheese, crackers and summer sausage."

Madi was talking to herself, rehearsing her mental checklist of what she should do at the helm: scanning 180 degrees for other vessels, debris in the water ahead of them, correct rpm's, depth readings ahead of them on the monitor, staying on course, engine indications normal, etc.

By the time Jess and Marie Ann returned to the helm, Madi had made the 155 mm.

"Steady as she goes, mate," Jess said and looked at the charts again. "Do we want to go up to Washington for the night or Belhaven? Check them out for us, First Mate, and I'll do a quick walk around the main deck and then top side. It might be nice going into port up on the flybridge. Wha'cha think crew?"

He stepped over and relieved Madi at the helm. Mari Ann laid the snack tray on the settee and filled a paper plate for Jess. Everyone had picked the Hazel Nut to drink and she poured three non-spill containers with it.

Madi stood on the port side of the helm with Marie Ann, watching what she was doing with the charts and information she was gathering. She was looking for points of interest related to treasure hunting in the area or a creek bridge they could get to for anchoring.

"Downry Creek Marina has nice comments from cruisers who have stayed there this year. Back in May, some weathered a hurricane with no damage. A lady by the name of Mary runs the place and the docking rates are great. Transportation to Belhaven is available or rentals can be brought in," Marie Ann reported to everyone and then ate another cracker.

"It looks like we should use that marina until the storm coming up from Florida is no treat anymore," she continued after washing the snack down. "I'll do more checking on a coastal watch activities in the Cape Hatteras area.

"I have my laptop now," said Madi. "I can do that if you have something else that needs done."

"At 150 mm we'll be back out in open water for a while," he sat on the edge of the captain's chair gazing off the port bow and then back to the channel ahead of them. "Heads up crew, we have a small speedster coming at us off the starboard bow." He pointed at the fast moving boat. It continued until it passed and circled them, coming up along the port side.

"Permission to come aboard, Captain Hanes," a voice boomed over a loud speaker from the boat. "U.S. Marshall needs to board you."

Jess slowed to just enough speed to keep them in the channel as Madi stepped out on the deck. A man holding a large box stood up in the small boat and handed it to her.

"Permission granted," yelled Jess from the pilothouse as he motioned Marie Ann out to assist Madi.

She dangled a rubber fender over the side and helped Madi assist the man on the aft deck. The speedster sped away at top speed toward the land area it had come from.

The new passenger helped Madi and Marie Ann take the large box into the salon to open. It was for Madi. *Why have another U.S. Marshal deliver it to her?* Jess thought. *I wonder why UPS did not deliver it to Belhaven's marina for us to pick up.*

"Hello, Dad, how did you find me?" Madi said and threw her arms around his neck. "It's been too long...six years?" She motioned to Marie Ann.

"Dad, this is a very good friend of mine, Marie—"

Her father interrupted, "Marie Ann Hanes and the Captain Jess Hanes is your husband. You two have been a very interesting couple to keep track of around this Great Loop you're on."

He extended his free hand from around Madi. "I'm Senior Regional Director out of Washington D.C."

He let loose of Madi and nodded toward the pilot's house. "May I go up and talk to Captain Hanes in private?"

"Dad, you don't have to be so formal out here. We all have a high security level. No secrets, Dad," she said with a tone of finality. "They have been cleared for anything we need to share. I would have thought you would have known that before coming on board."

"Listen to my youngest correct her father." He leaned over and kissed her on the forehead. "Well then, let us all go up with Captain Hanes." He followed the women up the stairs to the helm.

Jess set the autopilot and turned to extend a hand to Madi's father. "I was listening to your conversation in the salon. And, I didn't get your name, please, sir."

"Colonel Albertson Ash, A.A. for short with my friends," he said with a firm handshake and smile.

Jess stepped back and looked him over. "Hum, Colonel, would you show me a 360 degree."

The colonel was at least 6 feet 6 inches tall and a muscular 225 pounds. Gray hair protruded from his decretive hat. He twirled with the forefinger pointing to the deck.

"I've never seen a kilt this close before, and never aboard ship, mine anyway," Jess said and clapped his hands in unison with the colonel's dance steps.

"Jess, be more polite to our visitor," Marie Ann said with a smile and attempted to keep her laugh inside from showing.

"Madi, I thought you were from Texas, but your father doesn't have an accent from down there, but Scottish Highlands."

"Ah, my lad, you're correct all the way around. I just left a gathering in Massachusetts. This is an emergency meeting on your vessel, Captain Hanes. While I'm on board, I request permission to use *The Shallows* as a mobile headquarters until the threat in Washington D.C. is over. My clothes will be air dropped in about an hour at these coordinates, Captain Hanes. Would you proceed to my rendezvous point?"

He handed a small piece of paper to Jess, who in turn gave it to Marie Ann. "First Mate, locate this for me please. Second Mate, give me a bearing from here, and we will do it."

Jess turned off the auto pilot and took the trawler helm in one hand and with the other moved the rpm's for 20 knots. *The Shallows* jumped like it was shot off of a carrier deck by a steam catapult.

This fast reaction of the trawler surprised the Colonel and he grabbed for an overhead rail. "Yes, this is fantastic response."

"Should we be looking like regular cruisers, Colonel, I mean A.A.?" Jess asked. "If so, I would suggest putting on some dungarees of some kind, tennis shoes and a sloppy hat. ASAP."

He removed himself from the pilothouse and went down to the salon. It did not take him long to change and by that time Jess had the navigational information needed to find the lagoon the Colonel wanted.

He came back up and stood next to Jess at the helm. "Have you ever had the pleasure of steering a water vessel before, A.A.?"

"Nope, but I sure would like to learn when this meeting is over and the tensions are less," he said and kept looking out the starboard door. "I expect a black Hawk helicopter to appear from the north once we are to Dixon Creek Point break water on the starboard side." He pointed as the autopilot guided them to the inlet.

Jess turned off the autopilot and slowed their forward progress at G13 channel marker. "What specifically are we looking for, Colonel?" Jess asked with his hand on the throttle. "Should we have firearms handy?"

The colonel nodded to Madi and she came in from the main deck. "I'll get them Dad, from the box you brought on board?"

"Yes, but I don't anticipate any trouble here, but once we get back in the channel going north on the open water, we might have visitors."

"Like what, Colonel?" Jess asked as he motioned for Marie Ann to get her side arm. He took his from under the teak helm console, in its holster and put it on his belt.

"First Mate, get everyone a life preserver when you two come up," he ordered.

She brought them up with Madi.

At G4 they turned south into four feet of water and slowly moved ahead. The depth monitor showed them the deepest spot to sit idle. There were no currents to contend with and the wind was calm. Jess slowly came about with the bow to the north toward the channel for an easy exit.

It did not take long for the Black Hawk to arrive with very little blade noise. It hovered over the aft deck and lowered four black suited men with supplies. The helicopter left immediately toward the south.

The equipment and men were hurriedly put in the salon. Madi and the Colonel quickly organized the unit. With Marie Ann's help she located a spot for each of them for sleeping and showed them around inside.

Once back in the galley/salon area, Jess and Marie Ann were officially brought in on the details.

The Colonel related the situation to Jess and his crew: The unit is made up of Navy SEALs/marshals to be used for support of the president's leaving Washington D.C. by land, boat and not by air.

There is an attack of terrorist cells in the nation's capital, burning vehicles, bombing entrances to government buildings, tunnels, and railroads were blocked by explosions, and the airport taxi ways were damaged. The President's helicopter did not make it to the White House to get him and his family out of the city. They escaped by using two taxi cabs.

They were shuffled from different vehicles every five blocks and then to ambulances. Once out in the country they were put in Black Hawks to bring them to meet a submarine near where *The Shallows* was located.

The oncoming hurricane added to the threat of limited cover for the President and his family.

Jess hollered down from the pilothouse/helm to the colonel in the salon. "Why pick this Nordic Tug. It's one of the slowest vessels cruising the AICW. We are a sitting duck in a big pond?"

The Colonel stood on the bottom step up to the pilothouse. "I keep close track on Madi and knew she was on vacation somewhere on the AICW. Once I found your location, *The Shallows* was a perfect fit to our plans. Plus, I had a U.S. Marshal on board who I trusted.

"Your vessel is very mobile and you are a very knowledgeable man with vast military experience. Knowing Madi was on board, I convinced my advisors with the President to focus on your location as a point of safety to get the President and his family to a night boarding of a submarine off Cape Hatteras."

"But a nuclear submarine can't operate very well in the shallow waters inside Cape Hatteras. I wouldn't think it would be deep enough," Jess said as he headed the trawler toward Belhaven.

"We already have Navy aircraft flying at high altitudes above us to provide the President cover. There are two dedicated satellites tracking his movements as we speak, and your vessel is marked as a point of contact," the Colonel said and moved up to stand next to Jess at the helm.

Marie Ann continued to scan the channel ahead with her binoculars.

"Colonel, I would suggest the three of us move up to the flybridge so we can be readily seen, and the rest of you can be here in the pilothouse to observe from here," Jess said and turned around, pointing down the stairs to the galley/salon. "Your men can station themselves anywhere down there to watch to the side and rear areas. Outsiders will not easily know the three of us are not the only ones on board."

"My men are already at their posts with satellite communications set up," he replied to Jess.

"Dad, you owe us for this interruption of our vacation," Madi said as she came up the stairs. "I didn't know you were at the Pentagon now."

"That's been my front for a few years. I've been on the move continually since your mother died," he said and changed the subject. "I suggest you three get topside now. I can take the helm from here until you transfer control up there."

Jess reduced the speed to 6 knots and turned on the autopilot. "That should hold us until we're ready. We can communicate with that intercom," he pointed at it on the console.

The three went topside to the flybridge and took over. Jess returned to manual operation and increased the speed to 18 knots. "I forgot something to tell your Dad, Madi."

She came over close to him to hear because of the wind. "Yes, Sir Captain."

"We have that slip reserved at Dowry Creek Marina," he said and pointed to a monitor with marinas/anchorages of the location. "We can Med-moor at the dock with bow lines tied off to buoys. Or there is a good anchorage a short distance from the marina for us with 5 feet depth and a good swing for this 42 footer. We should make arrangements for topping off the fuel tanks, and groceries. Would you go down and ask your dad about it, please."

Marie Ann moved over close and put her arm around his waist to get some warmth. "It's a bit chilly up here. Do you want that windbreaker from the locker? I'm going to get one out."

He nodded approval and she handed him the binoculars. There were some pleasure sail boats ahead of them coming into the channel. He wanted to see what their 'tacking' track would be, and to stay way clear of them. There must be two dozen coming out of Belhaven heading straight toward them.

Jess put on the yellow windbreaker Marie Ann handed to him, it did make a big difference. The flybridge wind deflector did its job, but it had gotten cloudy with ten knots of wind from the south. He headed as close to the starboard shoreline as he dared in order to keep away from the sail boats.

"Are they in a race, they seem to be awful close together at a high speed," she said looking with the binoculars.

"I think so, love. See all those buoy markers for their course?"

"Aye, Captain, I see them."

Jess slowed as the marina came into sight.

Madi came up with three containers of freshly brewed coffee, setting them in holders in the helm fiberglass dash panel.

"Dad checked out the marina and its location. We can pump our own fuel and they do have a small grocery store at the marina. Once we are replenished, he suggested anchoring out. We want to be able to move at moment's notice."

"Okay, thanks, Madi," he replied and motioned for both ladies to get close to him. "Marie Ann, show Madi how to make up the lines on the bow deck and make sure the anchor chain isn't binding. We may have to anchor the fantail if there are waves from traffic."

Jess turned at the Dowery G-7 channel marker toward the marinas. He called the marina and they had reserved the first outside slip on the pier base and two assistants were waiting.

The Colonel came up the stairs and stood next to Jess at the helm.

Jess pointed. "Where the two men are waving to us is where we'll park." He slowed the rpm's and yelled to the women on the bow. "Get your lines ready for those guys on the first pier. We will back into the slip on the other side of the base pier."

Marie Ann hollered back, "Bow, stern, and two spring lines, Captain?"

"Aye there, First Mate," Jess replied and began turning the vessel around to back into the slip. "The satellite shows two lines for the bow and two aft with spring lines on the starboard side."

The first and second mates had the lines ready when Captain Hanes backed in *The Shallows*. He had to use both the aft and

THE SHALLOW'S DEEP SECRETS

bow thrusters to keep the port current from banging them into the pier before the starboard rubber fenders were over the side. Rudder was put to full starboard to keep from catching the current from the port side, thrusters off and the engine at full idle

Marie Ann hollered, "Port and starboard lines secured, Captain," as Madi secured the starboard spring lines. One of the pier crew grabbed the electrical lines Marie Ann handed to them, turned and hollered to Jess who had gone down to the lower passageway to change to shore power.

"Shore lines hooked up, Captain," she yelled and waited for an answer as she stepped inside the starboard pilothouse door.

"Shore power indicated lines are hooked up correctly," he hollered and started back up to the galley. He pointed to Marie Ann. "First Mate, switch to shore power."

She did and gave him a thumbs-up.

"Hey, Second Mate, we did that job in record time. I think that's worth a steak dinner tonight," she said stepping back out on the main starboard deck. They gave each other a high-five and came back inside the pilothouse.

A man's voice came from the pier. "Captain Hanes, U.S. Coast Guard, permission to come on board?"

Jess looked at the Colonel who in turn knelt and looked down to the salon and received a thumbs-up from one of his black uniformed men. "It's Chief Stanford, Colonel."

The Colonel stood up and nodded to Jess. "Captain, step out and welcome him on board and then in here, please."

Marie Ann had moved to the aft deck and Madi topside to the flybridge as they heard Jess give the Chief approval for boarding. They went inside and had a short conference, which the women were not privy to, but did get the details later. They stood their watch for any other out of the ordinary things to happen.

There was a Coast Guard cutter standing off to the south side of the channel waiting for the Chief to return. Two others were on the pier to assist the Chief; they had automatic weapons unslung at the ready. When the Chief departed, he gave the women topside a snappy salute, and joined his men in their inflatable dinghy/tender. They returned to the cutter and it did not take any time for them to be out of sight westbound.

It was that time of the day to set the lights for being in port. So they rigged one string of lights, which is called Med-Mooring lights, from the bow up to the flybridge railing, to the mast, across to the sundeck aft railing down to the transom railing, and plug it into a watertight bulkhead electrical box. There were enough lights to brighten the whole trawler down to the waterline. All the shades were kept closed and the drapes dropped to keep intruders from looking in should they walk by on the pier. Long distance binoculars on the high points around them were of no value either.

The two women took the barbeque pit grill out of the aft locker and stoked up the coals. The only way anyone could see what was being cooked would have been from a satellite.

Jess brought out his favorite marinated steaks and put them on the grill. Madi closed the lid and set the exhaust port on it. Marie Ann hung a mosquito light from the aft over hang near the grill. He went back inside as the two cooks sipped their iced tea.

Jess brought out his famous barbeque sauce in a deep saucer, stirring it, sniffing it, tasting it and set it down. "Be right back ladies, it needs just a spoonful of juice from those hot banana peppers. It would be too hot for ya'all putting anything hotter in it."

Marie Ann turned the T-bone steaks over and closed the lid as Jess came back with the jar of banana peppers.

"How does this smell First Mate?" he asked and then let Madi have a smell. "Does it smell food hot, not fire hot?"

"Nope," Madi said and stuck her finger in it. "Taste good too, but there is something missing."

Marie Ann had her finger taster up to the first knuckle into the sauce and sucked it right off without batting an eye. "Don't put too much of that hot stuff in it."

He opened the pepper container and poured a small amount of juice into a large soup spoon. "Smell that and take a small sample on the end of your finger."

They both smiled. "That's smooth stuff Jess. Where do you get it?" Madi asked and tried another sample.

"We can usually find it in most grocery stores," he said and filled the spoon, poured into the sauce, and stirred it. "This is a secret receipt I inherited from a Mexican tortilla maker on the Texas border."

"No, he didn't! It was from his grandfather who used to live in the Big Bend country of Texas," Marie Ann said and opened the grill for Jess to cover the steaks with the thick sauce. "This will be ready in about hour, thirty minutes on each side."

"I stand corrected. It was my grandpa in Terlingua."

He handed the hot peppers to Madi and with a tilt of his head and eye movement motioned her inside the salon.

"Please tell the others it will not be too long.

It was getting close to 8 pm and the bugs were getting thick. There was no wind to keep them away and they were massing around the night lights over the aft deck where they were cooking.

"I'll get the taco salad finished," Marie Ann said and went inside too.

After thirty minutes, Jess took some of the steaks inside to the hungry men.

"Now, some of these have been cooked on both sides over and hour, and some less than that… and there is more on the fire," he said.

"Man, I thought my throat was cut; smelling that steak cooking and those corn tortillas in here, plus whatever Mrs. Hanes is stirring up. My stomach is growling bad," one of the four men said and laughed when he stood up.

Madi laughed with him. "I thought it was a Drum or Gaspergou under the boat."

"What did you say? A Gasper… What?" One of the men asked.

"A Drum Gaspergou is a freshwater fish. I've caught them in the Devil's River of Texas," Jess said and spelt the name. "Good eating fish. While night fishing, with a lantern hanging over the side, they will school or collect while feeding. They have two stones of ivory in their heads that are rubbed together to make a growling sound."

One of the men stood to fill his plate again, "Sounds like a fish story to me."

The Colonel moved away from the aft salon door where he was watching out between the shades. "I haven't heard that fish name since we fished in the Buchannan Lake north of Austin. I think they had those fish in all the rivers and lakes in Texas."

"Dad, remember how they would group together under that ole *Lone Star* boat and make that horrible noise at night?" she said and put her arm around his waist. "It was a sure thing that those nights we would be bringing in a string of good eating fish."

One of the four black uniformed men leaned against the wall. "Sounds like you two spent a lot of time together when you were younger. It makes me homesick for my young'uns."

"Amen to that Sarg," one of the others said. "Plus I'm so under nourished I'm about to pass out from starvation. Does the cook need some assistance back there?"

Marie Ann went out with a large empty covered pot to retrieve the sizzling steaks. Jess opened the grill top and filled the pot with twelve large serried crusty T-bone steaks. While Marie Ann laid out everything on the coffee table, Jess closed the dampers to the grill for the oxygen to be chocked away from the hot coals. He anchored it in place to insure it did not tip over, and then went inside.

Jess did not hesitate. "Gentlemen, lock arms with us and we'll thank God for the food we are about to share. We ask Father for Your protecting hands over our country, our family, our men and women in Harm's Way, and for the secured safety of these men here with us. God bless you guys, and God bless America."

There were hearty Amens around the group and a few sniffles, which added to the taste of a good home, cooked meal; even though it was late.

The plan was made by military communications the five men had brought on board *The Shallows*. After the Med-lights were turned off, they left in the middle of the night, one at a time over the port side into the water.

They had changed into scuba gear, carrying communications equipment, weapons and supplies. The three-crew members watch them as they disappeared into the dark below. No bubble trails, no ripples on the surface could be seen in the disappearing moon light.

The hurricane was one hundred miles due south of North Carolina with the forecast expecting it to turn northeast before sunrise. If it did, political havoc would flourish with the good weather.

Jess put his arms around the ladies. "Let's secure and get some sleep. I'll check the weather to see what it'll be by ten in the morning. We can plan our route while we sleep."

He turned mumbling going to the pilothouse. "The AICW could be closed off because of the terrorist activity in Washington D.C. We may not be able to get to Norfolk tomorrow."

He escorted them into the pilothouse and all three studied the satellite weather report before turning in.

Jess detoured to the galley and was the only one who had a snack of crackers, crunchy peanut butter and sweet milk before getting into bed, and once there, it was no effort going to sleep.

All crew members of *The Shallows* were up, finished with breakfast, dishes stored, and getting updates on where then could go to stay out of the way of government blockades. By noon the winds had calmed from the hurricane that veered northeast away from the Carolina coast line.

There were no reports of damage from the storm on the AICW. The only information they needed was how close to

Norfolk could they get as tourist. Was it sealed off other than for military personnel? Even so, as a retired couple and Madi a federal marshal, why get on the naval base if it was not necessary? As tourist, they should find routes away from that area.

"I was thinking, if everyone is still interested, we could try our contacts up around Fredericksburg, Virginia, area for Civil War relic hunting. We should be able to get up through the Chesapeake Bay area, close to shore and up to Owens. Dahlgren Naval Weapons Station isn't too far if we need anything like a Base Exchange or commissary," Jess said, showing them an old 1943 military road atlas.

"Show us where you and the guys you were with hunted around Fredericksburg," Marie Ann said pointed to the different marked battle field areas. "Remember the display of Civil War relics back at the ranch in the den?"

"Yes, I do remember. And also, your research of family history placed your great-great-grandfather and mine fighting each other in a battle south of Nashville." She smiled at being able to recall, because it was six years ago when she was on their ranch in Texas.

"I don't think their regiments were involved out here in Virginia. They were volunteers early in the war, and November of 1864, they were in Franklin, Tennessee. Marie Ann's grandparent was with General Schofield who was trying to get to Nashville for needed support, and mine was with General Hood's Texas troops trying to stop him."

"You need to write a book about that, Jess," Marie Ann said and put her finger to her lip, "in your spare time, of course."

They laughed and he pointed to the map. "Madi, check the cruiser's Internet for a marina in Dahlgren or Owens on the Potomac River. They would be excellent locations to work from. We can get a rental vehicle to look for relic hunting possibilities."

He tapped the map where he was talking about; this area has been hunted for years. Many landowners now charge to detect on their land.[2]

---

[2]   There has been too much damage done by relic hunters who get on property without permission and leave damage from digging. Those who trespass are greedy and they are working above the law in metal detecting in areas they should not be in without permission. It reflects badly on everyone in the treasure-hunting hobby. Because of large deep holes left in battlefields, gopher holes in home lawns, churchyards, parks, and courthouse lawns, our generation and the ones to come will continue to be limited in metal detecting. Some people just do not really care about other's property.

CHAPTER NINETEEN

Belhaven to Fredericksburg, Virginia

After anchoring overnight at the AICW anchorage 57 the crew of *The Shallows* ate a small supper early and went to bed before 8:00 p.m. The weather was cooling down with northeasterly winds whipping up open water. Their anchorage gave them good blockage from the winds.

Jess was restless and quietly put on sweatpants over his pajama shorts and went up to the galley and fixed his usual peanut butter, crackers and a small glass of milk.

Then he went up to the pilothouse with his snack and laid it on the table behind the captain's chair. He turned the overhead monitor to check the weather. It was forecast clear weather to Norfolk, another 78nm.

There were no storms from the Atlantic Ocean and none coming in from the west. He turned the monitor off and settled back into the bench seat at the table.

He made his snack last as long as his taste buds would allow. He laid the empty glass on the table, turned on the seat and with his binoculars surveyed their southern exposure, and then looked north where the AICW would lead them in the later; no lights or movement of vessels.

He took his windbreaker jacket and stepped out on the port main deck with the binoculars. He looked at the distant Milky Way, Big Dipper and then to the southwest at the brightness of the half moon. By the time he walked around the deck back to the port door opening, he was chilled.

Stepping inside, locking the door, he whispered to himself, "Got yourself a nice chill out of that go-around Jess. Now, cancel that thought, you're not chilled, I claim victory over it, in Jesus my Lord."

"You better go snuggle up to Marie Ann and get warm again." He did without waking her completely; she was receptive to his coolness and let him snuggle.

She was up early and had breakfast fixed with the help of Second Mate Madi. The smell of bacon frying woke him. He stretched and slipped into their large bathroom/shower/head for a fast shower to wake up.

By the time he had dressed and entered the galley, everything was on the table for breakfast. "Boy, I sure time this right."

"Any longer, your crew would have left you in bed and we would have got underway without waking you," Marie Ann said and poured his coffee. "Your snoring would have covered the engine noise."

They finished breakfast dishes and then went up to the pilothouse with their morning coffee to look over the remainder of the AICW to Norfolk. Their plan was to stay overnight there and head up the Chesapeake Bay to the Potomac River up to Owen for some Civil War relic hunting.

Jess had contacts in the Fredericksburg area who were avid treasure hunters. He had not hunted with them for years, and was anxiously waiting for an answer to his e-mail.

Jess and Marie Ann made out a list of people to contact in Fredericksburg. "We can take on fuel, water and groceries in Norfolk." Jess said and put his arm around her shoulders. "I'll contact the Waterside Marina to find out if we can off load black and gray water."

"It doesn't show anything on the Internet for gasoline being available, or the dumping," Marie Ann said. "I'll make a call as soon as we are underway again."

"I still would like to take some tours in Norfolk before heading on up north," he said looking through internet info on the computer for tours.

Marie Ann showed Madi some photos of the ship's reunion back in September 11, 2001. She recited how they were getting ready to leave home and was watching CBS and saw the first plane hit the tower in Manhattan. Jess had thought it was a replay of a movie being made in downtown New York, until the second passenger liner hit the second tower and the TV hosts realized what had happened.

The reunion directors did not cancel plans to go to Norfolk, Virginia, beach for the reunion. There was a large gathering of the ship's crew to help show the terrorists that they could not shut down the United States solid Americans.

After four and a half hours of uneventful cruising up the AICW they tied up at the Waterside Marina in Norfolk. Rain and high winds kept them inside until the following afternoon. The marina made arrangements for gasoline to be delivered for the standby electrical generator and a rental vehicle for the crew.

The weather cleared but the winds were too high for them to cruise out on the Chesapeake Bay up to the Potomac River, so they made their own tour plans for Norfolk, Virginia Beach and surrounding area. It was almost like being in San Diego, California, other than no hills, high bluff overlooking the Pacific and mountains in the distance east.

It truly was a U.S. Naval Base community. Jess knew where most of the navy vessels went when they closed down Newport, Rhode Island Naval Base. Most had become scrap metal, others relocated to other bases.

Now in the cozy confines of *The Shallows*, the crew rested, read, watched TV, and watched people on the road and sidewalks in the marina. They took a couple hours walking tours twice a day to the local stores and parks just for exercise.

When it was not raining and the sun out, temperatures rose to the mid 70's, they went to the parks and metal detected. A large percent of the finds were modern silver cladded coins, and only six silver dimes. Total number of coins for the three treasure hunters, for three hours, was 143. Marie Ann found the most coins, Madi the most toys, and Jess found the most tokens and buttons. He did find two modern Officers Eagle buttons, which had some gold gilt, and one Pee Coat anchor blue button.

The days not metal detecting, Jess arranged to get them on board a dozen active duty vessels, because of being a retired veteran in the Navy and Air Force. They all three had government ID cars and passports when necessary when asked for.

A few times, the ship's Officer of the Deck or the Commanding Officer would start a tour for them, and then turned Jess loose to go anywhere on board he wanted to go. They always seem to be on board for chow time. The two ladies Jess had with him were always amazed at the preparations made for each meal and the amount of food served. The larger ships like aircraft carriers, battleship, cruisers, and service tenders, seemed to always have one chow hall open 24 hours to serve hot meals.

Marie Ann was still impressed with the cleanliness of the galleys and the absence of spoiled food smells. There were crews somewhere on board washing down the decks, bulkheads and overheads, because of the many detours in the passageways they had to take.

They had to run to depart from one missile cruiser; it had to leave port in an emergency without a full crew. Many other vessels got underway at the same time. They also noticed base security increased to Level Orange. The three departed the base to get out of the way, even Jess remarked, "In my opinion, we are safer on base than off. Maybe we should get a room at the transit hotel."

Marie Ann questioned on who would go first and who directed the traffic out of port. They remember the terrorist alert must have gone to "Red Alert'. Watching so many vessels going to sea at one time, made chills go up and down Jess' spine.

He remembered his 'alert and general quarters' days on board, not knowing what was happening and what was coming; just be prepared for whatever.

Jess, Marie Ann and Madi were advised to get out of Norfolk as soon as permitted.

The first and second mate hurried back to *The Shallows* and cast off line, while Jess got info from the Harbor Master. The lines were stored and the crew stood side by side in the pilothouse with the engine running. Jess was waiting for approval to head out into the channel to the Chesapeake Bay.

Once out in the shipping channel, they stayed out of the shipping lanes that were used for the large Naval vessels. Most of them had already departed and were out in international waters. If this situation became a major threat to the United States, Jess would have to put *The Shallows* in storage to finish the Loop Cruise on a later date. But, he was not too concerned as to where to store the Nordic Tug, but the safety of his crew.

After an hour cruising at full speed of 22 knots, Jess found a deep-water cove to pull into out of the high wind and waves. They dropped the bow anchor in shallow water near an abandoned small beach.

The radio, TV, and the Internet were flooded with information on the heightened terrorist activities. The three-crew members were listening and watching outside while it seemed the whole communications network was flooded with explosions across the United States.

Marie Ann monitored the navigational channels, Jess on satellite communications, and Madi on her cell phone and Ipad with the U.S. Marshal's offices.

She was to come off vacation, but stay where she was.

"Okay, ladies, I suggest we put on a high profile as possible. We want to make sure we have our larges flag flying from the fantail. Make sure we wear our authority badges where they can be seen by anyone from shore or on the water. Keep our ID and passport pouches on our body at all times. Wear canteens on web belts with sidearms. We don't want to be blown out of the water by some loose cannon. Once we find a port to store this vessel, we will buy a vehicle and get home. Madi, can you get transportation? If not we will provide you with a vehicle. I suggest whatever we get that it is not a new one but a late model four-wheel drive."

He took a deep breath. "Ladies, what can you add to the list?"

"Marie Ann, I can deputize you and give you one of my extra U.S. Marshal badges," she held up one finger to Jess and put it to her lips. "A marshal's helicopter has me located and will be here in thirty minutes. It's just enough time for me to pack and help you two for your search. I would suggest you go west as soon as you can, and store this nice vessel. But, don't linger, stay away from the big cities and get into the center of the US as fast as possible."

She grabbed Marie Ann and threw her arms around her neck. "It's been great and I love you."

Then she reached up and grabbed Jess' face between her hands. "It has been one great time with you, skipper, I love you too." She tipped toed and gave him a little kiss on both cheeks. She stepped away and saluted him. Tears flowed when she went below for her gear.

Marie Ann went with her.

Jess and Marie Ann waved to her until the helicopter was just a small dot in the blue sky to the west. There were white trails from high flying aircraft, almost horizon to horizon. North of their anchorage, they could see dozens of aircraft in the air at all altitudes. Navy and Marine jets flew low over them and from Norfolk.

Jess and Marie Ann stood on the flybridge, arm in arm watching the sun go down while the vapor trails could be seen for a long time after sunset.

"Lord Jesus, you are still our Lord and Saviour. We are still in your loving hands and know you will continue to protect us, our family and our new friends. He quoted Psalm 91."

Marie Ann said Amen, Jesus is Lord!

A cool breeze came in from across the bay and they hurried below for warmth.

"It sure cooled off fast," Jess said and took a windbreaker out of a locker and put across Marie Ann's shoulders. "Do we have any frozen chili left? It would sure taste good with a grilled cheese sandwich."

She put her arms around his waist and pulled herself as close to him as possible. "This isn't the time to be thinking about your stomach Skipper. I can take care of that while we discuss our move from here."

He held her tight. "Let me do some thinking while getting our outside lights on and make sure our anchor will keep us held. Keep the scanner down here in the galley turned on and your cell phone."

He finished topside and went down to the galley, securing all the outside doors as he went.

"I'm scared Jess, what do we do now, where will we go, what's happening?" she asked and sobbed.

He took her over to the couch and they cuddled up together. "Remember Psalm 91? Jesus has promised to take care of us and what does the Psalm tell us about our Father in heaven."

They knelt next to the couch and began reciting together the beginning of Psalm 91. "He that dwelleth in the secret place of the most High shall abide under the shadow of the Almighty. I will say of the Lord, He is our refuge, our fortress, our God. Surely He shall deliver us from the snare of the fouler and noisome pestilence…"

Early the next morning before sunrise, they weighed anchor and headed north toward the mouth of the Potomac River. Jess was navigating while Marie Ann was at the helm.

It was a cool pleasant morning without wind, but the swells were high and following. Jess had contacted an ole friend at the Naval Surface Warfare facility at Dahlgren, Virginia.

Marty Swartz, retired Navy Master Chief, was still in the civil service side of the facility and controlled all physical inventory. If you wanted to know where anything was stored, he would most likely tell you where it was without going to the computers. If it was not available, he knew where to get it, what the current price was and how long it would take to obtain.

When Marty got the e-mail from Jess, he contacted him by secured cell phone. "Jess it's good to hear from you. I'll make this short. When you're ten miles out call this cell phone number."

"I can do that," Jess said and wrote the number down of the transmitting cell phone from the indication on the face of his cell phone. "I've got it written down. Is there any craft warnings in your area.?"

"Not for your vessel, come on in."

"We'll see ya soon," Jess replied and closed his cell phone and put it in his front pants.

Jess turned to Marie Ann and put his hand on her shoulder. "Marty said we are clear to Dahlgren and to call him ten miles out."

He checked his chart made some measurements. "We can keep 18 knots and be there less than six hours. With this following sea, we shouldn't have any problems getting there this afternoon. But, we know this too can change out here in open water."

"How far are we off the port side from land?" she asked and used binoculars to search ahead of them. "I just don't want to get tangled up in a lobster pot this morning."

No sooner had she spoken a low flying sea plane passed over them going in the same direction.

"My goodness, what is it Jess?"

"Looking at it from the tail, I don't know."

He took another pair of binoculars and watched the aircraft. "It's not going much faster than we are. It might be a homemade kit aircraft. I'm not familiar with its small features." He watched it until it was out of sight when it turned north following a tributary.

They had to pay a lot of attention to commercial traffic and barges going and coming: ferry boats, tankers, supply vessels, and one large ocean liner.

Jess changed places with Marie Ann after the sun rose, so she could make brunch for them. They had decided to put *The Shallows* into dry storage for a couple of months while they went back home to Texas. Their ranch hands and manager/foreman needed their assistance on some projects Jess had sent them. They planned to be in Branson, Missouri, for Veteran's Week and on the ranch for Thanksgiving.

Arrangements were made with Marty to have *The Shallows* bottom cleaned and new zinc plates installed. He wanted to have Jess try out a diesel conversion for more power and speed that their research department had designed for hovercraft, at no cost. He felt the structure of the Nordic Tug would handle the stress. Jess and Marie Ann had looked over the design and approved for the work.

They told Marty they should be back late February to put the NT back in the water, and stay in touch every two weeks.

A Hummer limousine took them to downtown Fredericksburg to the Old Rappahannock River Hotel on the waterfront. They were just a short distance to the airport and very close to the Civil War battlegrounds.

Jess had hunted the Wilderness area some forty years prior and knew that relic hunting and the surrounding areas had changed drastically. It would be hard to get permission to hunt on private land, mainly because he had no contacts to guide him. The men he had hunted with years prior were either dead or no longer living in the area.

So that meant, knocking on business and private landowners doors to get written permission to hunt with metal detectors and dig on their properties. They had planned to spend two weeks

210

in the Fredericksburg area before having Mick Slater from Shuffleville, Indiana, to fly them home to Texas, their nephew.

Once in their room, Jess and Marie Ann set themselves down and checked the weather forecast for the next two weeks. The report was not for C.W. relic hunting, it was to rain for most of the two weeks with high winds and thunderstorms. He called the hotel's office and told them they would only be staying five days because of the weather and would leave early Monday morning.

Marie Ann called Mick about their stay; and when they plan to leave. He could not leave home, because his son was due to be born. Mick needed to be home.

Then she called the ranch and asked Aleta, their corporate chief pilot and head of the ranch's security, if the jet was ready for a hop to Virginia. It was ready and she made the schedule with Aleta to be at the Stafford Regional Airport on Sunday night to fly out Monday morning. She told her to bring Juan the foreman and his wife Lolita. Aleta reminded Marie Ann that Lolita did not like airplanes and would not fly. So that offer was dropped.

Jess and Marie Ann made up for being aboard *The Shallows* so long without much walking. They made their own tour of Fredericksburg on foot with a city map. The small stores, antiques shops, Civil War museums, restaurants, schools, funeral homes, churches and any other location that pertained to the Civil War, were circled on the map.

Saturday afternoon they took their pilot Aleta and co-pilot on a tour of the Civil War battle fields in the Hummer Limo. The two ladies were impressed with what had happened back in the 1860's during the Civil War.

When they checked out of the hotel Monday morning, they had a list of people who had invited them to hunt on their properties around the area. When they return in February, they would be equipped for two weeks hunting. Also, during that two weeks, arrangements for *The Shallows* to be taken out of storage and prepped would be made.

CHAPTER TWENTY

Fredericksburg to MJ Ranch, Texas

The flight back home to the MJ Ranch was smooth and relaxing in their recently purchased updated 2009 Hawker. The dealer's demo price on the Hawker Beechcraft 800XP with Jess' trade-in of the King Air was worth the haggling with the dealer.

Even though the King of Morocco paid the bill, Jess' MJ Ranch owned the aircraft by title papers. Jess still retained a certified aircraft mechanic and chief pilot. Aleta, Jess' chief pilot, with her crew were still based in Austin. She also flew the aircraft to Fredericksburg to pick them up.

There was a six-hour delay before Aleta could leave the ranch because of flight restrictions to Virginia, due to the bombings in Washington D.C. It was a long three hours wait before receiving authorization to leave. Authorization from the FAA to permit them to leave that area of Virginia, delayed them. Flying restrictions around Washington D.C. were tight, due to the bombings close to the White House and Capitol Building.

Before leaving Fredericksburg, they had to wait for a U.S. Marshal and an FAA inspector from D.C. to check the aircraft, baggage, crew and passengers.

By the time the inspection was finished, paper work done, it was too late in the day to leave. Therefore, Aleta had to update the flights departure until the next morning. They finally left at 8:00 a.m., after eating a good breakfast at the terminal.

The MJ Ranch looked beautifully green from the recent rains as they circled and landed on the 5,000-foot runway. The cattle along the other side of the fence line scattered as the jet taxied on the tarmac to the hangar. The two story white stucco ranch house looked as clean and new as the day it was built, 150 years ago. It was located two hundred yards from the hangars.

Juan met them as they came down the steps of the aircraft. His warm welcome with a bouquet of wild Texas flowers for Marie Ann brought tears to her eyes.

Stepping toward him, she gave him a big hug. "Thank you, Juan." And cradled the flowers in her left arm.

Jess shook his hand and also gave Juan a hug. "it's good to be home Juan."

The three got in an opened top old World War II army jeep and drove to the ranch house where Juan's wife, Lolita, waited for them at the kitchen door. There were hugs and kisses as the foreman's greeted Jess and Marie Ann back home.

Lolita was jabbering in Spanish so fast, Jess and Marie Ann could not keep up with her. Juan interpreted her in English, "Slow down and speak English."

"Oh my lands, I'm so excited you are home. There is so much to tell you about my grandson's birth and our oldest boy has joined the Marines, and Peter is leaving tomorrow for boot camp."

She grabbed Marie Ann's hand, led her to the kitchen table, and had her sit down pouring her a glass of sweetened iced tea. Through the years of being the ranch's main cook, she and Marie Ann had become very close friends. She had a lot to tell her boss-lady and could not speak fast enough in her excitement to tell Marie Ann all the happenings while they were gone on a 'big circle'.

Juan tapped Jess on the arm. "We might as well go out on the screened-in back porch to talk. We wouldn't be able to get a word in edgewise in here."

Jess poured them glasses of iced tea from the chilled pitcher of tea, and then they moved to the porch. The ranch house was on higher ground than the rest of the ranch and they could see for miles in all directions. The porch enclosed the outer perimeter of the ranch house. Juan brought Jess up to date on the ranch's business.

The first week home they spent taking care of a few big problems on the ranch. One was solving the problem of holding rainwater for the livestock. Drilling more water wells and/or dam more ravines. Unless there is a spring to drain into the ravines, the water will not last long after rains.

The second problem was cattle rustling. They were missing fifteen from one herd and five from another. If someone needed the meat for their families, Jess would arrange they would get the meat after butchering. Fences cut and some stripped carcasses left behind, but a few were just shot between the eyes and left.

The third major problem were illegals camping into deep ravines, leaving trash and other belongings when rushed to leave.

The border patrol and Texas Rangers were notified long before Jess returned home.

Jess and his ranch foreman, Juan, flew Jess' favorite slow flier, an ole bright yellow 1038 J3 Piper Cub to look at some of the ravines that would work to hold water. Over the years since his adventures in Morocco, his ranch was now the biggest in the county—2,300 acres of prime cattle raising land.

He and Juan flew over the ranch spread at least twice a week to keep an eye on the herds and mark on their maps any signs of rustling of cattle. Jess' *Lady Air Force* would fly at night using special night vision equipment, notifying authorities of any sightings. A few times, they herded a half dozen illegals right into the hands of Texas Rangers and U.S. Marshals.

The illegals were using caves to hide in on Jess' ranch. He had hidden remote motion detectors cameras inside the entrances that set off an alarm in Jess' hangar/ranch office and in the ranch house offices. Jess, with his ranch hands, would lead the authorities onto the ranch. Many times the Texas Rangers' helicopters took on the tracking at night.

On this one morning, Jess and Juan was in the Piper Cub over the east fence line when they received a cell phone call from one of his cowboys riding the north rim of Mule Shoe springs. Two men dressed in camos driving a four-wheeler had it stuck in the cattails along the west side of the small lake.

They were only two miles east of Mule Shoe and told the young cowboy, Rick, to watch for them. They would come in low and stay to the east, hoping to cause the two men to run, leaving their vehicle behind in the mud. Then, if they separated, Rick could get them.

Rick was using binoculars and saw the Cub's yellow wings reflect the sun as it banked toward him. He was located on a ridge that was mule shoe shaped with the small lake in the middle. It was a good spot to survey a long distance from horse back.

Jess and Juan had their cell phone ear plugs in place with their aircraft headset over them. They were on three way communications with Rick.

"We will pass low in front of the opening of Mule Shoe and come around to the north. Rick, let us know what happens."

"Yes, sir," he said as he sat comfortably in the saddle on his Appaloosa horse, Apple Pie.

Jess pushed the throttle to the maximum and sped the Cub at the fantastic full speed of 100 mph. Then he banked south and slowed his speed and came back toward the opening of the mule shoe, banking again he continued west, cleared the trees, and came back around to the north of the ridge where they could see Rick.

"The two trespassers scattered and left their long guns in the vehicle. I don't see any holster weapon. I can get one who is heading up my way. The other one is heading toward the opening."

"Okay," Jess replied on the mic, "we'll get the one running out."

Jess pushed in the throttle again gaining altitude and then dove down to five feet off the water heading for the two-legged trespasser. Jess had to pull up sharp to avoid mesquite trees the man ran under.

Juan turned in his seat as Jess banked. "There's enough clearing right between those cacti." He pointed for Jess to see the spot.

Jess set the little aircraft down for a perfect three point landing and spun around as Juan jumped out. He hit the ground and rolled then was up running toward the trespasser who still stood under the tree with his hands high.

In Spanish, Juan hollered for the man to turn around and clasp his hands over his head. Jess turned off the aircraft and got out.

When he got to Juan and the trespasser, the guy was frightened. "Mr. Hanes, I knew we would eventually get caught, but Dad said he had a right to be here."

Juan turned him around to face Jess. "I'm Gary Rowlen's son, your neighbor."

"Well, young man, how old are you now, fifteen or sixteen?" Jess said trying to remember the youngsters name. "Gary Junior, right?"

"Yes, sir, Mr. Hanes, and I'm fourteen."

"Juan, untie his hands, please," Jess motioned and called Rick on his cell phone. "Rick, get your man?"

Rick tried to talk, but the shouting in the back ground was too loud for them to hear him on the speaker. Then they heard Rick say something then the noise was over.

"Sorry, boss, but I had to gag this guy," he said a little out of breath. "He sure looks familiar—an elderly man, gray hair, beard and swearing like a sailor,"

"That's Mr. Rowlen, land owner to our east, across the county road," Jess said and gave young Rowlen some water from a bottle in the aircraft. They had walked under the wing for shade from the noon day sun. "Can you walk him over to us?"

"No, sir, I have him hogtied," he laughed; "Want me to drag him over."

"No, untie his legs and lead him over with a rope around his middle," Jess sort of snickered under his breath. "Don't bruise him."

Young Rowlen laughed too. "It serves him right. We've done this a lot, looking for deer or antelope. Your land is the only one close to home we can shoot and no neighbors would hear it."

"How long have you been doing this," Jess asked and turned to look for Rick.

"I've been over here twice this year, but found nothing to shoot at but Prickly Pears." The youngster said and shuffled his boots in the dirt. "Dad's hopping mad we got caught."

Mr. Rowlen was kicking at the dirt as Rick handed the rope to Jess. "Juan, loosen the rope and untie his hands. Now, young man, learn from your father's mistakes. Don't steal and don't lie for your father."

"Who are you to be telling my son what to do?" Rowlen shouted at Jess and swore. He swung his fist at Jess and missed, only because Jess figured he would do so.

He swung so hard he tripped himself and fell to the ground, Jess pointed at him. "Stay where you are! Otherwise I'll shame you some more in front of your young son. What's wrong with you Gary? I would have given you permission to hunt the Mule Shoe."

"It used to be my land, but you bought it on that bank sale," he said and stood up brushing his dusty face off with his neck bandana. "Just because I couldn't make my payments, the bank put this section up for sale."

"I offered to loan you the money when the bank wouldn't, but you refused me." Jess threw up his hands. "What do you want Gary?"

Jess handed a water bottle.

"Okay, Gary, I'll sell it to your son for half what it cost me; only if you start paying me directly every month. No interest, no strings attached, it will be in your son's name when paid for. Until it's paid, you can hunt here, but only when I know your over here. We have too many problems with rustling and illegals, just like you have on your ranch."

Young Rowlen stepped up to Jess. "I would be glad to work for you Mr. Hanes until I get out of school to help pay for this land."

"Thank you young man, but your father will have to agree to pay for the land, not his son." Jess looked at Gary. "You're not that unreasonable are you Gary?

Jess got a blank look of unbelief from Gary, who turned his back on Jess, murmured under his breath so no one could understand him. He kicked clods of dirt and put his hands on his hips, turned to Jess with a red face. "You're embarrassing me in front of my son. I don't like to be talked down to Mr. Hanes."

"I'm not talking down to you Gary. We were on friendly neighbor terms at one time. My name is still Jess, if you weren't so stubborn. You made your own way with this matter and got caught," Jess said and put out his hand to shake. "You're getting your land back, and what else do you want?"

"Don't fast talk me!" He replied and kept kicking the dirt, not looking Jess in the eye, and would not look at his son. "You making me pay for my land twice!"

"That's not true Gary, and you know it. You know that's your fault for not keeping your payments up with the bank," Jess said still waiting for Gary's hand shake. "You know the end results around here when ranchers are not current on their loans; they always try to sell it out from under you. When I paid off your loan balance, you were some $150,000 behind. I'm surprised they didn't foreclose on your whole ranch long before that."

"Dad, I didn't know you were that far behind," his son grabbed his dad by the shoulder. "Why didn't you tell me, I could have used my savings."

"No way son, that money is for your educations when you graduate from high school," he said and brushed his son's hand away. "I took your Mom's insurance and put it all in your education fund. That is the way the contract is written, the bank can't touch it."

Jess put his hands in his hip pockets. "What's going to satisfy Gary, short of me giving you your land back?" Jess waved his hands. "I can't give the land back to you, Scott-free! I've made too many improvements and we have oil on it now. You couldn't hold it long anyway; monthly taxes are too high now. But, I can make paper work out through a lawyer to have it turned over to your son. With the lawyer's guidance, I think your son is level headed enough to hold onto it."

"I wouldn't have any control over my own land," he swore and threw his hat to the ground. "What makes you think I would agree to such a thing?"

"Unless you have a better suggestion," he nodded to Juan to head for the aircraft. "I think you two should go home and talk it over and we can get together again."

"Sounds good to me; let's get out of here, son," Gary said to his young son. "Mr. Hanes, Jess, meet me at my place for breakfast in the morning about five thirty, and bring your lawyer." He finally looked Jess in the eye.

"We'll be there," Jess said and shook hands with Gray's son. "Nice to see you again, Gary Junior." He nodded to Gary. "Please mend that fence ya'll cut earlier."

Jess and Juan got in the aircraft, buckled in, and waited for the other two to get their four-wheeler out of the swamp end of the Mule Shoe lake. Once they were on the way to the gap in the fence line, Jess turned on the ignition and started the engine of the Piper Cub. It coughed and fired on the second try. Once the engine temperature was in the green, Jess checked the wind direction and made a short field took off. He leveled off a hundred feet above the trees and gained speed, heading for home.

Jess called his range scout, Rick, informed him what happened and to continue his routine watch. He then called his lawyer and explained the neighbor problem and agreed to meet Jess at Gary's ranch at five thirty.

Marie Ann was upset, and it took Jess awhile to get her settled down.

"I knew something was wrong over a year ago when he stopped attending church. His son would attend, but he wouldn't," she said and wrapped her dish towel over her arm, and turned to Jess. "I tried to comfort his Gary Junior who continued to go to church for awhile, and then he stopped coming. He sure misses his mom."

"Didn't you and a couple others from church, go over to the ranch for a visit?" Jess asked as he poured a cup of coffee, and then added two tablespoons of cinnamon cappuccino. "Gary turned down any support from the church. He's definitely a proud rancher, and hard headed."

"Yes, but we were not welcomed at all. Gary senior seemed to be blaming God for all his troubles and Junior was confused and upset with his dad," Marie Ann said and put ice in a tall glass for Jess to pour the coffee mix over it.

"Thanks, love," he said, walking across to the windows over the kitchen sink. "I think he's also blaming me for his loss of the ranch section, and especially when we bought it at the bank without a public notice." He stirred his cold drink and took a long swallow. "I appreciate your prayers for the breakfast tomorrow morning. I'm sure we'll be able to talk about the Lord. I know he misses Liz."

"I already have been doing that since you told me," she said and walked over and put her arm around his waist, looking out toward the western part of their property. "We don't really need all that acreage of his; do we?"

"No, but back then when we bought it, I thought it was a good investment added to our own property. Moreover, I wound up paying more for it because Gary was a good neighbor and a brother in our Lord. Even though we never were close friends, we always sat at the same café table and talked about ranching. Yes, there were times we talked about what Jesus had done for us in our past lives."

"Are you taking Juan with you?"

"Yes, he was invited too," Jess said and lay his almost full glass down and gave her a full tight hug. Nibbling on her ear lobe, he said, "I love you, sweet lady."

She giggled and pushed him away when he breathed down her neck. "You know that puts chills up and down my back."

He attempted to pop her with the dish towel. She turned and pointed a finger at him. "Don't you dare swat me with the wet towel. The last time you put a red welt on my backside." She grabbed the towels end and almost yanked him off his feet.

"Okay, okay, in here! Get out of my kitchen; this is no place for 'horsing around,'" Lolita hollered at them when she entered from the kitchen's back door. "I've got a cake in the oven and sourdough bread raising in the refrigerator.

"Dishes are done, Lolita," Marie Ann said and put the dish towel on a hanger behind the stove.

"I'm sure you two have better things to do than romp around my kitchen, go, go, I've got supper to finish" she said and guided them both by the hand to the dining room archway. She called her two helpers from the porch. "We'll have it ready at six."

Jess waved at her. "How many are you feeding tonight?"

"Twelve hungry cowboys, three of us, and you two...unless someone else shows up," she smiled at them as they left the kitchen. "We'll always have room for more."

She turned to her helpers holding up a slip of paper which she read from. "Senoras, tonight's menu will be tossed salad, country fried steaks, brown gravy, biscuits, corn and wheat tortillas, salsa, mashed potatoes, corn on the cob, green beans, chili red beans, beets and fried okra, banana hot peppers, iced tea, four pies and cake. There should be enough ice cream in the deepfreeze. I think we have enough fresh green onions to put on the table too. I'll put this list on the bulletin board above the counter."

The ladies went to work on the list. Once they had the list mostly done, they set the dining room table with two extra leaves installed to handle the seventeen places to set supper ware.

Mr. Hanes ordered for supper from day one. "Everyone who works this ranch will sit at my table, even if they have children; unless they must be on the job. Security will eat in shifts."

At 5:15 a.m. Monday morning, Jess and Juan was landing at Gary's ranch. His lawyer arrived at the ranch house at five thirty just as Jess walked up on the front porch. Juan flew the plane back to the ranch; Jess would have his lawyer bring him home.

After western omelets, biscuits and gravy were served, the three men retired to Gary's office. He started a fresh pot of coffee while the small talk continued and then sat at his desk. He placed two documents in front of them.

"Gentlemen, thank you for coming for breakfast and agreeing to this short meeting; it's the only way I could settle down and think this through. Before my son, Gary Junior, comes in, would you read the papers in front of you. It's short and to the point. I will sign it and you two will be my witnesses."

He smiled and continued, "Gary Junior will graduate from high school in six months and will be eligible for the military. He is not interested, at this time in his life, in ranching. After his enlistment is over, he may decide to attend college under the G.I. Bill. So, I'm backing off trying to ranch any longer and take an early retirement and find a job in town. I'll move into an apartment temporarily."

"What about your ranch lands that your living on now?" the lawyer asked, "Are you putting it up for sale?"

"No, it will be leased out until I know what Gary's going to be doing. Until then, that money will go into an escrow for him and half into paying for it. I'm not wanting any of the land that I kicked up my heels about yesterday. That was my fault for losing it and it's rightfully Jess' land." He leaned over and recited the document that was in front of them.

Gary Junior walked in. "Dad, sorry to be late for your meeting."

"That's fine, son, your just in time for the signing," he said and introduced Jess' lawyer and asked if there were any more questions.

Jess looked at his lawyer. "How long have we known each other Gary? I know yesterday's run-in was embarrassing for you. I don't think this was necessary for you to write up a formal document. Gary, we could have done this with a handshake. Besides, I would like for you to work for me at the ranch and not give up anything."

"I don't like handout Jess, you know that," Gary said standing up. He poured coffee for them all. "Junior, did you have breakfast and are you ready to catch the bus?"

"I was thinking of taking the pickup today. I need it to get feed this afternoon," he said and took the coffee cup from his dad.

"Yes, I had breakfast and my room is cleaned up. The clothes are ready down in the basement for washing."

"Good, thank you, son. I'll get that taken care of as soon as we are finished here."

"This document will make me feel better and it sets no restrictions on Gary Junior," Gary said and patted his son on the shoulder.

"Dad, may I read it too?"

"Sure," Gary said and handed him his copy, "I'll make you a copy as soon as everyone signs it."

Gary Junior smiled and stood up handing the paper back to his father. "Dad, I'm proud of you," he said and gave him a hug. He was almost as tall as his father, but not as heavy. "I told you our Lord Jesus would take care of us, He always has."

Jess stood up and shook Junior's hand. "Young man, you continue to stand for the Lord, He will continue to take care of you in and out of trouble. Some of us older guys need to be reminded, and often."

"Hey, I've got to go or I'll be late for my first class," he nodded to Jess. "See ya, later, sir." Then he turned to his father. "I'll call on the cell phone when I get ready to go into class."

"Okay son, be careful," Gary said and walked his son to the garage door. "Oh, you have lunch money for this week?"

"Yes, Dad, thank you."

Before he left, they bowed their heads and had a private prayer for God's guidance for the day.

Junior picked up his book's backpack and went out to the garage.

Gary walked back into his office where Jess and the lawyer were standing. "Gentlemen, what do you think about my decision, questions?"

"You've released Jess from all verbal offers made on yesterday's date," the lawyer said nodding to Jess. "It's short and to the point, I don't see any reason not to sign the document."

Gary signed first and then Jess and the lawyer.

They walked out on the front porch and shook hands again, and Gary held onto Jess' hand. "Forgive me Jess? Do you mind if we had prayer before you two leave?"

"Of course not Gary, do it!" the lawyer said.

Jess nodded his agreement. "Yes, Gary, You're forgiven and it's forgotten, in Jesus name. Thank you Lord."

They prayed.

Jess arrived back at the ranch about nine. The lawyer left and Marie Ann opened the kitchen door for him.

"Good morning again," he said and gave her a kiss on the cheek and slid past her to sidle up to Lolita, "Got anymore café?" leaned over her shoulder and sneaked a kiss on her cheek. "Got to keep all my sweethearts happy," and jumped back.

She jumped and her large rounded body shook as if she was shivering, then pointed the wooden spoon at him. "Macho, you full of bean!" She turned where only Marie Ann could see her face and winked.

"The electric coffee pot was just plugged in, so it will be a few minutes yet," Marie Ann said, laughing. "You're about to get a licking young man! Hum, doesn't 'macho' mean 'male animal' in Spanish? And full of beans! Wow!"

He slowly strolled over to check out what she was making, and Lolita pulled a large fork wrapped with steaming Mexican sauerkraut. "Senor open wide, open!"

He knew now what was coming when he got close to the stove. The strong smell of cabbage sauerkraut, but he had never had any made by a big Mexican *Madre* (momma). His eye watered before it was in his mouth and it almost took his breath away from its sourness. He stood there with his eyes watering, chewing and swallowing the delicious mouthful.

Lolita had learned from Marie Ann that he like cooked cabbage, so she fixed a large bowl of sauerkraut for him and anyone else that could get it passed their nose. Marie Ann had no liking for it at all.

Jess finally finished his first big sampling of the specialty and gave her a big hug, at least as much as his arms would go around her.

"Bravo, Lolita...Bravo!" He motioned for one more sample, which she served him with a shy silly girlish giggle.

Marie Ann clapped her hands and let out a yell, dancing around the kitchen table; Lolita followed her and then Jess.

Juan came in the kitchen door to find the kitchen in an uproar. "Senor Hanes, what is all the excitement?"

Jess stopped and wrapped a fork full and came at Juan. "*Amigo*, open up!" When he closed his mouth around the juicy cabbage and pulled it from the fork, he was snorting all the way out side.

Lolita was hollering at him not to spit it out, that Mr. Hanes ate all of his.

They came back into the kitchen with the cabbage in Juan's hand. He looked at Jess with a questioning red face. "You, Senor, eat this stuff?"

Jess could not keep from laughing, took the fork from Juan, and rolled more sauerkraut around it, put it into his mouth and chewed. "Hum, ya, hum, that's good!"

Juan came up close to make sure Jess swallowed what was in his mouth. Jess continued to smile as he downed the last string of cabbage.

Juan left the kitchen whispering Spanish under his breath and tossed what he had in his hand over the back fence. "Flies will not touch that!" he said in Spanish.

Thanksgiving, Christmas, and New Year's was in true Texan style with celebrations and festivals at the ranch for the neighbors and ranch hands on the MJ.

The little Baptist church where they attended did a nativity play on the lawn during the week of Christmas celebration.

The hill country people and visitors around Austin were invited through ads in the newspapers.

They began cruise planning when the new year 2011 broke all temperatures in the area with snow and ice from the northwest. The New England states were digging out of blizzards and hurricane winds along the coast. South Carolina north to New Hampshire big cities were shut down for car and airline traffic.

As long as the cattle on the MJ ranch were fed and watered, they survived. Only once, did Jess and young Ricky have to search for a mother cow and her yearling in the snow. They couldn't fly, so it was done the old fashion way by horseback.

One night under a pup-tent, room only for two men in two bedrolls, they survived the cold and found the lost cattle the next day around noon. It was a cold windy day with sleet and snow.

Rick carried the two-week-old yearling across his saddle with him and Jess led the mother cow by rope tied to his saddle horn. It was after the sun was down when they arrived at a corral built under a cliff overhang, to put them under a cover from the storm.

Back under the ledge, they used the tent to stop the wind from coming around the rock face of the cliff. It also stopped the wind getting into the cave cut in the rock. The back of the open corral shed helped block the wind, sleet and snow from coming further into the cave area. The mother cow and calf moved in with the two horses for warmth behind the barricade they had built.

In the early fall, Jess had his cowboys cut the dead trees for firewood. They cut a couple of cords stacked under the overhang. Ricky built a reflector from a stored tin roof that was replaced the year before. Then he laid logs along the bottom to help keep them in place and stacked more logs for the fire. It was not long before they had a nice hot fire with glowing coals to cook over.

Lolita had prepared them meals for cooking over an open fire and they savored every bite of steak strips wrapped in thick sliced bacon, fried with diced potatoes and onions. When they finished eating they broke up a bale of dry hay and spread it for the bedrolls. Then they broke up another bale of hay for the corral and horses.

They led the cow and calf to the water trough, broke the ice on top and they drank until filled; then they led them back into the warmth of the cave. After Ricky tied the mother cow to the fence in back, he took the horses to water after Jess had taken the saddles off them and left the blanket in place.

Finally, they all got bedded down for the night of rest, but the howling wind kept them all unsettled. By morning, the storm had moved on and the sun shone brightly across the snow and ice. Ice cycles hung from the overhang of the cliff where the sun was melting the ice.

The dripping of the water woke Jess just as his cell phone rang. "Good morning, love. How's things at home?"

"We are all inside and warm. Where are you two?" Marie Ann asked with some concern for them.

"We're at the south rim of the plateau where we rebuilt the corral and put a new roof on the shed. It's nice and cozy in the cave where Ricky built a nice fire for us all. It's real cozy in this bedroll."

"You're not undercover, Jess?"" Marie Ann asked. "You'll catch cold that way."

"Love, don't you remember the overhang from the cliff and the small cave back in here. It's where the old corral used to be. We have dry hay to lay on, warm fire, and a good supper cooked over the open hot coals last night."

"What's that noise in the background," she asked. "It sounds terrible."

"This yearling is getting breakfast from its mama this morning," he replied. "We better get our butts out of these bedrolls and pack up. It will take us at least two hours to get home, so we should be there by lunch time."

"Call me when you're in the saddle again and heading home," she said.

"Yes, love, I'll call ASAP."

The two cowboys broke camp and put the fire out, watered the livestock and headed home. The wind cut a good shallow trench in the knee deep snow toward the ranch house. The first hour went well, but closer to home the snow got deeper and the horses and cattle made slow progress.

By one thirty in the afternoon, they had everyone inside with dry warm clothes and hot Mexican chili, tamales, and cornbread.

Jess finished his meal, and for dessert, he had a tall glass of chilled sweet milk straight from the cow with crumbled cornbread in the glass of milk. Ricky's chili was poured over two fried eggs on top of cornbread; but no milk for him, he was allergic to it.

No work needed to be done, so Marie Ann gave them the rest of the day off. They both slept until supper time at six thirty.

All at the MJ ranch slept comfy and cozy that cold snowy night.

CHAPTER TWENTY-ONE

Winter months of 2010–2011

The Christmas and New Year's slowly came and went with all the excitement of children on the ranch and the football season ending. Jess and Marie Ann took some of the ranch hands to the Bowl Games in Texas and then to the Super Bowl in Indianapolis, Indiana.

The Texas Aggies, (Texas A & M) won the Cotton Bowl game in Arlington, and Texas Tech won the Ticket City Bowl in Dallas, so everyone at the ranch was happy.

The Super Bowl XLV at the Arlington's new cowboys' stadium on February 6 would have the Pittsburg Stealers and the Green Bay Packers. It would be a game Jess and Marie Ann planned to watch on their new 42-inch HD television in their den off the kitchen. All hands and their families were invited.

The blizzard of 2011 was just over, which punished the Southwest, Midwest and east coast with record snowfalls and ice storms. There was a major snowfall every week starting before Christmas and already continuing into February. The football teams were already in town and the game would be played even if the fans did not make it to the stadium.

Some of the ranch hands went home for the holidays, and a couple of them had their families with them on the ranch. The holidays were over except for the cold weather that had settled in. The winter weather forecasted additional snow with blizzard winds. Cattle had to be checked visually before the Super Bowl game, so Jess and Marie Ann bundled up and went out to inspect all the buildings on the ranch for running water, food supplies, and fuel. They were using an army surplus Hummer to travel in. They had an electric generator, front-end electric winch with boom-hoist mounted on the front bumper, and two weeks' supplies stored in the enclosed vehicle so if they were stranded, they would be secured.

Jess gripped the wheel. "Hold on, love, we've got a deep drift to go through in that ravine."

"I'm strapped in and ready, cowboy, but I ain't got no spurs on," she said trying to mimicking his Texas slang.

They hit the drift and the Hummer almost came to a halt until the special snow tires gripped and pulled them through to more solid snow cover surfaces.

"This is the last stop on our list," Jess said and pulled under the cliff hangover, where he spent the night under before Christmas. The snow was deeper now, and he wanted to make sure enough hay bales were out for the cattle. He wanted Marie Ann to see this part of the ranch she had not been to on horseback.

While pushing six large bales from the small barn loft, Jess noticed what looked like sealed wax packages in the corner. They were covered with loose hay/straw from the bales.

He went back over to the edge of the barn's loft. "Hey, love, is there a camera in the glove compartment?"

"I'll look, but I don't remember putting one in," she said and headed to the vehicle. She looked in all the compartments where a camera would be, but there was no camera.

She climbed up the inside ladder to the loft and could hear Jess pulling and carrying a bale to toss out. "No camera, but we have them in our cell phones."

"Thanks for looking," he replied and leaned against the other stacked bales. "This makes me short-winded in this cold air. Yep, I thought about the cell phones too, but a camera would take a better picture. Look over there in the corner behind those bales at the hidden treasure we uncovered."

"Oh, Lord above, not again, I haven't seen packages like this since diving off Fort Pierce." She took her pocket flashlight and got a closer look at the pile. "I count about two dozen. Why don't we use both phones to take pictures to insure we get good shots?"

"Go ahead. I'll alert Juan that we'll have Texas Rangers and border patrol coming out. Then I'll call them."

"Okay, I'll get as many as I can," she replied and took out her cell phone.

"Hello Juan—"

"Boss, we have some unwanted visitors," Juan interrupted Jess. There was some shooting in the background over Juan's cell phone.

"A van load of Mexicans took over the house and Lolita is being held. They want the drugs at the barn where we camped overnight."

"Who is doing the shooting?"

"I don't know, I'm in the basement…" Silence. "You still there, Jess?"

"Yes, are you armed?"

"No, I haven't had a chance to grab a firearm. They're out in the mare's barn shooting. There ain't no ranch hands out there that I know of Jess. They were all at the bunkhouse resting." He was out of breath, running to the fruit cellar door. "I'm going to try and get out the outside door of the fruit cellar. Then I can go around to the door into the garage shop."

"Good idea, there are two rifles and a handgun in the bottom of the big tool box," Jess said and waved to Marie Ann to come next to him. He put the phone on speaker so she could hear.

"Okay, boss, I'll call when I get the weapons ready. I'm worried about Lolita."

"We are too," Marie Ann said into the speaker.

"Mrs. Hanes, pray for her safety," he said and turned off the phone.

Jess called his friend at the Texas Ranger office in Austin and relayed the info. The ranger would round up the border patrol and state police. Jess also told them where he and Marie Ann were located and sent him the photos over the cell phone.

Ranger Captain Wayne said he got the photos and marked the location of Jess and Marie Ann on his map. "We will set up a parameter a mile out from the ranch house and get a helicopter to pick you up."

"How long will that take? I can be at the ranch in about forty-five minutes, if I don't get stuck in a snow bank."

"If we can get there sooner, we'll follow you."

"Land at the east end of the hangar and have them fly low," Jess said and held Marie Ann close.

"Take care, Jess, see you ASAP," the ranger said.

"We're on the way," Jess said and pushed the bales off the floor out into the corral lot. He then closed the barn door and waved Marie Ann over to help cover the drug stash with heavy bales of hay.

They got back in the Hummer and checked their weapons. Marie Ann poured him a cup of hot coffee from a thermos bottle. "Take a few swallows and I'll finish it. Let's go, Jess!"

He pointed to the map. "Let me look at that again. We can take the north road out of here behind Mule Shoe Lake and down that ravine to the east and then make a wide sweep across that open flats and straight down behind the hangars. Hopefully these people will not be using aircraft to get out of here."

He took a couple of swallows of coffee. "Buckle in tight, sweetheart, this may be a rougher ride."

He sped out of the cover of the cliff, dodging cactus, mesquite trees, rocks, and deep gullies. Their ride only took thirty minutes to get to the hangar. The rangers' helicopter was just settling on the deep snow when they all meet inside the hangar.

"Everyone over here…," Jess said, pointing at the wall map. "I have a detailed map of this area."

As Jess was unfolding the map, he said to them all, "Captain Wayne, I'm sure these people have at least one person captive, Lolita. Her husband, Juan, is my ranch foreman. My last report by cell phone, he's in the garage and armed. He is supposed to wait there until reinforcements arrive to help secure his wife's safety."

Jess pointed on the map he hung on the wall. "Here we are and Juan is in this part of the house complex. He can use a basement entrance from the garage, if you want some of your men to support him. I don't know yet how many intruders are in the house or on the outside. I do not know how many friends are with his wife. My ranch hands were in the bunkhouse, here." He pointed to the map.

"Call Juan on your cell phone. Hopefully it's on vibration now," Jess said to Marie Ann. "You and your men get a good look at this layout. I don't want to have this screwed up by not staying informed. How many others do you have coming in?"

"Jess, you have just us five. Can't get any more out because of the roads being closed. No snow removal at all and the forecast is for 6 to 8 more inches this afternoon."

"You men have a place to stay here in the hangar. I have additional men in the bunkhouse." Jess called the bunkhouse and told them what was happening. All seven were accounted for, armed, and were standing by for further instructions. "Okay, everyone, I have the bunkhouse crew on the speaker phone, also Juan can hear."

He paused to clear his throat. "Captain Wayne of the Texas Rangers is here with five combat experienced men. You three, Juan, Mrs. Hanes, and I will work with rangers headed to the garage and house basement. From there, Juan will head for the basemen stairs and then let them go up first to the kitchen. Is everyone armed?"

Everyone answered yes.

"Juan, can you talk?"

"No," he said quietly. "I'm right outside the kitchen door going down to the basement.

"Okay, Juan, stay calm and don't do anything until we get to you. I have rangers with me, understand?"

"Yes, boss," he said as he moved back away from the door into a pantry way. "Someone coming!"

Jess held his finger to his lips for everyone to be quiet and held the phone speaker high so all could hear. They heard the basement door open. A light switch clicked on for the stairs' fluorescent lights. Someone could be heard going down into the basement. Then he called up the stairway in Spanish to bring the two women down to him.

Jess held up two fingers to ensure everyone knew the number of hostages. They all gathered closer to Jess to hear the phone.

Juan could see passed the open door into the basement as Lolita and her helper were pushed down the stairs. Someone swore in Spanish about the women's hands tied and pushing them. Those two men could be heard going back up into the kitchen and someone else told them to leave the door open.

Juan was certain there were three men in the kitchen, but could not see enough passed the door's hinged edge. Someone wanted whiskey, but their boss told them to drink the Gringo's coffee or get water out of the sink. There was grumbling and they all sat at the table, at least all Juan could see. He wanted to linger to find out what they were up to and how many was around.

They were complaining about having to stay in the kitchen. One of them wanted to search upstairs in the bedrooms for jewelry. The boss was emphatic with his swearing they stay in the kitchen.

Juan settled in his own mind there were four men in the kitchen and only one of them seemed to have a firearm. He kept an eye on him through the crack at the door's edge. He could not see all four at one time. The gunman was the only one making demands and he could see the basement door. It was almost like he could see Juan looking at him. He stood rubbing his neck and looking toward the door; they seemed to be waiting for someone.

Who had been shooting out in the corral? Juan did not know and was worried that would be one not accounted for and would be number five.

There was a ledge along the top of the staircase where baskets of fruit were kept, because of the coolness of the staircase. It was dark at the foot of the stairs where it was out of the line of sight of the guy at the table.

Juan was tempted to walk the ledge until he was over the opening at the basement level, then lean over and grab the top of the doorframe and swing into the basement, hopefully landing on his feet. He trained in the 101st Airborne and spent time jumping in Vietnam; he talked himself into trying.

If he could do that and shut the door, bolt it, and untie the women, he could get them to safety.

He remembered the door was metal and was built to withstand tornados and flying debris. He put the cell phone on the shelf behind him with the speaker still on, and began his stepping over bushel baskets along the dark ledge.

He was getting ready to drop down to grab the top of the doorframe when there was a commotion in the kitchen. Their boss ordered one of the men to go down and check the women. Someone slammed the door of the kitchen as the man went down the stairs. He was swearing as Juan dropped behind him, knocking him to the basement floor, landing on the man's back. The weight of Juan knocked the man out.

Juan rolled over and ran to his wife, putting his finger to his lips for them to be quiet. He pulled his Army KaBar Survival knife from its sheath and cut them loose. Then he tied and gagged the man on the floor and then searched him. No weapons found, not even a cheap pocketknife.

Juan grabbed heavy shirts from the fresh clothes laundry basket for the women and led them to the garage. He gave his shotgun to Lolita and went back to the metal door of the basement stairs and bolted it shut.

He retrieved his cell phone from the ledge and ran back to the women and found them a good place to hide in the garage. He called Jess on the garage telephone, telling him where they were and how many men he thought were in the house.

"Stay in the garage. We will split up our force here and go into the house from the basement and rear door at the same time," he said loud enough for everyone to hear.

"Si, Senor Hanes!"

Jess pointed at the ranger. "Captain, you're in charge of this assault now. We have enough men, don't you think?"

"Good, we've got the floor plan of the ground floor and the location of the cellar door in the kitchen," he said and looked it over again. "Take three of my rangers with you into the basement, and I'll call you when we are ready at the front door. I have your key right here." He patted his jacket pocket.

"If we need reinforcements, they're in the bunkhouse," Jess said and then let the cowboys know what was happening.

"Marie Ann, come with us so you can help the ladies in the garage," Jess said.

He nodded to the rangers. "We don't want another Waco! Let's do it!"

One group lead by the ranger captain went toward the front of the house, using the rock fence for cover; the second group with Jess and Marie Ann entered the house garage from the rear.

Jess stopped his group inside the garage. "Listen, shush," he said and pointed to his earpiece. "They see a van out front with the engine running. It doesn't seem like anyone is in it. But they will have to approach it straight on or lose protection going over the fence."

"Wait, give us a few minutes to get in the basement," Jess replied as his group was ready to enter from the garage.

The man still lay on the floor where Juan had left him. Jess' group carried him into the garage and pulled the gag out of his mouth. He was talking in Spanish so fast Juan could not understand him. They finally got him to understand, if he helped, the Texas Rangers would take good care of him.

His eyes were wide and fearful of the Texas Ranger who spoke Spanish and finally calmed him. They searched him for weapons and took his wallet form identification, if he had any. He had no ID and he wouldn't tell them his name.

He got excited again when Juan took a large pocketknife out of his coat and then cut the clothesline rope from around his ankles and wrist. He put him in a chair next to a garage space heater and gave him some day-old hot coffee from the garage kitchen.

Jess pressed him for information. "How many people in house and van out front?"

He swallowed the mouth full of coffee. "*Cinco*—me and four up in house. Nobody in truck outside."

One of the rangers, Sergeant Thomas, suggested they flush the men out of the house toward the front and perhaps out of the front door.

"Tell your captain out front, sounds good to me," Jess said and sat on a work bench, wondering who hired the illegal Mexicans and why they picked his ranch to invade.

"Let's get all these people captured and then I have some more questions for them before you take them to jail," Jess said and waved the rangers toward the garage door to the house basement.

They handcuffed the man to an anvil welled to a metalwork bench and pushed a stool over for him to sit on. The heater was close enough to feel the heat, but he could not reach it to kick it over.

"We will be right back for you," Jess said and followed the men to the basement.

Marie Ann and Lolita were armed. The three lady helpers stayed in the garage with them.

The women talked to the man while the others went in to get the others out of the house. Marie Ann with her limited Spanish from high school tried to follow the conversation and knew Lolita was trying to get more information out of him.

Three of the rangers were to quietly go up the stair once Juan unbolted the basement door. Jess refreshed their memories as to the floor lay out of his home; then they were ready.

Sergeant Thomas called the captain and told them they were in place and were ready to charge up the stairs.

"Now," the sergeant said and the door was flung open and they headed up stairs. "Texas Rangers, you're under arrest."

The four men in the kitchen were still seated at the table, but had all fallen asleep on the tabletop. The noise and shouting caught them off guard and they froze in their seats not knowing where to go. They were all handcuffed in a few seconds and were on the floor, kneeling.

Captain Wayne charged up the front walk and up on the porch as Jess unlocked the door to let them in.

"Hey, Captain, that was a great capture. You rangers did good. How about some fresh coffee while you interrogate these men," Jess said and escorted them to the kitchen.

"Rangers, check the rest of the house," the captain ordered and talked to each of the four separately in another room.

Juan went down and brought the women and their prisoner up from the garage.

"Juan, put guards at the hangar, corrals here, and around the house," Jess ordered. "Make sure they wear extra layers of clothes. I don't want any men with frostbites. Get them relieved every hour or so. Once this is settled and the prisoners gone, we'll all get together for a meeting here in the kitchen."

Marie Ann cleared her throat. "Only after everyone has had something to eat. Lolita, get your special soup heated up with grilled ham cheese sandwiches. I'll get the coffee going."

Then louder over the kitchen commotion, Jess announced, "Everyone gets fed, even the prisoners."

Jess got Marie Ann aside and asked if she mentioned the drugs out in the Mule Shoe corrals to anyone.

"Nope, haven't even thought about them until now. Why?"

"I'll tell the rangers when we get them together, but not in front of the prisoners." He leaned over, kissing her on the cheek.

"Good idea," she said and started fixing the coffee.

Jess went in the room where the captain was talking to the prisoner. A couple of the other rangers were with him. He had them speaking in English, which surprised Jess. He took a seat across the room from the group and listened.

It seems these five men were to meet a truck on the highway and then follow it to get a load of drugs to distribute. It sounded like there was too much snow and they could not get off the road. It was the corral where Jess and Marie Ann had been that morning.

Supposedly, the information from the prisoners was they did not know any names of the supplier or location of the drugs. They knew that it was going north to another state and they would get paid half now and the remainder once they got to that location. All five men were illegals from Monterrey, Nuevo León, Mexico. They were to be given new identifications, driver's licenses, green cards, a place to stay, and free food for their families waiting for them up north.

A Texas Highway Patrol bus pulled up in front just as the prisoners finished eating. They thanked Lolita and Marie Ann for the food and then they were escorted to the bus. Border patrol and INS vehicles pulled up behind the bus and Captain Wayne talked to them. They all left the ranch except for Ranger Thomas.

Ranger Thomas, Juan, Jess, and the ranch hands sat around the huge kitchen table and discussed what had happened and what needed done. They were limited because of the additional snowfall prediction for the night, so Jess suggested he bunk with the cowboys.

Jess sent two of his cowboys out to the Mule Shoe corrals with supplies for six days. They were the most experienced hard weathermen he had and knew they would report any trespassers to Jess for further orders. They both were mountain hunters from Alaska.

A month after the illegals' ordeal, Jess decided to have the Texas Rangers haul off the drugs. He did not want them on his property anymore to bait the bad guys. Law enforcement picked up the drugs at the Mule Shoe corrals after no one showed up to get them.

The ice and snow lasted a month and melted. The earth's greens and browns appeared again. Then the greenery began to come out the first week in March and the hill country of Texas bloomed with the temperature climbing to the fifties and sixties. It would not be long calving and the new life of a new year would start for not only livestock, but also life for God's creatures.

Jess was happy to see the snow and ice leave; he was not a lover of cold weather. He could always bundle up with extra clothes and cold weather boots, but he did not like to play or linger in the cold. He loved the warmth of the sun and warmth of the ground around him.

March meant that Jess and Marie Ann could start planning for their return to the Intracoastal Waterways in the northeast coastline, beginning first with a week or more Civil War relic hunting in the Fredericksburg, Virginia, area.

Jess had already spent quiet winter nights rehearsing where they should go in March for permission to get on their properties, sending those landowners a search and salvage agreement. He and Marie Ann studied the Civil War battles and skirmishes lines west of the Blue Ridge Mountains. That covered miles and miles of uncovered property where a metal detector had never been.

They used old publications like the North South Trader magazine's first issues; old plate maps of early surveyors;, maps used by both Civil War Armies in conjunction with the twenty or more volumes of the Official Records of the Rebellion. Jess had purchased beaten-up copies of these records from old library discards. Marie Ann had purchased him a recent copy of the Atlas that was official document used with the Official Records.

They had accumulated six boxes full of papers with relic contacts and copies of maps. They made sure that wherever they received permission to hunt, that maps were clearly marked with current national park boundaries clearly marked. Each location would have a certified search and salvage agreement attached signed by the landowner. Some of those signatures came from landowners living in foreign countries or other states.

CHAPTER TWENTY-TWO

MJ Ranch – Hill Country, Texas

January and February 2011 were months of weekly snow systems dumping 6 to 12 inches of snow in the hill country. It was third week in February before the ranch roads were in condition for vehicles of any kind.

The Super Bowl party at the ranch was snowed in for three days before Jess and his ranch hands could open one lane to the closest paved Farm Road. Their 48-inch snow blower sheared a pin and had to make one from scratch in the hangar shop.

The real catastrophe came at half time of the Super Bowl game they were watching on a dish network. The snowstorm knocked out their local TV station. The ice and snow covered the ranch house dish, stopping satellite reception, which meant more tracking out in the snow to get snow off the dish. By the time they got the snow off, the game was in the last minutes of the fourth quarter. At least they all were back inside to watch the Green Bay Packers defeat the Pittsburg Stealers. Jess won his bet that the Packers would win.

One of his closest friends back in northern Indiana, Chuck Hernley, a lifetime supporter of the Steelers, has to take Jess out to a steak dinner at the Jalapeños Steak House. It would be awhile before he could collect, maybe in April when Marie Ann and Jess get back up to Shuffleville.

Two elderly chuck wagon cooks owned a restaurant originally from Stetson Hills, Georgia. Their story was as youngsters; they hired on a cattle drive in west Texas. They cooked for the cowboys who drove cattle to the railhead in Abilene Texas, back in 1903.

They got so good at cooking together, when the ole cook died who taught them and owned the chuck wagon, the two young men bought the wagon and supplies from the trail boss. The oil companies that had annual district picnics would have them cater. They did the cooking for almost thirty years, until cattle drives were no more.

They moved north to greener pastures and opened a barbeque stand. It did not take long before they had customers from Chicago ordering their marinated steaks, which, of course, were specially shipped from Abilene to them in Shuffleville.

The winter's months flew by making time for inside work, equipment maintenance and aircraft inspections took priority. Now, Jess assisted in the rounding up of cattle which had newborn calves in early April thru the first week in May.

Marie Ann and Lolita planned the early garden planting to have it produce vegetables, lettuce, spinach, onions, blackeyed peas, cabbage, strawberries, corn and potatoes.

In the fall they 'can' and have a good storage of fresh home grow produce stored in the 'fruit cellar' of the basement. This would help supply all those who lived on the ranch the year around. God always supplied the needs of all those on the ranch and an overflow to share with the neighbors when they were in need.

Texas growing seasons were sometimes very harsh, but the MJ Ranch crops had never failed to produce.

Branding the cattle came in May and they were heavily doctored with a Bag-Balm salve for fast healing. The salving of the cattle usually took a month after branding by the youngest of the cowboys. They were the ones, usually two, who would still be in school and could ride and shoot without endangering themselves or others.

Once the cold weather cleared, Jess sent out a crew of four to work the fence lines. Each year every mile of barbed wire fence and every cedar post were checked for brakes and rotting.

The old WWII power-wagon truck was adapted with a post-hole auger/digger, heavy-duty plow blade and front-end scoop bucket. It pulled a trailer with cedar fence post, rolls of barbed wire, other tools and hardware. It took at least four weeks of steady work to finish the perimeter of the ranch, and two weeks more for the other interior fences.

They graded and plowed the roads and repaired washed out sections of it. The barns, sheds, and corrals were the last to be worked because of extremely hot days.

Jess and Juan made the summer and fall schedule for the ranch hands. They had an annual barbeque on the lawn at the ranch house on June 1. During which time they announce any changes in the work crew for the balance of the long summer months.

It was planned for the crews to switch every six weeks for doing another crew's job. This helped when emergencies came up, everyone should know how to do the job at hand. If any questions or personnel conflicts arose, Jess and Juan would handle the final approval before finalizing the schedule.

The barbeque was always the best from MJ Ranch's kitchen, where Lolita ran the show. If anyone left hungry, it was their own fault. There was always plenty left over for the families to take home.

This summer would be different; Jess and Marie Ann were packed to leave for the northern Virginia area near Fredericksburg. The terrorist activity around Washington D. C. had quieted, but the citizens were still on high alert. They researched and received written permission to continue on up the Hudson River to find other places for treasure hunting.

There were a few restrictions, no removal of historical artifacts, no matter what lay in the ground or on it, no digging; salvaging to the public had ended anywhere near Washington D.C.

Still at the ranch, Jess and Marie Ann sat cozy in front of the fireplace in his den. The only light was from the burning cedar stumps they cut for firewood. It was quiet and peaceful, both in a padded double-rocker watching the embers and sparks of the fire. Two empty large coffee mugs set on the hearth in front of the fireplace.

She had leaned over, snuggled under his arm putting her head on his chest, curled her legs up under her, and then with a deep sigh, she closed her eyes. He pulled an afghan she had made off the back of the rocker and over her feet, legs, hip and arms.

The two lovers, full of spicy barbeque, relaxed, and almost asleep, were suddenly awakened. Marie Ann sat up, holding her stomach. "Is your stomach upset? I ate too much of that hot spicy meat. You want some crackers from the kitchen?"

"No, love, but I'll go get the cracker jar. Lie down and snooze awhile."

Jess scared Lolita when he came into the kitchen. "Oh, Mr. Jess, you surprised me." She had a half gallon of milk from the refrigerator pouring a small glass full, almost spilling it.

"Sorry, *Mamacita*, looks like you need something for your stomach too?"

She smiled and patted his arm. "Juan, mucho hot peppers with the tamales, red beans, and barbeque, she pointed at Jess getting the crackers, "You too?"

"Yes, we two…" Jess held up two fingers. They laughed as she poured another glass for them. "Rest good tonight, God bless you Mr. Hanes."

"You too, Lolita," he said and took the crackers and milk to Marie Ann.

He went up front and glanced out the bay-windows in the foyer before going into the den. Up the road to the west a vehicle had turned off the state road and came across the cattle guard onto the ranch, then stopped. Someone got out, leaving the door opened on the front passenger's side, and then walked to the rear of the vehicle. It was too dark for Jess to know the make of the vehicle, but the passenger got back in. The car backed across the cattle guard and onto the highway. Jess stood watching, wondering what was going on.

Marie Ann had walked into the hall behind him with the afghan around her. "Wha'cha watching so intently, Jess?"

"Someone came across the cattle guard and stopped, then backed out." He turned to her. "Is there a pair of binoculars in that foyer cabinet, bottom drawer?"

"No, that was the extra pair you left on *The Shallows*," she said and pushed up against him to see out.

"Careful, I've got milk," he said and pushed gently back against her.

"I can see the tail light on top of the hill, they are still going," she said and reached for the milk glass. "That looks good," she said as he gave her the glass.

"I smell peanut-butter," she said and snickered. "I would have bet you made some cracker sandwiches."

He handed her one as they headed for the staircase going up to the master bedroom. "I'll be up in a minute, want to get those binoculars in the den. I'll be right up."

He came into the bedroom and walked over to the balcony door which overlooked the front yard toward the west. The vehicle was still headed west. He looked toward the cattle guard and studied the shadows.

He took his handkerchief and wiped the sweat from one side of the window where he had breathed on it. Something was not right and he called Marie Ann to look.

"Wonder who is on the night rover watch tonight?" Jess said as he took out his cell phone. He dialed in the number and it rang only once.

"Yes, Sir Boss. Whacha need?" the voice asked with background noise of the vehicle he was driving. "This is Roberto with Slim."

"Where you located?"

"We're half a mile up the west fence line parallel with the state road. We just checked out the car that came on the ranch. He didn't see us. They must have thought they had a flat and didn't."

"Did you check in the cattle guard to see if they dropped anything in it?"

"No, sir, we didn't." Then he asked Slim if he did. "Neither of us looked. Do you wish for us to return and look?"

"It might not be a bad idea," Jess said. "I'm watching from the front balcony."

Still watching with his binoculars, he told them, "Red lights coming your way on the highway, behind you."

Slim turned on his bright lights and red flashers on the pickups roof. The state trooper pulled over and his partner walked over to the fence. Jess could hear the voice on Roberto's cell phone; he had it on the speaker.

"See a vehicle in the last five minutes going west?"

"Sure did, but they weren't in much of a hurry," Slim yelled back.

"Thanks, see ya later," the other voice said and the red lights sped on westbound.

"Did you hear that, Mr. Hanes?" Roberto asked.

"Go ahead and check that cattle guard. Make sure that nothing was dropped in it. Yes, I heard you loud and clear." He paused and continued, "Keep a good eye to the west and pass this along to your relief." Jess walked back to Marie Ann.

He had his cell phone speaker on too. "The state trooper maybe back, so keep a watch for him. Hang around the main entrance for an hour or so and then let your relief take it from there on the fence. By the way, how are the deer trails in the melting snow?"

"We're making a map and will complete it sometime tomorrow," Roberto replied and signed off.

They closed and locked the door from the balcony.

Jess and Marie Ann turned the bedroom lights off and opened the west curtains to watch. The Hummer used by the night rovers parked behind the high rock entrance wall and turned the lights off. They could clearly see to the west and not be in view from passing vehicles from either way.

Nothing found in the cattle guard after searching with a flood light. The morning crew would check it again.

The remainder of the night brought no trouble and everyone slept peacefully except for the night rovers who were always vigilant. All the full time cowboys had some sort of previous military security training.

The next morning at breakfast, the county and state Cattle Association along with the Texas Rangers, DNR, and DEA were all interviewed on local TV and radio stations. It was a state alert to all ranchers and cattle buyers. Drugs hid on, strapped to, the livestock on the open range herds. They showed photos of cattle wrapped with a thin quilt with drugs sown inside. The quilts were spray-painted the same color as the livestock being covered.

Marie Ann had just set at the table for breakfast as Jess pointed at the TV while he tried to swallow a mouthful of coffee.

He coughed and sputtered, grabbed a napkin to put over his mouth. He was choking, trying to breath. Marie Ann slapped him hard a couple time between the shoulder blades which did not help. Then she tried the Heimlich Maneuver and dislodged the air bubble in Jess throat. By then, they both were on their knees, as Jess was too weak to stand. Tears streamed down his face from the pain.

She had him lean back against her between her knees as she washed his face with a damp towel which Lolita had handed her. It happened so fast she did not know what Marie Ann was doing, trying to tease Mr. Hanes or kill him.

"Oh my Lord Jesus," Lolita kept repeating as she sat knelling next to Marie Ann.

"Jess, don't try to talk, just nod to me. Can you breathe now?" she asked and handed the wet towel to Lolita. "Fan him with this wet dowel, we got to get him cooled down. His pulse rate is still high."

Jess was white as a sheet and was trying to breathe deep. Every time he tried he had to force himself to not cough. His throat was sore from coughing so hard and too much. Marie Ann reached for the wet towel again to wash his face when he finally opened his eyes.

"Lord Jesus, thank you! I can breathe again," he grabbed her hand as she washed his face again. "I love you, sweet lady."

"We all love you, Jess," Marie Ann replied and squeezed his hand. "You scared us."

He tried to laugh. "I scared myself. I should know after all these years I can't drink anything and try to talk at the same time."

His breathing regulated as well as his heartbeat.

"Lolita, the blood pressure tester is in the pantry. It should be up on the top shelf with the first aid stuff. Would you get it for me, please?"

She got her large body from off her knees as if she was light as a feather. "Yes, yes, I know where it is. Yes, yes…," she said, going to the pantry.

It was a good thing nothing was in her way to the pantry and back, they would have been flattened to the floor.

She knelt to Jess' left arm. "Mr. Hanes, remember, I once was a full time nurse before working on ranches?" she said sliding the device over his arm. "Try to continue relaxing, Mr. Hanes. You are a good man; God is not ready to take you home. He has more plans for your life than what you could imagine." She held his hand to make sure he did not make a fist, and forced him to keep his hand open. Then she pressed the switch for the machine to pump.

Marie Ann felt him suddenly relax against her. Thinking he may have passed out. "Jess how do you feel now?"

"Just talked myself into relaxing some more," he said and smiled. "Your legs are going to go to sleep if I continue to lay here like this."

"Just be still until your nurse tells you what you can do?" she said and put the folded cool towel across his forehead. "I'm doing just fine."

"174 over 86 isn't extreme, but high enough for your age and physical shape," Lolita said professionally. "I'll fix you a light breakfast for this morning. How would you like two poached eggs on toast, half a cup of coffee, and then your daily vitamins?"

"Yes, ma'am, I can do that with no problem," he said and straightened up while Lolita removed the blood pressure machine.

"I'll hop right up from here and dance a jig," he laughed as he slowly used the table top and chair to lift himself off the floor. The ladies lifted under his arms to help. He pulled his chair under him and sat down slowly.

"I'm still a bit light headed," he said as Lolita massaged where he pointed over his shoulder." I think I loosened up some things between my shoulder blades in the back."

Lolita's thumbs and fingers worked tenderly like a good soft tissue Chiropractor would.

She ran her hand very close over his spine, looking for hot spots she said, "Hum-de-dum-dum, Mr. Hanes, you're still tight as drum. Take a couple of deep breaths and lean across the table with your arms reaching for the other side," she said leading his arm placement on the large oak table.

Juan walked into the kitchen as his wife found tender pressure points and massaged them. He walked over to Jess and whispered in his ear, "She is not for sale or hire!"

"Well, I was misled," Jess said and started to raise up. She gently pushed him back to the table top. "I'm not finished, just one more spot, right here."

Jess felt the pressure increase as the muscle and tendons relaxed. It hurt at first, but then the pain left "I'll go to sleep right here."

"No sir, not on my kitchen table," Lolita said and helped him set up slowly. "I will serve you in bed Mr. Hanes," and she was quick to add, "With Mrs. Hanes assistance."

She looked at Juan. "Please assist him upstairs. He had a bad coughing spell choking on coffee."

"Hold my arm Jess," Juan said, and lifted him.

The four went upstairs where they let him lay down with two pillows under his head. The other two went back to the kitchen, and Marie Ann stayed behind as Jess closed his eyes. She prayed for the Lord Jesus to put His hands on Jess for His special healing and peace. Jess dozed off. She sat with him an hour and then went down to the kitchen.

"What did Jess see on the television to cause him to get so excited and start to cough so violently?" Marie Ann asked Lolita as they both continued breakfast for the cowboys who came in by shifts.

"Something about drugs on cattle's back," she said and turned to Juan. "Did you see the news out in the bunk house?"

"Yes, they said there is a drug blanket that the drug cartel is using in the hill country to hide drugs." He replied and scooted back from the table after finishing breakfast. "Tell Mr. Jess I need to talk to him as soon as possible about the drug problems in our county. I have heard about this from our cowhands when they've been in town. We'll have to double check our livestock for this drug problem."

"Didn't you see anything unusual while branding," Lolita asked and took dirty dishes from the table.

Juan kissed her on the check. "Yes, we do check each one even if it needs branded or not."

He nodded and said good morning to the men coming in for breakfast.

Three other cowboys came in as Juan started to the kitchen. "Men, pass the word…Everyone meet me at the bunk house after breakfast…in an hour."

They acknowledged his orders and sat down for a hearty meal. After the kitchen cleared, Lolita started preparing lunch when Marie Ann came in. They talked about the drug problems flooding Texas and being a problem for all the ranchers.

"Jess will be down for lunch. So then we'll find out what he has in mind for our MJ spread," Marie Ann said while making a potato salad.

When lunch was over, Jess had all the ranch hands meet in the hangar office where he had a large wall map of the ranch. The snow was almost gone, except for the shadowed areas and the ground was not frozen. This made their efforts for checking each head of cattle much easier.

"We should be able to get this done today. Most of the herd is corralled somewhere and not out roaming around. I don't think this drug problem has hit our spread yet, but let's make sure they haven't sneaked in on us." Jess turned to the map and began assigning groups of coverage. There were six groups of three, either on horseback or in vehicles.

They would leave early the next morning after breakfast. Three meals made for each man in case some had to be out overnight.

"Okay, for the rest of today, make sure all your equipment is ready, vehicles, saddles, radios and firearms."

He raised his hands for added attention to what he had to say. "Gentlemen, you're professional cowhands, let's get the job done and back in safely. Be critical what you see that needs to be taken care of to prevent trespassing and injury to our cattle. This is your range too, you live here and it provides for us all, let's keep it that way." He raised his voice. "You younger hands be extra careful what you're pointing your weapons at, we don't want anyone shot. If you have time to do so, call in first before you fire at anyone. If you are shot at, return fire and call in, let the rest of us know what's happening and we'll come to your aid." He put up his hands again. "Understood, any questions before we separate?"

A young cowboy stood. "Mr. Hanes, if someone is shooting at me, should I shoot back to kill?"

"Johnny, if you don't, you better scare him to death with your shots. Remember, if someone starts to shoot at you on our spread, they shouldn't be here to start with. You have a right to protect yourself and those you're with. Get on the radio or your cell phone and let the rest of us know what's happening, okay?"

"Yes, sir, I understand Mr. Hanes."

"Anybody else have questions? If not, let's get to work," he said and waved Juan over to him.

"Take that young Johnny with you. We haven't been on this high alert since he hired on. Even though he was with the 101st Airborne Security in Afghanistan, we need to guide him some. I'm sure he has some talents he can share with us, but not right now, I hope. Feel him out about our setup. I think he will work out fine."

Jess walked back to the house thinking about what possibilities could happen and spoke a short prayer to the Lord, "Father, in Jesus name keep me, keep us, from being deceived. Keep your loving arms around our family here on the ranch. Thank you."

Jess had everyone assemble in the main house kitchen for a meeting before the evening meal. He needed everyone's detailed report on their day's search of the cattle. There were reports of drugs found on the cattle.

"All in all, we have good coverage of the ranch spread, so if you men hear or see gaps that need to be plugged, take care of it now. Please don't hesitate to let Juan or me know ASAP. We can stay ahead of the drug traffic through the hill country, but we got to stay vigilant and alert."

He pushed away from the table and stood. "Any questions?" He glanced around the table. "If not, okay ladies, you can have your table back. Let's wash up, guys."

It only took fifteen minutes for the ladies to get the supper on the table and called everyone back in to eat. Fifteen were seated on each side with two on the end, saved for Jess. He prayed and the meal was served. Jess also had thanked the Lord for the good report on the cattle.

The months flew by without any more unusual activities on the ranch. The April and May spring flowers and pastures green was beautiful from the moisture left from the abundance of snow. Jess and Marie Ann were now making plans to get *The Shallows* out of storage in Virginia and readied for completion of the Great American Loop Cruise.

CHAPTER TWENTY-THREE

Fredericksburg, Virginia, to Chesapeake City, Maryland

In Owens, Virginia, *The Shallows* crew finished loading fuel, groceries, and fresh water. All the systems checked out by the marina's staff were ready. Jess and Marie Ann were ready to drop lines and head out for the Chesapeake Bay to head north. The previous night they rehearsed the routes to take up to the Hudson Bay and New York City.

They would have to come back to Fredericksburg in the fall to hunt for Civil War relics. Construction of new roads, mall parking lots and new housing developments, caused metal detecting for relics to come to a halt. The areas hunted by Jess the last time in the area, some twenty years ago, just were not available to hunters of treasures left from the Civil War.

They left Owens, Virginia, at five and ate two fresh homemade breakfast biscuits with three thick slices of bacon and a fried egg inside. The biscuits washed down easily with two cups of fresh brewed coffee and enough to last until noon.

They headed straight across the Potomac River to Morgantown and then followed the coastline to Point Look Out, approximately 45 nm southeast. It was an uneventful cruise at 14 knots until the southern winds began to buff the starboard bow. This slowed them two knots, so Jess raised the rpm's to 18 knots.

When they turned north at Point Look Out into the Chesapeake Bay, they confirmed the course to Cambridge, Maryland, approximately 55 nm on the west shoreline of the bay. The wind now was following, pushing them. It had increased to 12 knots and they rode the swells up the middle of the bay. Jess began steering closer to the shoreline on the starboard side.

They tied up to the marina just before six thirty that evening in time for a lobster cook out. Even though Jess could not eat shelled seafood, he enjoyed the other fish served. Marie Ann had her plate full of assorted seafood's she had never tasted before; some she liked and others she promised never to pass her lips again.

By the time they got back on board *The Shallows*, it had been refueled and washed down. The wash down was a free offer to get cruisers to tie up to their marina.

Jess and Marie Ann wanted to see some of the historical sites in the area. Their plan was for an overnight stay and onto Annapolis, but the Yacht basin was filled because of activities at the Academy and over in Washington D.C., so they lingered in Cambridge for three days longer.

The trip to Cambridge was easy on the crew, no bad weather or headwinds. They slept soundly with only the continuous waves lightly lapping the marina wall.

The following morning the local Coast Guard Station posted a small craft advisory. They were actually in a 'safe haven' where they were protected from the southeasterly winds coming up the Chesapeake Bay. The low-pressure system was a slow one and it would be hanging around for a couple more days.

The Hanes' just hunkered down and stayed onboard *The Shallows*. They only did a limited amount of touring, spending most of the time on a tour bus. They spend a lot of time lingering in antique and pawn shops. The local community did not seem to consider the terrorist bombing in Washington D.C. was a problem for them to worry about; business as usual and no signs of people alert to any danger of questionable activity in their area.

They asked some of the shops owners and employees where they considered the best eating-place was located on the main street. They all said, "Two Anchor Bar and Grill toward the waterfront."

They found out while eating and talking to the people in the Bar and Grill about the name of Two Anchors that during a hurricane back in the 1800s caused the bay to flood the area. They actually had to chain two anchors to the building to keep it from floating away.

Their lunch specialty was a huge half-pound hamburger on a grilled half bun, covered with chopped unions, six slices of thick bacon, pepper jack cheese, sliced mild banana peppers, crushed corn chips sprinkled on top, sour dill pickles, and a taco sauce poured over it all. It had to be eaten with a knife and fork; juice's dripping soaked up the grilled bun.

The order was too big; they took half in a 'doggy-bag' back to the boat. Half of the order filled them both for $5.99. They had been warned ahead of time about the size of the meals.

The cook came out and talked to them for a while because he was interested in a Nordic Tug trawler. They asked him to drop by for breakfast the next morning, but he could not make it.

Jess' old contacts at business of Metal Detectors of Delaware were long ago closed and to find new friendly contacts was a chore.

"Did you read these state laws of Delaware and Maryland?" Jess asked Marie Ann while using the computer. "I've tried these last three locations in Delaware and no answering machines. I sent emails this morning and haven't received anything back. I'll try this FaceBook again. Maybe it will get me someone that will talk about treasure hunting up here."

She was on a bar stool at the kitchen island running her laptop. "I read them earlier. Some treasure hunters in the past sure had made the laws tight. The way I read those references, we better not be caught on the Delaware beach with a metal detector. Don't even kick over a sea shell or you'll be breaking the law."

"Over the last thirty-five years, metal detecting has gotten more bad publicity. How many times have we jumped someone who got on private property as though it belonged to them? Asking permission from the owner is no longer the thing to do."

Jess got up and poured more sun tea, offering to pour her some. She shook her head no. "That one guy told us, 'It's a waste of my time to ask. If I get caught, big deal.'"

"There is bound to be someone here on the Maryland and Delaware border we can contact. Let's spend another hour or so on researching and then eat that other hamburger we brought back. It's almost six. The news is on now," she said, stretched, got up and went over to him.

"This could get us stressed out again on the actions of such selfish people." She knelt on the couch next to him and massaged his neck. "As long as we continue to work the hobby within the laws, we can be at peace about doing our treasure hunting." She kissed him on the back of the neck and put her arms under his. "Listen, it sure has gotten quiet outside. I don't even hear the water splashing under the pier."

She moved away and he turned his computer off and followed her out on the aft deck. She was right, the harbor was like glass, not a ripple and the sky to the north was blue. The sun in the west was shining under a line of black clouds on the horizon.

She went back in and turned on the satellite TV and tuned in a local weather report, and then went up to the pilothouse and looked at the weather monitor. "It looks like we get some high winds again later this evening. We better check our lines again and bumpers."

She went back out; Jess had climbed up to the flybridge. She went up to him. "Did you hear me about the weather report?"

"No, love, I didn't hear you," he said, pulling her to him. "What did you find?"

"We may get a storm coming up the coast. Maybe it will go out to sea before it gets here," she said snuggling close again. "You hungry enough for that other half hamburger, or do you want to wait?"

"Let me see." He looked at his watch. "Six hours ago? I might be able to do a job on helping you eat half, with some more of your tea."

"I think we have some fresh corn chips, those on the burger are probably plenty soaked by now."

Jess escorted her down to the galley/kitchen again. "The cook sure fixed that up nice for us to bring home. It may not be soaked at all."

She got it out of the refrigerator and opened it. "It still looks good to me and it's not soggy."

"Gunsmoke is coming on," Jess said and poured the iced tea. "Notice at the start, Marshal Dillon never draws first. He always lets the other guy shoot first then he fires his 45 Colt…watch, here he goes." He pointed at the TV screen. "There, see that?"

"Yeah, I bet he does that every time they start the show," she teased. "Is he good enough to do that every time?"

"I bet he does it again tomorrow night," he said, and then snickers. "Bet he don't either, cause tomorrow is not the night he is on."

"He's on every night, what are you talking about," she looked at him. "Jess…you!"

They enjoyed the hamburger and Gunsmoke, and then settled in for a two-hour movie, National Treasure. It was going on eleven when they finally started to bed. It was 74 degrees and neither of them had worked up a sweat all day, so they did not shower before rolling into bed.

"We should have rode the stationary bike before getting in bed," she teased.

"Then we would have to take another shower," he replied.

She laughed out loud and poked him with her elbow. "What do you mean 'another show'? You haven't had one today."

"Yeah, I mean I had one yesterday, and tonight I would be taking the second one this week."

She elbowed him again. "Go to sleep feller. You're working up another sweat." She leaned over and kissed him passionately.

That did it!

They fell asleep in each other's arms.

After two days of rest and not having to fight bad weather at their marina's berth, they navigated out for Chesapeake City, on the C & D Canal. It was an uneventful cruise up the Chesapeake Bay even though they had choppy following seas and winds all the way to the canal.

They anchored in the Chesapeake Inn Restaurant & Marina area until a 65-foot cruiser left a berthing spot. It was only an hour wait, but worth it. They tied up to the outer pier with all the amenities for cruiser's vessels. From the Internet info Marie Ann had obtained, the marina was the best available before entering the Delaware Bay to go south to Cape May, New Jersey. Everything they read and heard from other cruisers, the Delaware Bay would be a rough 50-mile trip. They wanted to make sure everything was shipshape for the run and planned for a two-day layover at this marina in Chesapeake City.

Crews from two other yachts came in together, tied up at the marina and refueled. Jess and Marie Ann were watching them from the marina's restaurant's patio, which overlooked the slips. The crews took empty tables next to Jess and Marie Ann, who noticed how clean and well dress they were. They looked more like passengers than a working crew.

From the occupants that just sat at the two tables, Jess and Marie Ann figured they were on a pleasure cruise and were not the working crew from the two large ship's that just docked. The two vessels were flying British flags.

Jess tapped one gentleman's shoulder from behind. "Excuse me, please. Which direction did you come in from, Chesapeake Bay or Delaware Bay?"

The slight of a man turned. "Well, sir, the Delaware from the Atlantic. It was a very rough ride with following seas. And you, sir, what vessel do you command?"

Jess pointed passed the white jacketed gentleman toward *The Shallows*. "Our vessel is the 42-foot Nordic Tug on pier one, slip six."

He stood and then sat again. "Oh yes, the little white one out on the end. I'm afraid I would be deathly sick riding on that bobber. It's bad enough on that 72-foot dreadful thing we are on now."

The well-dressed lady next to him in a bright-colored flowered dress said, "Charles, don't be such a sissy. Just because you do not care for the tossing about, do not bother others with the matter."

"I am sorry, sir, for being so pushy about the rough water," he said and extended his hand to Jess. He tilted his hat to Marie Ann. "Sorry, madam, I'm not custom to such small quarters as we have on that boat. I'm a banker from Dublin, Ireland. I do need open space as I have back home. You understand, riding stables and all that?"

Marie Ann replied, "It took me a long time to get accustomed to the swaying and rocking. I've been sea sick quiet often." She reached out to him and offered, "I'm Marie Ann and this is my husband, Jess Hanes from Texas."

"Oh my goodness, a real Texan. Where did you tie up your mount?" one of the other ladies teased.

"Our little mount is the white Nordic Tug at the end of the pier, *The Shallows*."

"How fast is it, my dear?" the lady asked.

"It's built for leisure, not speed. We have a maximum speed of 20 knots and a draft of 4 feet 3 inches with a 650 horsepower diesel engine. It's range is 1,500 nautical miles at 15 knots. We can feed and sleep six passengers very comfortably, with all the amenities of home. Our little Tug will take us to most anywhere comfortably and safely. Commodore Hanes at your service," she said pointing to Jess.

The gentleman seated next to Jess clapped his hands. "Is she for hire…very good, very good." He turned to the lady that spoke to Marie Ann, "You are not very polite and you should be. Remember, you are not in Great Britain now."

She turned in her seat away from him toward Jess. "What can you tell me about Texas? I have never been there. Is it all barren country and dry like North Africa?"

"Yes and no, Texas is a large area, which covers beautiful shoreline, swamps, hills, plains, mountains, and deserts. It all has its own beauty, like Morocco, North Africa. They too have the Atlas Mountains, sea shores, rolling plains and hills, and then the Sahara Desert. They have very friendly people and a wonderful history. Some years ago, as you probably know, they too finally got their freedom and independence from the rule of France."

One of the other members from their table, a young man in his teen years said, "Sir, you speak as if you know the country of Morocco and the Sahara."

"Yes, I spent 31 months there while serving the United States. I took special commercial tours while there and then later I returned in my own mode of transportation and spent more time with the people." He sipped his iced tea. "I had a job to do with the Navy, but my off duty time I roamed the country from the beached cliffs on the west coast to the high Atlas mountains in the east. I've traveled by air, automobile, bicycle, and camel. And, I've been fortunate to travel the Sahara from Fort MacMahon to Algiers, Algeria."

Jess had all their attention when he said, "I'm not only retired military, but we," he pointed to Marie Ann and himself, "own a sizable ranch in the hill country of Texas. We also are professional treasure hunters. Searching wreckage of Spanish galleons to buried gold coins in Mobile, Alabama, to prospecting for gold in Arizona. We've hunted for buried munitions, bazooka rockets, to finding someone's wedding rings they lost and couldn't find. We have returned school rings that have been lost by graduates."

Marie Ann scooted closer to Jess. "We are now treasure hunting *The Shallows* of the Eastern United States."

The young lady with the teenage boy, maybe his sister, said, "Shallows, what do you mean 'shallows'?" Her eyes were getting bigger.

"The shallow waters of the rivers and lakes and the shores of the Atlantic Ocean to the shores of the Delaware Bay," Marie Ann said and produced a Cape May diamond, which hung around her neck. "We are going back to Cape May to find more of these. We not only use metal detectors, but sand scoop on the beaches."

The two captains from the two vessels the passengers were on arrived at their tables. They heard some of what Jess and Marie Ann had been sharing. They pulled chairs from another table and sat next to Jess.

One of them put out his hand to Jess. "I've never met you, but I've read your two novels about treasure hunting Mr. Hanes. I did enjoy them very much." He smiled and continued, "I'm Steve Rogers, skipper and owner of those two yachts we just berthed across from you."

He motioned to the other captain. "Captain Wayne Hurst, my partner, Mr. Hanes." Jess shook his hand. "What are you doing up in this part of the east coast, I bet it's looking for sunken vessels?"

"Only if it's in shallow waters, 30 feet or less," Jess said and sipped his iced tea again. "We are using a Hookah Rig, not scuba tanks. We have low-pressure air regulators with 125 feet of hose fed down to us, which is attached to an air compressor/pump. Two divers can work for three or four hours without worry of lack of air. We only come up for food and water. We have to do as much as possible before the weather and tides change."

Jess and Marie Ann were quiet, giving the others time to think about what they had shared. The two boat captains were growing very interested in what this captain of *The Shallows* had to say. The passengers had never talked to a treasure hunter, much less a Texan.

There were twelve passengers, three captains and a very experienced 1st Mate who moved their party to a distant long table for better privacy. It was along the railing where they could watch their vessels, because it was getting dark.

The waitress came over again to take orders. "We are going to turn on the colored balcony lights. Here is a box of clothes dryer napkins to help keep the bugs away, like mosquitoes. If you put them under the salt and pepper shakers they should be close enough to everyone to help keep them away. I put one under my collar," she said and pulled her shirt collar away for everyone to see.

"Is everyone ready for chow, we will serve you for three more hours, then we close the kitchen?"

Everyone ordered and the gentleman from England paid the bill. They continued the treasure hunting conversations until midnight. Finally, Marie Ann held up her hand and stood. "Hey, I vote to close this meeting for tonight and head for a shower and bed."

No one opposed her motion to adjourn. They agreed to meet for breakfast at eight. In all those hours, not everyone's name was shared, which Marie Ann promised would be addressed at breakfast.

Jess and Marie Ann put together a quick treasure hunting presentation for the breakfast group and went to bed. It was a short night, but they both slept soundly, too soundly... They were awaken at six thirty with a pounding on the salon aft deck door.

Jess grabbed his bathrobe and faced a local Harbor Police Officer. "Mr. Hanes, your lines have been cut and your boat is in the beach sand. I can pull you back to your berthing at the marina." He handed Jess the cut end of one spring-line, the other end still wrapped around the cleat.

"I'll get my clothes on and be right out. Thank you officer."

Jess ran back down to the Master bedroom and put his clothes on. Marie Ann was two steps ahead of him.

They went out on the main deck aft and surveyed the cut lines. It did not seem anything was damaged, just cut lines.

"Whoever it was either took our electrical shore-cables or they're still on the dock." Marie Ann pointed out to Jess and the officer."

He waved from his motor-launch as he tied the lines she threw to him for towing. Jess went into the pilothouse and turned on the engine. He then reset the electrical ship-to-shore circuit breaker that had tripped during the night. For some reason the alarm did not sound to warn them that they had lost electrical power from the pier. The wind had blown them across the small bay area.

The officer moved his motor-launch to tighten the lines attached to the bow of the Nordic Tug. By now, they had drown a crowd of watchers on the beach and cars on the street stopped to watch. Slowly the bow came loose from the sand slid back into the water. The officer pulled the Tug out into the bays deeper water and unfastened his end of the line, tossing it into the water for Marie Ann to take in.

Jess pushed the throttle to 'forward' and headed back to their berth at the marina. They had been blown across 400 feet of open water to the beach. In a short time, Jess had the port side against the pier. Marie Ann had taken new rope/line from storage and replaced the cut lines. They tied up and the officer promptly asked permission to go aboard.

"Sergeant Spivey, sir." He shook hands with Jess and Marie Ann. "This is the first 'line cutting' report since I've been on the River Harbor Patrol; some six years now." He pulled out a pad to write on and scribbled some notes. "I don't think we need to get the Coast Guard involved at this point. May I check the deck up and the pilothouse? You probably haven't had time to look over everything?"

Jess smiled. "We haven't even had our morning coffee, ain't that a shame?" Jess opened the starboard sliding door and waved the officer inside. "The small shore boat is still lashed down on top and I don't yet see anything missing or broken."

He opened the folder with all the certifications, title of the boat, insurance card and other papers, and then laid it on the helm counter top.

"I'm sure that is all up to date, Mr. Hanes," he reached over and closed the folder. "Did you seem to have any problems with the group you were talking with last evening at the restaurant?" he asked while looking at the monitors and instrument panel. "Nice layout in here Skipper," he said and turned to Jess.

Marie Ann brought up two cups of coffee handing them to the two men. "Officer, do you need sugar or cream?"

"No thank you, just black is fine," he replied and waited for a reply from Jess.

Jess looked at Marie Ann. "No, I don't recall having any problems last night with the group we were with. Everyone seemed to be interested in our sharing treasure hunting tails."

"Treasure Hunters, do you have a Maryland Permit for removing artifacts in this area?"

"No, sir, we don't mainly because we have not secured a location as yet. We've been interested in the Civil War activities and haven't been to the local museums and library for research. I haven't found anyone here in Chesapeake City who is a metal detector dealer. Usually, they are our first contacts to get leads as to where to go," Jess said and before either man could continue, Marie Ann spoke up.

"As professional treasure hunters we always make arrangements, after a lot of research, to contact local metal detector dealers, Civil War clubs, museums and law enforcement," she said and took a swallow of coffee while holding up her other hand's finger. "We also us a search and salvage agreement with the land owners."

Officer Spivey leaned against the helm's countertop. "It seems you two are not fly-by-night treasure hunters like we have around here. This I do appreciate and will inform my boss at headquarters. I have something for you that will authorize you on Maryland shorelines. May I see your driver's license and captain's certificate?"

Jess handed him the two cards and Officer Spivey wrote the information down and then used his cell phone to talk to someone in their headquarters. "And be sure that paperwork is hand delivered to the Chesapeake Bay Inn Marina ASAP. I'll be coming back by here to check that it's here. Thank you, Ms. Overton."

He handed Jess a receipt for the paperwork that was to be delivered, and put his hat back on his balding head. "Between now and the time you do any metal detecting, go on the Internet and read up on our state shoreline laws. Call me if you have questions or difficulty getting approval to get on property of the state or federal lands. I'm also a deputy U.S. Marshal with strings attached to most anywhere."

He shook their hands. "By the way, there is no cost for that paperwork. So, whoever delivers it, and they want money, tell them to call me. Marshall Madilene Ash said you were good people and for us to take care of you."

Jess and Marie Ann looked at each other. "Is she here, can we see her?"

He shook his head no. "She's on an Asian flight bringing back a hostage from Baghdad." He started to get up on the dock. "Also, this cutting of your lines is probably a local problem. We think it is some young kids playing around from a New Jersey school that is in competition with our local schools. They will slip up and one of these 'ole timers' around here will hang them out to dry." He waved. "I'll keep in touch, see you later."

"Thank you, Sergeant Spivey," Jess said waving back to him.

They turned and gave each other a hug. Jess kissed her tenderly and turned looking up toward the big crowd on the patio deck of the restaurant.

"Is there any reason we can't go get breakfast?" Jess asked and pointed to the two ship's crew up on the restaurant's patio.

The crews waved for them to come on up.

While Marie Ann plugged in the electric from the pier and turned it on, Jess went in and got their box of 'show & tell'. It was about treasure hunting for the British crew at breakfast. He then made sure the doors were locked and they headed up the pier for breakfast.

Walking up the pier to the restaurant, Marie Ann hugged Jess' arm. "Did you notice this morning, if the electric cables were disconnected and lay neatly on the main deck?"

"Yes, I did and dismissed it at the time because of the rush to get us off the beach." He hugged her back. "You're right, someone didn't want to get shocked by cutting those cables. They sure were quiet at their messing around."

"So, it could have been school kids that did it?" she added.

Jess nodded his head. "That's what the marshal thinks, but I'm not comfortable with his nonchalant comment about it, like it was not an everyday occurrence."

They mingled with the crew from the other yachts and found out they had arranged for a room inside for everyone. Breakfast would be served buffet style and everyone would feel more comfortable than ordering.

Jess and Marie Ann were motioned to the head of the line and they accepted the offer. The two yacht captains motioned for them to sit at their table close to the windows overlooking the anchorage. The table set eight, which offered for good conversation. Once everyone had finished eating and set back for fresh coffee to be served, the conversations quieted down.

Jess and Marie Ann stood, and then were introduced again formally to everyone, individually, as the tables were pushed together to be combined for laying the treasure finds on. Once arranged, they took turns telling the story behind each item and then passed them around for everyone to handle and inspected. They spread assorted sizes of Spanish reale and Escudo coins, jewelry, U.S. coins, small toys, date nails, Civil War lead bullets

(Minnie balls), small gold nuggets, and small 3-pound bags of Alaskan concentrate gold ore for sale.

These bags had small nuggets, not flakes of gold that needed a magnifier to find them. If they sold any bags of gold, they would not have to share the sale with the restaurant and marina.

Once the items had been discussed and passed around, they demonstrated one of White's Electronics' metal detectors, the Tracker MXT model, and then the Beach Hunter. They used some of the items on the table to show how the metal detector worked in the three modes: coins and jewelry, relics and prospecting.

After the show and tell, Marie Ann took three orders for metal detectors and Jess took orders for six bags of gold concentrate. It was worth their time to share treasure hunting to the sea travelers. Some wanted a demonstration of detectors on the marina's white beach; also half of the crew wanted to know how to use the gold pan for panning gold. *The Shallows'* crew was busy for the rest of the afternoon.

Before the afternoon was over, there was a large crowd of people watching from the beach and bridge. The marina restaurant played fifties and sixties music over their speakers for the beach. *The Shallows* crew made a hit.

When they got back to their Nordic Tug, they not only had cash for sales, but addresses, email and telephone numbers of the crew from both yachts. They had made friends with individuals and friends from Great Britain, plus both yacht captains were eager to keep in contact with them.

Through the whole day, there was only one person who was 'sour' from the time they got to the breakfast, until the end of the beach party with the detectors and gold panning..., Mrs. Worthington.

Mrs. Lacy Worthington was from England and could not believe Jess was a true Texan because he did not talk like a Texan. He looked and dressed like a Texan, but he had no real Texas accent. In her opinion, he was not like who she had heard and seen in movies of the old west. "Cowboys, real Texans don't ride on boats."

Marie Ann told Jess in private what Mrs. Worthington had said. Mrs. W. had on shorts to her knees and a gold pan between her skinny legs while sitting in the wet sand with her feet in the water, trying to gold pan.

Jess walked out ankle deep in the water and stood in front of her, watching. He knelt down in the water until his knees sank into the wet sand beneath. She looked up at him with a questioning frown.

"Excuse me Mama; would ya let me help ya find that gold ya got in that ther' pan? I'd be most please ta show ya," he tried his best to exaggerate his accent, but it got too much.

She lay her pan in the water and put her hands on her wet hip, staring at him.

"May I show you a trick to try?" Jess asked, looking her straight in the eyes. "Bet you a Pepsi you have gold in that pan already."

She squinted her eyes at him. "Young man, if there is gold in this pan, why can I not find it?"

Jess picked around in his deep shirt pocket until he found the small magnet that he needed. He held it up for her to hold and then picked up the pan, swirling the water over the black sand and gray ore in the bottom of the pan. As he washed the water around and around, the two colors separated. Tilting the pan, the heavy black ore moved to the lowest spot at the bottom edge of the pan.

He pointed to the black ore. "With your magnet drag it through the black ore and watch it grow whiskers."

She looked at him as if he had gone nutty or something. She cocked her head and still looking at him, she moved the magnet through the black ore. She then brought the magnet up between the two of them with her still staring at his eyes.

He smiled and took his thumb and forefinger pulling off particles of black ore from the magnet, held it out to her. She moved her hand over with the palm up, he dropped the particles into her hand.

"That is call black sand, highly magnetic because it is natural iron. It is said that where we find black sand, there should be gold. This black sand is considered a residue of gold. I can't explain why, it just is."

She drug the magnet through it again while watching what she was doing. The magnet was thick with iron particles.

"Now, when we are careful in removing the black ore, it may uncover or grab a small piece of gold with it. We have to be very careful. So, when we brush this black ore from the magnet, hold it back over the pan so we don't lose any gold it may have. Catch it in the palm of your hand first, before releasing it back into the pan. Make sure your hands have no oil on them, because the oil will cause the gold to float and the water will wash it away."

He asked Marie Ann for an empty peanut butter jar that had been steamed clean.

He motioned for Mrs. W. to drop her black ore into the jar and move it through the black sand again. This time they heard something scraping the bottom of the plastic gold pan.

She stopped and look at Jess. "I heard and felt something under the magnet."

"Slowly turn the magnet over."

As she did, there was a small nugget held to the magnet by the black ore. Marie Ann handed Mrs. W. a pair of tweezers.

"Easily and carefully remove the nugget and put it in the vial of water Marie Ann has," Jess said.

Her eyes were as wide as saucers. She held her breath until the small nugget hit the bottom of the vial, with a little tinkle sound.

Jess said just enough for her to hear, "Don't that sound and look pretty? That's your first yellow Mrs. Worthington."

She giggled like a young school girl. "May I buy this from you?" She had a tear in her eyes.

"No Mama, but all the gold you find in this pan is yours. Let's look for some more and show you an easier way to find your gold."

She had a big smile and kept looking at the nugget in the vial of water. Jess motioned for her to let Marie Ann hold it while she looked for more nuggets.

"Now, watch how I swirl the water over the ore?"

She quietly said, "Yes, I do."

"Now I'll tip the pan and wash the ore across those three ridges along the bottom surface of the pan. As I do, I'll wash out of the pan the material that is lighter than gold.

"Marie Ann, hand us that other pan, please," he said calmly.

She handed it to him. "Thanks, love. Now, Mrs. Worthington, we use this pan to catch any smaller gold that may have washed out. Then we can look through that again. But for now, let's keep washing this ore until we have only gold shining on the bottom of the pan or in these grooves or riffles."

He did it a few more minutes, knowing it would not be long before the gold would be showing itself, handed the pan for her to operated. It did not take long and she got the hang of it all. Finally, small glimmer of gold began to show on the green bottom of the plastic pan.

Jess motioned for her to slowly pour the remainder of the ore and water out of the pan into the other one.

"Oh Lord, look at all those little things, Gold?" She looked up at him with a big wide smile. "I have gold like the ole timers had."

"Yes, and whatever is left in that gold ore bag is for you too." She looked puzzled, Jess said, "It's all yours, you are the only one that has stuck to this panning. It's for you."

By now, there was at least two dozen watchers from the beach had gathered around to see what all the excitement was.

Jess looked up at the crowd. "Mrs. Worthington has found her first Alaskan gold." He clapped his hands and stood up.

Her husband sat down next to her in the cold water. "My dearest, we are rich now with Alaskan gold."

Jess said laughing, "Not rich, but where that came from is more, only in Alaska. You may have ten or fifteen dollars' worth of gold in her pan. By the way, keep the pan, it all comes with the gold ore."

Mrs. W. sat there in the water on the sandy beach, looked up at Jess and stuck out her hand. "I'm mighty proud of ya, partner, thank ya, sir. You are a true gentleman and an eye catcher."

Jess was still standing in the water, reached and shook her hand, tipped his cap to her. "It's been my sincere pleasure, ma'am. If you're ever out to the Hill Country of Texas, look us up." He handed her a business card. "So long, have fun finding you yellow."

The crowd began to thin out, but the two British citizens were still panning for gold.

It was getting close to sun down as Jess and Marie Ann returned to *The Shallows*. They lay their two boxes of treasures on the aft deck and then check the lines, electrical cables, and any other thing out on the deck to make sure it was all secured.

Jess unlocked the salon aft door and went in, locking it behind them. They put the two boxes on top of the engine room floor-hatch, and then turned putting their arms around each other's neck. Tenderly kissing, they snuggled into each other's arms.

"You sure feel good in my arms Mrs. Hanes," Jess whispered in her ear.

"I bet that's what you say to all the girls, Mr. Hanes," she replied with her girlish giggle.

"As a matter of fact…" She kissed him again before he could finish, but this time it was a lingering kiss.

He picked her up and went forward to the master's quarter for a shower. They worked up a good sweat today and did not even get a lunch break.

CHAPTER TWENTY-FOUR

Chesapeake City to Cape May, New Jersey

The early morning fog burnt off and *The Shallows* left the marina in Chesapeake City. It was April 1, April Fool's Day, and a Friday. As usual, there were early working fishermen pushing the waves with their trawlers as they made their way out into the Delaware Bay. Once out into the bay, the wind picked up as it came out of the south at 12 knots.

Jess and Marie Ann worked as a team in the pilothouse as he manned the helm and she navigated with the charts. The choppy Delaware Bay with the head wind did not slow the Nordic Tug. It was built for the heavy head-on collisions with the waves and did not lug down when hitting the solid walls of the waves. Jess locked in the autopilot for the distant channel marker and set the rpm for a steady 14 knots.

Marie Ann figured there would be a 6 to 7 hour run down to Cape May and dock at one of the marinas in the Canal Bay area. She had contacted the Mill Creek Marina and reserved three nights docking space. They wanted to go back to the beach area where in the 1980s they found Cape May diamonds. In the rough on the beach, the smaller pieces look clear and are called Angel Tears.

She spent some time on the Internet searching for a small shop in Cape May where they first heard about the Cape May diamonds. The first return she received was info on the diamonds and their history. She had forgotten that they were real close in hardness of the South African diamonds. They have a rating of 10 for hardness where the Cape May is 8. A black Cape May diamond had been found in the 1800s and was named, The Cape May diamond of great value, which was mounted in a ring. It was a 20 karat stone.

"Jess, was that store we were in the Sunset Beach Gift Shop on Sunset Boulevard?" she asked, moving her eyes away from the computer screen and scanned the water ahead of them with binoculars. "Did you see that vessel coming up the channel from the ocean? It's about three miles dead-ahead of us."

"Not yet, love, thank you." He squinted and took the binoculars she handed to him. "I can't tell what flag she's flying, but it's huge, maybe a tanker."

"You want to place a bet that it's a Liberian flag?" She said and took back the glasses.

"To answer your question about the store in Cape May, I think you're right. It wasn't a big place, but I remember they had a great selection of jewelry with the diamonds from those beaches."

He changed course to the starboard two hundred yards to give the tanker a wide berth to pass to their port side. He slowed from 14 knots to 12 and wait for the larger vessel's wake to come at them. Then he turned the bow into it so the Nordic Tug would easily ride over it.

"Depth 20 feet, now 16, 12," Marie Ann warned.

"We're getting out of the channel, so let's just wait for them right here." He kept the bow into the southern wind waves and slowed to match their speed, making *The Shallows* stand still. "It will be ten or fifteen minutes waiting if you want to contact that gift shop for information. Ask them where a marina was close by."

Jess did not like the fast speed of the larger vessel and turned the NT around and moved another 50 yards away and then turned around. The large tanker seemed to be coming right at them, and Jess turned again moving further to the west.

"Watch the depth for me," he said pushing the throttle for full speed, which was a good 22 knots.

"Look at the size of that monster. It looks to be twice the width of most tankers we've seen." He kept the other vessel in sight until he heard their air horns' signal for passing. He returned their signal and did a full powered turn about-face, 90 degrees off the tanker's port side.

It did not take long for the tanker to pass and Jess slowed their speed to 12 knots to ride over the wake of the tanker. They could not read the Oriental language written on the tanker to identify its name and owner.

Once over the main wake, he pushed the throttle forward for maximum speed again in order to maintain his control. They rode over the waves like it was not there and Jess set the course straight across to Cape May Channel entrance, ten miles to the southeast.

They contacted Channel Master for the latest information and informed them when *The Shallows* should be in the channel's west end. The Cape May Harbor was a little over three miles to the east. The info from the Sunset Beach Gift Shop was two good marinas to pick from in the Harbor. Marie Ann contacted them both after finding them on the Internet for their current prices of fuel and transit berthing.

The diesel fuel was up to $3.92 a gallon, but if you take more than 200 gallons, the priced dropped to $3.50. It would only take close to 100 gallons to fill up. So, they chose the smaller marina that gave not only senior discounts, but also veterans. Why not, 24 years of military service means something to some people, even if they were not veterans themselves.

Three dollars and fifty cents a foot of space to dock, was where the price started at the small marina they picked. Veterans not only got a free meal, but $3 even money, plus New Jersey sales tax. They docked at the Fantail marina slips for $1.50 a foot for overnight, and if you stayed more than two nights, the price dropped during the week to $1 a foot for vessels less than 45 feet, and $2 for those over 45 feet. Vessels longer than 60 feet jumped to $4.20 a foot. Something about insurance cost and higher maintenance of the slips.

Once *The Shallows* had been secured to the pier and fueled, they walked the eight blocks to Sunset Beach and walked the beach to the gift shop. They had a Sunset Beach Grille serving breakfast, lunch, and dinner seven days a week.

Marie Ann suggested they eat light. Jess got a toasted Tuna with Pepper Jack Cheese and Marie Ann did the same other than she order Cheddar Cheese. They got bottled water to take with them on the beach hunt.

She had brought two small highly magnified magnifiers, two tweezers, a felt pouch and two mess sacks to put 'finds' in. Jess brought two small probe metal detectors. Usually, they would wait after storms to use a more powerful detector. A storm warning was posted for small craft after 10:00 p.m.

They picked up any rock that looked interesting, even if it did not look like quartz. It was after watching the sunset in the west from the Sunset Beach Grille that they headed back to the marina.

It was mid-April and the evening winds cut through the jackets they wore. By the time they walked the eight blocks, the cold had chilled them both. Once they got back inside *The Shallows*, it felt like the furnace had been running. The had left the window blinds open and the sun warmed the salon to near 80 degrees.

"We need to walk like that every day until we get home," she reminded him of their gained weight on the cruise.

He patted his stomach. "I don't think we have gained much if any, just lack of exercise has cause an increase in the waist. And, you know I watch every bit I take."

"We both do, but that don't keep our weight down," she threw her arms around his neck. "We need to cut our meals in half; one order or meal divided between us." She looked up into his brown eyes. "we can try, right?" She squeezed him.

"Yes, ma'am, we can try again, and again, and again…"

She kissed him and held up her treasures from the beach. "I bet a steak dinner I found more Cape May diamonds than you did."

He pulled his bag out of the backpack. "Little lady, you've got a bet. By weight, I'm sure there is more in my collection than yours."

She spread a large bath towel on the galley cabinet top, and then they started to spread out their finds.

"Wait, I'll get another towel for yours," she said and went back down to the crews berthing.

She handed it to him while she began to spread her finds over the towel. He did the same with his treasure on his towel.

"You know, we should have washed these with that window cleaner for the outside surfaces," she said and turned to look in the cabinet under the sink.

"That solvent we have for washing the hull, would work too," he said and started for the storage locker out on the aft deck.

She hunted under the sink and could not find what she was looking for, but pulled out an plastic screen separator.

"Good idea," Jess said coming back in with the solvent bottle in his hand and some rags.

She poured her finds in the basket of the separator and put them in the sink. "A soup spoon full of that should clean all of what we found."

She mixed it with the water in the sink and placed the basket in the solution and shook it, and then stirred the rocks, shaking them again. Taking it out of the sink, she shook the basket and then poured the contents out on the towel.

Jess did the same process with his finds while she dried her treasures with the end of the large towel. He finished his washing and spread his load on his towel. They patted the finds dry.

"At least they smell better without all that salt and seaweed stuck to them," she said and grabbed his hand. "Look at all our treasures; will they be safe here for tonight? I'll get another large towel to cover them all."

"Yep, let's get a shower and go to bed," he said and turned out the salon lights and then the galleys.

They took a shower and lay across the bed, half way listening to the early eight local news. Both of them went off to sleep with their backs to each other. A clap of thunder woke them both, sitting them straight up in bed.

"Wow that was close! I'll check the electric and make sure shore power is still available." He went to the electrical panel in the hallway and went back to bed.

Marie Ann had the covers turned back and snuggled close to Jess. His warmth was soothing to her sore muscles from bending and twisting so much picking up her beach treasures; they eventually went off to sleep. The outside wind did not rock the boat because the large building along their pier blocked the southern wind.

They got up, dressed and finished breakfast at the marina's chow hall by eight. They rented a small vehicle and made a slow road trip along the coastline toward where the old hotel Christian Admiral was located. They had stayed in it back in early 1980s, but since then, man had demolished it.

The trip was twofold, one to check out the beaches and the Intracoastal Waterway. They stopped at three large marinas and inquired as to the AICW channel conditions from some of the transits crews in the lobbies. The local restaurants and grilles provided good up-to-date cruise conditions of the channel.

Marie Ann marked the beaches on her map for them to search; especially ones matching their historical sketches of the War of 1812 and Civil War engagements in New Jersey.

Some of their research papers revealed dates back to the War of 1812 Independence from Great Britain. James Madison was the first American president to declare war against another nation in June 12, 1812,. The war took place along the east coast of the

United States. Then too on the western frontier of the United States, the United States battled against the British and French. Both forces battled the United States on the Great Lakes and on the St. Lawrence River, then the French in New Orleans. The Mississippi River was a westerly marker where the war did not spread further to the west.

Jess and Marie Ann wanted to find a small engagement that was not prominent in the archives, where little interest was recorded. The information they had uncovered showed a Brigantine vessel with secret cargo and agents from Portugal hired by the British to get into Washington D.C., assassinate high-ranking officials and disrupt the city with explosions.

This group of six men and one woman were to put ashore near Gull Island, and then make their way by stolen horse carriage to Washington D.C. The blockade around the city was not tight enough to insure no undercover agents could pass. They paired off and each pair had a specific target.

The three separate targets were to steal pallets of gold and silver bars that were secretly stored in the large vault located in the Capitol building's basement. But, no gold was found by the British in 1812 after the rubble was removed from the fire. Whatever happened to it? Supposedly, it had been dispersed throughout the United States prior to the Civil War.

Then in 1937, President F. D. Roosevelt moved the silver deposits to West Point and the gold to Fort Knox. There have only been two presidents inside the depositories, Roosevelt and Truman. In 2009, reporters were escorted into the depositories to view and photograph the deposits. There has never been an independent audit made on either the silver or the gold deposits at their depository locations.

There are still questions by the American citizens, do we still have gold and silver in our depositories, or is it all in the hands of countries that are not friendly to our nation?

Jess and Marie Ann often discussed the question.

Again, was there evidence to work with about the gold stolen from the Capitol building's basement vault, after the fires were out when the British burned Washington D.C.'s government buildings? Jess and Marie Ann were not having good results on their own and began contacting friends and associates along the East Coast for answers. They lingered in Cape May.

After three days of searching the state archives and talking to old timers living along the eastern coast of New Jersey, Jess and Marie Ann took a day to catch up and rest. At least that is what Jess thought, but when they finished washing the breakfast dishes and had them put away, Marie Ann sat him down at the salon coffee table.

Standing across the table from him with her hands on her hips, she announced, "We have a project that I've been putting off too long and,… before you protest, it will only take us a couple hours of paperwork to get it finished." She turned and went down the hall and turned into the crew's berthing compartment.

He scooted back on the couch and spread his arms along the back. He could hear her making noise in the file cabinet in the closet. She came back up the hallway smiling that she had found what she was looking for. She laid a stack of six over-stuffed folders in front of him.

"We are over three-quarters finished on this cruise and haven't balanced our expense in the checkbooks. I'm sure it's a mess," she said and went back to the closet. "No matter how many deposits have been made, I need to show you in black and white the status of our financial accounts."

She returned with her bookkeeping adding machine that she plugged into the AC wall socket. Then she poured them both another cup of coffee and sled in next to him on the couch. She put her nose to his, and lightly kissed him.

"Now that I have your undivided attention Mr. Hanes, let's get this mess taken care of in record time." She went through them and put them in order.

"I'm glad you're retired from your accounting business, but this looks like you're opening up again."

"Very temporarily, Mr. Hanes," she said and handed him a folder with receipts. "Please put these in order by invoice numbers. That should keep them in some kind of date order. I'll mark off the check number to match as we go. While you're doing that, I'll get the laptop computer and hook up the broadband Internet. We'll have this done in no time."

She got the computer hookup and online, then they went to work. Like she said, it would not take long to get the paperwork done and out of the way.

Finally after three hours, she leaned over and planted a kiss on his cheek. "You can take me out to lunch now. I'm too tired to start something in the galley."

Files were stored in the watertight safe. It was noon. They put on some walking clothes for being on the beach and headed for the marinas diner. They both carried a White's metal detector and a sand scoop.

After dividing a 12-foot submarine sandwich and two iced teas, they purchased two bottles of water each to carry in their treasure pouches. They walked two blocks to Sunset Beach overlooking the Delaware Bay.

They visited the individual shops again in the stores and heard about the American Flag ceremonies every evening at sunset. Mr. Marvin Humm, the owner of the store, seven days a week, from Memorial Day to October, at sunset raises and lowers American flags that may have draped over caskets of men and women of our armed forces. Some have died during their time in service; others have died since serving their country.

Jess and Marie Ann wanted to make sure they attend those sunset services a couple of times before they continued their cruise north.

The beach did not have a crowd of people at this time of day, but there was a mother with her four-year-old twin daughters eagerly looking for Angel Tear stones. The two young long blonde-haired girls had deep tans like their mother from beach hunting long before this day. They did not see Marie Ann taking their pictures.

Their large brimmed straw hats whipped in the breeze, held in place by soft twine tied under their chins. They were so intense looking through the wet stones for clear glass looking stones that they did not know anyone else was around. The noise of the surf added to the breeze made them shout at each other about their finds. Their little fingers would brush the wet sand aside and then wait for a small wave of salt water to wash over the spot. The little ladies were giggling and talking to each other about what they were finding.

Their mother was helping them make good choices of stone to put in their pouches. Marie Ann had taken a dozen photos of them before their mother noticed someone else was around.

She was startled and jumped up. "Oh my, I did not know you were so near."

Marie Ann put her hand out. "We didn't want to interrupt your hunt. It looks like everyone is having fun. I'm Marie Ann and this is my husband Jess. He extended his hand to the two young ladies down on their knees.

"Look at that stone next to your heal," Jess said and leaned over moving the sand away from her heal. "You've got a keeper there young lady."

He stepped back as she slowly picked it up in her fingers, placing it in the palm of her other hand. "Mom, look at this one."

Then Jess knelt down beside the other daughter looking him eye to eye. "Look what you have under your knee."

She scooted back and leaned over with her hands next to the imprint of her knee in the wet sand. He pointed at something where her knee had been and pushed his finger down. She squatted down, put her head between her knees to where her face was about six inches from the sand.

"I don't see anything, mister," she said and Jess got down next to her with his little tea strainer and scooped the spot where he had pressed.

"Open your hand." He turned the scoop over and tapped it until it was emptied into her hand. She sat back on her feet, looked at him with a questionable took. He took his water bottle and began pouring water across the sand until the water uncovered a nice size stone.

"Do you know what that is?" Jess asked her and sat down in the wet sand, cross legged.

She shook her head no. "Is it just another rock?"

He shook his head and said, "Nope, you have a genuine Cape Map Diamond. This size can be polished, cut and then made into a nice diamond for a ring or broach."

"It sure does not look like much to me," she said and looked at her mother.

She knelt down between her two daughters. "I think Mr. Hanes is telling us that a beautiful diamond is hidden under this rough gray outside. Remember the butterflies cocoon?"

"It was not pretty at all before the butterfly came out," the other little daughter said. "Will my rock look pretty too, inside?" She looked at Jess.

"Yes, I believe it will. There are jewelry stores that may have a diamond cutter who could do the work for you," he said and stood up.

"The Sunset Beach Store is down the beach," he pointed. "They would be able to tell you where to find one. They cut stones too, but I don't know if he is in the store today."

"That would be expensive," one of the twins frowned and said to Jess.

Marie Ann cleared her throat and handed a business card to the mother. "Present this to the manager or owner if he is in. Have him call us and we will take care of the cutting and polishing cost." She smiled and then asked, "Would you write your name and the girls name on the back of that card. Then, Jess can sign it for you."

"This is very nice, but why would you do this for total strangers?" the mother asked.

"We observed you three having fun together and your display of love to them shows. Those stones will give you stories to tell years to come, and these two sweethearts can tell the butterfly story again."

"That is nice, but the expense must be great and that would cause us to be obligated to total strangers," she said and told the girls to keep looking for stones.

"Is this your first trip to the beach here at Cape May?" Marie Ann asked and offered them some water. The mother politely refused because they had their own water bottles.

"We were out here last night before sunset, but it was too chilly for us. That's why we are here earlier today."

"Are you out of state?" Jess asked and before she could answer, he shook his head and waved no with his hands. "That isn't necessary, that's none of my business. However, let me suggest, ask about Marie Ann and me at the store or grille. We are transit here on a trawler tied up at the Fantail Marina. We will be here for a couple of more days before heading north."

One of the girls saw Jess' metal detector. "Does that find treasures?"

"Yes, it sure can. You know, some treasures are nothing but junk, but others are priceless to some people."

He leaned over and pulled the gold necklace from under his T-shirt with a Spanish 8 reale silver coin dangling from it. "I found this on a 1715 Spanish galleon off the east coast of Florida a few years ago."

The twins wanted to hold it in their hands. They gently handled it and felt the weight of it.

"It sure is heavy, more than a quarter," one of them observed.

They were all kneeling next to Jess talking. Marie Ann explained the marking on the coin as Jess turned it over and back again. She told them these Spanish silver and gold coins have even been found on the New Jersey beaches, but not as often as had been found in Florida.

"My Daddy is in Iraq, he is a Marine," one of the twins said.

The other one nodded. "Daddy will be home in June for good."

"Grandpa and Mammy are at the motel right now. Mama, have they seen a Spanish coin before?"

The other twin spoke before her mom. "I do not expect they have." She informed them.

Jess, Marie Ann, and the twins' mother laughed.

"Oh yes, young wisdom can't be beat," Jess said and clapped his wet hands, spraying himself with salt water. He blinked his eyes and shook his head from the spray.

"Ladies, as much fun as we are having, we need to move on down the beach with our detectors," Jess said and stood.

Marie Ann leaned down and shook the girls' hands. "Have fun. You all come visit us if you're free this evening. The name of our boat is *The Shallows*."

Jess motioned with his hands. "Like shallow water; we stay in the shallow water to treasure hunt."

"What kinds of treasures do you look for," the mother asked.

"Well, really all kinds, depends on where we are. Like here on the beach, we look for metals that have been washed ashore, coins or jewelry lost by someone out here. In the city parks or parks along the beaches, we look for whatever could be there; either lost or purposely buried," Jess said.

"You can look at it like this, wherever people have been they will lose something or intentionally hide it. We are also hired to find wedding rings, wallets, tools, car keys and name it, we probably have looked for it."

"We have been called scavengers, beach hunters, treasure hunters, salvagers, junk collectors," Jess waved his hands and shrugged. "It doesn't matter; we have fun doing it anyway."

"Come see us," Jess said and turned on his detector and slowly swung the detector head/loop across the sand. Right off he got a signal indicating a quarter. He waved for the twins to come to him.

He unplugged his headset. "Listen to this," he said moving the loop across the target again. It beeped loudly enough for them to hear it over the surf and wind.

He pointed to the meter that indicated a coin and marked the spot with an X in the sand. "There should be a quarter right there, and maybe more. It's about four inches in the sand. Who wants to use my sand scoop to find it."

The mother asked, "May I try the scoop? Girls, this looks fun, doesn't it?"

They were on their knees next to the hole where the wet sand was falling back in after the mother made one scoop full. Jess moved the detector over the spot again and no sound.

"It must be in the scoop," Marie Ann said and instructed the mother to shake the scoop to force the sand through the round holes in the bottom. The holes were only half-inch heavy-duty mess screen, easy to let wet sand through. There was a large round magnet mounted inside the bottom edge of the scoop to catch small iron from dropping through.

She sifted the sand until they heard something metal or hard hitting the screen of the scoop.

"Look Mama, a quarter," one of the twins said and before her mom could reach for the coin, her little hand was in the scoop after it. Jess took his water bottle and washed the coin she held between her little fingers.

"What year was it minted," Jess asked her. She looked with a question at him. "Minted?"

"The year it was made, sweetheart," her mom said, pointed at the date mark. "It is two, zero, zero, six."

She looked up at her mom with a big smile and showed it to her sister. "Two thousand and six, the year we were born." The twins jumped up and down and dropped the quarter in the sand.

"Oh, Mama, I lost it," she said with almost a cry.

"Stand still ladies, it probably right over here," Jess said and moved the detector's loop over the sand again. "Right in the center of the hole of the loop; mark it with your finger under the loop," he told the twin who dropped the quarter.

She held her finger on the spot and Jess moved the loop away. "Now, Mom," Jess said to her. "It will not be very deep, so pull the scoop under her finger about four inches away. Now when the scoop gets close move your finger and the quarter should be in the scoop again."

They did the job and the quarter appeared again. Jess said, "Now, what do you have to safely carry that quarter in?"

"It's so shiny and new," one of the twins said. "I don't think we should put it with the stones."

Marie Ann said, "Good thinking, here try this." She produced a small folded plastic bag, one of six she always had in her treasure pouch. She opened its zip-lock crease and the twin dropped the quarter in. "Now, what is your name?"

"Sandra Lee, thank you," She smiled at Marie Ann.

Marie Ann turned and motioned for the other twin to stand next to her sister. "And what is your name, Sandy Ann Louckes."

"Well, this is only one coin, but it belongs to both of you, because it has your birth date on it," she said and asked, "What month and day?"

"November 20, 2006," they said almost in unison.

"I'll give it to your mother for safe keeping to put with the special stone you found today. Young Ladies, happy birthday, early," Marie Ann said and handed the plastic bag to the mother.

"I am so sorry; I didn't introduce myself, Sally Louckes. We are from Norfolk, Virginia, here until the weekend. We must be back Sunday. Thank you for your interest in my daughters. We think they are real special too."

"It is our pleasure, and your husband's rank and first name?" Jess asked as he showed Sally his military retirement identification card. "We will put him and you three on our prayer list."

In Sally's genteel southern accent, "God richly bless you both and have a safe trip home, wherever that is."

"God bless you too," Marie Ann said and gave the three a hug. "We will be on our boat all the way back to Benton Harbor, Michigan. Hopefully we will get there by September. That's where we started from cruising the Great American Loop, counter-clockwise, 6,500 miles, take a year or so to do it."

"My lands, how long you been gone now?" she asked while the girls went back to looking for Angel Tears again.

"Off and on for nine months, it will take us longer because of the long winter back home on our ranch in West Texas," Jess said.

She looked puzzled. "I thought you started in Michigan, not Texas."

Marie Ann laughed. "You are correct. We did, but our home is in Texas, and our boat was in Michigan. If we have a chance to talk again, I'll fill you in on the details."

"That's a date. I look forward to that story," Sally said and waved to them as Jess and Marie Ann headed down the beach swinging their detectors and watching for the Angel Tears and Cape May diamonds.

"I saw you drop that coin," Marie Ann said after thirty minutes of detecting and finding nothing. Jess could not hear her with his headset covering his ears. She waved her detector in the air at him until she got his attention. By then she was almost at his side.

He removed his headset. "How long have you been waving that thing in the air?" Smiling at her, he shouted over the noise of the heavy surf. "There ain't anything up there in the air!"

"I know that smarty," she replied and poked him in the side with her gloved hand.

"Careful there, gal, you might break my ribs," he teased and propped his metal detector against his stomach. "Wha'cha want, love?"

She had taken a swallow from her water bottle. "I saw you drop that quarter in the sand for the girls. They were too interested in finding Angel Tears to notice you."

"It was just a notion. I really didn't know how it would work to show them what we were doing with these detectors," he said and drank from his water bottle. "I haven't heard a sound since then either, what about you?"

She shook her head. "Dead, nothing at all. Why don't we head back to the boat and hunt that park on the way?"

"We've come about two miles, why don't we cut across the dunes, up there on the street level heading east and hunt the sidewalks too?" He suggested as they put their headsets over their ears and turned the detectors back on.

They moved up the sand dunes and over to the paved streets, detecting along the way. Going down the wooden walkway over the dunes to the street, Jess got a good signal and stopped. Marie Ann had turned at the street to watch him. He jumped off the steps into the sand, swept the spot again with the detector loop, knelt and scooped the spot. He motioned for her to him.

"It showed nickel or ring icon at 6 inches. This could be a nice find," he said and shifted the sand through the scoop's holes. Something rattled in the scoop and he handed it up for Marie Ann to take the target out. Then passing the loop over the spot again to check for additional targets, the detector sounded off again and he scooped a little deeper, because the target was 12 inches and showed a quarter.

"I bet this is a soda can as loud a signal at that depth," he said.

"What number was for this target," she asked before he got the scoop out of the sand with the second target. He felt something big when he pushed the scoop through the sand. "That was 18 on the screen for nickel or ring."

"You've got a nice ring and I think it's a diamond," she said and held it out for him to look at. "Sure is pretty, and look at that center stone, maybe a couple karats?"

"Nice fine," he said and nodded to her. "Give me a hand, sweetheart, and watch what is in this hole." He left the scoop in place and with his digging trowel he moved the sand away, making a larger hole.

She put the ring in a plastic bag and put it away. Then, she dropped to her knees next to the hole and took her small metal detector probe out of her pouch, and waited for him to finish uncovering the item.

"Looks like one of your black leather purses," he said as he lifted it from the hole. It had cracks in the leather from being in the moist ground so long. "Go ahead and check the hole again for anything else."

She used her Whites Bullseye probe again and did not hear a target.

"Nothing close. Let me use your MXT again." She turned her detector off and laid it in the sand. There did not seem to be anything else in the hole that would have been under the purse. "I wonder if this ring was in the purse and fell out."

"I don't think so. It's still snapped closed," Jess said and sat back in the sand to examine the purse before opening it. "It feels heavy as your purses usually are," he kidded her.

He brushed the wet sand from off the leather and with a brush from his backpack, he moved the sand away from the metal frame and latch.

"Ladies first," he said and handed the purse to her.

She carefully handed the plastic bag with the ring inside to him and took the purse. He put it down inside his tight pants pocket. Taking the purse from him, she unlocked the purse and carefully opened it. Her eyes became big as quarters.

"Oh my, Jess, look at this," she said and put the purse back in the hole to stabilize it from spilling. "Let me take a picture of this," she said and stood. She took out the digital camera she had in her pouch.

Jess moved his detector next to the hole so that it would be in the picture with the purse. She took several pictures at different angles.

"Go down to the street level again and take a picture up to here," Jess said and stood to stretch his legs, and helped her up onto the wooden walk.

A car with four teenagers pulled up next to Marie Ann at the street. They were laughing and having a good time. It did not seem like they were drinking or on drugs. They said hello to her, got blankets, lunch basket and a 'boom box' out of the trunk. Then they formed a single file up the wooden stairs, over the dune and disappeared down the other side to the beach.

One of them noticed her camera. "Tourist!" he shook his head and moved passed her with his cooler box.

They did speak to Jess, but did not notice the hole in the sand and metal detector. They evidently thought Marie Ann was just taking his picture on the dune.

She got her pictures and ran up to the top of the stairs, looking for the four youngsters. They were still walking along the beach, toward where Jess and Marie Ann had met the young ladies. She turned and went back down to Jess.

He unfolded another small backpack he carried when out treasure hunting, because you never know what you might find.

"I'll close the purse and we can check it out once we get back," she said and helped him put it in the backpack.

He lifted it up with the purse inside and motioned for her to help put it on his shoulders. He figured it should weigh at least ten pounds. They covered the hole and went down to the street and took pictures of the street sign. They went straight back to *The Shallows* with their treasures.

While Jess dug out some ole newspapers to spread on the salon table, Marie Ann made them ham and Pepper Jack cheese sandwiches. He then poured tea over ice cubes and sat them on the table. Then he took the purse out of the backpack and placed it on the papers, sat down and waited for her to bring late lunch over.

He pulled the table's drawer open and got a pen and paper to take an inventory of what was in the purse.

"I think this was a most successful day on the beach, wouldn't you agree?" he said and sat back on the couch.

She smiled and handed him his plate with the sandwich and chips. They asked the Lord's blessing on the food and what to do with the treasure purse.

"I can't wait any longer, you can eat, but I can't right now," she said and put her plate on the edge of the table.

Jess set a bathroom scale on the table.

"Take a sip of tea first," he said and patted her hand. "And have at it."

They did and she did, and lifted the black purse laying it on the scales. It indicated 42 pounds. He put the purse on the table for her and moved the scales to the edge. She slowly opened the purse, so it would not tear or break the dried leather. It was still a little moist on the inside.

She leaned down next to the table and pulled her hunting pouch to her. Slipping on her hunting gloves, she raised up and settled herself again where she could reach the purse.

"I'm ready now," she smiled. "Let's see what this ladies purse has in hiding. I'll lay all these loose coins over here in front of you if you want to build stacks by denominations and mint years."

He moved his plate over on the side table of the couch and put his gloves on. "Chow can wait!"

"There's rolls of silver dollars under those loose ones," she said and tenderly laid them over in front of Jess, as if they were glass. "What's this? Gold coins rolled in newspapers?"

She tried to pick up a roll of gold coins and the paper crumbled around them into her gloves. She let the paper slide off her hands back into the open black purse. Jess cradled her hands with his to make a wider place for the coins to slide. She turned her hands over letting the roll of coins slide into his hands.

"Let me get that plastic tray under the sink," she said and went to the galley.

"That's where we should put all the coins, bring two trays, love."

They removed all the loose and rolled coins onto the plastic trays, separating the silver from the gold. After all the coins were removed, she uncovered a felt pouch along the side and lifted it out.

"I'll guess this has gold nuggets or diamonds," she looked at Jess, and laid the pouch in his hand.

He weighed the weight in his hand. "It may be diamonds, because it doesn't seem heavy enough for gold."

He poured marbles out into the palm of his hand, poured them back in and set the felt bag on the scales; two pounds of marbles. "Marbles, you got to be kidding!"

They laughed, not really believing what was in the purse.

"That's forty pounds of precious metal. What else is in there?" he asked and moved the pouch to the side of the table.

'Hold on, what else is in that marble bag," she said and took the bag from him and poured all the marbles in the plastic pan. Then she turned the pouch inside out. Nothing more was in it.

She tilted the purse on its side and patted the outside, knocking the sand and paper loose, revealing a cloth covered line of oyster buttons compartment the full length of the purse. Tenderly opening the buttons, she pulled open the secret compartment. The inside was wax sealed to keep moisture out.

She took off one glove, reached into the black hole, lifted out a folder, like passports would be in. It had documents folded between its pages. An old garter had decayed, broken, and stuck to the inside. She handed it to Jess.

Jess lifted out an old blue passport with folded documents placed inside. It was issued in Great Britain in 1926 and another one issued in 1957 Diplomatic Passport. He read the information in them and they belonged to Edith Mayes Drummond, Senior Chairperson on Subversive Activities.

One of the documents gave her authority to transport $750,000 of U.S. currency, any denomination, with guarded escort from Washington D.C. to London, England, dated 1960, signed by some officials at the Pentagon. One envelope was not sealed with a letter:

June 12, 1960

To Whoever finds this purse,
    If you are reading this, I am a dead diplomat. Contact the United States FBI or CIA.

Thank you,
E. M. Drummond

"Yes, sweetheart, I know what you're thinking. I'll contact our U.S. Marshal and find out what we should do. Continue counting this stuff and take pictures. I'll help you with photographing the documents," Jess said and found his "special cell phone" for contacting Marshall Madilene Ash.

He came back from the safe in their bedroom closet and sat on the end of the couch next to Marie Ann. She had everything listed in her laptop computer and was waiting for him to make his call to Madi.

Jess was waiting for her to answer and got her voice mail, "Madi, Jess and Marie Ann are calling. Need your assistance ASAP. Remember Angel Tears?"

They took an inventory and photographed the different denomination of the coins, documents, and purse.

While Jess was storing everything back in the purse and putting it in the safe, Marie Ann transferred the photos into her laptop along with the information of where they found the purse. She got the satellite overhead picture location and saved it all. She then sent that file e-mailed to their home computer at the ranch in Texas. She then transferred the information to a 4G flash drive for Madi.

They cleaned up the mess they made and settled down for a late lunch. The bread of the sandwich got a little hard, but they did not fuss about that. They were both hungry and tired.

Not much was said about their discovery, just talked about how they enjoyed the twins and their mother looking for Angel Tears.

After their shower and in bed, she snuggled up close. "I've been thinking we may have found information on a woman who has been murdered. She wrote that over fifty years ago and buried it in the sand dune. I wonder if she was a spy or something."

"Madi will have some answers for us. Did she have a family here in the states or in Great Britain somewhere? Our total on the coins came to face value…?" Jess said and relaxed.

"It's close to $25,000, but at the going price of silver per troy ounce is $45.40 and gold is $1,534.90. I'm too tired to figure that even if I round it off to 46 and 1550." She sighed and turned over, putting her back to him.

Jess put his arm around her and pulled her close.

Jess' cell phone rang at 4:30 a.m., finding them both deep in sleep. It was next to the galley sink with its vibrator turned on. It jiggled over the edge of the sink into the aluminum bottom. This vibration was amplified and the noise made both of the Hanes to sit straight up in bed.

Marie Ann grabbed Jess' hand. "What's that?"

Mumbling incoherently, blurry eyed he stumbled and bounced off the starboard bulkhead and raced up the passageway to the galley. There was enough light from the pier night light for him to scan the galley and salon. Blinking and rubbing his eyes, he glared into the galley where the loud ringing and noise came from. He thought the garbage grinder was acting up, maybe shorted out or something. By the time he got his hand on it and removed it from the sink, it stopped its ringing and vibrating. By that time, Marie Ann was right up against his back, looking over his shoulder.

"Did you kill it?" she asked laughing.

"No, but where's last night's coffee I didn't drink," he said while trying not to laugh. "I bet it can't float!"

Then it rang and vibrated in his hand. Still not awake it startled him and he dropped it into the sink. He grabbed it again. "This time I'll choke you to death," he said while opening the receiver lid.

"You're going to what?" came a female voice over the speaker on the cell phone.

They both were laughing so hard they were crying and trying to talk at the same time.

"Hold on, just a minute until I catch my breath," he said and sat down next to Marie Ann on the couch.

She took the phone from him. "Hello, whose calling this ungodly hour of the morning? It better be good or over board you go!"

The female voice was hollering, "No, no, it's me, Madi… are you two okay?"

"Yeah, yeah, we're getting there," Jess replied, and still laughing. Every time he looked at Marie Ann, he started again.

"Oh my, Madi, you wouldn't believe the noise this cell phone makes on vibrate in the bottom of this stainless steel sink. It shot us straight out of bed."

"I bet we woke the neighborhood," Jess said and moved away from Marie Ann on the couch. Lights had come on the yacht tied up across the pier from them.

Someone called out to them, "Ahoy on *The Shallows*. Everything okay?"

Jess turned on the exterior lights and stepped out on the aft deck. "Hey Skipper, everything is great over here. Tell you all about it over coffee later, okay? Go back to bed!" he said and waved.

When he got back to Marie Ann on the telephone, she and Madi were laughing about the rude awakening. They finally got settled down and told her about their 'black purse' story. They made sure their conversation was quiet and almost a whisper, just enough for Madi to understand them.

"I have the weekend off, starting tomorrow after 1700. Turn on your tracker and I'll be there before sundown," she said and coughed.

"I'll add a couple of sick days for Monday and Tuesday," she said and coughed again. "I was at my nephew's soccer game yesterday in the drizzling rain we had. I yelled too much, but I'll be all right."

"Come on in. Marie Ann has a good tonic and chest rub that will take care of your problems."

"Great, and I'll do some snooping here in D.C., before coming up. I have some contacts in the archives who owe me."

"Okay, how are getting here," Jess asked.

She cleared her throat, "By aircraft, Rob owes me a ride in his seaplane."

"What kind of seaplane?" Jess asked.

"You'll know it when we do a fly-by around 1900."

"Great, bring some extra clothes and shaving kit," Marie Ann said, "Later."

"See ya," Madi said and they turned off the cell phone.

Marie Ann looked Jess directly in the eyes and could not hold it back, she started to laugh again, "The look on your face trying to handle that noisy phone."

They both were still in their pajamas heading back to bed, when Jess leaned forward and slapped her on her butt. She jumped and ran, leaping into bed. "last one in the pool is a turkey."

Two hours later, they were showered and fixing breakfast. After dishes were done and put away, Marie Ann washed clothes and put on fresh bed linen on the bed in the crew's quarters. Jess washed down the outside of *The Shallows* and checked the diesel engine vitals below decks. Everything was shipshape; inside and out. They were ready for their weekend guest.

Exactly at 1710, a low flying aircraft buzzed the marina over *The Shallows*. They both recognized the sound of radial engines from the aircraft. She beat him topside, watching the large seaplane bank to the south and come at them from across the ocean beaches. The pilot put in on the water about 100 yards going away from them. He crossed them from stem to stern and landed off their bow. It was a nice smooth landing. The Robin egg blue paint on the ole PBY-5 Catalina was fresh.

Jess hurriedly lowered their aluminum-hulled inflatable dingy, which was stored topside on the flybridge aft sundeck. They turned on the electric motor and skimmed out to the amphibious seaplane.

Madi was standing in the portside waist blister hatch. She handed her small amount of luggage to Marie Ann, and then helped her 'back-step' down onto the dingy deck. When seated, they pushed away from the beautiful seaplane.

Once they were away from the propellers backwash area, Jess saluted the pilot and he started the port engine. It did not have to rotate but one revolution of the props and it fired and came up to speed. The starboard engine was kept idling until ready for takeoff. Turning into the wind with full power, the Catalina gracefully skimmed the surface and broke the suction lifting above the water. It gained speed and altitude and flew into the sunset. It was out of sight when they came alongside *The Shallows*.

Jess tied off the tender onto the diving platform, and then helped Marie Ann board Madi. When she was on board the platform, she helped Marie Ann on board. The ladies went topside and swung the loading boom hoist over the side for Jess to fasten the tender for lifting. He then got out on the lower aft deck and helped guide the boat as the ladies turned on the hoist winch motor on the boom mast.

When they finally had everything in place and lashed down, the two gals collapsed onto the salon couch and relaxed. Jess poured fresh sun tea over ice and into tall glasses. He rimmed all three of the glasses with a lemon slice and then squeezed its juice into the tea. Handing them the glasses he took his and sat on the deck. Leaning back on a large pillow against the bulkhead/wall, he sipped the tea.

They shared the details of where the large black purse was found, and then Jess brought out the backpack with the purse in it. He again spread newspapers on the table in front of the couch and emptied the purse while Madi read the paperwork and passport. Marie Ann gave Madi the Flash drive.

"Very interesting discovery and I'm glad you called me. This could involve a lot of red tape, but I think I manage to bypass it. It may involve having to go to England for research," Madi said and sipped her tea. "Let me think this over while I make some calls. We don't want to stir up any undue questioning by snoopy authorities, just to get their hands on your find. But, I agree at this point, it's 'finders keepers'."

She went up to the pilothouse and started making phone calls. It was after sundown and the interior lights were off. The pier nightlights gave enough brightness for her to write notes.

Jess sat on the couch next to Marie Ann. "What do you think... did we make the right decision letting her know about this purse and its contents?"

"Why do you question it? We trust her, right?"

He rubbed his neck, "Yes we have, with our lives," and took a handful of honey roasted peanuts from the dish on the end table. He crunched a couple of peanuts between his teeth, "For some reason, I think we may have opened another 'can of worms'."

"What do you have against worms, their good for bait?" she teased and poked him in the ribs with her finger. "No, I agree, I also have an uneasy feeling about this, especially the British passport. This certainly may have to do with a murder. But, as usual, we really don't know."

"Let her chew on what we have given her. I think she enjoys these unknown factors we keep throwing at her," he said, stood up and went over to the pillow where he was and got his tea glass. "I hope she is not getting a cold, or worse."

"Jess E. Hanes, you know better than that," Marie Ann scolded. "Cancel that thought right now," she pointed her finger at him.

"Sorry! Lord Jesus, please cancel that comment I made. We continue to bind Satan and his ugly thoughts. In Your precious name we claim the victory. Father guide us in this matter of our treasure-find."

"Amen," came from the stairway up to the pilothouse. "Thank you both for that. I am definitely feeling better," Madi said and came down to the salon. She put her cell phone in her front pants' pocket.

"I have a friend in immigration and a trusty marshal in England," Madi said and turned to Marie Ann. "May I spend some time using your laptop. I didn't bring mine?"

"Sure, it's right behind you on the end table," she replied and smiled. "What else did you find?"

"Sweetheart, give her a chance to catch her breath. We've pushed ever since she's arrived," Jess said and asked if they need a refill on tea.

No one needed refills, so Jess took out the electric grill for barbeque pork chop sandwiches.

"Ladies, how do you want your hickory smoked pork chops cooked?" He turned around in the galley to get his answers. "I'll get them out to thaw overnight."

"Well done, sweetheart," Madi said out of habit with her fiancé. "Ops, sorry about that," she giggled like a high school girl.

"You flirting with my ole man again? You got a license for that, young lady?" Marie Ann teased Madi and said to Jess, "You know my chops have to be thoroughly cooked, over well please."

"Yes, ma'am, I've got a license for most anything I'm in need of at the moment. Wha'cha need?" Madi asked seriously and then laughed.

"I'll make up a list for ya after we get this research done," she replied and stood up, and then walked to the windows and began shutting the blinds.

Madi continued looking at all the silver and gold coins using a high-grade magnifier Jess supplied. "Some of these are really in excellent condition, especially the ones still in a roll. It's unusual for someone to cram so much into such a small handbag. It's almost as if the purse was soaked in water and then the coin pressed into place to stretch," she ran her hands inside and outside of the purse. "The leather formed around the coins lining the inside. How much did you say this weighed?"

He handed her the list they made, "Something over forty pounds."

Marie Ann reached under the couch and pulled out the felt pouch, "I'll bet you can't guess what's in this?" handing it to Madi.

She took it in the palm of her hand, weighed it up and down, moved the contents feeling the round objects under the felt, looked at Marie Ann, "Well, my experience is a bag of shoot'en marbles of different sizes; might be some agates in it too." She shook the bag. "Yep, marbles, bet you a steak dinner."

Jess and Marie Ann looked at each other. "Well I'll be…," he said and took the pouch from her.

He poured them into a large round glass bowl. "Now, that's right pretty, don't ya think? Add some water and gold fish." He set it over in the sink."

"Yeah, right, in the sink is where it would stay. Otherwise, it would be out on the floor in rough water," Marie Ann said.

They got a good laugh at that… all were getting tired and silly.

"It's getting near the bewitching hour," he said and yawned. "Let's put these bodies in the horizontal plane. Showers are hooked up in case you need it," he said to Madi.

He placed the coins in old towels Marie Ann got from their rag bag. While they were doing that Madi had stood up and stretched, and picked up the passport again. Leafing through it, memorizing as she went, she stopped and held it up to the light.

"This back cover is thicker than the front," she said and picked up Jess' high-powered magnifier. She changed it to the highest magnification, "We missed this earlier," she moved over to Marie Ann. Pointing to the edge seams of fine machine stitching, and then compared it to the front cover.

"You're right, it is thicker and the thin leather is stretched tighter across whatever it is inside. Can that be opened without damaging the cover?"

"What can we use to separate this leather where it's not stitched together? It could just be a hard backing of the passport cover, or again it could be something of importance in-between," she sat down again on the couch.

"That desk magnifier on the chart table could help. Then you can use both hands without holding the magnifier," Marie Ann offered. "That one may even lay on the other and still work. Let me close the blinds up there first."

Madi followed her up to the pilothouse. Jess put the empty purse and rolled towel of coins in the safe, and then locked it. He stood with his hand on the tall safe's handle, thinking aloud to himself.

"If we could check the newspaper archives in the local library while Madi checks for outstanding fugitives of those dates on the passport; then compare those results with Internet research with the names we find. Our military contacts can get us inside government networking..."

He twirled the safe's dial and closed the closet door. When he got up to them and shared his thoughts, Madi beat him with her thoughts.

"Yeah, we were just discussing the same plan," Madi said and smiled. "That's scary and excites me of the prospects we could come up with. This is fun, wish I had some more vacation time to help after this weekend is over."

"Who knows, this may cause you to be involved with a full scale investigation on an unsolved crime," Marie Ann said and handed the passport back to her with the back cover opened enough to see the papers inside.

"I'll let the expert hands of the U.S. Marshal's service remove this document," Marie said with pride of being able to separate the leather layers on the back of the passport.

"You know, it wouldn't be a bad idea just to leave it as it is for now. There is a good CIA forensics lab in D.C., and I personally know Director Valañce Hall." She was smiles from ear to ear, "Mind if I give him a call?"

"You're our leader on this, Marshal Ash," Jess said and sat in the captain's helm chair.

The map and magnifier lamps cast their body shadows on the closed window blinds in the pilothouse. It was now after midnight with no outside noise from traffic in the harbor or near Interstate. They could hear the channel buoy bells clang as waves hit them. Small waves splashed the hull below, giving them a slight feel of motion under them.

The three of them sat, waiting for Madi's contact to answer. They heard the answering machine turn on. She left a short message and hung-up.

"If that's all we can do for this morning, let's get some rest… if we can," Jess said as he stood.

The ladies turned off the light at the map desk, secured the pilothouse, and all retired below.

"Good night," Madi said as she closed the door behind her in the crews berthing quarters.

"Sleep well Madi," Marie Ann said going forward to the master bedroom.

Jess lingered long enough to recheck the security aft and then knocked on Madi's door. "If you remember, that smaller safe is open for the passport."

"Okay Jess, already have it secured," she said. "Good night, Captain."

"You too, Madi, sleep well," he said and moved on to his quarters with Marie Ann.

Kneeling next to the bed and partially laying on it, Jess prayed and went to sleep on his knees before he finished. An hour later, his tingling legs woke him and he crawled into bed. Marie Ann did not stir; she was long gone in sound sleep.

Friday morning was a cloudy, drizzly day. So the three investigators stayed on board *The Shallows* to continue their search for the owner of the large black purse.

Madi received a call from Director Hall and opened her lab for research. Her contact was a forensic scientist, Dr. Dandelina (Dee) Cohen. She and Madi had gone through the Naval Academy together in the early seventies. She had applied for the Navy SEAL program and did not finish the third week of physical training. She finished her doctorate at Yale in investigative/ forensic medicine. She had been with the CIA over thirty years, and now considered a senior citizen in the family of forensics.

They joined the CIA almost the same time; neither knew the other had applied for a job. It was only during the 9/11 terrorist invasion of New York that they were involved when the aircraft hit the Pentagon. They were among the fortunate ones with offices in the building furthest from the crash.

Like Madi, she liked the outdoors and was an avid coin collector. They had made trips together into Cambodia, searching for remains of MIA pilots.

Madi laughed and said, "Dee was a live-wire, talker and full of details. In her line of work, she was a walking encyclopedia. And it takes an athlete to keep up with her short-legged pace."

She was never married as far as Madi knew.

"I even tried wrestling with her on a mat after lessons in karate, but couldn't catch her," she laughed.

"I wonder if she has shift this weekend, they are working a lot of overtime because of the War in the Middle East." She grabbed her cell phone again, punched in three numbers and listened, "Haven't talked to her in a couple of months."

"Hey, Dee, it's Madi," she said and laughed. "Madi who? I'll black your eye when I get to town."

"What do you mean what do I want? I don't always need something when I call…at least most of the time."

"Yeah, I'm doing an unscheduled investigation…let me finish. No, it hasn't been authorized by the director yet, but that's what I need from you. If you'll stop trying to fill in my thoughts for me. You're never good at that, because you're not a mind reader, yet."

Madi waved her hand in the air, "Slow down and I'll tell you what this is all about. In short it could possibly be a diplomat, missing person, closed case that never was solved…that kind of stuff." She paused listening, then said slowly, "If I came over tomorrow morning, early, and meet you at the lab… zero nine hundred will be great… bringing two friends, so be prepared… yes, they have clearance… see ya."

Madi shook her head, "She's on a sugar high, couldn't get a word in edge-wise." She looked at her watch, "I can hand deliver the passport and be back this evening. Let me find my water-taxi Victor again, he might be in our area."

Before she could make her call, "Do you think it's that urgent for you to go now, you're on sick days?" Marie Ann reminded her.

"I wouldn't call in sick until late Sunday for Monday. I'm not doing anything strenuous, physically."

Jess came into the galley, "Don't forget, if you're flying, that will add to your sinus problems. I don't think that PBY has a clean air system to filter your low altitude air."

"Jess, I don't have allergies or sinus troubles. It's just the spring pollen in the air," she said sniffling and blowing her nose. "It happens this time of the year, every year. When the apple blossoms in D.C. bud, I can't see."

Jess walked over to her, put his fist under her chin and tilted her face, "Who hit you in the nose, and why are you crying so much?"

She sat down and put her head in her hands, "I'm just wishful thinking today. I'll stay in, don't need to get out in this messy dampness anyway."

Marie Ann had already microwaved a large cup of water and put it in front of her on the couch table. "Here's an assortment of teas, take your pick. I would suggest the mint to start with and breathe in the vapors. Here's a towel to put over your head to keep the vapor in your face."

"I'll spray her berthing compartment with Lysol and here in the salon," Jess said and went forward to their master bedroom.

They finally got Madi full of mint tea and Vick's vapor rub vapors. They put her to bed and set the inside climate control so they all could breathe a little easier. Jess and Marie Ann continued research on the passport and coins.

Jess had again found passport history on the Internet. He compared the one they had found with photos from England and Ireland. The one he had in his surgical rubber-gloved hand looked to be inside a thin leather cover. Its border was machined stitched with a waxed thread. The leather was treated with a water resistant wax or oil. So far, he could not match it to the photos on the website Madi had given him. He was anxious to find out what was inside, but closed it and put it back inside a large brown envelope. It fit nicely under the couch table drawer.

Marie Ann had stored the coins back in the safe, after checking Madi. She had a temperature of 100 degrees and was chilled. Marie Ann gave her a couple of crackers, vitamin C, and two fish oil tablets. The crackers were to help settle her stomach before taking the vitamins.

"Do you still have some of that all-purpose medicinal red wine?" Madi asked. "I think that will settle things more than all this other stuff. Vitamins okay, but fish oil didn't want to stay down."

"Sure we do, would you like it room temp, chilled or warmed," Marie Ann asked, and placed a damp washcloth on Madi's forehead.

"Room temperature should do it, thanks for your nursing," she said with a pale face smile. "This shouldn't last long. I think it's a result of malaria some years ago."

"Be right back," she said and went to the galley.

"Jess, we got a sick gal up there. I've got her covered with two blankets right now. She took vitamins and ate a few crackers. Now she wants some of our home remedy red wine," She said, and began looking through the galley-sink cupboard. "She had malaria some years ago."

"Love, the last I saw of that was up above the refrigerator freezer in with the canned goods," he said and stood up. "Need some help?"

"Nope, I'll use the little step-stool," she said and got it from the closet in the hall/passageway.

She had Madi all settled and full of wine and vitamins, covered and off to sleep. Her heavy sweating stopped and her temperature seemed to come down, at least by the touch of Marie Ann's hand. She closed the crew's berthing compartment door and went back up to Jess.

"I didn't remember her telling us she had malaria before," she said and poured Jess some more tea in his glass.

He stood up and stretched, took a swallow of tea, "Me either, love, how she doing now? I've heard that once you have it, you never completely get rid of it. With this high humidity, I'm sure it don't help."

"Her forehead is not hot anymore with temperature and she was off to sleep. I'll check her again in an hour or so."

"I can't find anything to match the passport on the Internet… yet. Let's do a search on the name through the Cape May archives of crimes, missing persons, special events, during the year of the passport date." He suggested and sat at his laptop computer again. "Unsolved crimes in Cape May during the year of 1933 and 1934 might be a place to start."

It was quiet for only a few minutes, "Jess, those were the years President Roosevelt called in all the gold from the American citizens and made a law against having it…correct?"

"It was in 1933, love. Wha'cha thinking?"

She went over to stand at the starboard window toward the bay, "What if…a rich lady had taken her savings out of the bank and hid it on the beach, back in 1933, rather than turn it into the government?"

Jess got up and walked over next to her, "If she either had it at home or in the bank, how did she get so much out of the bank. The bank would have to keep it under the law and not turn it over to the customer. How did that work if it was in a safety deposit box? Did the government put a freeze on contents of deposit boxes?'

"Well, let's find out on the Internet," she said and they went to work.

Jess sent a page for the copy machine to print. It finished and he turned and read it to her:

> Under Executive Order of the President, April 5, 1933.
>
> All persons are required to deliver on or before May 1, 1933, all gold coins, gold bullion, and gold certificates now owned by them to a Federal Reserve Bank, branch or agency, or to any member bank of the Federal Reserve System.
>
> Criminal penalties for violation of executive order, $10,000 fine or 10 years imprisonment or both.

Jess continued, "In the small print columns, the mention of 'hoarder' of gold covers a lot of areas of possessing any gold.

"Another article quotes the governments limit of owning any gold over 5 Double Eagles will be consider 'hoarding' of gold and can be prosecuted. This article is titled 'The Great Gold Robbery,' by James Bovard in1999. Looks interesting, I'll read more later."

Marie Ann tapped the table top next to her computer. "I bet that scared this lady who owned this purse and she hid her life's savings," she got up and started looking through their sheets of notes. "What was her name again? Did you write it down?"

"It's there somewhere, but the passport is under the drawer that's over the refrigerator. When Madi gets up, I'll put that passport in the safe.""

"Good place for it and here's your note." She smiled. "Edith Mayes Drummond. I'll use Google for a search for her name in 1933 and 1934."

Two hours later, they pushed back their computers and went up on the flybridge in the setting sunshine. The sun had dropped below the thick cloud cover and brightened the harbor anchorage and marinas.

"Did you see or hear our forecast?" she asked, and put her arm under his light jacket for warmth.

"Ya cold, love? Here you want to put this on?" He offered and she shook her head no and faced him, putting her head on his chest and snuggled tight. He wrapped her with the remainder of his jacket. "Sure is peaceful right now, like the quiet before the storm."

"No, I haven't any idea what we have for weather, but I will cancel your comment on the storm. My forecast, no storms on the horizon and none forecasted."

"Sound great to me," he said and held her tight. He was leaning against the padded railing, looking to the west. "Wonder how things are back home on the ranch, and up in Shuffleville? We haven't heard from anyone for about a month."

She softly said, "No news is good news."

"That's what they say, whoever 'they' maybe," he said while holding her tight, turned to put his back to the wind that had come up from the south. "Let's go down before we get chilled."

They secured the flybridge and went below.

"I'll check on Madi and then make some potato soup with some veggies in it. And, a grilled cheese sandwiches with a slice of ham," she said backing down the ladder to the aft deck.

"That sounds good to me, love. I'll be in shortly," he said motioning forward. "I'll check around the deck first and make sure everything is fine."

He turned on all the exterior lights and used his high intensity flashlight for the darker corners. He checked the water line looking from the pier, and then knelt on the aft dive platform and looked under it to the waterline of the fantail. Everything seemed in place, nothing unusual left lying on the deck.

He entered the salon aft door, went up to the pilothouse, and locked the side doors. He checked the weather digital monitor for the up-to-date weather report for the night. Showers, but no storming for the night hours; maybe small craft warnings for early morning if winds pick up.

He whispered to himself, "Nothing we can't handle with the weather."

Turning the monitor off, he went back to the galley. He pulled out a stool from the counter and sat down with his elbows cradling his face in his hands.

She began massaging his neck and down between his shoulder blades.

"I'll give you all night to stop that, if I could purr, I would," he said relaxing.

"Don't get too limp, you'll fall off your stool," she said and poked him in the ribs, and then pulled the other stool away from the counter and sat next to him. "Why are you so tired tonight?"

"It's just that time of the day. Lack of exercise, no walking done today," he turned and put his arms around her waist, snuggling into the nap of her neck.

"Don't you dare, that send chills up my back, Jess," she lovingly pushed him to arm's length. "Now look what you've done." She pointed to chill bumps on her arms.

"Turn the heat off from under the soup, please," she said and turned, going down to check Madi. She was still asleep, and no temperature.

They finished their light supper without saying another word, put the dishes in the sink, turned the lights out and went forward to their bedroom. Marie Ann stopped and listened to Madi's heavy breathing at her door and went on.

In bed they talked a little while about the black purse and Edith Mayes Drummond. They decided to look into the Cape May archives for deaths; maybe there is something of interest there. Marie Ann got up once to check on Madi and came back to bed. By this time Jess was fast to sleep.

After breakfast the next morning, dishes done and put away, they all went topside for the morning sun watch. Madi had regained her strength and had better color to her cheeks.

It was still chilly topside and they had on their windbreakers.

Marie Ann moved the coffee pot to the flybridge. They all had a full cup of coffee. They witnessed a quiet sunrise while they wiped off the controls and instrument panels. Jess started the diesel engine and let it idle for about twenty minutes, watching the instruments.

Jess and Marie Ann were standing close together for warmth when Madi squeezed in between them, putting her arms around their waist under their jackets.

"You two are warm as toast, mind if I split you two for a few minutes? Don't move, your warmth feels good."

"Don't chill," Marie Ann said and covering Madi's back with half of her windbreaker.

She squeezed them, "I'll enjoy this for a few more minutes and I think I should go back down."

She wanted to go back down and contact her friend in D.C. to look at the black purse. If it could be coordinated, she would leave on her flight to the Capitol and be back the next day. At the office there were reports she needed to read and make her recommendations, but the purse results should be finished on the night shift.

After only an hour topside, they were going back through their paperwork gathered about the purse and Edith.

With surgical gloves on, Jess was using his "mag-viewer" set up at the counter and continued searching the purse for any markings. Some areas of the leather dried and began flaking off onto the paper towels on the counter. He wanted to turn it inside out, but did not want to take the risk of it breaking open. Along the bottom seam of the purse, he found two bulges, where dried mud could have collected. It did not feel like a normal part of the purse's pattern.

With a small high-intensity Maglite and hand magnifier, he gently opened the purse as wide as he dared. Stuck to the bottom edge were two small felt pouches, similar to what diamonds could be carried in.

"Hey, you two, come over here, would 'ya?" he said and handed the two small, long-nosed pliers to Madi who was the first to get to him. "Should I leave those in place or remove them?"

"I suggest leaving them in place for now," she said and put the purse bottom on the counter top. With her rubber gloved hand she easily pressed her finger on one bulge to fell the size. "I think this one has cut stones of some sort. The other has a larger cut stone in it. We better not press them again, the felt pouches may come apart."

She handed Marie Ann the tools, and stepped around the counter to watch.

"Hum, let the experts in these matters give you an opinion," she too lightly felt the pouches and smiled. "Mr. Jess, you did it again. I felt those from the outside and mashed the leather together. I didn't investigate any further, just figured it was some of the newspaper balled up. I didn't even look inside."

Pushing back from the counter, she looked at them with a dumb stare, smiting her chest with her right hand, "Duh!"

They all laughed.

"Well, I'll put this all in my backpack and get ready. My flight should be on his way across here heading for D.C."

She went to her room and changed, while the other two straightened up the salon and galley from their scattering everything around. An hour later, her PBY dropped out of nowhere and buzzed them, turned and landed, taxing up to the end of the pier.

The three were waiting for the pilot to swing the tail around. He set the props to idle and came back to the port blister and raised the hatch. He tossed Jess a line for him to pull the aircraft toward the pier.

It pulled easily, and Madi transferred quickly. Jess released the rope. The two inside the amphibious flying boat went to the cockpit. Jess kept the fuselage from hitting the pier as it rocked in the waves. The pilot waved to Jess to push the tail away.

Jess and Marie Ann walked up the pier to get out of any backwash from the props when the pilot increased power. The PBY slowly moved across the surface beyond a channel marker, turned toward the east and almost instantly, it was off the surface of the bay. It climbed slowly, but steadily and then banked to the southwest.

They watched until neither of them could see the aircraft, and then returned to the comforts of *The Shallows*.

They watched the noon soap opera during a light lunch, and speculated as what was going to happen to the character. They had watched the stories faithfully on the cruise, whenever they could get good satellite or local reception.

They just got the great news of Osama Ben Laden being shot and killed by U.S. Special Forces Seal Team going into Pakistan. It was a secret group of forty men in two helicoters dropping into a walled compound, shooting him, and taking his body, files, computers, and info back to an aircraft carrier. They buried the terrorist at sea.

Now the question is, why not release the photos and video of the action. The President said no because he does not want to offend someone, causing additional terrorist uprisings. Uprisings will happen, whether he releases the information or not.

It is about time we finally got the terrorist behind the 9-11 Twin Towers' terrorists' tragedy, killing of those thousands of innocent people.

Jess and Marie Ann remembered watching TV on the morning of 9-11 while getting ready to leave for a ship's reunion in Norfolk, which started on the same day. The disaster did not stop them from going to the reunion. It was a unanimous vote from the ship's crew to continue with the reunion.

He whispered to himself, "Terrorists cannot stop Americans, 'You can't stop a man who keeps on a-coming, when he is in the right.' God's Justice will provable."

The missing person search Marie Ann did covering Cape May and the county it was in drew a blank. She even did a search covering the states of New Jersey, Delaware, and Virginia, without a clue. Towns in Alabama gave the closest names, but not the full name of Edith Mayes Drummond.

Jess was searching the archives in the area of England and Scotland, where her passport was issued. He did not come up with anything, except a small notice of a Edith M. Drummond who died in 1933. He went through their notes and copy of the passport, and it was issued in 1933, prior to the gold confiscation.

This may surely be a missing person who had no personal written history. Where did she come from? Did she get married, have children and grandchildren, a family tree, criminal record, military record, medical nursing or doctor records, etc.?

Jess fell asleep at his computer holding one key down. When he popped his neck after it dropped to his chest, the screen was full of zeros.

"Great," he said as he shook his head, gazing at the computer monitor's screen. "That's all I need, a screen full of one number."

"Did you fall asleep again?" Marie Ann asked raising up from the salon couch. "Go take a power nap. I'll wake you at five."

He hit the insert key and the letter "J" disappeared from across the screens. He selected the home screen and went after kissing Marie Ann on the cheek.

"Don't let me oversleep, love."

Marie Ann stood up, she was getting sleepy too. But, she could not get Edith Mayes Drummond off her mind.

Talking to herself walking over putting water in a glass coffee cup, "Was Edith a young lady, middle age or a widow? Was she married, and how many children did she have;? What are their names and where do they live?"

She put the cup in the microwave and set it for one minute, and then pulled out a box of assorted teas. She picked a lemon/peppermint; that should perk her up. "Pass up the sugar, you don't need it," she said to herself.

"What search should I work on now? And what was in those felt bags in the purse?"

The *beep, beep, beep* of the microwave sounded and she took the cup out and placed the tea bag in the hot water. While it steeped, she put a spoon on top of the bag to hold it to the bottom of the cup.

She walked out onto the aft deck from the salon and pulled up a lounge chair next to the open door. That way, she could hear the land-line telephone and the cell phone on the table. She should be able to hear Jess up front should he holler for her.

It was partly cloudy and had warmed up a bit. She watched the traffic to the east as it moved north and south on the Express Way.

The tea smelled and tasted great, just what she needed to perk up.

Suddenly, there was a big splash behind her, like a large fish had jumped. It startled her and she jumped out of her lounge chair, spilling the hot tea on the deck. She turned around so fast, she half-way stumbled over her own feet.

Someone from the pier over from them jumped in the water with an scuba tank over his dive suited back. He sank out of sight

318

because of the dirty water, but his bubbles marked his location. The bubbles stayed under the 85' two mast motor sail boat. It's beautiful sleek white hull design of an older vessel made it most appealing. It came in while they were on the computers. In fact, Marie Ann did not notice it when she moved out on the aft deck. She watched the bubble as they disappeared under the schooner.

She folded up the lounge chair and stored it. Then she went up to the flybridge and unlocked a storage locker next to the helm. She took out a pair of binoculars and scanned the surface around her side of the schooner. No bubbles, then she scanned the main deck and then up the mast.

Some movement on its far side on its main deck, drew her attention. A woman, perhaps in her forties, stood up wearing a light blue full dive suit. She was watching the water as she held a line for whoever was below her in the water. A member of their crew came to her side and pulled a boom on the boat around to them. He attached block and tackle to the beam, and then ran the line through the tackle back to a windless. She went to the windless and operated it while the guy directed her with his hand motions. They lifted a propeller out of the water and put it on the deck, lashed it down and stored the boom. Then they disappeared below decks through a hatch in the deck. Marie Ann could not see anyone else on deck or in the water.

"Wonder where the diver is?" she said to herself and moved her attention further west to the horizon. It was getting cloudy with rain clouds building from the west. She secured everything topside and went below to check Jess.

She did not realized how cold it was getting outside until she felt the warmth of the salon. She went forward to their bedroom and lay next to him. He was asleep and warm. She snuggled just enough to wake him for her to pull his arm around her waist where she could put her face on his shirted chest. She could do this for another thirty minutes and it would be six o'clock.

They were awakened by Jess' cell phone on the headboard. Marie Ann answered it, Jess made no attempt to move.

"Hello Madi, what's happening," she said and sat up, leaning against the padded headboard. "You sound good?"

"We are doing great. I'll make it short. We have ID on the passport owner. I'll explain details tomorrow morning when I get there. You'll be happily surprised as to who Edith is and where she is. Sleep good tonight, I should be there around noon. I will call when airborne. Love you two."

"Love you too," Marie Ann replied and heard the click from Madi's phone being closed.

She nudged Jess. "Skipper, you hungry?"

He rolled over and finally opened his eyes, "Not really, how about popcorn and a grill cheese and ham sandwich?"

"You're going to turn into a grilled sandwich," she said and kissed him on the forehead.

He grabbed her and held her to him, "You sure smell good. What's that perfume you have on?"

"Some of that cheap stuff you got me for Christmas ten years ago," she teased and slipped away from him before he could retaliate. "Meet you in the galley. What you want to drink?"

"Got any coffee left from this morning?"

"Yes, cold or hot?"

"Heat it up and put Cappuccino in it, and then pour it over ice cubes, please."

"Anything else, Master?" she said bowing to him as she went aft to the galley.

Jess thought to himself watching her swing up to the galley, "She sure is a pretty lady and she's married to me."

He got up and washed his face and hands, then went to the galley.

"Were you awake enough to hear Madi's conversation," she asked and put the coffee cup in the microwave?

"Yes, I did, she sounded 'up' and happy," he said and kissed her cheek. "She got a boyfriend in D.C.?"

"Could be, I really don't know," she said and got the electric grill out. "Hand me cheese and ham out of the bottom, please," she pointed to the refrigerator. "We will be the last to know!"

Jess turned on the TV and selected the local weather channel, "What's the weather forecast for tonight?"

"My forecast is rain, wind and colder," she said, remembering what she saw outside earlier. "Did you see the schooner at the other dock, port side? They had a diver in the water earlier and brought up a propeller."

"Was it off the bottom or from their vessel?"

"Don't know Skipper," she said and pointed to the microwave. "Your coffee's hot." Suggesting he mix his own Cappuccino.

"I made a fresh batch of chicken salad for sandwiches," she said, "Wha'cha want with it?"

"Chips and Pepper Jack, if we got some left."

"Coming right up, in about five minutes," she said and toasted the bread for sandwiches.

Jess checked the aft deck for flies and bugs, "We can lounge out here if you like."

"I like it up on top, if it's warm enough."

She could hear him go up the ladder to check out the flybridge again, and then heard him slide back down the railing and hit the deck. "It's a little breezy up there and you'll need your light jacket again." He stuck his head in the aft doorway.

"Okay, let's stay back there on the aft deck, coming." She had everything on a tray and he opened the lounge chairs.

He took a little AM/FM stereo radio, tuned it for easy listening and set it on the ladder. "That even made the reception better."

They prayed not only over the food, but remembered Madi and all their families back home.

"I sure enjoy this peaceful time together. No rushing around, looking at a time table, and just do what we want to, when we want to, and for as long as we want to…" Marie Ann said reaching for his hand and squeezed it.

"Me too, love, but look out to the west," he said and pointed for her, "There's sure a lot of lightening in those high rising thunder clouds. The forecast indicates it will stay west of us and go north."

"Jesus will keep it away until we finish a late supper," she said and thanked the Lord again. "It will stay to the west of us!"

They finished their meal, and just sat there enjoying each other's company. There was a program of old '50s and '60s music they sang and hummed along to, relaxing, watching the lightening play in the distant clouds. Every once in a while they heard the rumbling of the thunder.

Marie Ann would point her finger. "Don't you dare get any closer. We don't need your messing around here."

Jess said a hearty "Amen to that order!"

An hour later, the storm was way north and they were ready to hit the hay. They walked around the main deck and then put everything away, secured for another peaceful night.

They were not sleepy tired, just lay still listening to the soft music from the bedroom radio. "Skipper, I've been thinking about our Edith again. If Madi doesn't have any info on her, can we go back to that spot with our detectors again when she gets in?"

"Sure, I don't know why not," he said and turned toward her, "We've got three detectors, three scoops and three treasure pouches."

"What if Edith was murdered and buried right there close to where we found the purse?'

"Goodness, Marie Ann, what gives you those lines of thinking," he asked wrinkling his forehead, frowning. It was too dark in the bedroom for her to see his face, plus she was not looking directly at him.

"I don't know, just remembering her note in the purse. '… if you find this note, I am dead.' Wasn't that what she wrote?"

"Something like that… I haven't really thought about that any further, maybe we should. Let's ask Madi what she thinks," he said and sat up in bed, leaning against the headboard. "What if we find remains, which could cause a full scale investigation? I would suggest we secure our finds in a better place, like open a bank account and put it in a safety deposit box."

"Madi would know what to do with it for safe keeping," she said and sat up next to him. "What if… Here I go again. If she was not murdered or even died there with no one around? She may have been a survivor of a shipwreck and got ashore safely. But, if she was the only survivor once ashore; all alone, hungry, no water, and not knowing where she was; bad weather could have kept her from seeing further toward Cape May."

She turned putting her feet on the floor, putting her hand over her mouth, "My imaginations are running wild Jess. I don't want to think on it anymore tonight."

Jess went around to her side of the bed, "Let's go up to the pilothouse for a little bit, until you get sleepy." He put her light robe around her shoulders, and then followed her through the passageway, up the stairs to the pilothouse.

He helped her up into the captain's chair at the helm, and turned it so she would look aft, toward the couch in the pilothouse. The dim nightlight from the pier cause a soft glow into the compartment, making her shoulder length brunette hair glow with a soft brown. He sat across from her on the couch.

"You know what we forgot again today? Something we were going to do at least twice before leaving?" he asked and settled back with his arms folded, lingering with his next thought out loud to her. "My, my, you're a beautiful woman, Marie Ann. I do love you."

"Don't stop, I enjoy you telling me you love me. But what are you after, Jess Hanes? With a question like that and then almost in the same breath, a sweet comment…psychoanalyzing me?"

"No, I'm just wanting to help you relax and get your mind on other things so you can rest tonight," he said and laid his hands on the leather seat beside him. "All those questions you went through are valid, but you were working yourself in a dither. The more you talked, the higher your voice got."

He scooted down from the couch, walked over to her, putting his arms around her, "I do love you, sweetheart. Those what-ifs you mentioned were getting you knotted up."

"I know, I know, questions, questions...I can't seem to turn them off like you can," she said and pushed passed him. Looking through the pilothouse windows, she leaned against the edge of helm desk. "I'll get relaxed, just be patient with me, please."

He stood next to her, giving her room to move if she pleased. "This treasure hunting cruise is supposed to be fun and exciting, not to lose sleep over. May I make a suggestion, and I'll help you with it."

"Okay, Captain, *help*," she said softly, throwing up her hands.

He pointed to the couch table and took a tablet from one of the drawers and a two ball point pens.

"Let's do some brainstorming about the purse we found and its contents. Start by using the questions you had earlier, lets write them down and leave room for comments. As we come up with any answers, put them next to the question."

"We'll have a bunch of unanswered questions," she said and tore a couple of pages from the pamphlet. "We could give these to Madi at breakfast and see what she has."

"I really think this will help our process nailing down facts for our questions." He said taking the tablet with pen in hand.

"First off, what we forgot is that flag ceremony every night at sunset over at Cape May Point," he said and smiled at her. "Maybe this evening we can make our way over there?"

She nodded in agreement, "Number one, flag ceremony tonight."

They spent two hours back and forth with questions and some answers, until she started a lot of yawning. "Okay, Captain, let's

324

get some sleep before this night is over." She dropped her pen on her papers, he put his tablet and pen on top, then they went to bed.

It was three thirty in the morning.

Marie Ann heard stirring in the kitchen and sat up in bed. Jess was still beside her. *Madi must be up*, she thought and turned, looking at the digital clock. "Oh my, nine o'clock, we've overslept."

She slowly got out of bed, put on her robe, and went aft to the galley, "Good morning young lady. How long have you been here?"

She handed Marie Ann a cup of hot coffee, "Just long enough to shower and make a pot of coffee. I have a breakfast coming, it should be here in twenty minutes. Hope you're hungry."

"Goodness, you didn't need to do that," Marie Ann said and took the cup from her. "Thank you anyway. Yes, I am hungry after that early morning session Jess and I had up in the pilothouse."

Madi turned and looked up to the pilothouse, "What happened up there?"

"We had a brainstorming of questions to get down on paper, which we'll share with you after breakfast." She turned to go down the passageway to the master's bedroom. "I'll wave this under the captain's nose. I'll be right back."

Madi heard the commotion from the bedroom and water running in the head, rustling of clothes and they came to the galley.

"My, what a surprise, good morning Madi," he leaned over and kissed her cheek. "Thanks for the coffee, tastes great. So, we have breakfast on the way?"

"Yes, sir, Captain, we aim to please," she said and went to the salon aft door, stepped out on the deck and reached up to the pier, handed someone some money and brought back a plastic bag with breakfast.

They finished breakfast, washed up, finished dressing and met in the pilothouse. After they shared with Madi their questions she tried to give them some answers, plus info she had gathered.

"After all the time we have spent, we are still at square one. We cannot tie down any evidence of a missing person from a crew's manifest of vessels sank off Cape May Point. Nothing in the confidential government files I was privy to, and the local papers and police reports are nil, nothing, blank and zero that there ever was a person by the name, Edith Mayes Drummond. I went to Interpol and got no results, as well as Great Britain. Even though they did have large family trees of Drummond tied to the U.S., but not our lady."

"So, we still have a mystery lady, waiting to be found?" Marie Ann said and sat back in her cabin chair. She was disappointed, but still hungry for answers, "That means, she still is out there somewhere, dead or alive? Maybe, she never did exist. I went back to the Cape May earliest archives, in the 1830's looking for the last name, up through 1940's, and found nothing."

Jess nodded along with Madi, "Yep, it's a good possibility we have a factious name to hide the real person," he said and smiled at Marie Ann, "Love, the mystery continues."

"Here is the passport, and the papers from inside that we couldn't get out," Madi said, handing it to Marie Ann. "It's a faded photo that can't be enhanced, too much water was on it. We tried, but nothing."

She looked at the ole photo, "Shoot. I thought this was a clue." She handed it to Jess. "Now what?"

"You can put all this in a local bank deposit box for safe keeping, until more evidence is gathered. Again, keep it under cover. No one needs to know what you have. When you get ready to leave, retrieve it and be on your way. Right now, under the local laws of New Jersey and U.S. government, it's finder's keepers," Madi said and stood up. "That was fun. We need to keep doing it. We make a good crew, a stick-together team," she said and walked out on the main deck.

She went out on the pulpit, straightened the pennant, and returned to her seat in the pilothouse.

"Well done, you two. This has been interesting, even though we don't know any more about Edith than what we did at the start," Jess said and pointed to Madi.

He stood and placed his hands together on top of his head, stretching, "I have another question, if I use a ground penetrating radar unit, which would find any grave or disturbed ground, as well as anything metal, do we have to have special permission to use it here on the beach at Cape May?"

Marie Ann smiled at him, "Yes, we can, because we are a business that sell and services metal locating equipment. Under our legal license to sell, we can get a temporary permit from the state of New Jersey to use that radar."

"Well, listen to First Mate Hanes, well done shipmate," He clapped his hands. "See, some of your digging for info pays off."

"So how long will that take to obtain?" Madi asked, looking at Marie Ann.

"One phone call and we will have it tomorrow, and add all day to set it up and figure out how to use it." She pointed to Jess. "That's the Master's talent, not mine."

"We will all learn together, so let me make the call and find out the specifics," he said and took his cell phone off his belt.

"Jess, here, use mine, it's not traceable," Madi said and handed him her cell phone.

They put their plan in motion for searching the area where they found the purse.

Jess and Marie Ann searched through the Internet for shipwrecks off Cape May Point and for any vessels known to been beached in the area.

Madi searched through her internet contacts for restrictions on the beach and in the shoreline waters in depths of less than twenty foot of water at low tide. One listing showed all kinds of vessels from ones that had been sunk by mines, torpedoed by German submarines, collisions, beached by storms, and then those sunk out off the coast. So far, no archive history of a freighter/

cargo vessel or passenger liner sunk or beached on the east coast of New Jersey.

Jess tapped a pencil on the galley-sink drain board, "I've been thinking...I know that's hard to believe, but listen to this thought. We have assumed Edith was a survivor off a vessel at sea. Why not a misplaced person from a nursing home, or the last of a family and died around here somewhere, never to be known of again? Perhaps she rode a bus down here to Cape May back in the thirties, buried her life's savings, died on the beach edge at low tide, and then swept out to sea at high tide.

Or, we might have a false passport and this lady never existed."

Marie Ann looked at him and shook her head, "Well, we will never know until we exhaust our avenues of research. This may wind up being an open ended story... no ending."

"You both have good ideas. You're networking is great, but there are so many ways that we can research, and never find what we need to identify Edith's past, if there was an Edith," she stood and walked over to Marie Ann.

"This is a good example of why it takes so many personnel, so much time, tracking down false trails, empty avenues of details that go nowhere." She said smiling with her hand on Marie Ann's shoulder, "We may be wasting a lot of time and money. I suggest we hold off on that ground penetrating radar for now."

"Yeah, that might not be a bad idea," Jess said and put the pencil in his T-shirt pocket. "It's available if we ever decide to need it."

"Again, this is a suggestion, we are the only three that know about the valuables in the purse, passport, and where it was found. All the search by my contacts in D.C. has been deleted on their systems. I personally saw to that, so, put everything back in the purse and secure it in your safe until you return to the ranch. Or, ship it home and insure it like you would a metal detector."

"I could put it in a metal detector shipping carton," Jess said and nodded. "Not a bad idea, Madi. We may never be satisfied with this search until we find information on her. We don't even have a Social Security number if she became an American citizen."

Marie Ann turned her computer off, closed its cover and unplugged it from the wall. "Let's take a break from this. We been at it six hours with no good answers, but a lot of questions. I made a list of our questions and noted them as we talked."

Madi and Jess turned off their computers and put them away. Marie Ann put the coins back in the black purse with the passport.

"Madi," Marie Ann started, reaching into the purse and pulling out the two black felt pouches, "what did you find out about these?"

She poured the contents of the two pouches out on a paper napkin on the counter. Two different oval stones; a large red ruby cut for a broach, and the other a diamond looking crystal cut with different color veins.

From her small briefcase she retrieved her notes. "The red ruby is a Carnelian or Sardine Stone and the Jasper or quartz (cryptocrystalline) is considered a high grade diamond; both found as special stones in the Holy Bible, Exodus 28:15 -21 and Revelations 4:2-6.

They are very precious stones and have been cut and polished for mounting for pendants or broaches. I did not have them valued, but my own search indicates somewhere in the range of $2,500 per carat, gemstone weight. Gold is now $1,427 a troy ounce 24 carat, .999 pure."

She pointed at the gems. "You may have only $220,000 in both stones for their weight and size. I haven't weighed them."

Jess looked at them. "Beautiful stones, wonder what jewelry they were to go in."

"We'll never know, I'm sure," Madi said and sat on the salon couch. "This is fun and exciting to me. These treasures that relate to our Lord Jesus Christ, bless my heart. It's refreshing after being with the criminal element for so many years. You two are 'blessed stones' in my life."

"Well, praise the Lord for that," Marie Ann said, with a hearty "Amen!" from Jess.

"I'll get this stored and be right back," Jess said and went to the crew's berthing compartment.

"Are you going to be able to go up to New York with us?" Marie Ann asked and sat at the other end of the couch. "We'd sure like to have you along again."

"It doesn't look like I can get back on board for a least a couple months," she replied and patted the back of the couch. "This is a great 'get-away' for me. So, I'll be watching where you are all the time. I can find you with our satellite most any time of the day or night."

"Yeah, I'm sure your sophisticated electronics can lock in on most anyplace on the surface of the earth," she replied. "Big Sister is watching!"

"I don't think there is a spot in the U.S. that we can't view within four feet for a clear image. We can get license plate numbers using the satellites, and facial details."

Jess came up and scooted a galley stool over to where they were seated. "What's your schedule now? I heard you can't go north with us."

"My ride is refueling across the way and getting chow-to-go," she said pointing to the north through their starboard window. "He'll call before starting engines and taxing over."

"How do you like flying in that ole PBY?" Jess asked. "I've always had a liking to it. Never been in one, can we look when he gets over here?"

She jumped up, smiling. "Just one minute, Captain, I'll find out," she said and used her cell phone to call the pilot. She walked out to the aft deck for better reception. They could not hear her conversation.

She jumped back in. "Lock up, we're going for a ride up to Manhattan and be back before dark."

Jess grabbed her and gave her a big hug. "Second Mate, you made the grade today. Thank you very much."

"You don't know how long he has wanted to ride in a PBY. In all the air shows we have attended, there were never any opportunities for a flight. And now we go all the way to New York City and back, thank you Lord." Marie Ann was as happy for Jess as if she was going to enjoy the flight too, even though she really did not like to fly. "Thank you Madi, this is great!"

They grabbed their IDs, light jackets, bottled water, locked up, and waited at the end of the pier for the graceful flying boat to taxi over. They could hear the radial engines start and watched him taxi to them. There was a little chopping of the waves, but it did not hinder the aircraft getting in position to take them aboard.

There was a pilot and copilot up front, who they were introduced to before strapping into a comfortable leather lounge chair. "This isn't government issue, too plush." Jess said to Marie Ann next to him in another seat.

They had put on life-jackets before getting settled into a seat. Madi was still standing between the two pilots as they began to taxi. She moved back with them just as the PBY was turned into the wind for takeoff.

"Madilene Ash, this is fantastic, thank you," Jess said and tapped her on the shoulder, next to him. "Marie Ann, did you grab a camera?"

She turned back to Jess from watching out the blister-window, "Right here in my jacket," she said and immediately turned to watch their take off. She had a forward side view of the takeoff from the port side, Jess was on the starboard side.

Once they were in the air at about 3,400 feet, the bumpy ride stopped and smoothed out. They could move around in the padded fuselage whenever it was not rough.

On the intercom, the pilot told them to come up to the flight deck. They could stand behind the pilots and hold on to overhead rails. They had a beautiful ride all the way to the Hudson Bay and flew low up the Hudson River, landing and taxied to the Brooklyn side for a short docking time. The wheels were lowered and they rolled up a ramp out of the wate. They had to pick up two CIA agents heading south with them to Jacksonville, Florida.

Jess and Marie Ann got good photos of the Statue of Liberty and Manhattan Island as they flew up the Hudson River and back down, before landing.

"Jess, this is our tax dollars at work. Enjoy every dollar we are spending," Madi said and smiled. "We could send you the bill!"

"Nope, that would be double taxation, won't work," pointing to Marie Ann the tax lady.

They did not turn off the engines, and were back in the air after a ten minute stop; only leaving Madi behind at the ramp.

She had a call from her director to meet with him and a team of U.S. Marshals at the United Nations Building, immediately.

The flight back to Cape May was uneventful with a beautiful sunset and a low level flight into the harbor. One flyover to scan the area for small craft and then they landed, taxied, unloaded the Hanes, and was gone again. When they got back on board *The Shallows*, they sat in the salon for about ten minutes to catch their breath.

"What a beautiful flight, Jess," she said and clapped her hands. "I'm sure I got a chip full of good pictures. In addition, those two pilots treated us like family. That was absolutely a marvelous low level flight all the way."

She was still excited and would be for a week or so. She promptly plugged her digital camera into her computer for saving the pictures and picking the ones for her Picture Saver Gallery. She e-mailed the gallery of photos to Madi. She took over 100 shots in a three-hour flight and had the best seat on the plane for taking videos. Marie Ann was most certainly pleased.

After a shower, in bed they fell asleep holding hands, refreshed but tired.